Waste World

CW01176662

'*Government is not reason, it is not eloquence – it is force! Like fire it is a dangerous servant and a fearful master.*' (attributed to George Washington though possibly apocryphal)

'*A process which led from the amoeba to man appeared to the philosophers to be obviously a progress – though whether the amoeba would agree with this opinion is not known.*' Bertrand Russell

From Old English or Anglo-Saxon

'*Werod 1. n. throng, company, band, multitude, host, army, troop, legion*'

from: Hall, J.R. Clark: A concise Anglo-Saxon dictionary (4th edition, CUP, 1960)

'*Elsewhere Werod may be, and was, translated as bodyguard... It became much more, of course: it could indeed be said to have become legion...*' An anonymous scholar writing at the end of the 21st century.

ISBN 978-1-729414-00-2

Copyright © 2018 Charles R Waddington

All rights reserved. No part of this publication may be reproduced whole or in part in any form without the prior written permission of the author.

This book is a work of fiction. Names, characters, places, organizations and events or incidents are either products of the author's imagination or used fictitiously. Any resemblance to actual events or incidents, places, organizations or to persons, living or dead, is entirely coincidental.

PART ONE

Yggdrasil

1. *An Awakening*

The man sat and looked out with the vacant bleary-eyed stare of mental exhaustion. This look, uncharacteristic of his usual demeanour, had in his waking hours stayed with him for many days now. He was glad to see the light of day again, now in the small room in the topmost part of the tower, after yet another night of toil in the ringing oppressive silence of the basement library, the dungeon, as he was beginning to think of it. He was still absorbed, wrestling with his thoughts, and not just his thoughts, those of the other man too. It was those thoughts that held him as if he were under a spell.

The land was spread out in the distance, on the outside, like an intriguing and charming picture on the wall, viewing it as he was, its colours and rich vibrancy framed by the sandstone of the arched mullioned window. A touch of the old world, he thought momentarily; that is, the world long before the catastrophe - there was a sort of medieval fixed stillness about it. A picture, the fields and hedgerows colouring green, the sparkle of the thread of river, the distant church towers, the dark little spinneys, a faraway copse atop a hill, like a blackened crown, all under an azure canopy and in the invigorating warming light of a bright morning sun. Beautiful, yet in his present state of mind bringing little cheer. The problem was he could not cease thinking, cogitating, giving way by turns to anger and agitation, but also struck by his inability to comprehend. Perhaps a sense of proportion had slipped away.

'Who could blame me, or anyone like me?' he was thinking at that moment. 'I am after all one who has chosen to relive it all, for my sake and for theirs. The beauty of the day, the world outside, does not relieve me; it makes me think of a land waiting to be peopled. But that isn't the case: there are people here. I must hang on to that. I have a duty, a duty to persevere - they expect that of me. No, I shall not disappoint them, though I am tired almost to death. I shall grapple with him. I will understand him. I will get the better of him.

'I can see crows in the distance, or are they rooks. I cannot tell: it is too far. I shudder to think of it now, awake, and not in my nightmares. But I can still see, as though it were only yesterday. He has brought it all back to me with those twisted writings. An abomination... the crows, the crows... the battle of Hastings with the Anglo-Saxon rotting dead piled high, left by the Conqueror for the feasting of crows and ravens... yes, like that, only so much worse...

'His words compel and repulse in equal measure. All life encompassed, he believed, by the visions of his prodigious mind, his undoubted intellect. And the mathematics, which none here can fathom, encompassing in one way or another that life, and all life... an angel or a god of death... The whole of human endeavour throughout history reduced to an equation, an assertion of revealed truth, not through a spiritual epiphany but through a cold inhuman logic, or a superhuman logic devoid of humanity or of pity, and so to the terrible solution of that equation. Yet the true horror lies deeper, the possibility that he may have been... I cannot go there yet, but I must persevere.

'She is worried for me, I can see that now; for me and about me, as always my guiding light. But as I gaze outwards to the bright colours of the land, the awakening of spring - it is a cold bright hard April and the shadow remains within me. I must talk to her, I must. I fear him, God, I fear him even now... He could have done no more to put us in our place: us - *Homo sapiens*. He is not here, though his recorded thought is... recorded for posterity, I suppose... And, to match him, to contend with him, I shall set down these, my thoughts...'

The sound of someone learning to play an acoustic guitar, faltering, inept, but determined, was suddenly audible. The tears came unbidden and welled in his eyes. The smell of the dead of decades earlier filled his nostrils - his experience, his memory... not only a memory, a haunting. The multitudes...who would have thought Death had undone so many. He recalled the lines, linking himself to history, to literature, but nothing, nothing, nothing came to blot out the madness of what had happened...

2. *Leader?*

January 30th, an auspicious day, a day of reckoning or just another day. One's perspective on life mattered, one's circumstances, the conditions of one's birth, and one's life, Chance, Fate, call it what you will. For Ernst Röhm, tough and fearless veteran of World War 1, this date in the year 1933 was an auspicious one, a landmark in history: he was the most powerful man in Germany, leader of the *Sturm Abteilung*, the SA, the real force behind the new Chancellor, more powerful than the remnants of the standing Army, which had been emasculated by the Treaty of Versailles. He, Ernst Röhm, would ever have the ear of the new Chancellor, would ever be his right-hand man. He watched from a window in the Kaiserhof, his broad spade-like powerful hands at his side, thumbs tucked in his wide leather belt, watched the Leader descend the steps to the waiting car. He would soon return to set the new era in motion - History in the making, writ large. The others stood behind, a murmur of voices, whilst he was preoccupied with visions of the future, with what could be achieved. Soon the Leader would return to the room, free himself from the adulation of the masses. Yes, he, Ernst Röhm, a practical man, a soldier, would be indispensable. And so, thrilled as a schoolboy at the visions in his mind, he eagerly awaited the return of the Party Leader, and new Chancellor of Germany, Adolf Hitler.

3. *History, Imagination and the Missing Pigeon*

'The King is dead. They've cut off his head. The King is dead. They've cut off his head.' The choir of voices seemed to be singing or chanting. It reminded him of children in the playground - a repeated refrain, harmless like an old nursery rhyme at first but becoming more and more insistent and threatening.

The sky alternated between a livid overpowering grey gloom and a sulfurous yellow over the desolate plain. On the sandy ground the man was kneeling, his neck on the well-used and bloodstained block, his arms outstretched, the hands trembling perceptibly. His face was obscured by the curling locks of a black wig. It was strange: this was Charles II and when he had been standing, he had been Charles 1. Perhaps it was neither. The belching fumes from the volcano shifted and a dark river, dark as molasses, was revealed. The River

Styx: there were grey shapes of people on the opposite bank. The execution had taken place twice already but on this side of the river there was no sign of the axe-man. Then his wife appeared and handed him a credit card. 'This will all have to be paid for, you know.' He could not see her face, but he knew it was her. He remembered then that within a few minutes he would have to fight the invincible Achilles, whom he had earlier seen in the heat of battle mercilessly slaughtering at least ten Trojans. A cold sweat: he was afraid. He was no fighter anyway: Achilles would just cut his throat in a single impossible movement. Then there was a cat dead on the road and a pineapple. Someone was ironing, taking items from a pile of clothes seven feet high. All of a sudden a heavy thud from somewhere and he awoke, wondering whether the noise belonged to the waking world or to the dream he had had. He shuddered and was uneasy for a few seconds as he began to gather his thoughts.

His wife had gone to work at the hospital. He half remembered that she had said goodbye. Had that sound been the sound of the door slamming shut? It was a bright morning, nearly eight o'clock and the sunlight was streaming into the room. He could have an easy few hours: Ellie, his daughter, was sleeping over and he would not have to pick her up until noon.

That dream, the world of dreams, was mad; but was it any madder than the waking world? For one thing, the physicists told you that everything corporeal and solid that you saw before your very eyes was actually mainly made up of empty space containing some sort of electromagnetic web of energy! He had never been very good at science, or at least, to be charitable to himself, his interests for long years had lain elsewhere: history, literature, classical music, appreciation of, and yes, he was pretty well a fluent speaker of French, which did on occasion impress a colleague or two at the office. The office - if truth be told he much preferred now the work he did for a few weeks twice a year for the Adult Education people. In his full-time occupation he was in a sense still a history man. He had long been a history man: once upon a time, not that many years ago he had been head of history at Anytown Academy. It wasn't really Anytown; but he called it that, just as he called the town Anytown, mockingly and sometimes despairingly because, though a large Midlands town, one of the most populous in the country, it had for as long as he had known it, and decades before that, been lacking in ambition, reluctant to celebrate its few famous or half-famous sons and daughters, its councillors caring more about spending as little money as possible. At one time there was even talk in the council chamber about closing the town's only theatre... But he supposed it was like many a town, spoilt by fly-tipping, wind-blown litter, chewing gum-spattered pavements and a general air of shabbiness. Then there was the occasional headline-grabbing violent crime. In that, statistically, there were worse places to live. But the town had its sink estates, as they were charmingly referred to, and he was glad he and his family did not have to live in one.

Reality was strange when you stopped to think about it. And passing time was everyone's enemy, poor and comfortably off alike. A depressing thought... He had just turned fifty. The things that used to be, the things he and his wife used to like, the search for something new, and something to do, now that the kids were grown up or growing up. Only Eleanor, Ellie, left at home. She mocked them for their overly keen interest in her studies just as she did for their almost zealot-like determination to watch University Challenge every week; but she herself was clever and would go far, do better than he had done. They, he and Yvonne, had given the children a good start, but at times he feared for them more than he perhaps should, in a sort of motherly way. His understanding of people through his knowledge of history had perhaps warped his judgement, his view of the world.

That dream... It was in part linked of course to the series of six talks he was giving on alternate weekends, on the English Civil War, a course which took its finishing point as 30 January 1649, and the execution of the king. But unlike his dream there was no wig: Charles had had his hair tucked under a cap to expose his neck. Bizarrely too, as a mark of respect, Cromwell had allowed the head to be sewn back on again for the benefit of the mourners. History was full of brutal acts, the bloody torture and killing of helpless prisoners, the fatuous pronouncements of leaders, a lack of common humanity, whatever that meant... From the Byzantine Emperor, Basil II, who having captured fourteen thousand Bulgars, had ordered the blinding of ninety-nine out of every one hundred prisoners, with last being blinded in only one eye so that he could lead a maimed procession home; from this eleventh century atrocity to the murderers of Auschwitz, with their production-line killing of millions of children, women, the sick, the politically incorrect, and so on, in the supposedly more civilized twentieth century. You could not just blame those in charge. Some people obeyed orders out of fear, but there were always the sadists and the criminals devoid of pity and relishing their power. He feared that the world had not changed: there was ever a liberal sprinkling of the vicious, the psychopathic and the bullying in all communities at all times, just waiting for an opportunity that did not result in their own precious skins being brought to account. There was, he believed, an innate evil in a minority of people, just waiting for the right opportunity...

Next autumn he would have new 'students', listening to him talk about the Anglo-Saxons. He had already planned for his series of six lectures to end with the Battle of Hastings and the fall of Anglo-Saxon England. That last battle, the Saxon shield wall on the ridge, men standing ten deep in a line hundreds of metres long, the Norman charges, infantry, cavalry, terrified horses, attacking uphill, the smell of blood, blood soaking the grass, the cries, the gaping wounds, men on the ridge, barely finding the room to fall as they died...for hours on end... 'a close-run thing', as had been said of a later battle in history... had Harold held on for two more hours until darkness began to fall, a different history might have been born...

He himself had attempted a few lines of Anglo-Saxon alliterative writing, inspired as he was by a recent attempted re-reading of *Beowulf*: he thought he might try them out on his students in the autumn. Of course, it was not in Old English, nor was it poetry, more a sort of mock Anglo-Saxon prose story telling:

'Wulfhere stood, proud, ready, stock still in line. With strong-planked shield held sure on sinewed arm. He stood in first line, blue eyes of steady gaze fixed on middle distance. Full hour had he stood, shield locked on either side, in line of linked shield strength, on high, the high ridge above *Santlache* slope. Full hour to think on death or victory. Soon it would begin.'

Wulfhere... it was a name probably to be found among the Anglo-Saxon dead who lay on the battlefield for days, at the mercy of the crows and ravens. Wulfhere had after all been the name of the king of Mercia from the late seventh century, an Archbishop of York in the ninth century, and elsewhere further south in the land at that time the name of an ealdorman who had plotted with the Danes against King Alfred...

He was pretty pleased with it; but in the cold light of a few months' passing he might think differently. One thing was certain: he actually did like delivering his short history courses at the residential college in the country, with its fine views over the shallow valley, its wainscoted rooms, its simple well-cooked lunches, and its cosy little bar. He could smile at the council's new slogan 'Lifelong Learning into your Nineties', though one of his 'students' had taken it literally: he was a genial old fellow of ninety-two, whose grand-daughter would drop him off at the college and pick him up afterwards.

The principal form of employment for Adam Walter Plato, however, kept him for long hours, and sometimes well after hours, at the county council building, where most of the LEA officers were housed. Tomorrow, Monday, he would have to spend pretty much the whole day at the office, preparing for a series of visits to schools around the county during the rest of the week. He was far from certain that he actually made much of a difference to failing schools and felt that his intended advice on the delivery of the curriculum often drifted towards little more than a social chin-wag with an old colleague. But he always left plenty of written material: his assessments, his development ideas - and they could contact him at any time...

The office... His was on the top floor of the fifteen-year-old, pyramidal-type-design, red-brick building on the very edge of Anytown, with, it had to be said, wonderful views of the surrounding countryside. In an idle moment he could look out at a man-made lake, part of the town's flood defences, grazing sheep, a village church or two in the distance... Idyllic, but he was usually too busy: he was at his desk preparing documents, answering letters, sending emails, or on the phone-the lot of many, he supposed. He used the building's stairs as much as possible, preferring usually to go down to the ground floor coffee machine, where he would bump into, among others, Harry Lattimore. Harry Lattimore... He smiled now to think of him... Miserable, moaning old Harry whose glass was always half empty, as least as far as work was concerned. A little unfair, though; Harry had made him laugh on occasion.

Having dealt with the three S's - shit, shave and shower, as an accountant friend had once summed up the process of morning bathroom manoeuvres - he looked forward to breakfast and a leisurely look at the Sunday papers. Breakfast was fruit juice then a couple of Shredded Wheat with low-fat milk and a generous sprinkling of soya lecithin granules, which contained choline and inositol and was therefore good for the metabolizing of dangerous fats, or so the makers claimed; and it was probably scientifically valid. He had had his cholesterol checked. It was fine, as was his triglyceride count, something he attributed to the daily consumption of a glass of diluted lime cordial, a health tip he had picked up from a colleague some years earlier.

As usual when Yvonne was working the morning shift on Sunday, he picked up *The Times*, so as to leave her *The Observer* intact. Soon the various sections were scattered across the floor and the settee, as he alternated at first between skim reading and the morning political programme on TV before deciding to make a coffee and put on some music. He chose finally to play a CD of the St Matthew Passion, choruses and arias, and, his coffee by his side, began to read the news section. There was still a bit about the aftershocks of the

General Election. It still filled some column inches in the news section, and this time there was something in the editorial. The hung parliament was a reality, probably occasioned by the eleventh-hour scandal linking a Tory shadow cabinet member to dark dealings at one of those gambling, banking institutions: millions had changed hands. Anyway, the result was a continuation of New Labour in power, albeit as a minority government begging and cajoling support from the Liberal Democrats and others under the banner of uniting to deal with the national and global financial crisis. The Tories were up in arms about the political deals but still in the political wilderness themselves whether they liked it or not. At one point they were looking good for victory; but 2010 had not been a good year for them. Some of the enfranchised, a great many of them in fact, were beginning to say that it didn't matter because all the parties looked and sounded the same and had the same agenda. Harry Lattimore would often wax lyrical on this - perhaps lyrical not being the best choice of word. His view was that successive governments, despite the promises, had retreated from actually governing, preferring instead to delegate monies to the local authorities for them to waste on outsourcing services, PFI school building schemes being, according to Harry, the worst example, where naive local government officers 'negotiated' financially crippling deals with private venture capitalists that would keep LEA budgets strapped for cash for thirty years. And it was the same for the newly established Health Foundations and the building of hospitals. Harry dealt with contracts himself, contracts for schools, and was appalled by the waste of money. He knew the truth and had had the figures, he said, from a consultant employed by the council to monitor the contract. Harry...well, never mind Harry. Harry was always commenting on something or other.

Adam, sprawled on the settee, pausing to sip at his still very hot coffee, glanced at Business, which carried a mention of Simon Xavier Lacock, who had last week appeared in the Magazine, beaming out of the page from the lawn of his Devon country house, with his accomplished wife Elizabeth and their two children. Very, very rich... Not that he was envious: he had never really been that gripped by financial matters and knew he was lucky enough to be comfortably off: he still had no clear idea what the term 'hedge funds' really meant. In the glossy article the Lacocks, Simon and Lizzie, had stated their own admiration of their close friend Briony, a brilliant, absolutely first-rate biologist (or was it bacteriologist, or both - he could not remember) who was already doing some incredible research project at Cambridge and who was, the dons all agreed, a science star of the future, and probably had star status already. No, he could not remember exactly what the research was, and he could not now even remember her surname. But he remembered the picture of her: it had been taken in the house's grand conservatory: she had been standing with the elegantly dressed Lizzie Lacock. 'Lizzie' was good looking herself, but Briony, with her long blonde hair, symmetrical chiselled facial features, and intense blue eyes was stunningly beautiful... An accomplished pianist too... She radiated confidence, assuming that the camera did not lie in its telling of a frozen moment in time. The Lacocks had obviously wanted their young friend included in the article. They were rich: now they also had genius, if only by association, Adam had thought at the time, a rather unkindly thought he had decided on reflection. The fleeting nature of fame, or Sunday magazine fame and fame or celebrity in general... He had to confess that although he genuinely did not really care, he took a grain of satisfaction, not quite *Schadenfreude*, from knowing that many of the faces and names, bandied around and raised to exemplar or ideal status by the self-styled arbiters of good taste and accomplishment, would disappear with time. He felt that many in society were made unhappy by being so obsessed with trying to emulate such people; imagining for example that they had failed in life if they did not own a house like the Lacock's, or if their children could not match the achievements of someone else's children. Even the Travel section set impossible targets: take the kids to Siberia for six weeks this summer if you want them to have a real adventure. And Christmas? Lapland was almost passé. He was comfortable with his own life and really did not care about competing in this way. In any case, people, all types of people, were interesting. Live and let live was a good motto to carry with you. He was less comfortable, however, with the inevitable unbridgeable gulf between rich and poor: it always had led to trouble in one way or another.

Harry would have something to say about such matters as wealth and privilege if he dared to start him off tomorrow. But perhaps not: Harry's preoccupation at the moment was street crime and what he called, from something he had picked up in the media, the police's retreat from dealing with the issue of anti-social behaviour, another government abdication of responsibility. In truth, he was uneasy about this and had adopted an ostrich-like mind-set because he believed Harry was close to the truth: he recalled an article he had read in the local paper that very week about a man named Peter Dredge who had been tormented for months by a gang of youths and finally been badly beaten. His face stared out of the paper, gaunt, hollow-eyed. Alongside had been a picture of his dilapidated council house, in an area he knew (because he had driven through it many times when visiting a fortress-like primary school): the house probably still looked out onto an open grassed area strewn with litter and at least one abandoned burnt-out car: a wasteland at the best of times. For Peter Dredge, and his ailing, invalid wife, and probably lots of other people, life was a sort of hell that not even Dante could have dreamt up. Then there was the incident two weeks ago which had really infuriated Harry and made others in the office, his immediate colleagues, comment: a fifteen-year-old girl had lost an eye thanks to some moron with an air rifle, or as Harry had called him, 'some cowardly retard'. He preferred not to think about it... or Harry Lattimore, who would no doubt buttonhole him tomorrow with more of the same.

Harry was approaching sixty and could and would retire in just over two years on a barely adequate pension. He was himself in a much better position than Harry: still on the Soulbury Scale from his teaching days, he earned almost three times what Harry earned and would be able to retire very comfortably, if he wanted, at sixty and still do his history courses for Adult Education. Life was not difficult, but it was short: retirement made him think suddenly about death, or put another way, how long would his retirement last? Damn Harry and his talk of retirement and 'getting out'. Oh yes, he remembered ... *that* was what Harry had been talking about last week: he had lost his credit card, convinced in the first place that 'some scum bag' had stolen it. Then he realized he had probably lost it on a trip to the countryside park. The credit card, Harry's going on about his credit card: that explained part of his dream. And Achilles? He'd watched that film again recently. Heroes... Adam Walter Plato...he would never, he could never, be a hero. Such a thing was an impossibility, even though he himself always averred that nothing in history was impossible. Hastings, Troy (mythical history), Stalingrad: had he been there he would have crawled into a hole and died from fright. Oh well...

The CD of choruses and arias from the Bach *Passion* was getting towards the end, and he began again to relax as he listened, smiling and waving his finger in air as if conducting to an imaginary singer and orchestra as he listened to the aria *Gebt mir mienen Jesum wieder*! He glanced at a few more articles and sank the last now cold dregs of his coffee, deciding to make himself a second. Feeling a wave of contented, calm spirituality sweep over him, he went to the kitchen to the transcendent sounds of the final chorus, *Wir setzen uns mit Tränen nieder*, uplifting, heavenly ... He stopped in his tracks: on the large picture window was the dusty silvery spread of an angel's wings. The hairs stood up on the back of his neck. Then he realized: a bird, probably a pigeon, had crashed into the glass. It was not some divine manifestation at all, but it did explain the thumping noise which had awoken him from his jumbled historical nightmare. The marks were made up of a fine powdery residue whose overall effect was of angelic form. He thought that here might be a special name for this impact-related dusting, but if there was it eluded him. Strangely, he was almost disappointed by the simple scientific explanation. Then he searched outside for a dead or injured bird but there was no sign of the hapless creature. He felt relieved: he would have been phased at having to deal with an injured bird. The thought struck him that pigeons, it was usually a pigeon, were not that smart; unlike crows, which looked at you with a dark, baleful, knowing eye. He began to think seriously about Hastings, a vision of arguably darker times... Back to the present, he realized that he should tidy up a little before going to fetch Ellie.

Adam Plato felt good, on a high for the remainder of that day; so much so that his wife and daughter remarked upon it. In one respect, however, he was essentially like everyone else. Accomplished and knowledgeable student of history though he was, he could not of course see the future, or imagine how the world might learn from the lessons of the past, or not learn. If pushed to it, despite his good mood, he might have had more than a few misgivings about the future of humanity. Like everyone else, he simply did not know, could not have anticipated what was going to happen. But he did after all, apropos of nothing, recollect and say out loud with a self-congratulatory air, the name his subconscious had been searching for and eventually uncovered: it was a surname he should have remembered, the name of the architect of, among many other fine historic buildings, the mausoleum at Castle Howard in Yorkshire.

'Of course - Hawksmoor. I remembered it in the end: it was Briony Hawksmoor.'

4. *Politics without Power*

'Forget all that philosophy twaddle about the fate or destiny of mankind and the morality of power,' proclaimed Austin Summerville, Shadow Foreign Secretary and hard-headed party guru. Clean-shaven, his plastic-smooth cheeks glistening under the tea-room lights somewhere deep in the Parliament building, at forty-three he looked trim, vibrant and like a man ready to leap out of his seat at any moment. He took a couple of sips of his favourite lunchtime tipple of carbonated elderflower, squinting his pale blue eyes (to reveal character-making crows' feet) as he prepared to continue with his earnest outpourings. 'Let others get sidelined into metaphysical, ecological or moral debates. We can't do anything if we don't win power... What you're suggesting, Patrick, is all well and good, but these *fora* have a habit of getting out of control. Engage by all means, but only up to a point. We need to play it tight, keep our cards close to our chest...'

‘A sporting metaphor, Austin?’ Patrick Lansing held up a deprecating hand. ‘No offence. I do take your point. It is a fine balance. We know what the bloody media are like’. He saw that the other man was confused and irritated by his facetious question, however.

Patrick Lansing was slightly older, with hard chiselled features, smaller in stature and almost ferret-like in his appearance, but by general consensus a very able parliamentarian and always a considered and careful orator. He had held his seat in East Anglia for twenty-three years and though comfortable in being returned in successive elections with a large majority, he was never over-confident, worked hard for his constituents and was respected for it. His slim figure was tightly packaged in his pin-striped suit, and there was no trace of discomfiture in his steady confident brown eyes. He would not get caught up in the blood-pressure-raising high-octane world of Austin Summerville. Austin was one of the new men, newly elected, who would burn himself out in a handful of years. A different political animal was Patrick, and like Austin Summerville he was in line for the leadership when the time came, but unlike him he was not desperate for the reins of power. What would be would be, as they say, was his philosophy, his mind set.

Summerville has subsided somewhat and reclined now in the dark shiny leather-upholstered chair, but Lansing knew it would be a matter of moments before he launched into another spiel. He watched the other man’s face and pondered on how he could divert him from parliamentary business or sidetrack him from the subject of a General Election which might be as distant as three years away. After all, he'd had a hectic week and it was important to take a fifteen-minute break now and again.

The large low-ceilinged well-appointed room (albeit the patterned red and gold carpet showed some signs of fading) was almost empty of people: lots of chairs and low tables, the small walnut-wooded bar with dependable young Eamonn trying to look busy polishing glasses, a side table with the day's broadsheets, and the many-paned long windows looking out onto the terrace that in turn overlooked the Thames.

Lansing had finished his coffee and stood up, deciding that he would step outside and admire the view. He hoped, but did not expect, that Summerville, still cogitating, would not follow him. He made some comment, smiled and crossed the room. Outside, for a moment anyway, it seemed as though he had been wrong: he stood alone on the Riverside Terrace, leaning his folded arms on the warm stone wall, staring out at the sparkling broad Thames immediately below.

Summer sun and bright the colours of the craft that ploughed their way through the grey-blue water, and the people and vehicles on the far embankment. So bright, his eyes had ached for a second as he had stepped out.

He loved London, and particularly the Thames and its embankment landmarks. Never grew tired of it, and therefore, as Dr Johnson had oft been quoted, of life. There was still a magic for him in a Sunday morning walk through Covent Garden market, buying nothing, just seeing the stalls and life in general. On one occasion, there had been an opera singer, on the large side but young and not unattractive, her voice soaring to the rafters, with tourists staring down, appreciatively, rapt, from the walkway above. Another time, a quartet was performing, in the same area with tables and chairs where people could sit and listen close up, drinking their coffee, only this time only a couple of people were seated... The quartet was performing popular tunes. One of the seated people was an old man wearing a Jewish cap, an item of dress laden, imbued, with historical and cultural resonances and significance. The old man was classically or stereotypically Jewish, with deep brown eyes, a furrowed brow and a large hooked nose as though he had been lifted out of a painting by one of the old masters, and with a kindly twinkle in those eyes; a sort of lovable grandfatherly benevolent Tobit had been the image that had sprung into to Lansing's mind, as he had watched the old man clapping in time and grinning at the joy of the moment, the joy of life. This had moved Lansing almost to tears, as unbidden to his mind (because of a conversation he had had that very morning with a colleague) had come the thought of the Holocaust, the evil antithesis of Satanic proportions to this life and selfless abandonment to the joy of music. Lansing had been left with this unpleasant thought and had sauntered off into the bright morning, through the press of interested and relaxed visitors, down past the marbled halls of an ever-successful consulting firm he had worked for some years before, past and under the tall rectangular but ornate and in their own way magnificent buildings of the area, down through the quieter ways to the restorative Thames, with a life of its own...

If this Parliament, where he now stood, was the beating heart of this British democracy - for that is how he liked to think of it - then the Thames was so obviously the life blood of the city of London; a great open artery, once of a vibrant water-borne commerce that had now shifted to its embankments, from where the richest and greatest servants of new commerce could stare out and pay homage, and at the same time, though they may be unconscious of it, restore the life force of their souls.

Lansing watched the tiny figures on the opposite embankment, busy in their own worlds, then looked into the hazy distance to his left, past the ever-busy transit of people and traffic over Westminster Bridge and to the middle distance, where again on the opposite bank his lesser eye could not avoid the glinting vast London Eye where he fancied he could make out diminutive figures queueing, and far to his left was the shape of the dome of St Paul's, Wren's triumph, and beyond, the Gherkin, which he liked but could barely distinguish from where he stood (at least without his distance glasses) and which he thought was a modern masterpiece, the stamp of mankind's progress, the latest layer in the city's long history. St Paul's reminded him that he must really make the effort to visit the Tate Modern opposite, to see the new exhibition: he had missed the Rothkos last time they came - he liked Rothko but not really much else in the world of abstract art.

Just a few moments' reverie, then Summerville stood by his side. 'Admiring the view?'

'Never tire of it,' Lansing replied, staring ahead a small craft, black and yellow painted, with a small red ensign flying, her tiny bow cutting white shavings of water in the grey swell, an occasional glint coming from her metal superstructure. Lansing watched her wake forming, ever-renewing but always the same length of churning whiteness. Amid the sounds of the city near and far rising on the morning air, he fancied he could hear the sound of her small determined engines. There were several boats on the water in fact, more activity than usual, he fancied... 'I'll have to be getting back soon,' he said to Summerville, who stood intensely at his side, 'Jenny's sorted out some correspondence for me...' Does that ring true, he thought as he spoke, and why did I mention her? His mind ran back to the night of illicit lovemaking: it had happened only last week, and after all this time. Jenny, intelligent, attractive in a slightly severe way with her high cheekbones, the sometimes hard look in her grey eyes, until she smiled... bespectacled, efficient and smartly dressed to the point of elegance... Why had he succumbed at last? Fool, really. The flawed hero of the people...

'Seen a few things...' Summerville had broken his train of thought.

'Eh?'

'Seen a few things, the Thames... Viking ships, Nazi bombers, whales off course...'

'Yes,' Lansing agreed, smiling. For some reason an old memory of his first six weeks as an MP had surfaced, and at first he wanted to share it with Summerville because it amused him. The memory was of an irreverent middle-aged lady who had worked on the catering staff at that time, when he was starting out on his parliamentary career: young, green, and nervous Patrick Lansing. He wondered how these new men would have coped with her banter. He could see her now, or fancied he could, overly made up, and with bright red lipstick - it was Doris, Doris Preston or Presley - not sure, but definitely Doris. He smiled inwardly at the recollection, but at the same time, he did not now want to share the memory with Summerville, who was neither of the old days nor the old school of politicians. He let the moment pass, even at the risk of Summerville's hijacking the conversation: it was clear that the other man had an idea in his head and was waiting to burst out with it.

Lansing had a head full of his own problems, not all work-related... then there was his expenses return... Summerville was blocking his way, and clearly he, Lansing, would have to listen to something of what the other man was planning to bring up at the Shadow Cabinet meeting in three days' time. Summerville, sinewy but broad-shouldered, a bundle of energy, duly obliged.

'For the future, you know, 'he began,' I'm not sure that I'm interested in the party leadership. It's all a matter of whom one should support.'

'Not even given it a serious thought,' Lansing replied, honestly,' I know these things are bandied around and even I have had one or two things to say, but they've been superficial remarks, fluff, and guarded at that, social chit-chat...' He gazed abstracted over his beloved Thames which glinted in the clear air under a bright warming sun, and beyond, out over the hazier distance of the morning metropolis.

'Absolutely, one should be circumspect in these matters...' Summerville concurred.

'They don't qualify as *matters*, Austin: some things are best left unsaid, until the right time, for the good of the Party.'

'Well, yes indeed, you're right of course...'

Out with it, man, was Lansing's thought.

As if reading that thought, Summerville promptly replied, the index figure of his left hand coming up to press on his chin, his head lowered, a habit he had developed when he had something important to say: ' There are so many permutations and possibilities, with so many people coming through though... Geoff Allen, Becky Thorne ; and Louisa Harrington is of course presidential material if we want to run that sort of campaign in the future, but too young' (and stunningly good-looking he was thinking) ' ...Simon de Menzies, Charles Webster,' and here Summerville paused for breath and looked upwards as though seeking other-worldly inspiration, 'Dain Alvis, er...' He looked for a reaction in Lansing's keen eyes and thought that, for an instant, he saw a tell-tale narrowing.

'Best left alone at this stage - I'm sure you agree,' Lansing interjected, and, changing the subject determinedly, 'Anyway, tell me about the resurrection of the Road Map idea - there's talk of a summit in Cairo. What's our position on this?'

Summerville had a lot to say in response to this question, but Lansing was still thinking, 'Dain Alvis, I knew he was angling to get to Dain Alvis... sounding me out, the sod. I don't like Alvis, as he well knows. An odd name too, as I have always thought: as if anyone could have such a name as Dain Alvis. Quiet, determined and possibly ruthless Alvis...' His mind went back to two days earlier, when Alvis had cornered him in the Chamber... A hand tapping him on the shoulder, firmly enough to draw his attention, not so firmly as to offend, just like the succeeding comment, perfectly judged, insinuating, probing and yet seemingly the epitome of casual innocence. Alvis had had a purpose, and yet he had not: he, Lansing, wily old fox that he was notwithstanding, had gone away from the encounter feeling somewhat used and soiled, but in what respect he had been unable to fathom. Nothing had been said, really, and yet something had passed between them. Dain Alvis had had a purpose: yes, it was so, and yet it was not so. Then, as now, he remembered his Shakespeare: 'I think thou art honest; and I think thou art not.' Othello had been one man, of course: the Iago-like Alvis (for that was how he thought of him, fairly or not), if he were committed to some heinous design, could not fool the whole party for long... many people would be preferred in the future before him, and yet clearly he held Summerville at least in his thrall. Alvis was playing it safe, not giving too much away, but sooner or later his obsessive nature would reveal what lay beneath. His pet obsession, his monomania, with law and order, which he saw only in Draconian terms, might win over voters, but its intensity would surely make him less electable to senior positions within the Party, and probably even disqualify him from the one post that with his narrow focus he could aspire to - Shadow Home Secretary. And yet, here was the in-favour Summerville, Shadow Foreign Secretary, who was putting in, in a manner of speaking, a good word...

'I'm sorry, I wasn't paying close attention...'

'You looked as though you weren't listening at all, Patrick,' Summerville responded, looking a little miffed, but smiling anyway, his mobile beaming face shining as though polished.

'No, no, no, I picked up most of what you said. The PM's seal of approval? I agree: I think it's idle speculation at this point in time.'

5. *Country matters*

After the meeting of the Shadow Cabinet, the weekend after in fact, there was a quasi-social, or quasi-political gathering at Louisa Harrington's father's country retreat in the south of Northamptonshire. It began on a Saturday lunchtime, and was a grand-marquee type of event initially, but one that stretched into the afternoon and evening, when at last there would be a few speeches of a none too serious sort. A bit of a hotch-potch really, but an opportunity for some serious networking and a chance for the captains of industry and commerce, Party supporters of course, alongside local Party stalwarts, to rub shoulders with some of the Party bigwigs.

Those attending included... Daniel and Vanessa Leonard, brother and sister, fashion gurus, Charles Lovejoy and James Lovejoy, major figures in the banking world, with elegantly dressed wives in tow, respectively Pamina and Elspeth (Pamina, director of, and major shareholder in a publishing house, Elspeth a published writer on matters psychiatric and a former renowned practising psychiatrist), Sonja Brooker-Holmes, of the editorial team of *Horse Sense*, Mavis Kelling, Chief Executive of the local NHS trust, Jon Millar, newspaper magnate and his partner, Isabel Johnstone, popular author of romance novels, John Kelling (unrelated to Mavis), entrepreneur and leading light in the CBI, Ernest Halley, sports journalist , and Ruth Halley, his wife, Olympic 400metres silver medallist, Patrick Newton, leading geneticist, Veronica, his wife, pioneer in artificial intelligence and bio-mechanical science, Norman Chomsky and Davina Chomsky, of Royal Ballet fame, Richard and Diane Shaker, *the* Diane Shaker, star of stage and screen, a Broadway hit in her role in the new musical *Germinal*, and Richard, her husband, big in real estate in the US... And of course, there were many more, including local leading lights of the Party, Louisa Harrington's influential family members, her colleagues from the Party's second and third tier ranks, and a few Shadow Cabinet members...

It was a clear day, a bright day, a warm day, with a pleasant breeze which just stirred ever so slightly the flaps of the marquee. Champagne, caviar canapes, strawberries, in the early afternoon, and with a splendid, resplendent one might say, dinner to follow in the late evening for that limited number of guests, some invited and opting to spend the night at this country pile of historic Northamptonshire stone, which had links, it was said (as it was said of one or two other properties in the county) with George Washington and his origins, though with much less a claim on him, it also had to be said, than the nearby Sulgrave Manor.

A rather heavenly leisurely kind of summer afternoon under kind blue English sky, with all the very best of food and drink, catering with no expense spared, of course, and inelegant and coarse even to comment upon this, the view across the broad green striped lawns under the spreading trees, or seated quietly by the ornamental fountains, between the box hedging, admiring the roses, glass in hand...

This temporary paradise was a hell for Sidney Tew, the rather rotund, red-faced and ready-to-explode-or-implode master of ceremonies, as far as the car parking arrangements were concerned. It was his job, and that of his staff, to round up the chauffeured limousines after they had dropped off the invited dignitaries, leading lights and pillars of society, and see that they were carefully parked in an orderly fashion either on the hard standing to the side of the great house, close to the garages and stables, or on the grassed area set aside and specially rubber-matted for the occasion. The unobtrusive rubber matting grilles notwithstanding, Sidney Tew was never quite satisfied, never quite certain that all was well - Sidney Tew, uniformed, and aggressive and overbearing with his staff at times of stress, but obsequious and fearful with all but the meanest of those visiting, those meanest he determined to be some of the less experienced chauffeurs uncertain of the protocols on Sidney's home turf, though some older wilier hands at the wheel delighted in facing him down, getting a rise out of him...

The Leader of Her Majesty's Opposition arrived mid-afternoon and was accorded a warm welcome by Sir Thomas Harrington, the host. Harrington, of noble lineage dating back it was said to the Norman Conquest, was tall and heavy-boned, ruddy complexioned, and lantern-jawed, a long-limbed rudely healthy man in his sixties. Every inch the aristocrat, though a minor aristocrat, he had excelled both as a sportsman and a scholar at Eton, before going on to Oxford, as his father had done. He warmly shook the hand of the younger man who involuntarily noted the firmness of his grip. Perhaps this might have reminded him of his own firm grip on the Party, and its imminent call to power: one had to believe so given three by-election victories this year and yet another own goal by the government immediately prior to the recess.

At that point, another master of ceremonies appeared, Maurice Smart-Uffington, the baronet's steward, or estate manager. He too shook the hand of the Leader with the common touch, as other lackeys moved in to deal swiftly, silently, with the Leader's luggage.

Eliza, the Leader's wife, slim graceful and smiling, but conscious, despite the sunglasses, of what might be some sort of infection in her left eye, alighted from the car and caught the Steward by surprise, as he almost backed into her. He stepped aside awkwardly. Stepping forward herself, she greeted the baronet: 'Tom, how are you? 'The baronet answered, 'I'm so sorry, my dear ... What a delight to see you here. David hadn't told me of your coming, 'with a sideways look at Smart-Uffington, who looked guilty, 'The more the merrier of course. Louisa will be so pleased to see you...'

And so on. Just one more key person to arrive, the Party's spin-doctor-in-chief, Virgil Holmes. The hell of organising this important gathering, or at least part of that task, would soon be over for the now obviously and embarrassingly perspiring Maurice Smart-Uffington. It would be over with the arrival of Virgil Holmes who would in effect take full charge and shoulder, effortlessly it seemed, the responsibility of marshalling the minions. The evening, less people, though many a star in the firmament of society remained to shine, and shone in the ballroom where all were gathered, holding a score of conversations against the backdrop of a quartet playing Haydn and Mozart. Among them, many of those plotting and hoping to be running the country, officially, in the very near future.

There were three after-dinner speakers: one was Virgil Holmes himself. Patrick Lansing and his wife were two of those invited to stay over, and they sat near to the speaker. Lansing was glad that he and his wife were among those invitees, quietly pleased that they were not among those having to journey to the nearby hotel, ten miles across country to the luxury Lawsley Park. He felt tired from drinking and eating more than he usually did on such occasions when he was noted for his abstemiousness, and though he loved Lawsley and its beautiful setting, having stayed there some years earlier, he was keen to explore the not dissimilar grounds of Harrington's estate with an early morning walk. Most important of all, he wanted to determine this evening, if he could, just who was in favour with the Leader.

Lansing felt relaxed, ensconced here as he was. He was happy too. The day before, he'd bumped into Simon Lacock, one of his younger acquaintances, who'd given him some useful guidance, some 'information', on his share portfolio. Every little helped, and he quite liked Simon, whose wife Lizzie worked with, or should he say for, Pamina Lovejoy. Also comforting was the fact that his PA had gone on a week's holiday, so he felt as though his little indiscretion with her had flown further from his wife's knowledge with her physical removal, albeit for a short space of time. A breathing space for his conscience, or a recession of his fear of discovery? He wasn't sure. He was pleased too to see that Dain Alvis was not among this gathering. He thought he had spotted him in the afternoon, but then the impression was gone. Was the man haunting him? Or was he becoming obsessed with him in an unbalanced way? Alvis *shouldn't* be here, that much was clear: he was when all said and done a minor player on this stage. He thus put the thought of Dain Alvis to the back of his mind, hid it in the cupboard with his skeleton, and as he exchanged pleasantries with James and Elspeth Lovejoy, he squeezed his wife's hand. She looked at him, smilingly, wonderingly, thinking that he had been a little distracted of late, not his usual self.

The first two after-dinner speakers were, according to the general consensus, entertaining, especially, the second, a fabled raconteur who held most of them spellbound for long periods that were punctuated by laughter and applause. He was warmly applauded at the end by his audience which included the third and last speaker, Virgil Holmes.

White tuxedo, dark hair, rather hollow face, but animated, mobile, Holmes had intense baby-blue eyes and a beaming white-toothed perfect smile. He was quite tall, around six one, and seemed in control of his space: his polished enthusiastic talk was reinforced by expressive dramatic gestures of hand and arm. He was the picture of confidence and optimism. He nodded early on in the proceedings in the direction of Patrick Lansing, the darker-faced older man who eyed him intensely as though under a microscope. But Virgil Holmes, master of ceremonies, Party spin doctor, all smiles, was not really someone you could pin down on a metaphorical laboratory slide. Mercurial elusiveness would be one way of describing his particular way of avoiding a one hundred per cent commitment to any truth or fiction: what was true or fictitious was whatever suited the Party and his own career within the Party: those two conditions had to be met, to be always one in the same.

Silence - almost. Anticipation - certainly. But still a few chinking glasses, a muted hum of residual conversations, a furtive movement, a glance or a word at the tables. The last speaker, then to bed, or home, or hotel... the official close of proceedings in this last or latest chapter in the history of the assembled elite...

'You know,' Holmes began, 'I feel honoured to be here, honoured to be chosen to give this speech - which I assure you will not be too formal or long-winded - honoured to be following such distinguished and amusing speakers, and of course honoured to be a guest this evening at the home of our delightful host and hostess, Sir Thomas and Lady Hermione Harrington.' General polite, studied applause... 'I feel honoured too of course to be a member of this great historic Party, a cornerstone of this wonderful society of Great Britain...' Loud applause, as expected...smile and pause for breath from Virgil Holmes, working his audience already...'This Britain, that *is* wonderful, that *is* Great, and that will be seen to be *Great* again under the stewardship of this Party in three years' time.' A rising heroic voice at the end, and loud sustained applause...

'Three years ago,' more muted now, with Lansing and a few others scrutinizing him, but most rapt, wanting to be absorbed into the spirit of things, a few too tired or drunk to care...'Three years ago this great historic party looked down and out, doomed to perpetual protesting on the opposition benches,' pause...'but, you know, we've actually turned it around. We're going to win the next election!' ...Cheers and applause...

'But let's not forget the hard road that took us here, that took us to our by-election victories this year, our successes in local government elections, and the lead we now have in the polls... but first,' Pause for his audience to guess what might be coming... then with deliberate sheepishness, 'let me tell you about my schooldays. It's not easy to go around with a name like Virgil, especially when everyone's reading Dante,' Then the faintest flicker of hesitancy, of a lack of self-possession as his mind, just as at the time he had penned his speech, went back to when his head was held in the toilet bowl while someone flushed it nine times, at the time a seeming torment without end... he had hated his schooldays...'Nine flushes for the nine circles. There you are Virgil, lead yourself out of Hell...' He could still hear the words, after all these years.... At least it had given him an idea for his speech...those bastards...General polite applause...' It's a useful name now, however, because it enables me to remind you of our political fortunes as they were: internecine fighting, own goals, with people undermining all the hard work done at grass roots level,' A nod to the local Party members' tables and a ripple of applause... 'Yes, all that hard work undermined, the endless Party leadership debate, Europe - and I'll come to that in a moment - and so on. It was as though we'd hit rock bottom, Dante's ninth circle of Hell. But of course, that's to suggest that Virgil, this Virgil, has led you out.' Pause... 'But that's not the case.... We've done it together, we've all pulled together, and now we are out of the political wilderness, the Hell that is Policy without Power.' Pause, looking triumphantly at the expectant faces...'

We're back!' Thunderous applause and whoops of joy...

Then like a magician, Virgil Holmes conjured up, in brief and sparkling version, each of the major platforms that would win the Party the next election, and that would become policy and law under the new administration. He showed them, or rather reminded them, just how they would win over the electorate, convincing them that this would be the case across the land, and that this would certainly happen where it really translated into power, in the marginals...

He briefly covered: Health, with its usual mixed economy; Foreign Policy and Defence, with its emphasis on a strong and wise Britain that would neither fail nor forget its traditional allies, and that would be a world leader with a common-sense approach; Religion, briefly and with a witty little remark about preaching to the converted; Education, freedom of choice and standards and 'our young people', and before getting onto economic stability, the problem of Law and Order... Here he deviated a little from his prepared speech...

'You know,' he ad-libbed, 'our Party has a real strength in depth, not the least part of that strength in depth being the number and quality of young and zestful MPs and key players at the heart of our every policy... Law and Order is just one area I cite as an example...'

In his seat at one of the foremost tables Patrick Lansing unconsciously shifted uneasily, as though in autonomic response, and looked on intently with dark furrowed brow as Virgil Holmes, white tuxedo, expressive arms and confident smile, at centre stage, continued...

'I feel our message is getting through, and,' with a nod to the Leader,' David agrees with me.' The Leader of the Party duly nodded back in agreement, feeling, a little riskily it had to be said (because this part of the speech was new to him), he could trust Holmes's judgement.... ' And while some may have thought,' Holmes continued, emboldened, ' again, as one example, that Dain Alvis's comments at the Party Conference were too strident in tone, a little aggressive in their import, a little out of tune with the world in which we now live, they have nevertheless struck a chord with the British people, as our by-election and local election successes have shown...'

The sound of Dain Alvis's name sent a shock through Patrick Lansing. Sitting up, he looked around and behind as though seeking a soul mate who in equal measure might be sharing his unease. But look as he would across the tables in the plush chandelier-lit great room, there seemed no one else on whom the mention of this name had grated. So Lansing subsided in his chair and pondered on his obsession with this man.

Holmes had moved on to the Economy under the government in waiting, and it would soon be time for the Leader to say a few closing words of thanks.

It had been a successful event, Patrick Lansing had had to admit to that view of matters: plenty of glad handing, back slapping, mutual appreciation, smiles, laughter and good food in the very best of surroundings, with even the vagaries of the weather conspiring to be kind to the proceedings.

Into the early hours, there were a handful of couples, most young, but one or two individuals not so young, who, taking the opportunity of an event away from home, played away from home as the saying went, and in torrid hot embrace or bumbling half-drunken embrace with clothes strewn around, sought the self-abandonment of illicit sex. A much larger group, with their usual partners, most ready for sleep, briefly commented on the day's events. Not a few remarked on Virgil Holmes's laboured Dante analogy, with gentle and kindly or tolerant criticism: a few were more viciously mocking, like tormentors in that very Hell of Dante's imagining. Patrick Lansing was somewhere in between, jaundiced anyway by Holmes's mention of Alvis.

Lansing said to his wife: 'Holmes was a little over the top with his Dante allusion, don't you think? Ninth circle of Hell to describe a couple of years in the political doldrums... These new boys... Still, I shall think of him in a different light now. It makes a change to hear him talk about something other than his financial successes and the state of the market. If I think of Hell, though, it's some hollow-faced mother in a third-world nation nursing a dying staring empty-bellied child, or children in a schoolroom being hacked to death by machete-wielding drunken or drugged-up thugs with about as much humanity in them as a... a head louse...'

His wife, undressing, pulled a face, not wanting to go to bed on a diet of such images. She poured out a nightcap for them both and smiled at her husband. He in his turn suffered a pang of guilt, then laughed at himself for his choice of comparison. Then Virgil Holmes struck him in the next moment as a rather comic figure in his white tuxedo. Perhaps he was though leading them out of Hell after all.

6. *Silas Wood*

Silas Wood had an interesting name: it was officially Alfred Hector Erasmus Winston Wood. Someone, of course at least one of his parents Samuel and Ruth Wood, was hedging their bets. Would young Alfie (a diminutive he trialled for a time) become a great hero, a great scholar, the saviour of a nation, or even, one assumes, the King of Wessex and to all intents and purposes the King of England?

Of course, they knew full well that this last achievement was entirely beyond the ability or drive of a commoner in this modern age: for young Henry Bolingbroke (aka Henry 1V) it might have been possible to seize the crown, but the world had moved on... Nor would young Alfie need to become a 'tamer of horses' or be required to sacrifice himself to an invincible latter-day Achilles in order to achieve a form of immortality... And no one was really expecting another Adolf Hitler to arise and threaten these shores necessitating the emergence of another Winston Churchill to inspire the nation, to woo a US President and convince another Stalin... When all was said and done, these names were something of a burden, a curse even rather than a blessing... And Erasmus too: that was the name he was most ashamed of in case people should think, geek by name, geek by nature...

Yet Silas Wood did not have the misfortune of having to mix with the lower orders of society, as a few of his school-fellows were pleased to refer to them (though he himself thought this sentiment immature) and found that pretentious forenames were not all that uncommon amongst his peers. Perhaps, he considered, he was a born liberal and was embarrassed to be very comfortably middle class, upper middle class, in fact, if money had anything to do with it. Certainly, his parents were well off: his father was, cliché-like, 'something in the city', a phrase he found himself saying to his prep school classmates (though he was too young to understand what this implied), and his mother was a solicitor. His private schooling combined with his parents' management of at least some of his 'free time' brought him success at his independent senior school before he was then plunged into the hard work in English texts that Warwick University demanded of him.

Silas had for many years gone by the name Alfie. Appropriate enough and no one seemed to remember the film and song of that name, so it was all in all rather neutral, neither a millstone nor strikingly impressive -

Alfie Wood... Perhaps though a little down-market to its owner's taste...

In the 6th Form, some months before his exams, and with one eye on his place at Warwick (he had failed to get into Oxford but he still needed three As), Alfie, impressed unaccountably by the name Silas Marner (the eponymous hero of a book mentioned by his tutor as one he should look at as background reading) and feeling that it had a ring to it, duly adopted the name Silas, and so became Silas Wood, to all who knew him. The girls in particular seemed to like it, and it thus had a sort of talismanic effect on its owner. The new name may have played its part, he felt, in his losing his virginity at the age of eighteen, following an interschool 6th Form party at Meehan's nightclub... Amanda Morton... walked her home, to her aunt's house, to which she had a latchkey... no one at home...a nervous kiss...her hot, sweet and nervous lips (her first time too), guilty haste to the bedroom and guiltily within... She had supplied the condom and the towel spread over the sheet in case of any tell-tale bodily fluids of lost innocence... then her aunt had come back earlier than expected... They were downstairs in such a hurry they hardly knew how they had gotten there... hearts beating so fast and loud that auntie could surely hear the thumpety-thump... trying then to try and make small talk about the aunt's theatre trip, feeling each of them that they were wearing a big sandwich board announcing their discovery of original sin, thinking too about their own secret pleasure and the achievement of a milestone on the road of life, formerly a millstone that had made them feel inadequate among some of their, allegedly, more successful and experienced peers.

'Silas' Wood therefore went to university without, from his perspective on life, the hang-up of never having 'done it'. He'd gotten his three As too, gone to Warwick as planned: everything was falling into place. At 'uni' he was relaxed, easy-going and popular, he believed. He had a mop of dark-brown tousled hair then, a student's special sense of self-importance laced with uncertainty, and a good sense of humour. Some of his male peers, in the freshers' year certainly, looked, he thought, compared to him, like rabbits caught in the headlights. His relationship with Mandy had now cooled: it was conceivable, probable even, all along that she had used him as much as he had used her, but that did not shake, offend or bother Silas. He could now talk about her as an ex-girlfriend back home, which, he felt, made him both more interesting and available. The difference between confidence and diffidence, between success and failure, was no more than the thickness of a paper wall that people broke through or not. Time made him forget this, that happenstance had played its part, and he grew used to his own person and his luck, so that like people he thought less successful socially, he was just as incensed about a low mark in an essay and felt just as keenly a sense of injustice.

Silas did in fact become a little opinionated, and also prone to mood swings, especially when everything failed to go his way. His heart remained however, as most would aver, in the right place. Even some who thought him arrogant, or imagined he was acting as 'God's gift', could not doubt his enthusiastic support for the rights of the individual in society, and the genuineness of his anger at governments home and abroad who either blatantly disregarded freedom or else chipped away at it, or acted as a dripping tap, looking to erode freedom over time. In addition to his studies then, Silas contributed to the student newsletter, spoke vehemently at NUS conferences, and yes, let us not forget, after a couple of one-night stands in his middle year, found himself a steady girlfriend, whom he loved and who in the short space of a week was introduced to his parents: 'Mum, Dad, this is Lindy...' Lindy Took's forename was Rachel, but she was so deliriously happy about a day at Lindisfarne when the family had been holidaying in the Cheviots when she was eight years old, that her parents had taken to calling her Lindy, and the name had stuck.

University was over, for the time being... the impromptu parties, the chaotic mess at the rented house, the groggy mornings, the nights watching the matches on Sky, the occasional missed lecture, the reading up for essays and exams, that last push towards finals, his dissertation on Lawrence, which it seemed he would never finish on time, with his tutor's demanding insistence on deletions, additions... the cogency of his argument came under criticism too... In the end, he'd had enough of Ursula, Gudrun, Rupert and Gerald, though now, as he looked back, he was pleased as punch that he'd done it, and pleased as punch with his 2.1; especially given that now, with hindsight and, if he was honest, he said to himself, he could have worked harder... This was untrue, of course, his excuse for not getting anywhere near a First. In fact, in his last year, despite the delightful distractions of Lindy and the occasional riotous evening with his male friends, he had worked very hard indeed, fearing that he might finish with a 2.2.

It was over: three great years, he often reminisced... he knew, or thought he knew, that it hadn't been so good for others, even if their smiles and hugs and back slapping on graduation day had suggested otherwise. He was, in truth, smug: he felt superior, invincible; he felt that he, Silas Wood, was actually much, much better than the average, that he was destined for great things where others were not.

Silas had spoken glibly, especially when well-oiled, about 'doing something in publishing' or 'going into politics'; or, he would 'see how the land lies', or, with even greater self-deception he would harmlessly deceive others with, 'Oh, I have a few irons in the fire' or 'one or two things in the pipeline'... His father was ever poised to intervene, to find him something, but knew he would be blamed if it all went wrong, so he held back to see whether Silas could find his own way.

Lindy, too, had gotten a little concerned about him. She knew, or knew of, the unforgiving nature of the real world, and hard-headedly, as well as in the marrow of her bone, knew that you had to work at one thing, really work, to be something you wanted to be: that, or you would become nothing, just one of society's pawns, or a bit of flotsam drifting from one job to another, relying not on Providence, which she felt favoured the determined, but on luck alone. She wanted to be safe, secure, which is why she had her career as a biochemist mapped out: degree, research, post-doctoral research, a foot in the door, and let them carry her out dead at the end if they wanted rid of her, whoever *they* might turn out to be. She knew that she was a very clever girl, but she knew that Silas was clever too, in his own way - but he must learn to focus. She hoped that after a year out, he would focus and register for a PhD. When he took himself less seriously as a man of destiny he would probably make a good lecturer. She would always smile at his man of destiny speeches: they usually followed a good intake of vodka, or lager, just as her father's disgruntled (he was quite contented as a rule) fireside diatribes about the state of the country were fuelled by expensive red wine, and now too by the more insidiously working onset of middle age.

Silas thought a lot about Lindy. He had initially hesitated, very, very briefly, to commit but... Lindy was beautiful in his eyes, lively and positive about life, what he needed and what made him feel good. She was not that tall, bordering on petite in fact, but with a perfect figure... Drawn by the physical first as are many, he first noticed, he told his friends, her firm little boobs, her flat midriff... a shapely little backside, well-shaped legs... But he was always really attracted by faces first, and hers was a radiant open face with large dark-brown eyes, a face framed by flowing, cascading dark-brown shoulder-length hair that smelt as sweet as new-mown hay, as he liked to comment... Lindy laughed at his jokes too, but could be serious at times, when it mattered to him, and was passionate about all the things he cared about... She was passionate in the bedroom too but was never clingy or possessive... 'Lucky Silas', his friends began to call him, and he hoped that that had not been the deciding factor... that instead she had seen real qualities in him. The upshot was that Silas began to find the future inconceivable, impossible without Lindy at his side.

And Lindy was right for him and right about him: her faith was rewarded. Silas suddenly became aware that he was in danger of becoming a drifter and a day-dreamer. Suitable work was not so easy to come by, much less the big breakthrough he had promised himself. In truth, he had put in little effort, and he knew it. But he had managed to pick up a bit of temp work at the local council, helping with a backlog of data entry related to long-term adult care assessments. The ageing population... It was true. It was also true that that this work was not what Silas had had in mind. He was young: the world and time stretched out before him...

The sunlight, bright, golden, warming his right cheek and his denim-clad leg, streamed softly through the south-facing French doors of the comfortable late-Victorian terraced house, his sister's house. Silas sat meditating, relaxed, sprawled, in an easy chair. He always liked to visit his ever-busy older sister Hope, who, however busy she was, always delighted in seeing her little brother, and would always make time for his visits, dropping temporarily all the jobs or errands she had planned. If Silas happened along when she was due to pick up the children from school, then, with a rush of enthusiasm, she got Silas to tag along. For Silas, the novelty of picking up the two youngest of his nieces, Siobhan and Charity, soon wore thin. He found the babble and screaming of the 3.15pm pick-up at the nearby primary school grated on his nerves: the waiting amongst the crowd also irritated him, and it seemed that his nieces were the last, or almost the last, to come out. The push-chairs, the toddlers, Hope's fellow young mums, a sprinkling of grannies and granddads, the odd incongruous older father... After a couple of trips, he was bored with it, though he loved to see his nieces. 'It's all a bit random,' he said to Hope by way of comment, not really knowing what he meant by this. His perceptive older sister knew, however: she knew that Silas needed a few more years of 'freedom' before tying himself down to a family. She hoped Lindy felt the same, as appeared to be the case. 'Silas, with a family!' she had said to her husband Ben's cousin Ryan, when Ryan had been trying to get to grips with who was who in the Blenkin household. Then he'd gone back to Australia after five weeks in Europe, two of which had been spent in England. He never really fully grasped the network of family members on Hope's side. It had been the second time around too, as he had been a guest at Ben and Hope's wedding nine years earlier, in 2005.

'Soon be your birthday, Silas...in three weeks. Any plans? Going away anywhere?' Hope, five feet four, now with blonde tumbling curls, was a bundle of energy, and of questions for her little brother.

'Yes, the May Day boy, always easy to remember... not that you would forget, Sis...' Silas had been smilingly staring contentedly at the sunbeam patterns being woven on the surface of the new blue-grey carpet of the comfortably furnished cosy lounge, with its mix of mainly faux antique and a dash of modern functional. 'Lindy and I will go out for a meal, I think.' Silas suddenly looked preoccupied with his thoughts.

'What's up, Silas?' Hope stopped still, holding in the air, like a symbol, the cup of tea she was going to hand to her brother. 'Oh, yes, here,' she said, handing it to him at last, looking at him intently and awaiting his answer. He would always confide in her: she knew that, and he knew that.

'Oh, it's mum and dad - well, mum really,' he responded, with an element of gloominess, or perhaps he was looking for sympathy. 'Mum's always going on about a job and the future. It's true she's better now, now I'm bringing some money into the house. It's funny, with school, it was always dad going on at us, and now with work and careers, it's mum.'

'You'll be OK,' she warmly reassured him. 'Things have a habit of working themselves out. A bit of a cliché I know, but it's true. I always worry about the children, but Ben's much worse than I am in that way... You know, the sort of world and all that, but we can't wrap them in cotton wool, as they say... It's a comfortable and safe life, really, living here. Not much crime, and because we're back from the road at the front - we've got gates and things as you've seen anyway - the cars ...well, you know, this road's not so busy...not a rat run.'

'Yeah'. Silas, now reassured and cheerful again, the effect Hope usually had on him, looked out and studied the garden with the weathered bird bath in the centre of the little lawn. 'It's a nice spot you've got here, 'he said,' lovely family home... lots of character...'

She laughed. 'You're moving into estate agent mode: mature four-bedroom terrace in quiet residential area...But, yes, I couldn't really think of anywhere else I'd rather be at the moment. It's great... Did you want to sit outside? It's chilly but it's bright...'

'I'm perfectly happy here, Sis... How is Faith doing at the secondary?'

'Well, she's in her first year there. We had a little bit of trouble, but it's all been sorted: it's a good school.'

'Trouble?'

'The usual I suppose - a bit of bullying. It was nothing,' Hope's momentarily furrowed brow, a cloud passing swiftly over her usually sunny face suggested that it had not actually been nothing; but she quickly overcame the memory that troubled her. 'Really, it's all sorted. She's perfectly happy there now.'

‘A mother at eighteen, Sis... Bit of a shock for mum and dad, ‘laughed Silas.

‘They’re over it by now. Just as big a shock for them that I’d already decided not to go to university. In fact, they still talk about that as I’m sure you know...’

‘They’re probably thinking you took the right decision, when they look at me,’ he shuffled in his seat and smiled a mock rueful smile.

‘Oh rubbish! You’ve done well, *very* well... It’ll work out.’

‘Yes, in fact it will,’ proclaimed the brother determinedly, sweeping back his brown locks with his right hand as he was wont to do at such moments. ‘I’ve as good as made up my mind to go back, register for a PhD, do some lecturing... by hook or by crook, do what I should be doing...’

‘Great! Well done.’ Hope plumped down on the settee opposite him, feeling, and consciously appreciating the sun’s warmth on her face. ‘I told you you’d be OK. And the politics? Still as interested?’

‘Yes, of course...er...yes,’ Silas replied a little guiltily. It was one of those things he had let slip, his political activity, but his interest was still there, and his views were still as forthright. He felt guilty because he knew that a man of destiny did not just think and say but actually did something to make a difference. His sister knew him well, however...

‘Well, ‘she suggested,’ I suppose you’re not so involved, now that you’re no longer at uni, the hot-bed of activity,’ laughing, ’politically speaking, that is.’

'Yes, yes,' Silas laughed, feeling at once relieved and less self-critical,' but it was never like I imagine the LSE to have been ...I suppose in the sixties, seventies, and eighties, was it, of the last century... Life's so much more complicated now. For one thing, it's not so easy to shock anymore. A paradox really, when politics has become so bland, and has been for years, so that you can't tell the difference between one party and another. Well, except for one or two extremists or out and out characters. But no, that actually isn't true: things are suddenly beginning to change... one or two things I've noticed over the last year to eighteen months. And yes, I am part of the change. I was part of a splinter group, a faction, at uni, wanting a more socialist approach, outmoded though it now seems. There's been an erosion of personal liberty, no doubt about it... and too much tax, too much information held. Of course, there are threats, but we've been there before. You remember, fifteen or twenty years ago and more...Weapons of Mass Destruction, a form of words as far as I can discover created in the lead-up to convincing everyone that Iraq should be bombed. Of course, such weapons always were that, but no one had used the words in that way, as buzz words, as they used to call them, to popularise a cause. Interestingly, Bush senior, the first George Bush, talked about the new world order, though his accent came from the wrong part of the States: he meant new '*woild*' order... and where has it got us... and there's an interesting point,' (as if he had never said it before and his sister had never heard it before) 'the only country that has really ever used weapons of mass destruction on a civilian population is the US in 1945... As they say, History is written by the victors... Then of course there was Libya, and Syria...'

'Whoa! Slow down - you're preaching to the converted. Not that I'm anti-American, and nor should you be. We'd both be glad to see American marines turn up if we were being held captive by terrorists... though I suppose that that's simplistic, if not a bit racist, and what we're conditioned to think... Anyway, what is certain is that most Americans are people just like us. If you leave out governments and the military, and the arms dealers, most people just want to live their lives without a lot of unnecessary fuss and trouble.'

'Apart from the vociferous minority, eh, Sis,' laughed Silas, visibly relaxing. 'But it is true none the less that it is an ever more complex world we live in: black and white standpoints are harder to see, solutions so much more difficult. At least global warming seemed to have taken a week off ...'

Hope, however, would not at first be drawn. 'Yes, a cold late spring - the frost nipped some of my patio plants, but it's warm today. Sure you don't want to sit out?'

'No, I'm fine here, but I'd like to have a little wander in the garden before I go - see what you've been up to...Where were we... yes, global warming: another hose-pipe ban this year do you think?'

'I hope not. That does annoy me. When we took the children to Spain last year there was no sign of any shortage, and yet they don't have half the rainfall we have...'

'Not so many people either, not so many conurbations, and concentrations of industry... well, perhaps that's not true anymore, I don't know. Out of my depth there, but the world's problems are massive. Lindy says that she'd heard a visiting speaker from Hoffnung Pharmaceuticals say that it was all to do with entropy... Lindy's tried to explain what that means, but my brain cells tend to shut down when it comes to science and maths.'

Hope looked with almost a mother's tenderness at her little brother, now a young man nearly half a foot taller than her.

'Come on,' she said on an impulse, 'let me show you the garden then. After that I'll make us another drink and break open the digestives, even though I'm trying to be good.'

'You don't need to lose any weight,' Silas frowned, at the same time patting his own middle.' Actually, I don't either...'

'You! I should think not. Silas, now I've had three children, I find I need to be a bit careful; but you, you're like a rake...'

'The rake's progress,' he laughed, passing a self-congratulatory palm over his designer-stubble chin.

The compact little town garden with the high brick wall running along the back, and close-board fencing six feet high on both sides bordering the neighbours, was sheltered and private, a haven. Beyond the high rear wall, partly ivy-covered, was a broad walkway, tree-lined, with another row of large Victorian terraced houses fronting the walk across the quiet street. The garden was coming to life: the cherry tree close to the wall was beginning to blossom, as were the dwarf azaleas in the corner, while the grape hyacinths, poking through here and there in the borders like vivid little knobbly spears, were at their peak, and competing them was a scattering of newly emerging bluebells. The daffodils were past their best, but a few narcissi clung on to their self-regarding splendour. All across the patio, whereon stood a round-topped blue-green marble mosaic table with two distressed metal chairs with wicker seats, pots were strewn, in various stages of preparation for planting out.

'You really are happy here, aren't you, Sis?' Silas' s eye had caught a yellow plastic bat and a soft red spongy ball in the corner. 'And the kids must love it, too', he added. 'Lindy and I will come round and see you very soon, for a proper visit, in the evening. I really would like to see you all together. It's a long time since Ben and I have had a chat, and I'm sure the girls would like to see their uncle Silas... and Lindy has been insisting that I sort something out... You know, it's a good life if...'

'You don't think about it too much,' Hope interrupted, sensing that her brother might cross into becoming maudlin. Then at the same moment she gave him a big hug.

He laughed, genuinely happy, in the moment... 'Ah, yes, I didn't tell you: in August, Lindy's parents are taking us with them to the Switzerland for ten days.

Wengen - in the Bernese Oberland, right up in the mountains...'

'Fantastic. But why didn't you tell me before...great. You need to enjoy it and forget about the world and its troubles for a couple of weeks.'

'You're right, I do think too much, have something to say about everything, worry too much... Yeats was right: he had it stuck on his gravestone: "Cast a cold eye on Life on Death/ Horseman pass by"'.

'Sounds a bit grim,' laughed Hope, frowning a little none the less. 'I'm not sure about being cold about the good things in life...'

Silas stared lovingly at his vivacious, uncomplicated and aptly named sister. Had she missed the point though, or had he?

7. *An interview to remember*

The studio was tense and taut with anticipation. There was a palpable atmosphere like the crackling in the air before an electrical storm; at least, so it was in the minds of those present: a memorable event about to take place.

Lighting, sound, the studio's producer, cameras one through three, transmission, make-up... all getting ready for the interview, all getting ready to get it out to the nation... start on time to the second and finish on time... well practised at this... And the nation, blasé as a result of decades of live broadcasting, could usually take or leave these late night politically focused head to heads in spite of the no-holds-barred style of the eminent broadcaster who had become a national institution, even a national treasure because of his uncompromising and sometimes confrontational style of questioning. Gerald Goodman, journalist, broadcaster and political biographer of note, who had made many an Honourable Member blanch and stammer under the studio lights and under the camera's eye in his time...

Two high-backed leather seats, with gleaming stainless-steel arms, faced each other under the glare, across a glass-topped low table, a scene shown always empty as the opening credits rolled up, the show's trademark. A civilized confrontation was planned, in this executive office minimalist-chic setting. The focus would of course be on the verbal combatants: the technical wizardry, and the fruits of the weeks of planning and organising, the behind the scenes hard work were naturally taken for granted.

Given the growing interest in Gerald Goodman's larger-than-life, outspoken guest, who had never before deigned (a homophonic newspaper pun on the day) to be interviewed in such a fashion, wholly in the spotlight and by so formidable a foe as Goodman, anticipation was high that ratings would be boosted this evening. Tomorrow's newspapers might actually be saying the words 'good television', or 'TV licence money well spent…' A moment in TV history, or perhaps a footnote in history itself, history writ large?

The interviewer took his seat, stage right. Still a long lean frame, and dark wavy hair, now greying around the temples. A more livid face, but a long hook-nosed powerful face, deep-brown intent eyes under a shrewd and furrowed brow. The confident relaxed air of a man who knew his business: a celebrity in his own right and a two million a year man. In his faintly striped suit, a lightly patterned blue tie and pink shirt, he adjusted his long, crossed legs a little as he glanced at the sheaf of notes in his lap.

Then opposite... opposite... and lured into Goodman's interviewer's den at last, the other, the guest, the victim, if that were not too strong or fanciful a word, which of course it was, given that this was just a bit of TV... Opposite, also in a suit, blue suit, wearing a white shirt and diagonally striped two-toned blue tie, sat the other man. Shoes were shined as well as those of Goodman, even though, aside from the opening and closing shots, and a couple of long shots during the proceedings, no viewer would be able to see their feet. Still, nothing could be left to chance, and you never knew when a press photographer would pop up uninvited, in spite of the heavy security: one had always to look one's best, to be dressed appropriately for the occasion... Hair, dark-brown hair, a little lank, face oval, unremarkable really, the nose a little long, but the eyes, a deep radiant blue that at one in the same time seemed vacant and fathomless yet whose gaze could be penetratingly warm like a summer sky, or blue-hot, like the fire of a burning star, and seemed always probing or knowing, as though he were looking through you or deep into your soul... this man of the people. Man of the people? Sage? Executioner? Taxman? All these labels had been attached to, but none really got to the quintessence of the man whose particular form of personal magnetism belied his average height, his compact tidy, broad-shouldered and muscular frame, that of a gymnast, it had been suggested. His thin bloodless lips could widen into a winning smile, causing a dimple in his left cheek. The teeth, not brilliant white yet devoid of caries, were not perfectly aligned, were not those of a Hollywood star, but such attention to physical perfection was not, he would often avow, his business: he was, he said, with all his imperfections, a man of the people, and above all a man for the people...

The Interview 23.01 hours 15 June 2015 BBC 2

'Dain Alvis, you've been quoted as saying - and I'm quoting from your maiden speech in the House' (Goodman adroitly picked out the relevant piece of paper as he spoke in his slow deliberate fashion) '- that your Party will bring order to the streets. Hasn't happened, has it?'

Alvis, apparently relaxed, eyes staring into those of the interviewer, was slow to reply. He was either preparing himself for a long answer or deliberately creating suspense. Like Goodman, he was a consummate performer.

'You're absolutely right, Gerald,' he began, slowly, deliberately. Everyone in the studio gazed with rapt attention...' absolutely right, except in your emphasis and context: I did say that the Party would bring order, but within that context, that I would make this my personal mission.' He leaned forward here with a look of increased intensity, the blue eyes piercingly fixed, as when he spoke stridently from the rostrum at the Party Conference...' My personal mission, 'he repeated,' as a representative of and on behalf of the law-abiding citizens of this country...'

'Well, that makes it even worse, doesn't it?' suggested the interviewer in a cool matter-of-fact way, ready and waiting too with his sheaf of papers, the relevant statistics to hand therefore.

'I respectfully disagree, Gerald: violent crime and intimidation has stabilized, the upward trend has levelled out.'

'Is that what you meant by bringing order?'

'If you'll let me finish, I'll answer your question fully. Of course, the viewers watching tonight' (a smile) 'will be aware that this issue will take time: it isn't going to happen overnight... But if you go around the former no-go estates as I've done, you will see that people are noticing an increase in the number of police officers on the beat. You'll hear from people - as I have - who say that the tougher attitude by the police in the dispersal of gangs...'

'But the overall crime figures...'

'One thing at a time, one thing at a time: the people of this country understand that. The real issue of concern for the law-abiding majority is that for decades now no one has addressed this issue. You know, Gerald, I don't have any children, but I understand the caring parent who for years...'

'You said decades - does that include the negligence or failure of your own party?'

'As I said, and this is important, people understand what I'm saying, and my view will not change... Caring parents who have nurtured and loved a child, brought it up responsibly, to grow into a fine young man or woman, with the future in front of them... These parents are terrified that their beloved child will fall victim to these dirty little street cowards, because that is what they are, these mindless worthless louts... And it is a matter of respect for life and for one's fellow citizens.'

'Of course not, your view will not change' interrupted Goodman, aware of the harsher tone in the politician's voice, 'but how are you really going to...'

'Gerald, these cowards, these craven apologies for human beings who enjoy violence as long as they are able to carry it out with little risk to themselves, and perhaps because in the past they have felt safe from real retribution, real justice... They feel safe, or have done for many years - until very recently... As I've said, loving parents don't bring up a son, for example, attend parents' evenings at school, take him to the doctor anxiously when he's sick, encourage him to get on in life and become a responsible citizen, to see his cherished head kicked like a football by a drunken cowardly excuse for a human being; or a daughter...'

'You're talking, Mr. Alvis, about your proposal that such killings, which don't involve the use of a weapon such as a gun or knife be...'

'Murders, always murders,' interrupted the politician passionately, with an almost predatory gleam in his eye, sensing the watching nation, 'they are murders just the same.'

‘Yes, well, fine, murders, let’s stick with that word, since you insist upon it; and I’m sure many will agree with you... But how will you...’

‘There will be no mercy for these people.’

‘You’ll bring back the death penalty?’

‘I didn’t say that. I said there will be no mercy for these people.’

‘But surely that’s what you implied, isn’t it? And surely the issue here is that your party, the party of government, won’t let you go too far. Isn’t your party the party that said it no longer wanted to be seen as part of the “flog ‘em and hang ‘em brigade”?’

‘A derogatory and hackneyed label, but not applicable here...’ Alvis, louder and more strident, was none the less controlled, measured in his responses. ‘Ours, mine, is a completely new approach to this matter, a determined approach. I believe that as a party, we were elected to deliver on this issue as much as any other.’ And now he half glanced at the camera, at the people, sensing their attentive presence at the hearthstone, in the home. ‘I will not let this matter rest: I take personal responsibility for the solution to this problem, insofar as the power rests in me.’

‘Isn’t that a little self-aggrandising, a little arrogant, Mr Alvis? Come on, there was a Cabinet reshuffle recently and you were ignored for the post of Home Secretary.’

Dain Alvis beamed a smile beneath his lank dark hair, and purposefully it seemed gave a chuckle, as if amused by Goodman. ‘As you will no doubt tell me in a moment or two, Gerald, I'm only thirty-one and perhaps not ready for full Cabinet responsibility.'

'Is that your leader's view?'

'The Prime Minister has a view of course, and far be it from me to question his judgement. But there is still time. While the people of this country continue to share my concerns, support my position, and I thank them for their good judgement in that...' He hesitated, but only for a second... 'There will be other cabinet reshuffles.'

'Do you ever see yourself as Prime Minister?'

'Everyone likes to do the best for his country, and the higher one goes in government, the more one can achieve for a people that wants a government to tackle the issues head on, and not just talk about it, as the last government did.'

'As did your own party, as you've already implied,' Goodman added in passing before saying: 'Isn't it true that you're perceived as a bit of a maverick, and that while you appeal to popular sentiment, it doesn't matter really because your own party will never fully accept your extreme views?'

'It matters to tell the truth about the state of the nation, Gerald - that's what matters. And of course, you're wrong to say, or suggest that I lack my supporters within the party...'

'You're talking about Austin Summerville's support of you at the last Party Conference?'

'Austin, yes, and others; but I'm not running for the leadership yet, Gerald,' he laughed. 'As I've already suggested, I'll have to wait for another Cabinet reshuffle. But I can wait, and,' he looked briefly towards the camera,' my view on this and many another issue will not change.'

'You've a strong opponent and voice of opposition in Patrick Lansing, the Home Secretary, isn't that the case?'

'Patrick and I have differences of opinion: that's true of any democratic party, and any party where lively debate is encouraged...'

As Alvis spoke, Goodman was thinking: 'Is this interview tough enough?' Should he deviate from his script? People were sitting in front of their TV screens at home, or less likely but possible, one or two pubs might be showing this, such was the interest aroused by what in his secret and personal view was a cold and cunning, inordinately ambitious and, if the truth be told, rather unnerving and even spooky individual sitting calmly opposite him in the glare of the studio lights...

'You know,' Dain Alvis continued, 'people are watching this' (Goodman felt as though his mind had been read) 'and thinking, will this man be true to his word and continue to push for action on the all the important issues within government? And the answer is, yes, of course he will.' Alvis smiled, feeling that his star was still in the ascendant. Then he looked coldly, insolently almost, at or rather through Goodman, who re-crossed his long legs and shuffled his papers. He sensed the Goodman did not like him and felt that this gave him the edge over the renowned bruiser of TV journalism.

‘You’ve been accused of many things, Dain Alvis.’ Alvis smiled his thin smile. ‘Some accusations may seem a bit wild, that, for example, you have racist leanings... and an overly, some might say, pro-German stance on Europe. One of your own Party even called you, or at least implied that you reminded him of Adolf Hitler...’ Goodman barely got the name out, and it turned to sawdust in his mouth: he hadn’t meant to say it, to go down this line of questioning or criticism, even though his source was accurate, as everyone knew. It was a cheap shot, though. Alvis did bear some resemblance to the German *Führer*: more handsome certainly, his hair less dark; but the eyes, the nose, the mouth, the forehead...a rounder face though, and more inclined to smile...yes, more handsome than the unprepossessing Austrian...

Dain Alvis stared, another insolent hard stare at Goodman, but lost somehow on camera and only directed at Goodman, or so the newsman felt. And his reply seemed an age in coming.

‘An odd story,’ he smiled. ‘I must confess I am surprised that a man of your experience, integrity and professionalism has stooped to lift that old chestnut from the gutter, Gerald...’

‘It has been said, though,’ retorted Goodman, palpably embarrassed, red in the face and on the defensive.

‘Yes, and I should answer it. But first of all, I should like to make a point, one that I’m sure you’ll agree with: being a Germanophile does not make one a racist...’

‘Of course, I wasn’t trying to suggest that’... Goodman was recovering but was not quite back to where he wanted to be.

‘Every nation has its racists,’ Alvis elaborated,’ and emphatically I do not belong to that group of people in this nation. I do admire the tenacity and hard work of the German people who have consistently performed well economically since the horrors of the Second World War and the difficulties of reunification, and who have tried to move on from the awful legacy and stigma inherited from the person you named. Germanophile? yes, I freely admit it; but I am a European and I also admire the French, the Italians, and of course the Welsh the Scots and the Irish who make up this Great Britain. But you will be aware, or should be - and I’m sure you’ve done your research,’ nodding to the sheaf of papers on Goodman’s lap, ’ you will be aware too, Gerald, that I have German ancestry on my mother’s side, and that more importantly as a nation, or at least part of the nation, we share a common ancestry: the Angles and Saxons came from Germany, as every school child doing History knows or should know...I should add that twenty-five per cent of Americans can trace their ancestry back to Germany. But I understand that relatively recent history, Dunkirk, the Blitz, the Holocaust, remain potent symbols; and other European countries, like Poland and the former Soviet Union will no doubt have bitterer memories than we have... But the world does move on, and if we are going to talk about history perhaps we should also remember that

Prussia played its part in the defeat of Napoleon at Waterloo... But it is today's problems...'

'Yes, well, without dwelling on history...' Goodman had recovered much of his poise but knew he had yet to recover the initiative.

'On a personal level, I will also freely confess, Gerald,' Alvis continued,' that I study, or perhaps dabble in Anglo-Saxon, or Old English, the language, and that I admire the music of Bach, Beethoven, Brahms, Handel, Mozart and Haydn... the last two Austrian, of course.' He laughed, in control but wanting to get back to his political agenda, but not before he ended on a lighter note...' Oh, yes, and occasionally I drink German wine which is, by all accounts, immeasurably better than it used to be... I do like a pint of good English real ale, however...'

'I think we can all agree on that point,' Goodman joked impatiently.

'A final point on this matter,' Alvis added with a serious frown. 'One of the tabloids made great play of the fact that I have two Germans working for me. This is true. One is a reliable chauffeur, Horst, though I have another chauffeur, Aaron, who is Jewish, and who is every bit as reliable. I also have two Arabs on my household staff... All, apart from my parliamentary secretary, who is English, are paid for by me and not by the tax payer, something to note for the morning editions...' He smiled again and waited for Goodman's next question.

'So, your call for an end to immigration has nothing to do with, as one of your close colleagues called it, England for the English?' Hawk-like now sat Goodman, but he no longer felt like the predator here.

'The country is full, Gerald, that's my take on this matter. Whoever is here now, legally here, is British. It is neither socially nor economically viable to let more people into the country... We have a duty, as a government, to look after the interests of the people of these islands; and it is my firm belief that we can no longer afford an open-house policy. To paraphrase Churchill, an iron curtain will have to come down...'

'And the Prime Minister and his Cabinet share this view, do they?'

'I believe action will need to be taken sooner rather than later...'

'You know this? This is the Prime Minister's view?' Goodman, feeling better, feeling that he was setting the pace... though Alvis, watching and waiting, knew better. Relaxed in his chair, young, athletic and muscular, his strong hands resting on his lap, his fearless blue eyes resting on his interrogator.

'It is my view. I am one voice in a democratic government. I also happen to believe it is the people's view, whatever their ethnic origin. Everyone's life will suffer if immigration remains unchecked...'

Goodman made as if to speak...

'Resources are limited,' Alvis continued, his strong hands gesticulating with carefully timed gestures, punctuating his speech: 'action needs to be taken as a matter of urgency.'

'Very well,' Goodman conceded, but then he shifted the ground,' on the matter of resources, or management of resources, your government has made little or no impact on carbon emissions, has it?'

Dain Alvis thought hard for a long pregnant moment before coming out with a slow deliberate, almost menacing answer: 'My government will have to act,' he half-turned to the camera, as though aware he was almost about to give a prime-ministerial broadcast. ' Year on year we've talked around the world about reducing emissions, since the very first years of this century in fact... and, yes, we've failed as a government, as a society, as a nation, as a world... Half a per cent reduction last year, here in Great Britain, after a year on year increase, and a year on year increase everywhere else in the world, is just not good enough. This issue must be addressed.'

'Plans and fine words are not enough, are they, Mr. Alvis?'

'I wholeheartedly agree: plans and fine words are not enough. There will be a breakthrough on this issue - which affects us all - and over the generations to come the effort to reform our habits will continue, just as surely as there will be a breakthrough in regard to moral lassitude and moral turpitude, and to genuine fear, which is strangling the life out of our communities. That's beginning to happen, as I've indicated, but not quickly enough for my liking ... But global warming ... 2014 was the hottest year on record... the heat wave of 2014 that killed 300 people, possibly more, in this country alone, thousands in Europe, combined with hosepipe bans, and standpipes in the north east and East Anglia, the winter floods, the freak storms in Canada and Australia...Action will be taken, action will have to be taken...' Dain Alvis was impassioned, wholly convincing, simply because these issues were obsessions with him; and such issues demanded the emergence of the right man at the right time to deal with them.

'But how are you, how is the government going to get the people of this country, the businesses of this country...'

Goodman hesitated. He had suddenly lost his composure: in fact, he looked shocked. Off camera there was pandemonium, a sudden movement of people on the floor, the floor manager waving his arms, and there was a sudden flurry of activity in the production control room. 'I'm sorry, 'Goodman said, waving a long-fingered placatory hand towards his guest, as the other hand pushed at his earpiece. 'Look', he said, his head lowered, bowed as though talking to no one in particular,' is this true? I have to be certain...'

This was an unprecedented interruption. Dain Alvis, upright in his chair, like a fighter before the beginning of a round, was alert but appeared duly mystified. He lowered his gaze as though not wanting at that moment to be the focus of attention, since something vitally important was clearly going on. Meanwhile, more news, or reiterations of the same news, seemed to be pouring into Gerald Goodman's earpiece. The interviewer sat serious-faced, his head cocked to one side, listening intently.

There was excitement and stunned disbelief throughout the studio. Many, including Goodman, knew the political significance of the news, some knew *him* personally, and there was the timing of this news... It was, in broadcasting certainly, one of those moments... a moment in history...one to give you goose bumps... Where were you when...?

Goodman had recovered but looked grave.

'I'm sorry to have to tell you, Mr. Alvis...and,' with a solemn and suitably downcast look at the camera, though he was genuinely shocked,' and those of you at home watching, that Patrick Lansing was killed tonight in what I'm hearing is some sort of road accident. As yet the details are sketchy, but it seems that there is no doubt that Mr. Lansing, the Home Secretary, has died this evening.'

Dain Alvis looked drained of colour and completely in tune with the nation's sense of surprise and shock.

'Under the circumstances, Dain Alvis,' Goodman continued,' I don't think we can consider continuing with this interview. I am sure, though, that you would like to say a few words in tribute...'

'Indeed, 'Alvis began slowly,' I am very, very saddened by this news... Let us hope that there has been some mistake... But I share your view, Gerald, and I am sure people will understand, that under the circumstances it would be wholly inappropriate to continue with this interview.' A pause... 'I will say finally, however, that if this terrible news turns out to be true then my condolences go out to Heather, Mrs. Lansing, and to the whole family. 'He threw out his hands in rather a limp gesture of helplessness, as if to suggest that words were suddenly futile at such a moment, though he added for emphasis of the point: 'What can one say?'

At the edge of the studio, where the light was less revealing, Alvis was met after leaving his seat, by his two aforementioned chauffeurs, blond and cropped hair and blue-eyed Horst, the German, and curly haired, square-jawed Aaron, the Jew. Both were strapping athletic men, over six feet, and built like Olympic javelin throwers. Alvis walked between them, small in stature by comparison, but tough, square-shouldered and obviously in command, as they ushered him away from the scene of the aborted interview. The chauffeurs were well able to deal with any waiting press hounds who would be outside, quick off the mark, and they were soon flanked by others whose task it was to protect their leader.

Goodman joined his own entourage, or colleagues, production team and so on, the general studio throng... Lots of words were exchanged, a babble, as though words by their very utterance might bring the world back to order.

In a quieter moment, later on, as far away from people as he could manage, Gerald Goodman, feeling that he was close to the end of a long career, feeling old in short... He had been genuinely taken aback by the evening's events, and he philosophized to himself about how life always managed to surprise from time to time. And as he did so, he gazed at a long-legged fly moving slowly up the magnolia painted wall: both he and the fly seemed locked in a frozen moment of silence and contemplation.

People would go about their business tomorrow, and a minority would comment on this event. The morning editions would run something different now from the story they might have written about the Goodman-Alvis encounter, and pro or contra partisan comments about Alvis would probably have to be put on hold, for a time, while in due deference respects were paid to the long-serving Patrick Lansing.

It wasn't true of course that everyone was interested at that time. For example, at that time, at that moment in history, in the unremarkable place that might be called Anytown, someone called Harry Lattimore, a minor local government officer was consoling his tearful wife who had that day been diagnosed as suffering from advanced emphysema. She, and he, were alternating between moments of forced optimism and determination on the one hand, and on the other, talking through the consequences, the implications, the prognosis... the horror, the real horror, when to think that only a week earlier he had been raging about politics ... Retirement would have to take a new turn... Their reason and human spirit would be forced to come to terms with a darker future...

Silas Wood had had a long and busy day at work, from work, driving through town, watching people from his car in the hot stationary traffic: the black mother standing by the traffic lights, holding her little son's hand, next to her and overweight man with sunburnt tattooed arms, in a vest, and unshaven, looking unwashed too. He was walking a bicycle. He, Silas, had been able to see that that they were not together, yet they shared a joke, the man's belly shaking as he laughed: it had made Silas smile appreciatively, and lightened his mood during the short-distance but time-consuming journey... A moment...

Like a significant minority, Silas was that night watching the interview. He was at his parents' house with Lindy. They sat cuddling on the settee, relaxed, young, with a sense of invulnerability in each other's love. From time to time, Silas would delight in a loud but brief rant about Dain Alvis. The young couple did not like him, thought him a threat to liberty. Silas's parents, comfortable too in their own settled and contented world of rather splendid suburban cosiness, were more conservative in their views and concerned that someone should really govern the country, as Alvis was advocating. Silas was politely bullish in response to this red rag, which was not being waved deliberately in any case. He even agreed himself that more action was needed on the environment. But, at bottom, was

Silas's own realization that he had underestimated Dain Alvis. He was not just a Tory Party maverick. He now saw him in a different light, found him rather... disconcerting.

The sudden news about Patrick Lansing made them all gaze in stunned silence at the large flat screen and then at one another…

Suddenly, Silas was thinking, the world of bland contemporary politics had been jolted in its orbit. He could not say why exactly, but he felt that this night was of especial significance. Thinking logically, in a matter-of-fact way, a politician had died and that was that. That was the way Silas could have viewed it. But instinctively he felt the event meant more than this: he felt that a way forward had suddenly been opened up, or would open up, for Dain Alvis. There was a sudden awful inevitability about it.

8. *A man to be reckoned with*

You could say that the future stretches out like a giant staircase that reaches to the clouds: one model that could be employed for the passage from the actuality of birth, or certainly the consciousness of self, to the certainty of death... And so, you begin... You are drawn on, or you persevere... the further you go, the higher up you go, the greater the distance from the relative safety of childhood; though, truth to say, for many a childhood is neither safe nor happy, but just is. Many join you on this journey upwards, onwards, but should you avoid mishap, holding determinedly to the central way, to avoid plummeting into the terrifying dizzying gulf on either side, the fall into nothingness, then you see others disappear... your relatives, your friends, your associates, even those whom you despise or hate... Consciousness, of individuality, separateness, vulnerability, a feeling of being isolated, alone, grips you, even if in only rare isolated moments, as you go on... There may be nothing at the end, nothing: you may travel ever on, knowing that it is not in fact forever, and there is no way back, not one step is allowed... You know that to go back is impossible, to go forward is...

Without the comfort of God, some would say, the end is unthinkable.

And yet another view... The future is a flat land of many paths, forks, turnings, a maze with no clues, a puzzle without solution, featureless but always with the capacity to surprise, humble, terrify or please... In the end the result is the same... Your companions on the way are gone, or you must first leave them, with no second chance. You are alone, the carrier of what immortal truth about life there is, your life experienced but the truth veiled, the meaning half perceived. What drives you? Certainly, to stay alive, to live the longest and best life possible; unless the loss of others along the way brings you down, destroys your will, your desire to lengthen this life's journey, even for one more day...

For some though the quest, the monomania, the prophecy, the hand of Fate, is all in all. Fate has chosen you, you believe in your own importance, the significance of your contribution. You will drive on past all despair and beyond all hope. Beyond reason too... Reason, which might seem to inform the quest at the outset - 'Clearly, the case seems to be this, or this, and this or that action needs to be taken' - this reasoning in the obsessive soon becomes subservient to the mad blind drive for perfection in the complete execution of the plan, a no-compromise state. In the end, in only the most extreme cases, humanity as expressed in the common, the ordinary pursuits, ambitions, hopes and fears, will be entirely sacrificed to this no-compromise state of mind, which will abide no obstacle. Both Life and Death, one's own, become an irrelevance if unconnected to the Grand Plan... no time to worry about figurative staircases or forking paths...

In political history extreme cases of obsession with the quest seem rare, but are noteworthy and transcend the world of politics, leaving an indelible mark or stain. Hitler was one such case, and on the opposite end of the good-evil, moral-amoral, peace-war scale was Gandhi. The apparent annihilation of a real humanistic self that is without real empathy and concerned only with the abstract, a self-willed delusion, and that bends its whole being to serve the will to power and to self-aggrandisement in Hitler's case: the abnegation of self, the elimination of self-importance in Gandhi's case to achieve by peaceful means a country's independence... Both beyond the run-of-the-mill political, the seemingly possible, but creating a new possibility none the less... the quest of the driven... This is shared by the mathematician giving over his or her life to the proof of a theorem, to the point of nervous collapse, and it is seen in the madness of Van Gogh, some might say. The goal is all, praised if for the common good, sometimes praised anyway. Einstein... $E= mc^2$... a masterpiece, a Sistine Chapel of Physics, but at the theoretical heart of Hiroshima and Nagasaki... The driven do not dwell often on the thought of Death, their own death... Just as the more mundanely busy and striving for their own goals, they do not have the time to ponder on mortality, not until the goal is achieved, the business settled. But the driven, the obsessive, with the grand impossible scheme that might never come to fruition, are different from the everyday, and are sometimes to be feared... Such a man, with grand ideas and a fixed purpose, on which his eye was ever fixed, was Dain Alvis. But was this really the case, or was Alvis just another politician, another ephemeral pleaser or disappointer of the people, a footnote in history?

An interesting moment not yet recorded. Not of great significance it seemed, and probably of no importance at all... no evidence whatsoever that this was soothsayer's truth, a prophetic moment... probably, it was just a moment of madness pure and simple...

It was something Austin Summerville had had on his mind in the period immediately following the by-election successes, but before the Party was returned to power at the General Election... some years ago now...

He had meant to mention it at the time to Virgil Holmes, that slick, charming master of spin, but had thought better of it, realizing that for one thing his bizarre moment had had no place in the business of his life, consumed as that life was then in the gathering that had had been due to take place, and did take place a week later at the Harrington mansion in Northamptonshire. The reasons he did not mention the occurrence were strange in themselves, beginning with a reluctance to seem to be admitting that he had been selected as some sort of victim or target. Why him? Then there was his failing to mention it: was he ashamed of something, and was his failure to admit to the event, as time wore on, an indicator that he himself had something to hide. Then there was the possibility that someone might see in this, if he should disclose what happened, either some sort of plot against Dain Alvis, or at the least some implied criticism of him. Yet logically, when he thought logically about the bizarre occurrence, it seemed so trivial, even if so odd and so oddly portentous, that it was nothing... and so why hadn't he mentioned it straightaway as a silly little story? And so, the wheels turned in his mind until the little bit of nonsense had grown all out of proportion.

It truly had been nothing, really... He had on the day just been within walking distance of Westminster and fancied that he would, on so bright and pleasant a day do just that, walk to his place of work. Even politicians have to eat, and he had, he remembered it well as he looked back, popped into Prêt-a-Manger and bought himself a mozzarella, tomato and basil baguette and a coffee. He had decided to eat in and felt in buoyant mood as he sat down and quietly in a corner consumed his impromptu meal, relishing both the food and the coffee. He had been hungry and in need a caffeine boost, so it was in truth a feast. He looked with idle curiosity at a newspaper someone had left behind, so as to not be approached by members of the public, so as to remain incognito. To his relief and very mild feeling of chagrin no one had recognised him, or if they had it was not obvious, and he had managed to get away without having to speak to anyone. Something in his 'free' paper had reminded him as he walked away that he needed to get a copy of *The Times* that day, and before he got to the House; so a couple of hundred yards and just around the corner he had stopped at a kiosk and bought a paper from the vendor, who did say:' Mr. Summerville, thought I recognised you, sir. Have a good day and I hope your lot win the next election.' Pleased at the recognition, and on a high too because this had been a supporter, but also comfortable in feeling that he did not have to stay around to chat, he had thanked the man, wished him well, and hurried off. It had been a bright day, a hot sun, and dusty pavements... paper litter stirred by an occasional light breeze...

He hadn't gone far, then he had stopped in the middle of the pavement to look more closely at an article that had caught his attention, the one he was expecting to see in fact. Then he had moved off, preoccupied by what he had read, or so he remembered, heading again in the direction of the Parliament building. He had been deep in thought, gazing absentmindedly down at his feet on the broad walkway.

He had been aware, he remembered afterwards, of a shadow coming towards him from the opposite direction, but he did not step aside and had only half looked up. But then he had become aware that the man had intended, or so it had seemed, to bump into him deliberately. He had at that point looked up, to see the strangest shabbiest looking old vagrant whose dirty bearded face was shaded by a black hood that had reminded him then, and thereafter, of a monk's cowl. In the shadow it cast, he had just been able to discern that the vagrant had only one eye, the place where the right eye should have been being just a black sunken wrinkled socket.

Summerville, unnerved, had started and stepped back, all sorts of sudden alarms jangling in his head, and he had just stared at the man, whose mouth had broken into a carious yellow-toothed grin, that had seemed more a snarl than a smile. Then surprisingly the voice that had eventually come out was controlled, but harsh, accusative...

'Tell your master he will fail.'

That was all he had said, and then he had simply stared. Summerville had stared hard back at him despite his discomfiture, nonplussed at first; but as he had become aware that passers-by were glancing or looking in curiosity at the 'meeting' of such opposites, he had quickly stepped to one side, and shaking his head as if to say, you could only meet a lunatic like that in London, had walked on determinedly and turned his back on this Elijah, this prophet of doom...

It had unsettled him at the time, as any incident of unwarranted aggression or intrusion would have done, but it had become for Summerville a spooky, out-of-the ordinary little incident. He had told his family over dinner that night but, oddly, had sworn them to secrecy. His wife had assumed that this was due to the fact that he had no wish to be ribbed by his parliamentary colleagues about it. And he had kept it from Virgil Holmes rather than simply forgetting to tell him. A strange but unsettling little incident... And the question had tormented him: What had the man been talking about? It was probably a case of mistaken identity, but if not, who was his, Austin Summerville's master...the Party Leader? Or had he been referring to Dain Alvis? And fail, what had he meant by that? Mistaken identity... just a lunatic... But strangely, the incident had made him think long and hard about Dain Alvis...

And Dain Alvis had thought long and hard about himself, his ambitions, his life, his world view. Was he just a career politician, or could he really accomplish something, or would any small change he made lead the country in a better direction? He felt that he did have a mission, a quest. His holy grail, however, was he felt even more nebulous, and could not be reduced to finding the cup of Christ. But then perhaps, he reasoned, all holy grails were really like this. But would he make a difference, do some good in this world? It would have to happen in steps or stages, a planned and purposeful campaign.

It began in his mind, with an obsession with repeated incidents of violent and so-called mindless, but in his view, simply inexcusable and sadistic crimes. He saw in these acts the manifestation of the barely controlled vicious tendencies of the species *Homo sapiens*. It was a jaundiced world view, he knew some would say that , resulting from his being bullied at public school, and before that being psychologically tormented and humiliated by his father. Whatever the reasons, and of course in his mind there were no reasons - he was simply right in his assessment of humanity, he had a grim outlook on the way society had developed., or failed to develop, and he trusted no one, or almost no one.

Alvis had not remained a victim, and in fact never really was one, because he had had from the outset a determination that made him want to fight back, and justly punish the aggressor. Though of medium height, he had always been naturally physically strong and robust; and as he grew he had trained and hardened his body through gymnastics and weightlifting, and later had been an Oxford boxing blue at light-middleweight. He had then developed and redirected his tendency not to flee a physical challenge into the more diplomatic but still rather unnerving method of standing his ground and fixing people with an icy stare from his brilliant blue eyes, as though he might freeze the beating heart of his opponent. He carried this into politics but added to it a certain polite and respectful 'charm' which he had used to allay the fears of many a doubter but did not allow this ability to detract from his undoubted drive and fearlessness which at the same time won him many supporters. Yet there was no doubt that many of his peers still found him disturbing or simply did not like him.

His remarks on the Goodman Show, about Germany and the Germans were, some thought, uncharacteristically unguarded and lacking in judgement. Yet others, of his supporters, saw this as taking head on the charge that he was overly and oddly pro-German. But Dain Alvis, whilst abhorring the racist policies and actions of Nazi Germany, had yet a sneaking admiration for Adolf Hitler's rise to power, from nonentity and penniless Viennese vagrant to German Chancellor in twenty years. He had no liking for Hitler, however, but had been amused by Goodman's *faux pas* in suggesting a physical resemblance between himself and the German *Führer*, an obvious piece of tawdry and lazy journalism which had given him, and not Goodman, the advantage. But what was in any case the truth was that Alvis was not so much interested in twentieth century Germany as in the common roots of the two nations, in a way that conformed to his own interpretation of history. Here was the beginning of an obsession, if he let it run its course...

Yet Alvis had more, much more than this to consider and weigh on his scales of justice. Alvis's view was based on the belief that people failed to treat one another well if they were not forced to do so through self-interest; and that too much freedom had resulted in confusion and despair: people needed to be led. He saw in the tedious but inevitable isolated incidents of violent crime a failure of government to lead and to act. He saw himself as a defender of the innocent, and the idea occurred to him that he would be just that, if only he had sufficient power. A student of history, he pondered on how Stalin's political commissars could go out and effectively not only stand up to but strike fear into the officers of individual army or air force units, so that in the end the Soviet party machine of political control was more feared even than the tenacious and ruthless Nazi invaders. He pondered too on how, with an iron hand, the SS and the Gestapo had held sway over the German people, while the *Wehrmacht*, the German armed forces, were bound by their oath to Hitler : unspeakable atrocities at home and in the conquered lands had been dutifully committed, occasionally with sadistic glee, or perhaps more often with mechanical inhumanity born of their creed and that oath to their *Fűhrer*, and even at times, in rare cases, with a sense of disgust and self-loathing.

Such power had existed, in the mid-twentieth-century dictatorships. What if, Alvis reasoned to himself, something like this power were applied to the elimination of the little gangs of thugs, and feral youths who had for a generation or more terrorized with virtual impunity so many citizens and made them live half-lives, fearing to step beyond their front doors? And then there were the drug barons and dealers, and the fraudsters, the con men, the intimidators of the elderly on their very doorsteps, the internet fraudsters, the tricksters, all the aggressive products of a weak system in which they, the offenders, knew their rights but felt no responsibility, no duty towards the state or their fellow citizens. And there were the corporate criminals who always managed to escape meaningful censure and punishment for their abuse of the citizen. They through their lobbying groups, and not just in Britain, were endangering the very future of the planet itself by their failure to seek and implement strategies that would combat global warming, and by their success in blocking real change that might impact on their profits...

Dain Alvis had pondered long on these matters and was now firm in his conviction that the iron hand would have to be applied without, as they say, throwing the baby out with the bathwater, a hackneyed metaphor he enjoyed and would often repeat. Alvis too virtually willed a belief and an interest in Teutonic and Norse mythology, as though through this exercise in perversity in a nominally Christian country he could demonstrate to himself that anything was possible through will, determination and effort.

It is dangerous some might say to play with beliefs, however arcane, archaic or anachronistic, and though Alvis knew in his heart that these willed beliefs were silly, and that grappling with an Old English primer and trying to learn the language of the original Anglo-Saxons was a waste of his valuable time, he persisted in the latter for a while, feeling that it gave him, well, a unique perspective on things. There were practical steps to be taken, however, even if lurking at the back of his mind was a vague jumble of English history that had itself turned, in 1066, from Scandinavian and northern European influences to a more southern European world view... Alvis, notwithstanding this historical event, felt that his mind could draw on any number of useful sources; Norse and Teutonic gods, Teutonic Knights, the Order of the

Knights Templar, Stalinism, anything that might infuse and inspire him under his banner of being a champion of the people.

Alvis was intelligent enough, logical enough, to know that his ambitions were not wholly feasible or achievable and that they were fundamentally flawed: one could not be the driving force for good through ruthlessness alone, and without some compromise along the way. The question was, how could he force through change without turning himself into a Hitler or a Stalin when in fact he wanted to be more like a King Alfred? It was not logical to think that this could be done, a bloodless revolution, and yet obsession, the grand idea, like sexual passion, will always master reason when the point of no return has been reached. He could not, would not, allow the state of things as they were to persist, whatever the consequences. It would be for the greater good.

There was no doubting that Alvis was intelligent: he had achieved a comfortable 2.1 at Oxford with diligent and consistent effort but without feeling the desperate urge to strive for a First. His had been a rounded student existence: academic endeavour, sports - boxing, rowing, rugby union, athletics - politics (inevitably), socializing, and occasional sexual exploits but without commitment, encounters which became ever more discreet as he learned the value, for him, of trusting and confiding in no one about his private life; and bragging about a sexual conquest was distasteful to him, and he looked with cold pensive hostility on those who did, as if he might decide to put their names in a little black book of his own.

Of his parentage he always spoke very little, and increasingly less and less as he became conscious that he was beginning to cut a dash as an enigmatic figure. His father, William Alvis, could and did trace his ancestry back to Anglo-Saxon times, the seed of his son's interest and bias perhaps, while on his mother's side, his grandmother had some link to France, possibly to Normandy. Alvis was less enthusiastic about this strand of his lineage, preferring to side with the eventually maltreated underdog of the eleventh century, perhaps a reason for his liking the book *Ivanhoe*. More importantly, in the real world, as it was often simplistically labelled, his family's money, acquired variously over time through land ownership, wool, slave trading and cotton manufacturing, had enabled him to go to good schools, kept him very well supported at Oxford, and its well-established nature and that of his family had given him the links and introductions to the Party, and certainly did not hinder his advancement through its ranks, nor his ability to keep himself, as much and when he chose to be, in the public eye.

And what of the world that Alvis was so intent upon changing? There were so many questions, issues, that he had to visit and revisit. His vision for the future and his ambitions were shape-shifters, ever elusive and allowed him no rest. He knew however that as long as he made steady progress, was energetic, determined and if necessary ruthless, he could, one man though he was, make a difference even in this complicated world, with its lucrative advertising and marketing, its ostentatious wealth, its culture of transient celebrity, its vested economic interests, its glad handing, its disparate groups of the disadvantaged, its lawlessness, its lip service to climate initiatives, its lauding of democracy and opportunity for all, and its failure to deliver that opportunity, its hiding behind tradition, in particular that of the monarchy, its negativity and its media focus on predictions of doom juxtaposed with trite little news items to raise the spirits... above all, what had caused Alvis to become impassioned and helped to clarify for him his objectives, his targets for action, was the political system and what he called its modern Pilate-like washing of its hands, its abdication of real responsibility, instead devolving responsibility without power to inept local authorities in Health and Education, for example, yet still claiming credit for anything that by chance alone managed to work. A bleak view of his fellow man was that of Dain Alvis, and an even bleaker view, laced with anger, of the political system that he felt had betrayed the people of his country. Alvis would say to his closest followers, in the early days, with great care not to appear anti-democratic: 'Democracy and the growing wealth of some sections of society in the western world have created problems that democracy in its now weakened, even moribund state, can no longer solve. What is needed are control and leadership, leadership and control - these will be the twin pillars that will support a new manifestation of government democratically elected...'

England, Great Britain, the United Kingdom, would be a mighty challenge. And beyond?... Foreign policy... there would need to be massive changes: would the United States, the big brother partner with a vested interest stand idly by? And Europe? What precise shape would the new Europe take when faced with a new United Kingdom? Vague notions, dreams only perhaps, were beginning to take shape in the mind of Dain Alvis, but his was a pragmatic focus on immediate goals. He intended to focus like a bird of prey, hovering with concentrated intent, knowing it must return to feed its young, intent now upon a speck of soon-to-be-extinguished life scuttling across the ground below.

Finally, science... This was writ large too in Alvis's plans for the future: he was convinced that science would play its part in the unfolding of the new world, but only dimly aware of what could be achieved. His own achievements in this area were modest by any standards. Academically, he had virtually abandoned rigorous study at the age of sixteen, apart from studying biology for a further year, after which he dropped to four subjects to be certain of his grades. But he still took a layman's keen interest in scientific advances and resolved that, as well as keeping up with the latest technological and theoretical advances, as best he could, he would through his political career forge links with the scientific community and actively encourage lobbying where he felt this would benefit the world.

Allies in this sector would be useful, ranging from the pharmaceutical companies, through university researchers, to the military. Science would play its part, he had decided, in the mechanism of control.

And so, Dain Alvis, naked from the waist up, facing a full-length mirror in the wainscoted little room he used as a gymnasium-cum-reading-room, staring back at himself with his piercing blue gaze, his dark hair sharply cut, flexing his honed square torso, and practising a gesture or two for his next speech... flexing his muscles, yes, but also demonstrating to himself that his was an indomitable spirit. Politics, science, growing influence, powerful friends... Seen though at that moment, with his posturing, some might have thought that, though clearly athletic, he cut a rather comical figure as would-be challenger to the established order. Others might have thought in their turn that such an assessment was wide of the mark and a terrible and grave error of judgement.

'Silas! Wake up, sleepy head.' This was the sound of Lindy, as the darkness cleared, and the myriad photons of light found their way into Silas Wood's wine-stupefied consciousness.

He moved his heavy head across the pillow, his brown hair looking more mop-like than it usually did. He made as though to return to sleep, closing his eyes with purpose and grabbing at the duvet. Lindy's voice continued to punish him for the over-indulgence of the evening before. A bright, fiercely bright morning, after yesterday's torrential rain, did not help matters, particularly as the love of his life had pulled back the curtains to their fullest extent.

'You know where we're going in a couple of hours. I told you, you were drinking too much. It's fatal to try and keep up with John and Alex... Anyway, there's some news you'll be interested in...'

'What?' came the muffled reply.

'The Cabinet reshuffle... Dain Alvis is going to be the new Home Secretary.'

Silas Wood pushed the covers back, then said, 'Ow!' and held his head. 'Bloody hell... you'll have to drive, my darling... Home Secretary...'

9. *Silas and his diary*

'Prime Minister... Prime Minister... Prime Minister...'

It rained, an incessant steady rain, all through the night, and through the early hours of the morning as the first results had come in, indicating something sensational; a wild swing from both Conservative and Labour. An incessant rain, dripping still at dawn from the lilac bushes, once bright mauve blossoms now past their best, browning and water-laden, but with their leaves with pendant droplets glistening. The cherry blossom too had all but gone, a limp dirty-brown drooping farewell from what was once pink splendour heralding the spring. But in the steamy air the ceanothus, with its own tight bunches of dark-green hard-ribbed leaves was beginning to show its cornflower-blue blossoms. And so, a cycle of weather, but an exaggerated cycle, from the bright and blinding sun of the previous week, when the temperatures had soared to a record for the time of year, all was green and wet again: it was, everyone was beginning to sense, increasingly, a climate of extremes.

Prime Minister? An absurdity, and incongruity... One eye open in the grey wet morning light, Silas peered at his alarm clock, which he had forgotten to set; but it didn't matter because he'd booked a day off. Lindy was still sleeping soundly beside him, warm and safe like an animal, deep in its den. Prime Minister... a waking dream. Lindy gave a little snuffling noise in her sleep, as though confirming Silas's sleepy simile. He looked at her head of dark ruffled hair - her back was towards him. He was full of love for her, and strangely, fear for her in the perfection of this moment. In his recognising the moment of perfection it was gone, and in their cocoon, he began to think of her safety and that he and she were sheltered from the happenings of the world outside.

The clock said 8.30am. They had wanted to be up earlier, so as not to waste the day; but it didn't really matter, and Jonas was not at nursery this week.

Jonas was quiet, in his room, along the landing. Silas sat up and stared at the bedroom door, which, ever since Jonas had come home with them from the maternity wing, had been kept ajar at night. He heard a movement: Jonas was stirring. Gnawing away in Silas's mind were those words cot death, even though there was no history of it in either of their families, even though he knew no one personally who had been visited by it, and even though Jonas was now four years old. True he had these thoughts less frequently now and the gnawing would go away from time to time, unlike those first anxious days when he had hardly slept, but he did wonder when he could stop worrying. Of course, he, Silas, had now become a worrier. And Lindy had discovered last week that she was definitely expecting a second. Again, Silas stared at her lovingly, protectively, gratefully. He reached out a hand to caress her hair but decided at the last second not to wake her.

Silas Wood, twenty-nine, father. Sometimes, even now, he had to pinch himself to believe the second of these things about himself, and it still sometimes thrilled him: the first fact, equally undeniable, he was less enthusiastic about. 'I thought it was women who worried so much about their age,' Lindy would taunt him, laughing. Silas would reply that it was not age as such but rather what he was doing with his life: he hadn't achieved anything of note in his working life. 'And that is a male preoccupation,' Lindy would tell her friends, and then report the less personal bits of the conversation to Silas, adding: 'Women are too busy to get such hang-ups'. This would lead to a bit of banter, suburban pop psychology about the gender differences, about how men could become obsessed with a single goal, and how women just got on with things and would actually find the butter, or the cholesterol-reducing spread in the 'fridge, even if it had been moved from its usual place.

Silas's dissatisfaction with certain aspects of his life was just that, a dissatisfaction with certain aspects; and superficially at least, he, they, he and his little family, appeared to be getting through life rather well.

'Stop worrying about things that need to be done. The only time there's nothing to do is when you're dead. And stop trying to over-analyse your life.' That was rich, Silas had said, coming from a scientist.

The house, the house they were living in and were buying, their family home (Silas had gotten used to the idea now, after four years, but still felt as pleased and proud as punch whenever he invited friends round for a dinner party or a barbeque). The house was a four-bedroom mid-Victorian terraced house, set back slightly from the footpath in the quiet road at the front, and having a small enclosed garden to the rear; a house not unlike his sister Hope's but slightly roomier. The road at the front was pleasantly lined with mature trees, though the council, or someone, had had to take out a couple of diseased individuals, leaving gaps.

They lived in North London, not far from Highgate Cemetery, and could only afford to live here because the market had been in free fall when they purchased and because, and more to the point, Lindy's brother had given her half a million which she'd put straight down as a deposit. Also, she was now a relatively high earner at Hoffnung-Larousse (formerly Hoffnung Pharmaceuticals), where she was currently doing work on new influenza strains, having done three years with another company on similar projects. She loved the work, which really was well-paid, though she found her senior manager, and Assistant Head of Research and Development, Briony Daniels, tough and uncompromising and a company climber. She did not really like Briony but respected her for her brilliant mind, which, during the long working hours at least, seemed wholly focused and never wavered from her current work on monoclonal antibodies as receptor tyrosine kinase inhibitors (revisiting an old area of investigation) in the search for new wonder drugs that might make millions, or, might not.

Lindy was clever in her own right, of course, but made a point of saying very little about her work to Silas, primarily because of its confidential nature - her contract did swear her to secrecy - but also because he would have been unable to understand it anyway. Silas could take some consolation in that he was now at last a *Philosophiae Doctor*, even if he was slightly dissatisfied with his university associate lectureship position, and did not have far to travel to work. It was true that his contract had recently gone to eighteen hours a week, but this meant a lot of preparation and, sadly, a lot of marking. He did feel he was more used than useful in an academic sense, at least when he had time to sit down and think about it. There was a certain amount of prestige in the job and he had come a long way from the Silas who had met Lindy for the first time; and a long way from the dull jobs he had had to work through in his early days as a postgraduate student. He knew though that a *proper* contract would secure his future so that he could plan to publish more than just a reworking of his PhD thesis. However, other things in his life were going well: there was the open prospect of his future with Lindy, and there was his beautiful son Jonas, with his black wavy hair and large round brown eyes, darker even than those of his mother, and now there was the child to be. They had the house too, a good house, a lovely house that would hold its value and that was well on the way to being paid for. He knew indeed that he was very comfortably off compared with the vast majority of people in these islands, even if he sometimes wondered and worried that a jagged rock of Fate might suddenly shatter his barque's midstream smooth and steady progress. Even the recent water shortages, and the need to use standpipes, seemed to be the lot of other and the poorest people, and not his lot or that of his new family.

Silas had made a point of not speaking to Lindy about her work, just as she did with his. It did rankle a little that she earned at least four times as much as he, but the real reason he knew not to ask about it was because he knew her work was commercially sensitive and that she had binding confidentiality clauses in her contract. So, the less he knew the better. He knew when she left for work, when she returned, when she was on holiday or having a day off, whether she had had a good day or not, and that was it. He had seen where she worked, both the locations, because he had dropped her off on a couple of occasions, but that was all he knew - just so long as she was happy, and, if he was honest about it, bringing in the money.

Apart from work, and getting Jonas to nursery, or round to his friends or taking him to the park, which was a little safer now (which he had grudgingly to admit when his instinct was always to criticize the efforts of central or local government on anything they attempted to do), or enjoying playing games with him, their busy life, his and Lindy's, was focused on one another, and they would speak of anything but work if they could and were in tacit agreement about this. And when he had time, though he was far from conscientious about it, Silas tried to keep a little diary about his life and times, times which, egocentric though it might be, he found historically important, significant, of landmark significance in fact, and, disconcertingly, full of portents and dire warnings: he felt too, probably because it made him feel important, that his diary might actually be of historical interest.

One of the things that Silas and Lindy did talk about a lot, and talked about it with their friends too, given what they all saw as the strangeness of the times, was the political situation in Britain, which seemed to be undergoing phenomenal changes that no one would have thought possible or even dreamt of ten years earlier.

Silas was wide awake now. How had this happened? How was it possible? He tiptoed across the bedroom and then went to look in on Jonas, whose little frame lay softly in repose; then he went downstairs to make a cup of tea, and in fact, to find his diary. Something made him look for it as a priority even before he went into the kitchen to fill the kettle, normally his very first task.

There was the black diary for this year, 2022, just peeping out on his desk from under a pile of scripts he had still to mark. He opened the week-to-a-view book on the 23rd and the 24th of June: the 23rd simply read,

'Election night! Surely not?' Under the 24th he scrawled, as though for posterity, and improbable even now as the whole thing seemed: 'It's true - it's happened. And what will happen now? Dain Alvis, Prime Minister of this Great Britain.'

Silas had a penchant for the over dramatic, the portentous, and knew his diary style was a little self-conscious, even pompous at times, but the last few years had seen major changes to his personal life and major developments in the wider world outside...

2016 Diary of Silas Wood (extracts)

August 23rd Getting married to Lindy! Still can't believe it. Only 3 weeks away now.

August 25th Checked tickets for Antigua - again. Hot here - nice barbeque with Josh, Simsy and the others last night. Not sure a stag is going to be such a good idea.

August 28th Getting closer. Lindy looked especially lovely last night but harassed by all these arrangements. We'll soon be away, and she'll be Mrs. Silas Wood - is it still OK to say it like that, I wonder. No time for anything else, even politics. Note, however, official enquiry - at last - into the death of Patrick Lansing. Government has got the jitters - talking of which!!! Dain Alvis's speech criticised - for lots of reasons... 'We'll build 50 new prisons!' Ha!

2018 Diary of Silas Wood (extracts)

<u>January 2nd</u> Meant to start this yesterday - missed over a year. Never mind. Probably won't do this religiously, every day - we'll see. Good Christmas - glad Josh and Beth will be staying over for another couple of days.

<u>January 23rd</u> My great grandmother's birthday as I recall. If she'd still been alive she'd now be - The Battle of Rorke's Drift - 1878 or 1879? Good pin number next time around - not now I've written that down. Lindy loves her job... definitely worth her while persevering with her PhD while she's sort of working. Not all that comfortable that she's linked to a pharmaceutical company, but that was always going to happen. Real world, Silas -

<u>May 7th</u> WOW! Half a million, HALF A MILLION from Simon - that's brotherly love and we can move house just like that. Still be a biggish mortgage; but we'll be OK - Lindy doing well - and that lead for the job at the university looks promising. Lindy - Hoffnung etc. - we're lucky, more than one lucky star, then... And the economy nose-diving again. What is going on in the Cabinet? Prime Minister's Question Time - what a riot. The abandonment of fixed-term parliaments as a sort of demonstration of good democratic intent - well, that experiment didn't last long... That Alvis is a fanatic, I've always said so - keeps banging on about Middle England, and talking about a breakthrough in law and

order, a breakthrough on the economy, a breakthrough in the Health Service, in foreign policy... Seems he thinks his leader and his party are doing nothing right. Keeps on saying breakthrough. Certainly (*Thinks: I'll have to scribble this in tomorrow's entry, so he marks with an arrow and continues*) Likes the word breakthrough, just as he keeps banging on about Middle England. Is he setting up a leadership challenge? Spooky guy - every time he speaks in public now his entourage of bodyguards and camp followers seems to have grown larger. The inner core look like hardened thugs, smartly dressed though, not like the extreme right's, the silly fringe extreme right's people. But Alvis's team do look like a bunch of Nazis, but he's definitely not a racist, I'll have to give him that. And he's passionate, madly passionate about the environment and Europe. Still keeps his German and Jewish links among his followers - just to spite Gerald Goodman I suspect! (*That's enough - I'll be into the next page - squeeze this in though*) Fires in California - out of control- still 38 degrees there, and winds gusting. Brighton 35 degrees, and Paignton and York close. Floods in South Australia - 40 dead or missing. Jesus!

June 1st Alvis - wow! Resigned as Home Secretary last week and walked out of the Conservative party, taking half a dozen with him, including Summerville. Vote of confidence which the government has LOST. General Election called. Alvis doesn't stand a chance (does he?) with his Breakthrough Alliance Party - the Party for Middle England. Reason for Alvis's action? Continued and repeated rejections of his radical proposals for reigning in the 'scum of society' and the failure to impose climate change initiatives...

September 23rd It happened - should have entered this before. Breakthrough Alliance Party trounced at the Election: Government scraped home with an overall majority of seven. Still, Alvis got 11%, which is massive for a new party. London Eye shut for maintenance - why have I put that in? Anti-Alvis protesters beaten up last week by his multinational 'werod', as he calls them. Picked up by the press: 'werod' - how bizarre, an old Anglo-Saxon word meaning company or throng, or troop or legion, or bodyguard, depending on who you believe. Won't rush out to learn Anglo-Saxon, though ... Alvis protests his innocence, his bodyguard, or 'werod' acted to protect him against criminal gangs or those paid by criminal gangs - a sort of rent-a-mob. Still consistent with his demand for 50 new prisons, which his old party wouldn't sanction (*Arrow onto the next day's space*) I can see him now, with his squat body and those unearthly blue eyes. Alvis quote for posterity- well, for my family anyway: 'The old parties have accused me of wanting to push up the prison population. And, of course' he laughed and leaned forward, and with an imperious gesture,' it's true. If they are needed we'll build fifty new prisons (to a crescendo of noise, then a thunder of applause from the converted, with whoops, whistles and cheers thrown in, USA style) and I tell you what, we'll take these drunken little street terrorists out of the picture for a long, long time (more cheers). The people of these islands, who have fought and toiled over the centuries, deserve better. That's why I resigned! That's what this new party is about!' (Cheers) 'We will clean up the streets in weeks, not years - that is my promise...' Hope posterity likes my reporting. I must stop being fascinated by that monster, if monster he is... (*Into the next day now. Still, what does it matter? Apologies to posterity. But I don't keep up with the diary as I should anyway.*) Let's see if he's as good as his word one day. God, if he exists, help us! Still, he's right about some things. A fireman was beaten to death after his team was lured into an ambush ... drugs are finding their way into our primary schools… a murdering youth was apparently grinning the other day as he was sent down and led away to a life sentence, or half a life sentence if he's a good boy - out in seven years, or something like that. Maybe Alvis is right about some things, but he still looks like a Nazi - the mud thrown by Goodman has obviously stuck. But that Party emblem or insignia - and the flags ... A rune, for God's sake, a Viking rune. It looks like this…

ᛞ

It's called Dagaz and it means Day, Dawn or Breakthrough, with other shades of meaning around these. They stick on their flags and their little metal badges. On the flags it's black in a big white circle on a blue background. A runic Breakthrough logo - corny, but scary and un-British. Still, 11% ... I wholeheartedly agree with his banging on about global warming - I will - there, I have written it down, so I can't get out of it - I really must join the Earth Conservation Trust - only twenty quid... Another increase in carbon dioxide - and now methane... Forget Alvis, that really is scary and scarier still is that Lindy, with all her science, thinks so too.

October 11th On holiday in Yorkshire - little stone terraced cottage in Kirbymoorside, near Helmsley. Glad I brought the diary along - Lindy's missed a period and thinks she might be!! We have been trying - WOW! If it's true. Lindy well into her PhD and will probably take the minimum time off. She says that there's a new girl at the lab whom she really likes. Her name's Hannah, and a little bit older, about thirty. They're getting on fine, but it seems Hannah is getting bullied by the boss Briony. Lindy says Briony sees her as a threat, but what kind of a threat she can't imagine. That's all I hear from the lab, and I don't want to hear anything else - I wouldn't understand it anyway.

2019 Diary of Silas Wood (extracts)

June 9th At 1.57 pm Jonas was born. I'm a dad!!!! Seven pounds and twelve ounces... Three days after D day, the scan date, that is. New life, life, a new life... Can't say any more -to the 'phone again.

July 1st Panic stations. Jonas had a blister like a bubble appear on his top lip, in the middle of his Cupid's bow. But panic over - it's a feeding blister apparently. It's 11.00 pm - only just got round to writing this.

July 2nd Jonas is OK, of course. Torrential rain and violent storms overnight and he slept through the worst of it. It's 5.30am and Lindy's feeding him now. It's still hammering down outside. Need it after nearly three weeks in the nineties. Terrible flash floods in Hull, York and in the West Country... Together with yesterday's news about the Arctic ice cap and the loss of a strip of East Anglian coastline... well, what can one say?

July 23rd Dain Alvis gaining ground if the opinion polls are to be believed - a couple of percentage points. Warming up again. New role at the university next year, but more responsibility. Must do some work on the thesis but enjoy the holidays too... Earth Conservation Trust newsletter interesting but scary. Lindy agrees something must be done - and soon; for Jonas, for his generation and beyond. Shopping tonight!

2020 Diary of Silas Wood (extracts)

March 25th I'm bloody angry. This used to be a good neighbourhood. One of our neighbours, Jimmy Osborne, was beaten up at the Crown and Anchor.

Minding his own business - set upon by a dozen youngsters, teenagers, whatever, little shits - might lose an eye. Only married last year, driving part of his job. Perhaps someone like Alvis is what we need... (*Shall I leave that in or cross it out?*)

April 13th A proper Spring day again, if there ever was such a thing. Saw an interesting programme about the suburbs of Delhi last night. You don't think about how life's going around the world. A different sort of hustle and bustle. How would you ever start to describe the complexity of the world of people, the never-ending activity of people scattered across the globe, all doing something or other at any one moment - 7 billion people. Waxing philosophical, Silas. Ha, ha!

May 21st Lindy's had a promotion of sorts and I've got some extra hours. Had a scare a few nights ago... Jonas started breathing hoarsely and barking like a seal. Had the doctor out after ringing Mediline. It was croup. Nearly steamed all the old wallpaper off one end of the kitchen. Must get round to that decorating. Yuk!

May 22nd Lindy's mum and dad came round. Decorating? We really could afford to pay someone?

August 4th The new Community Special Police (just paid expenses or are they paid properly?) seem to have made a difference. I did see two of them getting lip from some yobs, but the courts are beginning to get a bit tougher. Government trying to stave off Alvis with these new initiatives, but both the major parties, or the three major parties, are beginning to look jaded. Economy is a mess - again, or so they say. Now threat of standpipes being introduced here. Earth Conservation Trust meeting next week. Must go!!!!

2021 Diary of Silas Wood (extracts)

March 21st A lot of Germans, or half-Germans, or pro-Germans, in Alvis's 'Werod', also French, Israeli - lots of others including Thiakoupolis (spelling?) the Greek - a regular United nations, but predominantly British - mainly English - and German. Alvis seems to be being invited by the government to join a lot of working parties including that for the Community Special Police (CSP hereafter). Smart idea perhaps, inviting Alvis in: one way to try and draw his sting. Polls put him ahead of the traditional main opposition and two points behind the government - I can't believe it! He's getting a lot of fanatical support from a lot of fed-up people - the rallies in Manchester, Birmingham, Norwich... - he's going everywhere around the country as though he expects an election tomorrow. This government could last a couple more years to its full term. But a scandal could finish him... one or two of the 'serious' papers are trying hard... (*Writing smaller, these spaces are too small*) but the government seems to be having all the bad luck at the moment.

April 17th Jonas really is a terrible two - even though

it's a couple of months away. Drives us mad sometimes. Gets an idea in his head and that's it...

April 19th Moaned at by Dulcie, the child minder, for getting J. late to her house. She only wants to get to school early so she can chat to her friends in the playground, so Lindy says. Hmm... try getting the terror ready ...then dashing off in the morning traffic, still digging up the road near Fishmonger Street... to the Uni. A day's work before I start - I'm probably not the only one who thinks that... But Lindy can't possibly do it now: Hoffnung etc. Might be having a grand new research facility so it's probably going to be another eight miles for her... At least if it comes off, she'll almost be in the country...

May 17th In two things now - Earth Conservation Trust has a political wing. Think I'll abandon the New-New Opposition... What is the opposition? *The Globe* alleges that Alvis's agents, with the knowledge of the CSP and even the Met and the County Constabularies, are stirring up trouble in the sink estates to flush out the troublemakers - *agents provocateurs*! Hard to believe that; although looking at the way his gang has grown, anything's possible. If it is true, it could bring him down, but the government can't be seen to chase this - they might then appear soft on crime, particularly as the new statistics show such a small improvement on the last set of figures....

June 9th J. Is TWO!!! Party time., Jonas! Lindy has a day off - we'll go out for a pizza.

June 18th Alvis's 'Terrorism of the streets' speech, and all his talk about the betrayal of the people has gone down well. Bring the troops back from Syria and Afghanistan to help, to work with the regular constabularies, and the CSP, based on 'the information that has been collected' (by the Werod among other agencies) ... Jesus! It might backfire on him; but he's getting a lot of support on global warming as is our new group. Temperature here last week was a record thirty-three for the area.

July 31st Catastrophic split in the Arctic ice cap!!! Greenland ice still on the move too. Lindy getting together all the information she can -networking with her international colleagues until nearly three in the morning. A year-on-year increase in carbon dioxide and methane worldwide. The US is perhaps beginning to wake up - another terrible hurricane season looming. But they really don't like Dain Alvis. Watching closely his links with Europe, particularly Germany, France and Russia: they're obviously scared of an economic shut-out.

August 1st Ice cap split not as major as the headlines suggested, so we're now being told. Looks bad enough to me... It's all heading in the wrong direction.

September 18th Alvis again. Bring the troops home. Home security all important. Tries to pacify the US with recommendation that a token force .... and so on. Won't wash, Dain!

2022 Diary of Silas Wood (extracts)

April 18th A heat-wave in April. Standpipes. A woman killed yesterday in Stafford, fighting to defend her position in the queue. A general water shortage - this will destroy the government. Global warming - Alvis is right when he says that they've been soft on big business with the self-policing approach to carbon emissions... Renationalization of water, he's suggesting...

Again, June 24th 'It's true - it's happened. And what will happen now? Dain Alvis, Prime Minister of this Great Britain.'

Silas did toy momentarily with the impulse to scribble through his entry for the 24th but was at a loss as to what else to say. He closed the diary and stared for a moment at its black moleskin cover. Two thousand and twenty-two: he was twenty-nine. Instead of giving in to a feeling of foreboding and self-pity, however, he shrugged his shoulders and decided to make a cup of tea before going for a shower.

10. *Cabinet and revolutionaries*

There sat Foreign Policy, or its Secretary, and there sat the Economy, or its Chancellor, there sat Education, or its government mouthpiece, there sat Health, young in a suit, with a sniffle, there sat - a minute-taker, there sat Energy, looking a little listless and playing with his expensive pen, and so on, at a long, beautifully polished expensive wooden table, bums on newly upholstered seats of leather; smiling, or rueful, or nervous eyes on the new Leader, or just with blank or frozen stares. A big job indeed, running a nation.

Defence heartily congratulated the Leader, which was as good as patting himself on the back for being a loyal supporter, and Law and Order or Justice, commonly called Home, seconded, as if to pat herself on the back, too.

At the head of the table, in a manner of speaking, where quite probably great Winston had sat, was the would-be King Alfred, perhaps saviour of the nation, perhaps even the world, it had been suggested.

The first Cabinet meeting of the new Breakthrough Alliance government... Dain Alvis held sway. This was his time, not the time of Walpole, Pitt, Peel, Gladstone, Disraeli, Lloyd George, nor the time of Churchill, Thatcher or Blair. He thought not about the illustrious and sometimes scandalous past: instead his eye was fixed on massive change and he thought only on the future. For all he cared, democracy could turn to dust, and in fact it might as well hurry up and do so, for though it would take time for his plans to materialise, this Cabinet of the elected from the elected would, whatever the issue, do his bidding.

The cameras were allowed in, briefly, for the now traditional new Cabinet-at-work shots for the evening news. In truth, to the people it all looked much the same; business as usual, the sideshow of government that affected their lives only in small ways, even though, of course, this had never been true. Cabinets of the past, governments of the past, had sent sons and daughters to their deaths in war, praised the victories of the brave soldiery, had been slow to spend on medical advances, or had moved quickly to eradicate disease, had ploughed money into properly educating some, at the expense of others, had overtaxed, or under-spent, or the opposite, had embraced technology or failed science, had allowed lawlessness or had dealt with a problem, had been just or unjust, had a system of checks and balances for the management of finances, or had blundered, but in all this had an army of civil servants and their statisticians to put the case for the government and to manage the whole business of policy administration, not to mention the Police, Hospital Trusts, Courts, Local Education Authorities, County, District and Borough Councils, and Business, the Banks, and venture capitalists, waiting to pounce, waiting to serve the public in the interests of the taxpayer, or so it had always been claimed... And at a discreet and discrete apolitical distance, the monarch, the titular head, still much loved by many, though less powerful since Oliver 1, or Cromwell, and since King William of Orange, and at a greater distance too, but still a valuable social glue, those of the monarch's kin on the Civil List, promoters of Britain, and as such players in the game that this would-be King Alfred the Great was wary of, by their very existence in this tradition-steeped land. Just as their Lordships in the other place, the powers that be, or some of them, wanted a collar and leash on this squat, blue-eyed Anglo-Saxon-loving newcomer to the top commoner's job.

But not so his Cabinet, a Cabinet of the politically faithful; though some at this stage fell under the heading too of the self-serving, a course of action or intent that might well lead to their falling headless, in a manner of speaking, in the future.

Alvis, with the cameras gone, and after the pleasantries and the plaudits, and before the first item of business, but setting the tone, and in fact governing all that would follow, laid the ground rules for the management of affairs.

People had been loyal thus far, he said, and hoped that they would continue so to be, through all the difficulties, obstructions, and frustrations that must surely lie ahead. He reminded them that there would always be opponents and others that would criticise them just for the sake of criticism. These last did not really matter: the real opponents were the ones to be reckoned with and there had been such a one in the early days of his career. But Patrick Lansing, he added, was no more. And then he paused.

Austin Summerville, his plastic face more wrinkled now, but his blue-grey eyes alert as ever, was the one who raised his head at the mention of Lansing's name. Summerville was Foreign Secretary, just as he had been under the old government. His gamble, his decision, to follow Alvis into the new Party had been vindicated, at least so far and in the outward show of his career. Virgil Holmes, smiling vacantly, younger than Summerville, and more animated in that moment, looked interestedly at the Leader. Yes, Lansing was no more, Alvis continued, and they all knew that the inquest into his accidental death had failed to uncover a conspiracy to kill him, and they should all believe in the inquest's findings. Then he added that it was odd that unfortunate things had always seemed to happen to those who opposed him.

The old clock ticked, and the room, the historic room, grew chill at that moment, as outside, beyond Downing Street, in Trafalgar Square, beyond into Leicester Square, Oxford Street, the Strand, and so on, London busied itself on this warm and pleasant day;

and the tourists gazed, wondered, smiled and squinted, sauntered and ate ice cream. The chimes of Big Ben, and Alvis in his position of power, added, before the detail of business began, that none of his followers, his *true* followers, he stressed, should be afraid of what others, and of course what he himself had termed his Werod. It just meant, after all, a company of friends, well-wishers and yes, perhaps bodyguards - to be sure, the Old English word, the Anglo-Saxon word simply meant just that, though it could also mean 'army' or 'legion ', and some had suggested, had they not, that it could mean 'mead' or 'sweet drink' ... He laughed at this point, seeming in an instant to be looking at all at the same time, though none could abide his gaze for long. 'It is nothing,' he said, with a dismissive wave of his pale hand, a smallish but strong sinewy hand, like that of a climber, 'it is nothing, nothing... You, my friends, should not have to worry about the Werod.'

Every word he uttered seemed to them to have special meaning. One or two grew pale. This was the beginning of the business of the new government.

Lovely evening, near the canal: narrow boats, two moored, one moving slowly by, sun low in the blue-violet summer sky. Sitting outside, at a benched table, Silas and two of his friends... Around them the other tables on the sloping lawn were gradually filling up; but they had a prime spot close to the sparkling water, gently undulating and lapping at the sides with the passage of the passing narrow boat.

Beside Silas sat pretty, pert-mouthed Eleanor, whom he and his other friends called Ellie, and opposite, the gaunt fair-haired Michael Sims, or Simsy. Ellie's fiancé, Tudor (Ashtonhurst) and Josh (Joshua Mann), Silas's best and oldest friend from his university days, had gone to get a second round of drinks. Glasses, with dregs and crushed crisp packets, two of these neatly squashed into little balls, were evidence of the first round.

How to fold a crisp packet into a little, irregular ball? Silas hadn't known the trick: Tudor had demonstrated. 'Make a circle with your thumb and forefinger facing up, like this, like you're holding a pole, or about to do a job on yourself...' a smile, then, after, a moment's hesitation, the group laughed, though Ellie shook her head as she laughed, her soft downy cheeks reddening perceptibly. 'Lay the packet over, then, push it down into the middle with the fingers of your other hand. Then, still keeping a slightly tighter circle now - squeezing the bishop a little...' another ripple, Tudor milking the joke,' fold each corner inwards and push down hard into the hole, and squeeze and release - hey presto!' He had triumphantly tossed the little ball into the air and it had landed in the dregs of Josh's pint. 'Well, it's my round next anyway,' he had added with a flourish, and a flush of self-conscious success.

While they were gone, Silas had tried with another packet, and then turned his attention to Ellie, whom he liked and was attracted to. He always felt a frisson, a glow, from close proximity to young attractive women and always savoured such unique precious moments, even while knowing that as a loving husband and father, things would not get out of control; or at least knowing consciously that he did not want them to. So as Ellie, younger by a year than Silas, showed him half a dozen holiday snaps of herself and Tudor in Rome, Silas would look from the photograph of the smiling faces of the recent past, to steal a glance at the short-styled , layered mousy brown hair of Ellie in life, hair with subtle highlights, with her tiny, perfect half-obscured ear and her sharp little profile with the light catching her slightly moist lower lip as she spoke. A symmetrical fresh eager face, with bright green to hazel eyes... Her arm, bare, extended, lifting the photograph, showed the faintest of fair downy hair, caught and tinged with colour in the slanting rays of the low sun. A moment...

And a moment later, Tudor returned, and Josh. Silas's spark of guilt was just that, dying as quickly as that of his delicious heightened admiration of Ellie... This was quite simply the finest company, Silas was thinking - the company of friends.

Tudor was taller than Silas, with cropped springy jet-black hair, a pale-complexioned square face and dark eyes, mischievous eyes. He was handsome and self-assured, some might say smug, if they were being down on themselves, insecure, but smugness was just an impression he sometimes made on people. Josh, not quite as tall as Tudor, but a fraction taller than Silas, had a shock of mid-brown hair and a long bony face that matched his skinny frame. His eyes were big, brown and hopeful, like those of a loyal dog. Intense, intelligent, often shy and occasionally silly when he had had too much to drink, Josh was and always had been a person Silas could talk to way into the small hours about everything and anything.

They set the drinks down: beers, a white wine for Ellie, and a pint of orange juice and lemonade for Tudor, who was tonight's chauffeur. 'Yes, you guys,' said Josh, his brown eyes widening,' we were trying to remember: which King Harold was it at Hastings - 1066 - with the arrow in the eye? Harold the First or Second, I mean... '

'Harold the Second,' shouted Silas, 'Harold Godwinson - er, I think...' He knew this, but how and when he'd bothered to pick it up, he couldn't remember, and he didn't want to look like a show-off.

'Whoa!' they all said, and clapped; and Tudor, his strong pale handsome features wearing an excited expression, suggested: 'Hey, maybe we should form a quiz team?'

'Don't know about that,' Silas demurred, though the notion did briefly excite his interest. 'I don't know where that answer even came from...'

'The Collective Unconscious?' suggested Ellie.

'Carl Jung,' joined in Simsy. And as they looked at him a huge cheer and explosion of clapping arose from the neighbouring table, around which a large motley crowd had gathered, in a celebration of some sort.

‘Wasn’t that clever,’ Simsy declared, but standing up to take a bow as though the applause was in response to his demonstration of general knowledge.

Silas was quietly enjoying the moment in an almost unconscious reverie when all of a sudden he noticed he was being stared at. Close by, at his side, a blond toddler with clear blue eyes and cropped hair was looking unblinkingly at him.

His friends noticed and began to smile. ‘He’ll call you dad in a minute,’ Josh suggested. They all stared at the still unblinking little boy, who obviously had some fixed determined notion in his head. Silas, a bit self-consciously spoke to him at last: ‘Sorry, I’ve got one already and another one on the way - no room at the inn.’

From the edge of the group at the noisy neighbouring table, a young woman in a bright floral dress shouted, ’Wayne, come here!’ She moved across and grabbed him by the wrist. ‘I’ve told you not to wander off - you could have fallen in the water.’ Besides Silas’s group, other onlookers were a large red-faced man with rolled-up shirt-sleeves, and his bespectacled equally large wife who looked on from the narrow boat that was moored close by. They, too, were smiling, kindly appreciative smiles. The mother of the little boy was apologetic and embarrassed: she need not have been, as everyone here at the canal-side rendezvous was enjoying the warm evening and the convivial outdoors and showing the better side of humanity.

‘Hey, that reminds me, Ellie,’ Silas began, though he wondered what had reminded him,’ Your dad’s a hero, unless I’m much mistaken. Don’t know why I didn’t mention it before...’ Ellie blushed, seeming to know what he had been going to say, probably because others had talked to her about it.

‘Yeah,’ added Josh enthusiastically, while Simsy looked mystified, his gaunt face questioning. ’I saw the name Adam Plato, but it didn’t register at first - pulled a little girl from a burning car - could have gone up at any time...’

Ellie blushed, again, was embarrassed but very proud. It was the first time they’d all gotten together since the incident the week before, an incident that had appeared subsequently not only in the local paper and on the East Anglian regional TV news but had also made the nationals. There was talk that week of her former Education Inspector father appearing on national television and being nominated for a bravery award. And so, she went through it all again with her friends wowing at the newly revealed snippets... Tudor of course knew it all and was the necessarily proud would-be son-in-law - reflected glory indeed. But the timing of the news, for it was news entirely to Michael Sims, or the general discussion of it, was freakishly coincidental as it turned out.

They had sat and chatted for at least another ten minutes when, just as Josh had begun talking sport, Silas began slowly to stand up, apropos of nothing, and seemed to be staring down at him, or more accurately right through him. Then, all of a sudden, Silas launched himself across the table so that glasses and beer went everywhere and his friends, particularly Josh, shrank back in alarm.

Nearby, a woman screamed a terrible, strangled, piercing cry, helpless, desperate.

Silas leapt between the seated and amazed Josh and Tudor, took three rapid bounding strides and threw himself into the canal a yard or two from the stern of the narrow boat, and half disappeared under the water.

A number of people pushed forward. The woman was still screaming: short stabbing cries imploring help.

Up came Silas, and with great effort hauled a tiny figure onto the bank. The little boy started spluttering and then bawling out loud as his mother hugged and kissed him and sobbed uncontrollably in relief.

Wearing a pair of much-too-big-for-Silas trousers, a pair the pub landlord had loaned him, and an old winter sweater of the same provenance, Silas, the new hero of the moment, made his way back to Tudor's new car, stunned as anyone else by what had happened; the cheers, the plaudits of the onlookers still ringing in his ears, visions of strangers hugging him and shaking his hand, and at the back of his mind a chill recollection of the cold filthy water in which he hadn't been able to see a thing.

That night a celebration of the hero's deed was held at Tudor's house, a celebration which Silas was uncomfortable with, since he felt, and knew, that he had just acted without thinking. And after all, he said to the others, the water wasn't that deep at the edge.

But the incident would haunt him for a long time. He had a recurring dream: he had kept on groping around in the water and had been unable to find the boy, and then the boy, the stranger's boy, had become Jonas, and it was Jonas who was drowning, and he couldn't save him. What, he would wonder too, in the waking hours, if I had not acted, or been a fraction of a second too late?

Nevertheless, that night, back at Tudor's, or Tudor's parents' house, which he was looking after while they were away in France, it was a time to relax and celebrate; celebrate the surprise event, yes, but mainly to toast the culmination of a couple of days together as a group (excepting Michael Sims who had been able to join them on the last day only).

When he got home the next day, Lindy asked him if he had enjoyed himself and was stunned and pleased by the revelation of his exploits.

11. *Chequers and the Dark Disciple*

Not everyone welcomed Dain Alvis's accession to power, though he was seen by many as a potential hero and saviour. Some did not like his extreme views and liked less the look and 'feel' of some of his supporters: of his supporters, they felt some fell into the category of fawning politicians, self-servers who had changed sides to further their careers rather than out of principle; but they were probably more concerned, the generality of liberal thinkers, that is, about the non-elected swelling ranks of Alvis's entourage, which disparately comprised, besides economic advisors, which was to be expected, scientific advisors and what looked like , what felt like , out-and-out henchmen. To their concern, the henchmen and some of the co-opted advisors were becoming more and more integrated into the mysterious Werod, of which more anon.

As yet, however, immediately prior to his successful election to the supreme executive office, and during the post-election honeymoon months, most enthusiastically welcomed Alvis as a breath of fresh air or were prepared to give him the benefit of the doubt, such was the parlous state of the world as viewed from inside the United Kingdom. They hoped this would be a genuine breakthrough into the light, or at least genuinely light at the end of the tunnel.

Still obdurate crime figures, baking reservoirs and standpipes (with fears of worse to come), a poorly performing pound, inadequate housing, too many people being packed into our green and pleasant land, mishandling of public finances, and a general drift and a lack of vision, had all contributed to the voting in of the new man for the now not-so-new century. Alvis had said: 'When you are sitting in your car on the packed and stationary lanes of the M5 motorway wanting to travel south beyond Bristol, and it's hot outside, and your air conditioning's packed up, and you can't move, and back at home the water's been cut off and your job's under threat, you look across at the other angry and sometimes aggressive motorists, and then up at the RAC Traffic Control building, and you say to yourself: " My God, is this Britain, is this what life here has become?"' And for many it had become a matter of seeing life as grim, and he knew he had struck a chord with the common man, whether it was the holidaymaker used to the struggle to get to the south-west, or the those commuting daily to Bristol from the Cotswolds and beyond, and all those who felt crammed in and trapped and maltreated in the kingdom, and who thought: 'Yes, he's right. How well he understands the world in which we live: how well he understands the struggle.'

Alvis, still trim, squat and strong, directed his gaze out of the small window and across the burnt-off grass to the sorry brown fields of Coombe Hill, and he momentarily recalled, with his thin-lipped smile, those very words, or something very close to them. 'Ha!' he uttered out loud to himself, then wheeled round and strode off to join his guests. There were plenty of them at the traditional Prime Minister's retreat in Buckinghamshire that weekend; a real assortment of well-known and lesser-known political figures and their wives or husbands, as well as a gathering of more shadowy figures who were ostensibly on the fringe of things, politically speaking, but who were closer to Alvis than any of the more obvious associates. And there was an air about these people that spoke of privilege of a special kind, and of growing influence. Some but not all were linked to the Werod, but all made their more perceptive fellow guests feel somehow uncomfortable, nervous to a certain degree. And yet Alvis, the buoyant purposeful genial host strove to make all feel at home and was in great measure successful in this.

The guests were assembled in a manner of speaking, spread through a number of rooms, though a few lingered and sauntered outside in the glowing shimmering sweaty heat of the mid-afternoon. Stepping out, they stepped as if into an oven, the house too sucking in a brief hot breeze as the doors were opened. The glare viewed from the darker rooms was initially like that of a spotlight. The sun in a cloudless blue sky: beneath, browning lands in this late summer. The heavy downpours were expected, hoped for, but seemed reluctant to materialize and give relief to dried-up Nature.

In one large room the chatter of thirty or more guests, most of them male, sounded as a continuous murmur punctuated by the occasional laugh, or loud declaration, or the chink of crockery and silver cutlery. Tea was being served. Some took it hot, some preferred, quite naturally after the protracted hot spell, iced tea, the coolness of the dark old room notwithstanding. Iced tea was greatly in fashion now, having been previously in recent times all the more so across the Atlantic. On that theme, one or two risked a little alcohol in the form of a version of mint julep: no doubt some of these were readers of great fiction or devotees of bygone America.

Serving people, a handful, male and female, busied themselves among and around the sprawling group (some members of which were not actually sprawling but standing ill at ease, trying to attach themselves to a conversation), dispensing chinking cups or chiming glasses beneath the ornate embossed ceiling. Long-serving Horst was one of these, not actually dispensing drinks himself, but watching those who did and keeping one eye on his master, who sat now on the arm of a red-leather chair, swinging a leg as he chatted sideways to Austin Summerville. Summerville, looking still pretty trim himself, but aged, with his plastic face tending to sag a bit whenever he was tired, seemed at ease most of the time though discomfited at that moment by the fact that his leader had what he thought a less comfortable perch than he.

If the truth be told, unlike Summerville, who was relaxed, more than one of the senior government figures present looked uneasy; or perhaps wary rather than uneasy. Often, they could be seen stealing a glance at an unknown neighbour, perhaps trying to ascertain or understand who the person was or whether he or she had any connection with the sinister Werod organization, or group, that seemed to be so important to the Prime Minister. Some present in that very room were known members, and some could even be identified by the 'Dagaz' badge on their lapel, or the ring equivalent on a finger of their left hand; but not all were so open. One eye of course was also kept on the leader himself, since few felt wholly comfortable in his presence, though at that moment he was smiling broadly as he shared a joke with Summerville.

A woman entered and crossed the room, unobtrusively. She was tall, elegant, attractive, and looked untroubled, businesslike. She ignored the admiring glances from what she probably regarded as the seedier ageing males, and even the admiration of the younger males. She made straight for Alvis, who casually inclined his head, so that she could whisper her message to him. He nodded, and some took notice as he stood up, half-ceasing their conversations to observe. When it was clear from the leader's demeanour that probably nothing important or untoward was happening, they palpably relaxed again as though at some unspoken instruction from their master.

Alvis, pleased with the way the weekend was developing, was not even bothered overmuch by the oppressive heat. He had become used to it in his early years travelling with his uncle and aunt around the countries of North Africa. With a spring in his step, then, he made his way through the old building, pausing as he often did at the famous stained-glass window. A few moments later he stopped at one of the darker turnings, darker only perhaps because he had just glanced outside at the glare of the day as he passed the windows overlooking the pleasant but now parched grounds. He had stopped at a display case containing memorabilia of Oliver Cromwell, and as he did so he tried to make out a large figure at the head of a short staircase, a figure dressed rather oddly in dark, loose-fitting garments. He knew who it was, of course, for it could be no one else. The sudden, stealthy appearance out of the shadows of this rather ungainly, almost misshapen figure of a man might have unsettled momentarily a less steely man than the unconcerned great leader.

'Alec!' Alvis announced, moving forward towards the shadowy figure, who now himself advanced into the brighter light. 'You are most welcome. I hope you had a good journey. You can if you wish join the throng' (though I know it's not your wish, this seemed to be saying), 'but you'd probably like a few words first. We've a bit of catching up to do, eh?'

The visitor was, it has to be said, odd to look at, strangely amorphous and faintly repulsive. He was quite a bit over six feet tall but without quite appearing to be a giant. His round-shouldered bulk of a frame swayed as he walked, in somewhat shambling ungainly fashion. As to his facial appearance, he had almost vacant, misty, grey-green eyes that often looked, unnervingly for some, expressionless. The face was puffy, the skin dry to the point of beginning to deteriorate, as though its owner were a regular eczema sufferer, which in fact he was not. The nose was almost bulbous and largish above a red fleshy and moist full-lipped mouth. His ears were small for the large head, which was poorly thatched with thinning, fine light-coloured hair that might or might not be receding at the temples. Beneath the face with its pale watery stare, and beneath the jowly chin, the man had a prominent Adam's apple. The visitor appeared to have overly long arms, hanging in an ungainly fashion at his sides, arms which ended in enormous white and puffy freckled hands, which everyone who met him attested were clammy always to the touch but incredibly strong. All in all, there was something not quite right and rather repellent about him, though this was mitigated by youth: he was nowhere near the age some might take him for.

Alvis was quite aware of the effect his visitor could and usually did have on people, which was one reason why he had given him, despite his age and complete inexperience in dealing with politicians, the opportunity to sit in from time to time on the first few meetings of his now rapidly forming Werod. One aspect of his role was planned to be that of a sort of reserve or understudy to the person responsible for state security, as it was termed within the shadowy new organization. Another aspect was, ultimately, to carry out similar duties in the area of the advancement of science, a task for which he was admirably qualified. In truth, as things stood at the moment in practical terms, he would appear as an auditing apprentice sitting and learning at the back of a master-class.

Security, or law and order, and science were, as they say, strange bedfellows, but they were perfectly well accommodated in the unlikely-looking person of Alexander McLennan (more properly Joseph William Alexander Sergei McLennan) whose soft slow deliberate voice showed little trace of any Scottish accent, even though his father was half-Scottish and the family had lived in Scotland for the first six years of his life. McLennan's genealogy showed an interesting and varied pedigree, that over a century and a half or so, encompassed a number of European countries, and there were distant influences more exotic, from even further afield. This did not really concern him, and he rarely referred to his progenitors. The past however perhaps did manifest itself in that he had troubled to learn passable German, a considerable amount of French and some Russian. His intellectual bent was, however, towards science: he had taken a First in Natural Sciences at Cambridge after sailing through a first year doing Mathematics with Physics. He was working through his PhD with a single-mindedness and ability which astonished his supervisors. McLennan was a first-rate mathematician, and, according to his academic mentors, and his peers, he was, at twenty-three, quite simply a genius. The plaudits of the scientific community would, those in the know who knew these things said, be an inevitability.

McLennan did not care: he was indifferent to such praise: he just absorbed himself, though not exclusively, in his scientific and mathematical pursuits; and equal in measure with his love and mastery of science and mathematics was his support for Dain Alvis, the great leader he had attached himself to, as a limpet to the rock. He would get on with shaping his own analytical view of the world alongside his active furtherance of Dain Alvis's power and the hoped-for changes to society. There was in any case something of the laboratory about this whole business of politics which afforded McLennan inner satisfaction.

So, he followed the smaller, squarer, more confident-looking Alvis into a small room where he and the Leader sat down opposite one another.

Alvis stared unblinkingly into the younger, larger man's watery eyes; daggers of piercing blue ice lost in a deep fathomless pool, where it seemed the exuberance of youth and even the normal social drives and conventions seemed to struggle for existence. McLennan had a view of the world that was extreme, even by Alvis's standards, and it would often sound wholly clinical when he spoke about it, strangely devoid of the usual emotions and concerns that a young man, however socially inept, might be expected to display. Fifteen years separated the two men, but McLennan looked older than his count of orbits of the sun; which was how he often thought of time's passing - in terms of distance travelled... a simple calculation until you tried to take into account the movement of the sun and planetary system around the galaxy, and in turn the movement of the galaxy, and the universe itself from its Big Bang origins, the very Big Bang theory that McLennan ambitiously hoped one day to disprove... (it was wrong, and had always in his view been an error, to base theories on the observable part of one universe).

'You are changing your name, I hear?' commented Alvis, coming straight to the point, pre-empting the younger man who, despite his peculiar form of self-possession, was a little discomfited.

'Yes, Leader, with your permission I shall now go by the name of Alex Quellan.'

Alvis smiled, and his eyes narrowed as he pondered this. He was used to being addressed as Leader, in private, by McLennan and a handful of other followers; but it was not that which gave him pause for thought: for one thing it was odd and almost touching that the strange young man should ask his permission as though he were speaking to a close family member or a bosom friend, but the other thought was the overriding one - that he half recognised the new or adjusted surname as a familiar word.

McLennan leaned forward in his chair and extended his arm, a scrap of slightly crumpled white paper in his clammy white paw.

Taking the proffered note, and unfolding it, Alvis read, in that quiet room, that inner sanctum, what was written thereon: 'Alex Quellan from Joseph William Alexander Sergei McLennan. Quellan, the infinitive of the verb, which should be written Cwellan.' Alvis racked his brains, and McLennan, now hoping to be Quellan, was anxious now not to appear to have been testing his Leader.

'*Cwellan*, an Anglo-Saxon word? Yes, quell... but it meant something more than that, I recall, so I can see why you changed it... Very apt, given the work we may be required to carry out, if I recall the meaning correctly... You've deliberately used the infinitive - 'to kill', am I right? 'McLennan slowly nodded his large head, as if to say his Leader was correct on both counts, and a smile of appreciation played around his thick lips. Alvis, scrutinizing him, analyzing him, continued: '*Cwellend* means killer, so changing to the infinitive and changing the spelling of the infinitive too... softens the ending and it sounds, I must say, quite contemporary, quite plausible... This is how language develops of course... And our Anglo-Saxon ancestors had another word, spelt with one 'l' less for the infinitive of 'die'. It has a ring to it, and it makes you sound, well, less regional. Alex Quellan... mm... Very good. I like it.' The odd-looking young man who filled the chair opposite was pleased; pleased by his standards, that is, for he never seemed to display much emotion, rather soaking up other people's like a sponge. 'I shall mention your new name to the full Council of the Werod this very week.' It was the

Leader's turn to feel pleased with the process of naming: the 'Council' of the Werod had only just been established by him, in discussion with his close followers, and already it seemed to him to be a working entity and to possess the capacity for organic growth, a shadowy but very real complement to the public face of government. Alvis had big plans for the Werod. So far, its membership included only one MP (the Minister of State for Science and not a full Cabinet Member) but then that was not its purpose: it was an unofficial body by design, and its job would be to steer policy in the areas that mattered to the new Leader. Yes, Alvis thought, this young fellow will keep the Council (that word again, pleasing...) on its toes, even if they don't like him sitting there, huge, dark-clad, all lumps and bumps. The very idea certainly did amuse him, and he had already received muted murmurings about his presence at earlier meetings: now, Alvis had decided, he would become a permanent fixture. In any case, his focus would be Science...

The windows blazed like luminous paintings, but they did not wholly illumine the entirety of this dark wood-panelled room, something of a refuge from the heat of the day, wherein the squat, energetic and dapper and fearless Alvis consorted with his large zealot of an apostle.

'You are preparing the list, Alex?'

McLennan, or Quellan, looking at ease now in his chair, said belatedly to the point of being apropos of nothing: 'Thank you, Leader.' Alvis peered with a steely blue searching gaze into the large face with the watery eyes. His ill-favoured apostle was just being appreciative: he felt something like a stab of sympathy for the young social misfit who idolised him, or at least who slavishly took on board his ideals, but who was never importuning, always keen to keep a respectful distance. Obsessed with science, mathematics... living was incidental, a means to an end: that was the Leader's cold assessment of him.

'You are preparing the list, Alex?' he repeated.

Quellan, for Quellan it now was, was still quietly pleased by the way in which his new name had been so readily accepted and approved by the Leader, and the fact that he was straightway using it. Yes, Alex, and no longer Alec, implying the rest of the change, the surname.

'Yes, sir', replied' It is well-advanced. We have a thousand agents - most of them glad to work for free - getting the names of those we would call, and know to be, enemies of the common good. That is what they are - enemies of the common good. And shall we start looking at the schools?'

'Of course,' Alvis replied, with a narrowing of his eyes.

'Good ... with respect, I had anticipated that this would still be your view, so I've taken the liberty of including those, male and female, fifteen years and over. Most are surprisingly law-abiding. However, for those...' He shrugged, and trailed off, wanting eagerly to impart some extra news.

'I have something else,' he began again, facing the unsmiling Alvis, whose now stern gaze was fixed.

‘I have extended the search - because we have so many willing and eager, and efficient helpers - the search will now cover back editions of local newspapers throughout the land, to see where the perception of the people is that sentencing policy has failed the people; occasions when the vermin were allowed to get off lightly for their crimes. This of course will call into question too how we are to deal with a corrupt, rather should I say, lenient judiciary...but perhaps it’s just a case of new laws...’

‘A little bit of both, I should say, Alex. But be circumspect in your choice of words, at least at this stage, outside of our infrequent conversations *in camera...*’ Alvis noticed a flicker of disappointment in the heavy face of his apostle, so he added: ‘Your enthusiasm for the cause, as ever, does you credit. But relax, young man.’ This was said with a sort of cold affection which pleased ‘Quellan’, his face showing not a trace of suspicion that the Prime Minister was patronising him. ‘And let me know how your ideas are developing. You may come to the position of formally auditing the activities of the Werod Council, when you are free so to do; but I won’t throw you into the lion’s den just yet. And don’t worry - we shall prevail. Society and the world will change... But I see some doubt in your eyes...’

The comment hung in the air, and the young man shuffled his bulk in the deep leather armchair. Alvis took the opportunity to study more closely the young man’s strange garb: black boots and baggy trousers above which a voluminous dull-grey shirt, more like a smock or a frock-coat hung down, pulled in at the waist by a thick leather belt; some sort of black, faux leather waistcoat completed the ensemble. McLennan, or Quellan, reminded Alvis of old pictures of pre-revolutionary Russian peasants in a history book he had read quite recently; or had it been a biography of Tolstoy, who himself liked to be seen dressed as a peasant. He was uncertain as to where he had seen the photograph; but what was certain was that it would not really be possible for his young protégé to go on the podium at the Party Conference, and give a speech, dressed like that.

'No, Alex, no doubt as such,' Alvis hastened to continue, sweeping back his brown hair with his right hand, and with a determined look. He was now thirty-eight, and his bright steely face as yet bore only a few lines of care and age. 'My idea is that people can be made better and happier by strong and if necessary ruthless government. Is your view still that it is possible only to contain or punish the evil-doers of this world and not reform them? Speak freely, as you can nowhere else.'

The young disciple cast a deep watery glance to one side as though contemplating the oblong of glaring brightness that was the window onto the outside world, aware that his mentor was studying him.

'I understand your meaning, Leader...'

'Call me Prime Minister: you will find it easier. We don't want the world to get the wrong idea...' Alvis was aware that he had interrupted, but he was cautious over the title 'Leader', used in this manner, whether in front of the less zealous or wavering of his followers, or his opponents, or even in front of the die-hards of the inner circle. Its German translation would certainly upset the Jewish, and German, elements of his bodyguard. After all, a handful of mischievous newspaper scribblers, and celebrity newsman Goodman, had compared him to Hitler; and whilst he did not object to the comparison in terms of the power that had been wielded by the *Führer*, he most certainly objected to it in that Hitler had abused and misdirected it, against innocent Jews, Gypsies, Slavs and the conquered peoples in general, and in generating a global war. Interestingly, Alvis recalled, at that particular moment, that his large disciple, formerly with the Scottish name, had had in fact a great-grandfather of Siberian origin, who had fought on the Mamayev Kurgan in the Stalingrad battle, and who had lived to see the Germans defeated there. But McLennan was a mixed bag, with, as well as a Scottish father, he had English, Irish, Russian, German and Swedish blood, somewhere along the line over a two-century span. In fact, when pressed, he would usually express his sympathies for the trapped, frozen and starved German 6th Army, in equal measure with sympathy for the Soviet defenders, his maternal great-grandfather included, whenever Stalingrad came up, whether in came up in conversation with a Werod member or in his presumably limited social life. He was loyal only to what he calculated to be the truth of the matter.

An ancient clock ticked loudly in the polished dark Tudor room, and the wooden walls of Old

England listened intently, breath held: a speck of dust caught in a shaft of sunlight fell, undirected, purposelessly, on McLennan's black-garbed right knee. He did not notice.

'I understand your reasons, Prime Minister; and to tell the truth, your proper and public title does come out easier...' He smiled a thick-lipped smile.

'Very honest, Alex...' Alvis returned the smile, thin-lipped in his case. 'Would you like a cold drink? I'm having one,' he added quickly. 'Gunther!'

The door was opened in an instant and a tall young German stood in the room.

McLennan admired the command in his master's voice and was in equal measure surprised by the sudden appearance of the German, a nephew of the head of Alvis's personal bodyguard. The young man was smartly dressed, and McLennan studied him from his seated position, fixing on the pale blue eager eyes of the politely smiling newcomer. Two iced teas were ordered, in German, by Alvis, the Prime Minister of the United Kingdom. As Gunther left to carry out his serving duty, Alvis, sitting back down, smiled at the thought of this, and his mind continued on in the same vein.

'You know, Alex,' he began again, waving his hands side to side in grand sweeping gestures, for emphasis,' this whole business of Anglo-Saxon, German roots, even the Werod, or its name rather, our party emblem... it's all a game in a way. Amazing how people will follow anyone, believe anything, if the conditions of their lives are improved or in prospect of being improved. Even now, some people live in fear, or are apathetic, despairing... They are without purpose. They want to believe in something or someone... Since the virtual disappearance of organised religious belief and practice, there has been an incurable spiritual malaise... But you believe, don't you, based on your analysis, mathematical, scientific, that the situation is even worse? I agree with you of course and that is what drives me to succeed.'

'Yes, Prime Minister.' McLennan took the opportunity to speak.' I believe the world is running out of control. I have no belief in any god, and believe there to be no divine purpose.' He was rapidly becoming animated, but trying, it was plain for Dain Alvis to see, to keep his own particular form of ranting in check. 'God was an invention conjured up out of fear of the dark - the eternal darkness, I should say. Many people believe this, many people...,' he continued breathlessly, before taking a gulp of air, and aided by a calming gesture from the older man.' I believe it is the tendency of matter to become ever more complex wherever and whenever it can, and that life itself is one manifestation of this process. Religion and complex social systems are other manifestations. The more complex a species, the greater this urge, this drive towards complexity; and thus, through to the manifestation of this ever-developing state...so the greater level of entropy. There must come a point....'

Here, he halted, as though to go on would somehow be disrespectful to his host.

Alvis changed the subject, while at the back of his mind he briefly pondered the implications or the meaning, if any, of McLennan's view of Man and Nature. Inanimate matter, 'the tendency of matter'... what on Earth did that mean?

They spoke then of lists, other lists, and of far more far reaching plans which were of necessity as yet in their infancy. They spoke too of the need for greater and greater commitment and a collective will, but a collective will that should be subservient to and answer only to the Leader. There must be no fudging of the major issues to pacify or satisfy minority concerns. There would be no pandering to democratic lassitude and indecision. The danger that was global warming, climate change, call it what you would, was fast approaching a tipping point; both men believed this, McLennan having no scientific doubts. Climate danger alone would provide sufficient justification for *anything that needed to be done*; but there was also the matter of bringing in real justice, Alvis's key election platform and pledge. McLennan, Quellan, was no less interested in this, no less passionate. The Werod, from its twelve-person Council downwards, and across every important area of society, would be the real agent of change, and at its head, Dain Alvis. The name of the Prime Minister, and the reputation of his official, Breakthrough Party would of course need to remain untainted by the actions of the Werod. The Werod, as an executor of the rule of law, would be praised where the public expressed approval of its actions; and should an *extreme* circumstance arise, giving rise to public concern, then the Prime Minister would disavow and deny with a sense of public outrage any involvement, at the same time ensuring that no blame attached itself to the Werod.

Quellan, large and animated, pausing incongruously to sip his iced tea in an overly dainty way, enquired and made suggestions relating to the Werod Council's at the moment tenuous links with the forty-plus Chief Constables, the Armed Forces Chiefs of Staff, MI5 and MI6, and the Universities: in respect of this last group of institutions, so important in so many ways to Quellan and to the country, Quellan expatiated on the range of PhD research projects that might be of use in not only the broadest technological sense, but in a military sense, to protect the nation, to anticipate the research likely to be conducted by other countries. There would also need to be strong links with the prison authorities, the media in all its manifestations, and, oh yes, the pharmaceutical companies such as Reed International or Hoffnung-Larousse... And so it went on, with Alvis marvelling at Quellan's seeming grasp of affairs. Given his youth, his limited experience... The ungainly young man even seemed less repulsive when he spoke, less of a misfit. But then for the first time Alvis noticed that his protégé seemed to be wearing makeup of some description, a foundation or powder seemed to have been disturbed by a bead of sweat. Clearly, the poor fellow, unprepossessing as he was anyway, had some form of skin condition. As if to confirm this almost, Quellan self-consciously took out a handkerchief and gently dabbed at the bead of sweat.

Much of what needed to be done could be legitimately agreed and officially sanctioned by Parliament, but there were some things that would need to be accomplished through the Werod and its agents. Recruitment to the Werod would have to be on the mark: the selection process, currently being addressed by the Council, would be rigorous. Everyone would need to be made aware from the outset that betrayal of the common cause would be dealt with swiftly, in the appropriate fashion, for the good of the people.

'Patrick Lansing had his own point of view, as have one or two other people along the way,' Dain Alvis said incidentally, though with particular meaning: McLennan, or Quellan, understood the importance, he said, of adherence to the true path, of loyalty to the new order.

Alvis had studied Quellan closely as he was talking, freely now, confidently and passionately, with vision, but also in a controlled way. The man who was Prime Minister recalled a story that he had overheard the young man relate: he recalled that it had been on his, Quellan's second appearance among the group, two years earlier, before the formation of the twelve-person Council of the Werod, of course, and at a time when secrecy was perhaps less important than now. At that time they had envisaged the spread of the Werod and its ideas, originally his, Alvis's ideas, as being like the spread of the Cistercian monasteries of the middle ages, as pyramidal model, based on the establishment of ‘daughter houses’, if he had his history correctly, a process which had been dedicated in one respect to consigning Odin or Woden and the Norse and Germanic religions to the past, for good and all, a process not just carried out under the Cistercian model of Christianity of course, but going back to the time of the Emperor Charlemagne, for example, who roasted Saxons in cages if they refused to convert. McLennan had engaged then, like the other would-be members of the Werod, in talk about historicity, about the nature of religious monopoly of truth and so on, but what had strangely stuck with Alvis, without really haunting him (since that was not allowed in his mental make-up), was a disturbing little tale he overheard McLennan telling another delegate:

‘I sat next to these two men in a pub. I’d been there some time, on my second pint, when they came in and sat down at the table next to me. They looked at first like labouring types, but as I listened, I realized that it was a lorry driver and his mate. The lorry driver was older, a fat man, heavy set. He was probably in his forties. The other was younger, about twenty or so, new to the job... He didn’t have much to say. Eager to please, and keen not to offend the older man who spoke slowly, softly, as though uttering words of wisdom...

They began talking about rats. I can’t remember how the subject arose. Anyway, the younger man was obviously a bit squeamish or sensitive, from what had already been said. The

older man then broke into a story about how he'd once caught a rat alive by its tail:" We had this barrel of maggots, full it was, and I dangled the rat over it and let him hang there for a while, squealing..." The younger man already looked as though he didn't want to hear any more, but was trying not to show it, so the fat man held back for a moment, for effect, the denouement of his story. He was taking a sort of sadistic pleasure in holding back, upsetting the younger more sensitive man. I could see the young man's face, sense the other man's pleasure. Then the fat man said, with a chuckle: "Oh, he knew where he was going, all right, so I kept him hanging there, squealing...Then I just dropped him in and he disappeared. Eaten alive as he suffocated."

I must say I found this disgusting fat ape, so delighting in his enjoyment of torture, both of the rat and the sensitive young man, one good example of the what sort of vermin hides, or can hide, in the shape of a man. Casual cruelty... towards another creature, to validate one's own worthless existence... Interestingly, the story made such an impression on me, that I made it my business to find out the fat man's name and where he lived, the names of his children and so on and so on... Now it's a hobby of mine, gathering details of people... As you will guess, I don't really like some people, and in fact despise them as a form of subhuman... And whilst on occasion, I might complain about heavy-handed state violence, I do abhor casual acts of cruelty

committed by individuals... Yes, I think the moral of the story is that there is a significant minority who enjoy cruelty, if they can practise it without risking their own miserable cowardly hides. I should really like this flaw in *Homo sapiens* addressed on a massive scale, once and for all, whatever it takes... yes, whatever it takes.'

Dain Alvis studied his young protégé now, the reminiscence of that incident rising unbidden in his ever-active mind. 'Yes', came the thought, a thought, a view he had held for some time now: 'I can use this driven, obsessive misfit. He certainly can play a role in the work of the Werod. We can expect great things of him, I believe. An unlikely manifestation this McLennan-Quellan, an unlikely manifestation of a dark angel of retribution.'

The Prime Minister, recalling his other guests and his duty as a host, wound matters up with a few pleasantries and showed the younger man, large and awkward, to the door. Then, after fixing a date for Quellan to sit in with the Council, he said goodbye. Feeling rather pleased with himself, he prepared to rejoin or track down a number of his other guests, thinking he would tell some members of his Werod Council now about Quellan; among the many other weightier matters of business he needed to discuss.

As he parted from Quellan, he had an afterthought, and turned to say something to him. But Quellan was gone. He had already turned the corner at the end of the short corridor and disappeared into the shadows. So be it. It could wait.

Chequers shimmered in the heat, in front of a burnt, blistered Coombe Hill. Soon the rains would beat down and the very land would audibly, greedily suck in the life-sustaining water, and the flash floods would form pools and rivulets and create havoc in the dips and hollows of the kingdom. Still waiting for this, it seemed, two dusty carrion crows sat hunched up, bedraggled, close to one another. They sat mournfully almost, on a ridge tile, close to one of the many old brick chimneys, on the roof of this country retreat of Prime Ministers. They could have been watching, listening, ready to take wing with any news...

Odin's ravens, for the time being saying nothing. An early autumn, and then winter, and spring, repeated over and over again, but the differentiation being warped, blurred by vast invisible changes. A world turning with its myriad human desires, dreams, terrors. The awful passing of unyielding, unsparing heedless time, ticking away and taking away... The quotidian world with its innumerable cares, its delights and its inconveniences, work, rest, to sleep and dream, chance, luck, and all the scheming and planning leading towards that finality of all finalities, yet always towards and within the continual cycle of rebirth. Did humanity really hold its breath for what was to come, or would it be fanciful so to suggest?

12. *London's burning...*

Carbon emissions had been reduced, in Britain at least, for the first year since the issue had become an issue at the beginning of the century. Dain Alvis's government had achieved that much, though the scientific consensus was that global warming was none the less continuing apace, with the United States and China in particular continuing to make the most detrimental contributions, and India not far behind. Still, new technologies were being introduced and it was hoped that by... and so on. Methane, too, was being released now in volumes vast as the Siberian permafrost was gradually but, in geo-climatological terms rapidly being consigned to history. As had always been the case, however, most people concerned themselves with their daily struggles: the environment meant their immediate environment, their immediate, their localized struggle.

The Breakthrough Party still ruled, with an absolute majority, and was in its second term; and contrary to the dire warnings of all the doom merchants of the liberal press, the Union Flag still flew over the kingdom, and the runic Dagaz flag was waved only in the shadows or at the Party Conference. In those shadows though the Werod had grown immensely strong and was continuing to infiltrate all the key institutions of the land. To use its coded terminology,' all the *placement targets* had been achieved': commissars of the Werod, called *liaison advisors* were now to be found in all areas of the Civil Service, in ministries like Education and Health, and in Defence, at individual universities, in the Bank of England, working with the Police, and with the Criminal Justice System, with the Armed Forces... However, as yet, there appeared no clear pattern, whether clandestine or open in nature, to the attachment and involvement in these various areas of state organization.

Paradoxically, as the power, or the potential power of the Werod increased, so in almost equal measure, as though by some mathematical inverse law, the popularity of the Breakthrough Party wavered and appeared to be diminishing in the middle of its second term. It was by no means certain that Alvis and his government would be returned to power at the next election.

The prison population had increased with the building of twenty-three new prisons, a little way short of Alvis's promised fifty; and whilst the number of all recorded offences remained steady, the number of serious crimes of violence had fallen dramatically, despite the continued existence of large pockets of deprivation and an increased level of desperation in some quarters; though many streets, estates, backwaters remained, to use the more extreme end of Breakthrough parlance, polluted, and had yet to be thoroughly cleansed and scoured. This notwithstanding, investigative journalists, those brave enough, were still trying to get to the bottom of scores of mysterious disappearances of hardened career thugs, who had tangled with the Community Specials, who in their turn had reported them. Often the wrongdoers had then, quite simply, literally disappeared, as though off the face of the Earth. The estates where these thugs had once held sway had become better places to live, so those who had kept silent in the past through fear, perhaps now kept their silence in gratitude for their deliverance, perhaps also through potential or real menace from another source. The upshot was they did not want investigative journalists rocking the boat, now that life was better.

Silas Wood was now thirty-seven and thought he could detect the first signs of grey hairs at his temples. Lindy was a few months short of thirty-seven and had a more philosophical view of ageing, though she had in no wise 'let herself go'. On the contrary, she was, despite having lost the soft downy glow, or the bloom of youth, still a good-looking woman who had worked at keeping her figure, even though she had returned to full time work at Hoffnung and continued to be the mother of three children. Jonas, the eldest, was now a robust if slightly shorter than average tousle-haired ten, with his mother's dark eyes; and he had been joined in this world by a brother, Leo, now eight and unaccountably blond, and a sister, Nancy, who was now five and shared her elder brother's dark good looks. The children were in excellent health, and in this respect, the family had so far been blessed with good luck.

They still lived in their homely Victorian terrace in North London. Silas was now a Senior Lecturer and naturally had permanent tenure, but still earned less than Lindy who had moved on in the pharmaceutical industry, having had two promotions at Hoffnung-Larousse. She was now in research and development terms at the right hand of Briony Daniels, who was the brilliant intellect of the company and respected throughout the world. The pressures of work, however, were beginning to show on Briony: her once shining determined youthfulness had become tarnished and the years had begun to make her look careworn. Her slimness had given way to a tendency to appear undernourished, though she fought against this by a deliberate policy of eating the right foods and exercising; unfortunately, only when work allowed her the time. She remained a good-looking woman, even strikingly so, but time was making its mark sooner than it might have done. The pressure she found in her work was, she knew, and Lindy Wood and others knew, in part caused by extraneous 'unofficial' government interference, as the company sought to secure new lucrative defence-related government research contracts, or at least 'preferred contractor' status. These people put the fear of God in her where nothing else did, but she felt certain that this would advance her career to an even greater degree.

Lindy did not get involved in any of this, nor was she invited to. She was busy herself with her section's own developmental work on a new anti-viral drug. In truth, Lindy was a bit tetchy at the moment. Two things preyed on her mind, or at least gnawed at the back of her mind from time to time. One, her colleague, the obliging, ever eager and reliable Hannah, whose recent marriage had changed her surname from Stacey to Lyle-Richardson, had left for a new job, effectively a couple of rungs upwards rather than a sideways move, a job with Reed that meant a move to France, near Grenoble; Lindy was not envious, just sad to lose a friend. The second area of concern was Silas, who she felt might be about to fall victim to a mid-life crisis. She had been disappointed by Hannah's leaving but was fearful on the other count; that Silas might succumb to the young charms of one of the swarms of attractive students who passed through university each year on their way to something else in life. She did not want to lose Silas, much less lose him to someone else's phase in life, for lost she determined he would be if he ever did anything like that. Of course, it might not even be a student: it could be a waitress or a solicitor's clerk; who knew? And yet it may not happen, and Silas was a bit young for that sort of behaviour, having been, as far as she was aware, loyal up till now. Her friends insisted that forty-two or forty-three, from their knowledge and experience, might be nearer the mark. Well, she had thought at the time, *that's* something to look forward to. They were all talking as though it were inevitable. He had grown older, but then so had she. What was more to the point, had he grown too accustomed to her? To the back of her mind these thoughts would have to go. In any case, Silas did love her, she knew it, and he would most likely not stray so long as everything else in his life moved along without complication.

Thus her train of thoughts ran against a background of lab work, the writing up of research findings, departmental e-mailing, chilly one-to-ones with Briony, school targets, parents' evenings, theatre, holidays, Christmas, Sainsbury's, Waitrose, and, occasionally, Lidl; and to her mind, to her recollection, only one complication had arisen: the time Silas had visited the police station, and all because of that damned burglary.

It had preyed on *his* mind ever since, she knew that. Only yesterday he had woken up in the clichéd cold sweat. Rather, she had awoken him because he was talking loudly in his sleep. He had dreamt he was shouting that he knew nothing and pleading to be set free. The white room, the bright lights, the bars on the window, the little table and the man with the notebook on the other side, with a couple of goons standing behind, ready to hit him again with what they called a blackjack, a kind of club. He was stripped to his underpants, cold and shivering, an insect on a shiny glass slide.

When Silas had come to, from his disturbed sleep, and when the blue-grey light of incipient dawn began to make shapes in the room distinguishable again, he had realized, as he had before when waking from this recurring nightmare, that the reality had not been, physically at least, like this. Mentally, yes: his interrogator had gotten into his mind.

The burglary had happened at the end of March. A couple of rooms had been ransacked and bedroom drawers pulled out, their contents strewn everywhere. There was not much damage, malicious damage, no excrement smeared on the walls and such-like: papers were missing, bank books and cards, and a few expensive-looking but actually worthless, in terms of their market value, ornaments which did have, however, some sentimental value. Everyone was upset, returning like that from a pleasant night out at the theatre, where they had been to see a musical. According to Silas, it was though Fate had said to them: 'Don't enjoy yourselves too much - you never know what's around the corner.' It had seemed particularly hard to take because burglaries overall were beginning to fall in that area, not that the problem had ever been that great there by national standards. The Police had been called, they had been given an incident number, the insurance company had been contacted, and, the next day, the banks and the building societies. 'That's what I hate,' Silas had said,' It's such a buggeration.' Lindy had smiled, almost laughed; 'That's an old and very odd word for you.' Somehow it had struck her as really funny.

What had surprised Silas, and Lindy and their friends, was just how quickly their case had 'come up' for action. On May 7th Silas was summoned to the local police station for an update, though why the news had to be communicated in that way, with his needing to make a visit, he did not know. It just hadn't been what he, or they, had expected.

It had been a bright, clean and crisp, fragrant spring day: the various white, pink and red blossoms shouted out their joy at the arrival of a new year, another new arising. Silas had been requested to report at 9.30am, had managed to get cover for his morning lecture and tutorial, and was looking forward to a quick visit, perhaps the recovery of his possessions (some hope), and getting back home after the return ten-minute walk that fine morning, for coffee and toast, more a second breakfast than a brunch. He had made up his mind, as he made his way up the concrete steps of the old station, that if they offered him a drink he ought really to refuse, so as not to spoil the anticipation of his 'real' coffee and his toast at home: an odd and singularly focused cosy notion he had thought afterwards. He remembered having smiled to himself at that point: entering the police station and thinking about his second breakfast.

There was a black woman in the waiting area, looking anxious and with a motherly eye on her rather vacantly gazing twelve-year-old son. They were waiting to be seen. Silas walked up to the desk and the duty officer looked up with eyebrows raised and an interrogative facial expression.

'Mr Wood - Silas Wood. It's about a burglary at...'

'Yes, sign in please, er, Mr Wood.' The officer looked suddenly a little flustered, trying though to mask some anxiety or at least unease, by a strict adherence to his oft-repeated procedure.

Silas duly obliged, saying as he did so,' 'Well., I didn't realize I might be some time... But, no matter,' he added, thinking that however bureaucratic this moment seemed, he still might be required to stay for only five minutes or so. 'Have you found some of our stuff then, Officer?'

'In a manner of... er... speaking,' the officer, young with black eyes and hair, and a round eager pale acned face, replied. He seemed oddly to want to say something else. He pressed buzzer under the counter. 'Someone will collect you in about five minutes, sir.' He returned to his paperwork and alternated this task with another that required his staring at the computer screen.

Silas waited. There was some to-ing and fro-ing in the rather welcoming, warmly lit reception and waiting area; and before long the mother and son were greeted by a smiling young woman. A solicitor? A welfare-worker? When they had gone he kept on looking up at the clock and felt an unaccountable growing sense of unease. He felt his heart beating and felt as uncomfortable as some people do when waiting to see the dentist. Here, however, there were no magazines. For a change he looked not at the clock but at the various posters neatly decorating a part of one wall. There was a harsher tone to their admonitions about wrong-doing than he would have expected; though this made him pleased rather than otherwise.

'Er, Mr Wood, you can go through now. They said just to go through. Open the double door when I buzz and it's the second door on your left - room eleven. Just knock...'

The officer definitely looked anxious, and keen not to catch his eye. 'Just knock?' Silas echoed, feeling nervous and looking around nowhere in particular for support. The officer did not answer, did not lift his head. The doors buzzed, and, fumbling, Silas pushed the wrong one of the two so that the officer looked up and pressed again. This time Silas found the correct way to open the left-hand door and found himself in a short well-lit carpeted empty corridor.

'This is ridiculous,' he mumbled, 'What sort of service is this?' But why was he getting angry? He'd half a mind to turn around and leave the beckoning but chillingly empty corridor; but being a law-abiding citizen, he dare not, and felt it would be wrong. Silas did indeed feel that this was ridiculous; or more to the point, that he suddenly cut a ridiculous figure: here he was, a mature man in his late thirties, fearing to knock on a door. 'What on Earth am I afraid of!' he shouted in his mind.

Steeling himself he moved to the second door on the left - there were about five doors on each side. It was Room Eleven, no doubt about it. He knocked. No answer. He knocked again, a heavier knock this time. 'Enter!' came the slow purposeful commanding voice of authority. Like going into the bloody headmaster's study, Silas thought angrily.

Beyond the door, the room was a pale-yellow colour with a carpet of nondescript grey. It had been newly decorated. He picked up the smell of fresh paint. He later felt he would always smell the paint thereafter. The morning sun threw lines from the half-open vertical blinds across the light carpet.

Two men were in the room. A large man sat in an upright chair by the only window, on the right, his hands resting on his thighs. Ahead was a small plain wooden table behind which a smartly dressed man with fair hair and a freckled hollow face sat and stared. Beyond him was some shelving with box-files. What focused Silas's attention was the stark white-finished wooden chair this side of the table, the chair he would be expected to sit in.

He hovered on the threshold: something was not right.

'Come in, and close the door behind you,' said the man behind the table, smiling coldly it seemed to Silas.

He moved forward uncertainly towards the table, as though in slow motion, in a dream

'You have news about the burglary, I understand,' he forced himself to say, but was thinking,' Why don't they introduce themselves? Why the silence? 'Have you recovered...'

'Sit down, Mr Wood,' began the slight man, slighter even than Silas; bony really, but clearly having a composure, an inner strength that he, Silas, certainly did not possess at that moment. The man motioned to the plain white chair which was some four feet back from the table, as though not even belonging to it, isolated.

He sat down, reluctantly, but he knew only too well, obediently, trying to stare like a dissatisfied customer at the annoyingly self-possessed upright figure across the table. For a moment, Silas Wood, Senior Lecturer in English, upright citizen, was overcome by a wave of annoyance that made him forget his trepidation. He felt his blood beginning to boil. 'Look, I came here today... Who are you, Officer?' He stared hard at the man's hollow freckled face and his dapper suit; and as he did so he noticed a tiny badge on the lapel with its Dagaz insigne. At that same moment the man tossed a black file or something onto the table. At first sight Silas thought it *was* a file.

He sat there, feeling like someone unprepared at a job interview. Worse, the man's insinuating face made his self-esteem sink, his feeling of vulnerability rise: more and more, Silas Wood, university lecturer, felt like a little boy. He looked down at the knees of his sandy-coloured chords, then purposefully glanced at his watch, trying to regain the upper ground, the ascendancy, with a feigned nonchalance. Then he looked again at the black file. Matt black. Moleskin bound. Not a file. It was his diary!

Silas knew his face had gone suddenly from a subdued pale to a blushing guilty pink. He glanced nervously at the man in front of him: how he hated his gaunt, freckled face and his thin lips, which had a dappled chilled look under the stark fluorescent lights which were surely unnecessary on so bright a day. And Silas was suddenly more than ever aware now of the other man to his right, by the window; the silent heavy, he had now decided, with a spasm of fear.

And so, the questions and answers:

'You recognize that, don't you, *Mis*ter Wood?'

'Yes, it's my diary, I think.' Silas felt that his voice was noticeably trembling.

'I think you know it's your diary. Well, what have you to say?'

'Nothing. Where's the rest of my stuff? I came here thinking you'd cleared up a burglary and recovered my stuff...'

'That's what you were supposed to think. And I'll ask the questions, Mr Wood. Those other things that we have and that were - recovered, we'll let you have later, provided of course,' with a sideways look at his silent heavyweight colleague, 'that we are happy with your answers.'

'Look, look, what is this?'

Silence...and then... 'I've told you, I'll ask the questions. Are you aware that you've written things in there', pointing down at the diary, 'that could be regarded as treasonable?'

'What do you... no, I don't think so.'

'You don't think so, or you don't know? What are *we* to think? No, do not answer. You question the motives of our Prime Minister: you regard him as an extremist, even though you give grudging

praise about his and the government's progress on crime reduction and our efforts to reduce carbon emissions. Are you in league with anyone, Mr Wood?'

Silas wanted to anywhere else in the world but that room, with its bars, its fingers of sunlight stretching over the plain grey carpet.

'No, no. I don't know what you mean, sir,' he felt instantly the shame of having called him sir, 'I've done nothing wrong.'

'That will be for us to decide.' The officious man got up, walked slowly around the table, looking down into Silas's eyes as he did so, then he stood behind him for several seconds, finally resting a hand on his right shoulder. A palpable shudder ran through Silas's whole frame, his knees were trembling, and a horrible sensation gripped his pelvic area. From behind, the man moved his warm, clammy hand closer to Silas's face, so that a finger or two rested not on his clothing but on his very flesh, on his neck. Was it the jugular vein or the carotid artery that he touched? He then brought his repulsive skeletal head close to Silas's right ear, his voice getting louder and louder.

'Do you know what we have to put up with, Wood? Well, do you? People like you haven't any idea.' To Silas's relative relief he moved back to the table. 'In your comfortable little middle-class houses, and your soft jobs...' (I work bloody hard, Silas was thinking, but I'll say anything he wants.)

'Getting money together for your children's education, are you?'

A pause... The man sat down opposite again and looked across at his colleague.

'You have to understand my annoyance, Mr Wood. We deal on a regular almost daily basis with the vermin of society, assisting our colleagues in the Metropolitan Police in the restoration of order...' (Who were they: MI5 or MI6, he did not know the difference, the Army, the SAS? He had heard rumours and was trying to shape his jumbled thoughts.) 'As you condescendingly put it, we are making an impact, an improvement. We have made life better for people on estates that were ruled by lawlessness. These people were victims on a daily basis.' He smiled grimly, knowingly,' but not anymore. They are truly grateful to us: not like you who know nothing, condescending in your attitude. So, I'll ask you again: are you in league with anyone, Mr Wood?'

'No, sir.'

'Do you believe a conspiracy exists to overthrow the government? '

How to answer...how to answer...how to answer... 'I've never thought it, I mean thought of it, as a possibility. Some people might, it's the way of the world...' (Why did I say something so glib, so trite? Silas thought. I'm not making sense... God, that was the wrong answer...)

'The way of the world,' laughed his interrogator, 'you're bringing Congreve into the picture, are you?'

Silas looked confused: he was alternating now between hot flushes of guilt and cold spasms of fear.

'Yes, you see, you're not the only educated man here. I too know a little about the Restoration dramatists. In fact, I have a soft spot for the arts. But not all of those,' he glanced meaningfully at his colleague by the window, 'who strive for the common good of the people are cultured and sometimes this makes them a little cruder in their methods, you understand. I'm sure you understand. Mr Alvis, he who in your diary you come perilously close to defaming, *always* works within the letter of the law, but some of those, some of us who admire and follow him... I'm sure you understand...'

Silence. A long silence. A trap?

'You should respect our Leader. There are strict rules in place, procedures to follow. You should bear in mind that there are other people whom Mr Alvis would restrain if he could. I am sure this is the case...hmm... When you were at The Prince of Wales, three weeks ago last Wednesday, did you not make some comment about Mr Alvis's "lap dog", and did you not also refer to Mr Alvis's "pet"? It was linked to a conversation you were having about your university's science funding, was it not? '

'I...I...', Silas stammered. He felt ill: his head was buzzing, and he was afraid he was going to faint.

'You need to be careful, Mr Wood; there are eyes and ears everywhere. I see you are surprised. But consider this: what is a man of your education doing parroting in a loose-tongued fashion the scurrilous remarks of the gutter press... you know where you read it, a man of your education and good fortune... Our informant could not be certain however whether you were in fact referring to a minister or to someone else... You need to be *very* careful, Mr Wood... be careful how you go...'

Silence. The 'prisoner' looked ill.

'You have a very beautiful wife, Mr Wood, who is doing some excellent work I understand at Hoffnung-Larousse... and you have three fine, healthy children. Of course, you want them to stay that way... The State can be, and is, very supportive and protective of the dutiful citizen and his or her family. You need to remember that, you really do...'

Mr Wood could think only of escape: an almost neurasthenic sense of vulnerability was making his skin crawl.

But, unexpectedly, it was soon over, and Silas Wood, with a plastic bag stuffed with his belongings was hanging from his tense left hand. The knuckles of his hand were white, as he tried to grip the bag tightly to compensate for the swimming sensation in his head. The interrogator's final words of admonition were ringing in his ears: 'I warn you to

say nothing of this interview, nothing; not to your friends, not even to your wife...'

He was dazed. The light of the bright morning blinded him. He sank to the pavement and put his head between his legs until the buzzing in his head subsided and he felt he was able to stand up again. One good Samaritan asked him what was wrong, and somehow, he just thanked them and said he would be fine. Soon he was up again but still shaking. Numerous vehicles, including two buses, one advertising the new Bond film, passed him by. This aside, he was not really taking in anything as he drifted aimlessly along the pavement.

It was incongruous, impossible, surreal: some sort of state counter-insurgency agents working out of a police station. That diary, that damned diary! But it wasn't just that: someone had followed him, listened in to his conversation in the pub, reported him... The rumours of clandestine operations were out there somewhere in the ether... Had he really believed any of it until now? And why him? It was not right. He was not a criminal; but he felt like one. He felt dirty, ashamed. They were working out of a police station! Was this how the government was getting results! Who was getting results? Who were they? The question came back again and again as he walked along in a daze... the Army... MI5 ... the word Werod came to him... the badge...it just linked the man to the Breakthrough Party...surely this was the case... so ashamed of my fear, my guilt, he was thinking...

A car horn blared, and Silas, as they say, jumped out of his skin. It hadn't been directed at him, that noise, but now the passers-by on the pavement came into sharp focus, vividly, loudly dressed and inquisitive it seemed to him then; and the busy street with its shops and its people and its press of noisy fume-spewing cars seemed to crowd in on him. He was feeling ashamed of the vulnerability, the fear he had shown in there. That bastard!

He needed a drink, even though it was barely ten-thirty in the morning. He had to pass The Prince of Wales and as he did so he stared at its ornate doors, with their stained-glass upper panelling: with a shudder, he passed on by. He trembled still, and felt dirty, with his plastic bag of incriminating evidence... He began thinking: he was too ashamed to tell Lindy what had passed. Besides, he must not breathe a word to anyone - they had said...

He later told Lindy that he had been questioned, about the burglary, and that though the Police had found their stuff 'damaged', they had had a couple of queries, that was all, linked to information about the *modus operandi*, so they could tie the incident in with a spate of burglaries in the area. She knew something was wrong, however, and, at bottom, that was why she began to think that Silas's behaviour, his occasional preoccupied distant look, signified a possible involvement with another woman. He seemed too to have lost interest in other things: only six months earlier he had ranted about the whitewash that was the supposed new public enquiry into the death of Patrick

Lansing, a death which had occurred years earlier. If he was interested in anything, it was unexpectedly, suddenly, her work, and specifically whether she was being 'bothered' by anyone at work. Perhaps *he* was jealous and suspected *her* of something! They needed to talk about it; but in truth she did not want to go there. Perhaps it was better not to know.

Silas for his part was for a long time haunted by his experience. His subconscious linked it to all he had read a few years earlier about Stalin's 'Terror', and about the interrogations that went on in the Lubyanka Prison, and elsewhere in the old Soviet Union. That was probably why, in his dream he had tried to form a picture of something called a 'blackjack', a flexible club that people were beaten with. In reality, mere words had been enough to terrify him: he could not begin to imagine, or rather he could begin to imagine, the horror of a sadistic physical interrogation. He wished he had never read a single word about the 'Terror', or anything to do with Stalin and his purges. Unwillingly, his memory supplied him with a vague picture of someone, a dwarf, nicknamed Blackberry, a sadistic torturer who in his own turn was executed and whose legs had trembled and who had cried for mercy when he had been taken off to be shot in a basement with a sloping floor, sloping so that the blood could run down the drain and be hosed away; and there had been someone whose name began with Abuk, or Asik, who always rolled out an old red carpet before he began his sessions, so that the blood of his victims would not spoil his new Persian rugs. Nightmares...

Today, however, was the 13th of June and it had started without the cold sweat, and there had been no nightmare: perhaps the dreams and the demons would haunt him no more.

His sister and her family were coming round that evening, and Lindy's brother Simon, most generous brother Simon, might also be popping in. It often occurred to Silas that they owed Simon so much; too much in fact: they would forever be in his debt. Lindy did not see this as an issue: reciprocal sibling affection and generosity was all that was important - repayment in its crudest sense did not matter one jot.

So, there was last-minute shopping for a few bits and pieces after work - that always happened. He could get them: he was finishing at three today. Ah, yes, he absolutely must not forget the vanilla essence for the sticky toffee pudding, or was it the rum and raisin pudding...

It turned out to be a splendid evening after what had been a hectic and busy day for both Silas and Lindy, at the university and Hoffnung-Larousse respectively. They could now relax, and did. The music, classical, jazz and popular and all sorts, including 'world music' sounded out, as they chatted, laughed, hugged, enjoyed the food, the wine, the moments in time. The weather was kind, too, a bright long evening, very warm and ever so slightly sultry, so that, with doors flung open and kept open, they could spill out into garden, where Silas, aided by brother-in-law Ben, manned the barbeque. The garden, which Lindy had clearly modelled on that of Silas's sister, was beautiful, enchanting, in the soft light of the midsummer's evening; a gentle walled oasis, 'far from the madding crowds' of London's bright and busy centre. Laughter, like a tripping melody, or the flow and babble of a brook, familial bliss, out of doors, the garden as a wide and spacious new room, a real extension to the living area... A time of joy and forgetfulness...

Hope's husband Ben, looking older now, heavier set and with a lot of grey hair vying with the black, talked a lot about politics, but more about the days-out he and Hope had had recently; and though he was by nature sober-looking, he seemed perfectly relaxed and genuinely forgetful of his newly diagnosed hypertension. Silas likewise laughed and joked, and Lindy was pleased to see this after his recent apparent depression. Their children were in high spirits, too, and interested in cousin Faith's expected baby. Hope's eldest was nineteen, four months pregnant and beginning to show. 'Like mother, like daughter,' Silas whispered affectionately in his sister's ear.

Simon, Lindy's brother, did drop in with his new bride, and second wife, who was two years older than Faith. They stood apart somewhat, but no one was judging them here, even though it was still a new circumstance they were getting used to.

The television was on and off: Jonas kept putting it on, his mother switching it off. But there was no chastising, nothing acrimonious: it became more of a game in the convivial family atmosphere.

A rosy picture made all the more so with hindsight and measured against what could go wrong. Perfect family moments... They talked of Ben's and Hope's enjoyment of the previous year's Last Night of the Proms, their first visit to the Albert Hall. Silas and Lindy had seen it on TV, wondering if they would spot them. This reminiscence had led to a short discussion about great British traditions which had been maintained against the changing social and political background, traditions which in themselves, albeit at a superficial level only, suggested that, fundamentally, Britain would never change: the Last Night, the Boat Race, the Grand National, the FA Cup final, the Festival of Remembrance, Black Rod, Christmas carols, Stilton cheese, cheese rolling, Cheddar cheese, black pudding, Walsingham, the traditional expensive wedding, Children in Need...

Perhaps all was superficiality, and there were things far more fundamental even than society itself: people were beginning to sense a change in the pulse of Nature. The evidence for what some were calling the imminent catastrophe of the natural world was beginning to look chillingly overwhelming. Yet even these people were in denial and said to themselves: that which has always been must be. And there was Dain Alvis's government, which had made some impact, and was starting to influence other governments, albeit the smaller nations, but probably too late in the day to save the polar bear. And against this looming terror, the old traditions had indeed been maintained; and though there was talk about things 'going on behind the scenes', Democracy with a big 'D' was alive and kicking. It was true, however, that Dain Alvis might well lose the next election. The old parties were becoming popular once more, if the opinion polls were to be believed. Certain business sectors were beginning to champ at the bit, resenting as they did the snooping of unelected government, unrepresentative agencies, loosely termed Alvis supporters, who were 'attached to DEFRA', or 'supporting Trading Standards', or 'supplementing the work of the Community Special Police'... How many ways had this been said? The Breakthrough Party and its government and its leader Alvis - how good or bad was he for the country?

Silas was silent on these matters as they were briefly, fleetingly discussed, and Lindy, with her big brown inquisitive eyes noticed this and was puzzled, especially when she too mentioned 'interference' at her place of work. Silas the sympathetic but Silas the silent... Yet in the family atmosphere of wellbeing, plenty, and warmth the conversations around 'politics' and 'nature' and science were quickly passed over in favour of family matters, albeit family matters whose optimism-inducing glow of certainty was viewed through an alcohol-induced mist. There were the school holidays to come - still an important issue for Hope to expatiate on, and yet more important for Lindy, whose young brood would have to be catered for.

The sun gradually went down, it grew a little cooler, and the young children grew sleepy and irritable at last, and were put, finally, to bed. Now the adults could really relax, one of them switched on the TV and the news: 'Isabel Stewart, popular romantic novelist, has passed away at the age of seventy-three... In 2027 she was diagnosed with... Patrick Newton, Nobel Prize winning geneticist, has criticized plans to... A seventh case of malaria has been identified in Somerset, a spokesman for the Cheltenham Hospital said... the number of fatal road accidents attributed to speeding has fallen, a new report ... government policies and tougher sentencing, plus the ban on car advertisements which...'

It passed them by that evening, the drift of events... Their minds were full of their family bonds and interests: the sleeping children, the Chinese Mars probe, bargains in the High Street, holidays, the best sun cream, the best and cheapest holiday insurance, shopping in New York (still popular - one of Hope's friends had been quite recently), the good spring-summer, which was not yet too hot, but would they be spared this year the drought and heat-wave that had been so damaging and debilitating last year? Like millions of Britons, all the millions who like them passed into the artificially lit night of that thirteenth of June... As it grew dark they lit two long outdoor candles in the garden: flames in the gloaming and then illumining the pitch of night and throwing circles of orange flickering light over the green lawn, reminding those who chose to ponder of the flames of long ago in the history of mankind, of unrecorded moments of its quiet family occasions, elemental flame put to good use. A comfortable family of Ancient Rome, sipping their wine, they too might too have stared wonderingly, meditatively, at living torches in their gardens piercing and defying the enveloping darkness... so long ago...

Faith's husband saw that she was getting tired and so they left. Hope, Ben, Lindy, Silas, Rachel (Simon's new wife) and Simon moved into the lounge. With the French doors still open they could still look out to the flaming torches, flickering and waving as the air cooled and the slightest of warm breezes stirred. Fire - it had been a night for barbeques up and down the country, from the more affluent and comfortable suburbs to the mean streets, wherever they might be.

They talked and drank and continued to snack, and Lindy noticed now that Silas was more his usual self, even to the point that he just wanted to 'flick' the TV back on. Perhaps they could put a film on later? Simon was in agreement. Ben was silent and smiling and said he wouldn't take sides. The question was, would it kill the evening or be a pleasant way to prolong it into the small hours of the fourteenth of June?

Silas managed to dodge Lindy, who was trying to block his route to the remote. They wrestled like children as the others laughed, with Silas saying: 'We can just catch the end of the vampire film on BBC 1...'

They laughed and then were silent. They were suddenly silent as the flames of the garden torches waved and guttered audibly in a quickening breeze.

There was no vampire film. Instead, scores of emergency vehicles were crowded into the Mall and within the grounds of Buckingham Palace. A myriad of blue lights and of red lights flashed hypnotically. There was the sound of a helicopter hovering above the scene, and from time to time this showed an aerial view. The Palace was burning: great flames swayed and leapt into the dark sky dwarfing the figures that scurried below. The reporter on the scene looked harassed: soldiers, firemen, police and ambulance staff moved about in the background, in the darkness, and in the darkness the lights of their vehicles shone out, and their red and blue beacons winked intermittently, all amid the swirling smoke. Then the scene shifted to the Parliament building, where a greater fire raged, and the faces of Big Ben were extinguished in the darkness while the Thames below furnace-like glowed a vivid red. Around the vast old buildings on the fire-illumined roadways scores of emergency vehicles flashed their oscillating beacons, lighthouses in a swarming sea of desperate shadowy figures scurrying to and fro... rushing to help. There were reports, as yet unconfirmed, of an attack on at least two royal residences, and on the Scottish Parliament building and the Welsh Assembly building... Huge explosions reported in Birmingham, Manchester, Leeds and Bristol... and there was talk, increasingly credible rumour, of attacks using chemical weapons. There was as yet no news on casualties and the fate of all the members, all the members it was stressed, of the Royal Family was unknown. Much of this, however, was exaggerated media hysteria in the face of both ‘reported’ and very real events.

From one disaster to the next and back again: a worsening situation. Even the news-hungry, hard-bitten journalists, broadcasters and reporters looked visibly shaken, unable to cope.

What could Prime Minister Alvis do in the face of this chaotic night's shocking events? He was in Downing Street, from whence a column of shadowy grey-black smoke rose up into the night sky of the City. He was at his desk, slumped backwards in his chair, a smile it seemed frozen on his thin pale lips. His blue eyes stared, fixed, glazed, as though in wonder, yet at the same time frozen, empty otherwise of expression, frozen like pools of eyes on which a glassy film has formed. A tell-tale dark red circle was in the middle of his forehead. Dain Alvis could, and would, do nothing: Dain Alvis was dead.

At 9.00am on the fourteenth day of June in the year 2030, while across the land they counted the bodies, searched for the missing, and put out the fires, Alex Quellan, a spokesperson for the government, declared that a State of Emergency existed in Great Britain.

13. *The New Order begins*

A diary of somebody or other, relating to these events

'Britain is leaderless. We are all paralysed, wondering what will happen next. For two days hardly anyone has dared to venture out to work, or even to the shops. It is fear, yes, but also it's a sort of morbid curiosity, if I'm honest. The news broadcasts, television in particular, though radio has played its part, are still continuous, round the clock. Each day is bringing a new shock and a new revelation.

Who on Earth is Alex Quellan? Suddenly he's a spokesman for the Government...He has given out instructions to the emergency services and the security services, the army and the air force... A couple of ministers I have seen before have come out to say that for the moment he is the man we should listen to. If I'm honest, it's very scary - what will happen to us?

Who is to blame for all this? All the armed forces are on high alert, we're told - why weren't they before it happened? Who are the terrorists? Which country is involved? Will this lead to some kind of war? How many are dead, and what has happened to the Royal Family? Can it be true that the Prime Minister was killed in a gun battle at Number Ten? That's what they are saying... so no one is safe...

All we can do is keep the children away from school: thank goodness my mother and sister are close by. But what about food - it's getting low, and what if they target the water supplies? I never liked this estate but at least we've got good neighbours... The water, though, what if they poison the water?

I feel sorry for people in hospital or with sick people at home... They're telling us all to sit tight... I wish we could see someone round here to tell us everything is getting sorted, the army the police, anyone... I'm worried about the water... Still, keep the TV on ... They could have picked a nicer looking man than this Quellan to tell us the bad news... Some odd-looking bloke with steel-rimmed glasses... He looks like a throwback to the middle of the last century... And that red-blond hair looked like a wig... He wasn't very old, though, just not very photogenic...

It was bright yesterday, but now it's raining outside, grey dull and mournful... Chris says this place looks like a wasteland at the best of times...

The emergency services have done a great job - they always say that, but it's true. The man, that Quellan, talked about a relief plan and an emergency plan being put together for food, water, electricity and gas - ours is still on, that's something, I suppose. I wish we knew more... Cheryl's coming around for a cup of tea and a chat... still got a few biscuits left if the kids haven't found them.

Don't understand all this about a joint Cabinet and, what is it, werod council, taking over for the time being ... What's a werod council?

Alex Quellan has been on again saying that the terrorists will be caught and punished for their monstrous - monstrous is an understatement - crimes... Still trying to work out which country was involved in this attack, or whether it was intended as some kind of protest or something. He looked different somehow this time, not that I could ever fancy him.

News of deliveries to the supermarket... That was quick... Noticed a few more people getting out and about now... It's been six days now...'

Quellan had convened, and chaired, in Alvis's stead, a new Council of the Werod; in the Midlands and well away from London. Among those who had picked up on the 'new arrangements', some said the Council had met or was meeting in Stratford, others said Evesham, others Oxford, and others yet, Northampton. Speculation was rife, as Quellan supposed it would be.

They met in a large hall, a school hall, with an area curtained off. A large hall was needed as the new, virtually self-appointed temporary or emergency stand-in leader had with him a cohort of one hundred heavily armed and dark-uniformed bodyguards, twelve of whom, tall and strong and impassive, had been appointed to stand behind the twelve chairs of the members of the Werod Council. The number of Council members remained at twelve as it had been in the very beginning. Of their number two only had been ministers of the Alvis government, though other members of the shattered administration were seated away from the chosen twelve: still important, but not as important; and among this group, three Alvis Cabinet members. The new government men and women, ostensibly former Alvis sycophants (though future history in its unravelling of these events would categorize them differently), were long-standing members of the Werod organization. The Werod of course could now be numbered in its tens of thousands and had had people for some time now in hundreds of key positions helping to manage, to run, the machinery of state. A government still existed: it was here, in this hall, still vowing that it would continue to carry the torch for Democracy.

Beyond the curtained area, the seventy or so of Quellan's most efficient and loyal bodyguard either stood sentinel in the remaining areas of the hall or patrolled the buildings and the grounds outside, where their number was massively supplemented bemusedly but loyally, by SAS and Paratroopers: their orders had not been clear, nor had their understanding of the overall situation, but local commanders made the decision on the ground that the key task at this point in time was to support the interim government as the best way of restoring order and the confidence of the civilian population.

Quellan, dressed in some loose-fitting black garment, sat darkly at the head of the Council table; darkly except for his large pale head with its thinning hair. He looked older than his thirty-one years, but trimmer (even though he wore his usual baggy outfit pulled in with a belt), and his voice had noticeably deepened with age. He spoke without smiling. He was not intending to discuss matters with his Werod Council: he had his directives to issue and they, the new Council, expected no less. And yet, as each member was menaced, as well as protected, from behind by an armed dark-uniformed Werod fanatic it was clear that none was wholly trusted by the new leader. Quellan, without betraying a hint of a smile or a glint of pleasure in his deep fathomless eyes, was pleased at the sight that met them. He would indeed trust no one, though he did not really fear his newly appointed Council: it had been formed as he had expected it to be formed.

All flights were grounded, he advised, and a member of the Council duly confirmed this position. All flights except one, that is: the exception was the one that would be landing in Washington DC at any time carrying special envoy Eamonn Carter-Jones to meet and reassure President Kramer, not to inform him that all was well, but that all was being done to control and manage the situation, to apprehend the terrorists and restore, as the Americans were fond of saying, a 'state of normalcy' in terms of financial operations and foreign policy. The assistance of UK-based American forces would be most welcome, particularly in the guarding of the ports, the nuclear facilities and the water supplies, as UK forces were, he would understand, stretched to breaking point. There were, in this request, implicit assurances that the special relationship between our two great nations would not only be maintained but actually strengthened. The US had put its armed forces on the highest state of alert, he knew, and in his calls to the President in the evening US time, and in the first hours of the crisis, Quellan had paved the way for Carter-Jones's visit. He had calculated too that an old Etonian Oxford blue, and allegedly a distant cousin of the King's into the bargain, with a begging bowl, would be just the man to win over the American President and his Chiefs-of-Staff.

At home, Quellan announced to his Council that there would be a curfew: anyone caught in the streets after 22.00 hours would be arrested, no matter what their excuse. Traffic and travel permits would be issued, and were being issued to all who would need to use rail and road services to carry out essential work, including all military personnel, medical staff, utilities staff, key administrators including and especially Civil Service key workers, emergency planners from every higher-tier council, and so on. Quellan, and his own staff, experts by now in drawing up lists, seemed to have thought of everything. Schools and universities would remain shut to students and staff for a week, except for access for those university staff who might be able to assist in the reconstruction and in the restoration of order. The hospitals would remain open. The banks, and the London Stock Exchange, would be closed for two working days only, tomorrow and the day after, 17th and 18th June. Then there would be restrictions on trading activity, to prevent profiteering, for the foreseeable period: this would be made clear by the Government under its emergency powers.

France, Germany and the other EU countries, and Russia and China, all the major players, were being kept informed of developments. The terrorists, Quellan said, seemed not to have disrupted the communications systems, which was their fatal mistake. True, things had been difficult for the first few hours when all the networks seemed to have gone down due to volume of use, but now plans were being put into place.

What was now clear, Quellan went on in a mournful monotone, was that the First Sea Lord was dead, as was the Commander-in-Chief of all Land Forces, along with a number of senior commanders and members of Cobra. Condolences would be sent out to the families though it was not yet clear whether the families had survived.

Parliament would have to be dissolved. It was essential now to be a step ahead of the terrorists: protection of the people was paramount. There was the need to ensure that Britain did not suffer an invasion from outside. The purpose of the attacks?... the motive?... the origin...? - these questions would have to wait. Britain had been in a tight corner before and would not be panicked by these murderers.

Dain Alvis, Quellan announced, had died bravely by all accounts, at his desk, refusing to cower before the terrorists. His bodyguards had fought to the last, as their bodies and those of their enemies had testified. Special mention should go to his longest serving retainers, Horst Schweibling and Aaron Rubens: bullet-riddled, their bodies had been found at the very door of the Prime Minister's room. They had sold their lives dearly and a number of dead terrorists had lain close to them. A German and a Jew respectively, they had fought as brothers in the defence of their leader: they had fought like the Anglo-Saxons defending King Harold at Hastings, he said. They had fought fearlessly, even without hope, for Democracy and for Britain.

The Council and the ministers, and the rest, applauded at this point, in this most incongruous of meeting places for government. After a few moments Quellan continued. The King and the other members of the Royal Family would have to be protected. The nation would pray for its King's continued wellbeing and his family's safety.

All this, less those elements of the briefing deemed important to withhold for security reasons, was broadcast to the nation in the form of a speech read over the radio by Alex Quellan himself. He subsequently made a television appearance that day dressed uncomfortably in a suit with a black tie and black armband. He wore a short blond wig which seemed to fit him well, and he was made up to hide his blemished skin. The strange menace of his eyes was ameliorated somewhat by a pair of light-rimmed spectacles which gave him the air of a tax inspector. He appeared, in all, not likeable but trustworthy, a sober sort who would cover in the interim, until the King returned as figurehead, and Parliament proper and therefore proper government could be reconstituted.

Quellan returned to his temporary headquarters, a stone-built hotel standing within two acres of wooded grounds, where work on fortifications and troop emplacements was frantically being carried out. His advisors accompanied him. There would, he had said from the outset, be no use of mobile phones until he could be certain of American intentions. He asked, with an air of urgent wholehearted truthfulness (though nothing could be further from the truth) how many terrorists and saboteurs had been arrested or killed. The names of all those enemies of the state had been drawn from lists of drug traffickers and gangland barons, who had long been under surveillance and whom no one would mourn. They would never come to trial: they would be given bogus identities and 'disappeared'.

What had happened had been of course a *coup d'état*, long in the planning, unremittingly ruthless and clinically efficient. It would now be dealt with, under the imminent news blackout, as just such an event, 'addressed and dealt with' by those very people who had engineered it. Quellan was legion, for within the multifarious Werod his word was law, and he alone could be said to constitute 'those very people'.

There would, Quellan said, not letting his guard down even to himself when in the company of his willing executors, there would be a reopening of Parliament when the circumstances permitted. A statue would be raised in Parliament Square to Dain Alvis, a great Prime Minister and innovator, who had shown the world the way forward with his stance on law and order, and on climate change. Quellan fully meant this: he was grateful to Alvis as the architect of change in this first phase, and could genuinely praise his accomplishments, even though it had been necessary to remove him. This capacity for double thinking to achieve a desired outcome was embedded in Quellan's mental make-up: he really could, in the same moment, genuinely praise and be planning to destroy the object of his praise. He went on: the key, the most high-profile members of the Royal Family, the King, those closest in line to the throne, were safe and under protection of the armed forces. Constitutional monarchy would soon be fully restored. When the news blackout ended, for he would have to announce a news blackout to come into effect soon, before the free press and media got to work, they could update the nation on the state of things.

Quellan retired to a quiet inner chamber set up as a makeshift office with two communicating doors, one accessed by his closest aides; all save one, his Deputy, a bulldog-faced Englishman named Bateman, were *not* members of the Werod Council: the other door, facing his large polished mahogany desk, was for visitors, for those charged with the restoration of order in Britain, for those required to report directly to Alex Quellan and no one else. This door remained accessible to the constant stream of parliamentarians, deputy chief constables, civil servants, the military, MI5, MI6, and so on. This large disparate mass of organizers was marshalled into ones, twos, threes or small groups as determined by another set of Quellan's staff. Whoever they were, whatever their status, they were required to knock before entering. None objected to this: those still confused by events saw Quellan as an exceptional organiser and, after all, he had had the ear of Dain Alvis so in that sense it was a continuation of government, and as such Quellan's 'orders' could be tolerated: someone had to pull things together and it seemed he knew exactly where the priorities lay. When the situation improved some form of status quo could be re-established. Quellan understood this, these people, and played the part of the self-effacing administrator well.

Notwithstanding that access via this door was controlled, so that he could deal with one problem at a time (everyone understood this), he had an inner sanctum, a small dark room, with shutters closed, which could be accessed by a third door to the right of the 'leader's' desk. It was to this room that he retired after three hours standing, giving orders, instructions and advice, on the hoof, by turns coldly commanding and plausibly humble, impressing all; those who knew what was going on, those who thought they knew, and those desperate for information on how best they could manage their own delegated responsibilities: in one way or another, he impressed them all by his absolute grasp of the situation and his ability to find brilliant interim solutions to the seemingly impossible or intractable, and this too after a moment's reflection. Someone actually said that were it not for his unprepossessing appearance the young man would one day have made an outstanding Prime Minister in his own right, albeit he had just been an advisor to Dain Alvis.

Quellan needed twenty minutes to himself, within the inner sanctum, a physically separate environment where in his view one could experience to the full the absence of other people: it was too a statement on the human condition - one really was on one's own in this world of conscious self-reflecting existence. Just some time to reflect on events also, to plan, to engineer... the plot, the drive to the end game. Even then, he probably knew that there was only one way, that it would only end one way, but consciously denied it as a real option, for the time being.

He opened a cupboard and gazed at the mirror set on the inner side of its door. Standing at the washbasin, he checked the make-up which was supposed to be hiding his blemished skin. There was no time to unmask and then disguise himself again. His eyes watery, yet with a play of many colours showed little expression at first, then as he looked back in the mirror, he thought to himself: 'Not very prepossessing, but human none the less - Alex Quellan.' He gave a brief rueful smile. As ever, his intelligence was processing all the events in a logical sequence: this must be done and then that must be done... The plan, first of all, to complete the task Dain Alvis had set himself, then to further establish the Werod, and then...to consider... the wider perspective...

Alvis had shown the way. A truly great man; but he would certainly have been voted out at the next election, betrayed alike by those in the great democracy who either thought he was moving ahead too quickly or by those who thought the opposite. It was important that Alvis went at a time when the Werod had established itself as a hidden power in the land, but before it became complacent and could no longer be used as the executive arm of the revolution ... Now there would have to be scapegoats: these had already been prepared for sacrifice... It had been a pity however to kill so many innocent people, as the world would view them, but this was a world of people that continued to tolerate the existence of evil and the despoliation and continuing destruction of the planet. If this one hurdle now were to be cleared without compromise, then the sacrifice of relatively few innocents would have been worthwhile. This was after all a war, the war; a fight to the finish...

Quellan gazed into the future allowing himself a snarl of a smile, a rare smile, as he poured out two fingers of Scotch. One every other day, a tonic, it burned his throat as it went down. He could stop there, seemingly blemished skin, seemingly uglier than he actually was, sunken mobile watery eyes, an incredibly strong if poorly conditioned body, with great hands whose grip could squeeze a cooking apple to pulp, and, absolutely, an iron will. The whisky was both a test and a tonic: he tested himself thus - he never took a second drink. He smiled again, a rueful smile, as he contemplated the recent events. Let us pray for the success of the new government in this enterprise and in the safeguarding of Britain's unique and historic democratic principles. The days and weeks to come would be of critical importance; but he knew this, and he did not fear this time. The chameleon and the fly...

The days passed and the news blackout that had been imposed on days seven and eight, was lifted, and it became clear to everyone that Britain had a new leader of sorts, Alex Quellan. Strangely, however, after decades of celebrity worship and visual images of the latest overnight stars, few were certain that they knew what he really looked like: he appeared different somehow on each of his broadcasts, and he did not convince as attractive and charismatic, though there was something hauntingly forceful and compelling about him, rather like a conjurer, though perhaps more like a hypnotist. Some commented that in these troubled times people wanted to believe in someone and that someone could be anyone, just so long as they could sort out the mess. New leader he was, accepted widely as a tolerable stand-in until the crisis passed; a steward rather the owner of the estate, was one way of putting it. But new leader Alex Quellan was. A meeting was arranged with President Kramer, and Russian Federation President, Alexei Koniev, to take place in Reykjavic, to be followed five days later by an Anglo-Chinese meeting in Beijing; then visits to Tokyo and Sydney were scheduled, with the return to Britain from the Sydney visit being via Paris and Berlin.

These visits were a gamble: the forces of reaction, however, Quellan persuaded his advisors, were as yet disorganized, and would not be able yet to move or speak with a common purpose; they were still in the grip of paranoia and indecision, not knowing whether he, Quellan, was friend or foe. Thus far, the Werod had done its job. Besides, he, Quellan, had been keen to stress the interim nature of his leadership under the emergency powers, and had given more than a veiled hint of a relatively swift return to full-blown parliamentary activity.

The days passed into weeks, and the threat to Alex Quellan and his Werod-dominated interim government receded. Trade and commerce began to flow again; and if some people did look with genuine concern over their shoulders, a state of normality, superficially at least, appeared to return, and the high streets, shopping centres, retail parks, roads, ports and railway stations became busy once more as though nothing had changed. There were rumblings in the media, but there was apprehension bordering on fear. At the same time, the government strengthened its position by the promise of tax cuts but won real popularity with a 15% increase in pay for the armed services, the police and the fire service, and all qualified nurses. These pay measures were rushed through and were devastating blows for any would-be opponents.

Some people naively looked still for a sinister threat from abroad. Many guessed what had happened and quietly and nervously accepted the situation as a *fait accompli*, particularly given the feeling that the formerly depressed economy seemed suddenly reinvigorated. And there was too the success and acceptance of the new leader on the international stage, ably supported by the cream of the Diplomatic Service. There were people who felt guilty about the fact that 'nothing was being done about this atrocity', yet too many difficulties blocked the way forward for a challenge to be mounted. The Werod organization seemed to have people everywhere: would it simply just collapse if Quellan were assassinated? But how and why would that help matters? And so the time passed.

The people began to see more and more armed soldiers in the streets and at all the transit points; a legacy of Dain Alvis's government, with the return of troops from Syria, and a reduced presence in Afghanistan. This had happened in some degree with the emergency powers, but the security role of the army at home was now more in evidence. This was however more a comfort than not, given the real initial fears of widespread anarchy, of unchecked violence and looting that might well have taken place. People were getting used to seeing a military presence, and even took little notice of the black-uniformed, and armed, Werod advisers and commissars who were sometimes to be seen alongside the soldiery.

There would always be some, not taken in, not to be taken in, and even a few determined to do something about it; yet fearful or uncertain how to proceed, especially how to communicate with other like-minded individuals.

There were yet others who sought to take advantage of what they saw as a breakdown in order; 'criminal elements' who had roamed the outlying run-down estates of Britain, who had so far evaded the effects even of Alvis's closer attention to the state of policing and control. These pockets of disorder had continued to thrive, some of them remnants of the old days, others the next new wave, a small minority of the young, a hardcore of vicious disaffected or opportunistic youth, used to getting its own way; just a controlling few to whom the agents of the Werod were concocted bogeymen, as much a threat to their activities as the old ASBOs had been. So drug dealers, petty criminals and gangs of thugs still roamed the old sink estates; and some of those who terrorized and made victims of other young people, of the elderly and of the nervous alike, bethought themselves, cock-of-the-walk-like, that they need never fear this Werod, and that in the post-Alvis confusion, opportunities to do just what they liked when they liked would continue to present themselves. The Werod meant nothing to them, it was just politics, and they were not interested or concerned. Such pockets that remained were not really aware that elsewhere, in other areas just like theirs, a new order had been established, and crime of any sort was being ruthlessly ‘phased out’. Where they heard rumour of this, they did not believe it, and believed rather in their own invincibility, because it had always been like that. They laughed over Alex Quellan’s early comments about continuing the work of Dain Alvis and bringing order to the streets, about ‘bringing reassurance and hope to the hard-working, honest people of Britain, and instilling respect.’ They laughed and then forgot. True, this message was given less prominence by the re-emerging but increasingly pro-Quellan media, because major political developments dominated the news; but only the wilfully ignorant, the uneducated or the contemptuously arrogant could fail to see that something fundamental had changed and changed irrevocably. Not a message immediately obvious, or writ large on the side of a lager can, these words, ‘changed irrevocably’... Of course, it has also to be said that few, very few, understood the true menace of Alex Quellan; and none, other than he, knew the all-encompassing nature of his vision of the future.

14. *Werod justice*

In early October of that year it was unseasonably, uncomfortably hot; though it was becoming more and more difficult to make comment on what, and what was not, in line with the seasons of the northern hemisphere. Flowers were still in bloom, new roses showing forth, and you could even spot a dwarf rhododendron sporting a blood-red blossom, anticipating the spring. At the same time, the reservoirs were dangerously low, and Nature seemed to be keeping to her own strange new agenda, wholly separate from the comings and goings of mankind.

Anytown, or so we may call it, continued in its slumber and its anonymity and its mediocrity, whatever the rest of the world or Nature happened to be doing: its citizens hoped for little beyond the everyday and aspired to little, while its ruling borough and county councils sought to avoid the limelight because this might incur cost, and on this basis, that of not spending money, they continued to oversee services rated as one star by the still-active monitoring bodies. But in spite of the low profile, the troubles of the world could descend on the town, but equally, quotidian life could go on for many who wanted no more from it and were quite happy to be left alone, thank you very much.

The lingering, or newly returned evening warmth, however, lent even lethargic backwater Anytown a kind of sparkle, a sense and aura of well-being. Taking advantage of the pre-winter fine weather, more people were abroad in the early evening, or late afternoon, when after the four o'clock rush from schools and the first rush from work; and when a while later, when the low, blinding sun would sink below the horizon, and when a reddening disk in a purpling dusk would give way to comfortably warm darkness, they, a few anyway, would 'fire up the barbeques'. People knew that this weather probably would not last for much longer: the cold rains would come at any time, a freak snowstorm, or a hoar frost, and the change would have happened.

It should have been for everyone a pleasant time, and yet Anytown stubbornly remained one of those places where anti-social behaviour had not been fully 'addressed'. Two incidents falling close upon one another, however, served to demonstrate that the new reality had at last paid its visit, and with a new and purposeful vigour, to this old industrial town, this throwback to the past. The first was a relatively minor affair; the second, some would come to call an outrage, others a marker, a signpost, to a new intolerant justice, a new order...

The cemetery lay in the centre, facetiously in the dead centre of the western suburb of Anytown, on one of its hedged and fenced borders at the end of a cul-de-sac: its pair of wrought-iron gates (vehicular access for funerals) were closed. Adjacent to it was a pedestrian kissing gate, whose hinges gave low metallic moan whenever it was drawn back. Flanking the entrance, and grown black against the dark night sky, were two conifers, whose lower branches had been removed, so that they stood like great lollipops.

The cemetery was generally well-kept, better than some old country churchyards, wherein some areas long grass obscuring stones indicated a long-extinct or a long-departed old family. So it was tidy, this cemetery, with a few leaning stones, and even one broken in half, but with many in almost pristine condition, some grey, some black, some with urns, empty or with old or new flowers, a variety of inscriptions to send the deceased on their way, and to remember them whilst their living relatives remained here... A comfort at the time, on the day and beyond... In the daytime, the grey squirrels could still be spotted, running in and out and between the serried ranks of stones, pausing to look up nervously at a passing dog-walker then fleeing for the safety of the trees; and overhead the finches and sparrows flitted, or a crow or two would gaze down and give its raucous call. It was a place half-lit or thrown into long shadow at night by a row of houses whose short rear gardens backed onto it along one side. Pleasant by day, at night it could sometimes appear as an austere and chilly place. There were lots of children's graves here, at both ends, because the originally designated area had been filled. They sat with fluttering windmills sometimes and cuddly toys that grew wet and discoloured in the rain.

Not always quiet this place at night. Sometimes small gangs of local thugs would hang about under the dark trees, the other side of the garden hedges and fences, a place where in daytime perhaps a group of disaffected but harmless teenagers would stop for a smoke and a chat, or to put off the moment when they would have to start another day at the nearby secondary school. At night, however, it was sometimes different, as the neighbours had often complained.

That evening, in early October, as it eventually grew dark after a hot day, a group of a dozen or so youths was gathered noisily under their favourite cluster of trees, positioned about halfway through the cemetery, at the side boundary, in the shadow. They were dark figures under trees, but occasionally stepped out into the brighter light cast by the houses: there was some pushing and shoving and someone was pinned on the ground, and a few lager cans were strewn about. The alpha male in this group was a nineteen-year-old called Lee McIlroy, shaven-headed and hollow-faced, with a broad freckled nose and black eyes set close together. He wore a light tee-shirt, the better to see his muscled arms and single tattoo. The fashion for piercings had faded, but he still had one through his left nostril, though above it, his left eyebrow just sported the marks where a ring had once been.

McIlroy had a history of petty crime, leading up to a conviction for grievous bodily harm, but had got away with a number of assaults and regular episodes of intimidation because none would speak up against him: his violent nature was well-known, and matched by the notoriety of his large family who tormented their neighbours. Thus far he had served only six months at a young offenders' institution... McIlroy drew support from the small, stocky, dark-complexioned Domenic Savoy. Savoy was vicious, sadistic and bitter, and his brown feral eyes were always on the look-out for trouble, always on the look-out for a victim. The CSP and the police were alert to the nuisance and real menace of this pair and the gang who followed them: they searched for evidence linking them to a recent spate of muggings and unprovoked attacks, they were looking for witnesses prepared to speak up... Stiffer sentences had been introduced under Dain Alvis, but the courts were inconsistent in their application. The police wondered where these people were 'in the system', the 'system' being the new way of recording possible troublemakers. In fact, their names had reached the lists of the Werod some months earlier, just before 'the attack on democracy itself,' and had now been 'processed for action'. The local constabulary was generally in the dark about such matters, however.

There was a lot of whooping, and the occasionally loud cry into the night, with a 'this fuckin' and a 'fuckin that'. For a second time, Savoy wrestled one of the younger gang members to the dark ground, in the shadow cast by black tree. He pressed his foot over the boy's groin.' Shall I tread on his nuts?' he shouted.

McIlroy shook his head: 'Nar,' he said; then 'Hey, look at this. 'He pointed to a gravestone and read its inscription aloud:

'Peter Dredge, Departed this Life, 21 October 2017, Rest in Peace

'This lager really goes through yah.' McIlroy proudly took out his penis, long and pale in the half-light, already boasting, he would proclaim, a number of notches, and he waved it around for all to see. Then he urinated long and noisily, plashing on the stone. 'Ha, ha, ha, Rest in piss!'

'Hey, what's this,' someone shouted.

In the distance, in the half-light therefore, close to people's houses, but in the garden of the dead, a lone figure moved, hobbled almost, along the wide path that ran from the right, the main road end of the cemetery, heading for the kissing gate at the other, eastern end, between the two conifers. He, for it was a man, moved slowly, unaware of the peril he was in. The hunter Savoy narrowed his dark eyes, and grinned. 'What have got ere,' he shouted, so that clearly the man had heard, and visibly stiffened a little. 'Entertainment time!'

Savoy then bellowed. The man seemed to hurry forwards but was still not moving fast enough.

The group, about twenty-strong, moved quickly, skirting a low hedge which cut the cemetery in half, moved to head off the slowly moving figure. McIlroy was smiling: Savoy was working himself up into a fake anger that he could use to justify to himself any action he deemed fit to perpetrate upon the hapless stranger.

McIlroy, swaggering, approached the man, who appeared to be just above middle height, and probably in his late thirties, younger then than he had seemed at a distance, probably because of the limp. So much the better, thought McIlroy. Close up, in the half-light, the man looked nervous: again, so much the better. 'Got a light, pal?' said the pack leader, holding out a cigarette, as the others formed a three-quarters circle blocking the man's path. The man did not answer. 'Oh,' continued McIlroy visibly grinning and turning this way and that, playing to his audience. 'Nothing to say? I said…' he leaned his head forward until his snub nose almost touched the other man's, 'have you got a fuckin' light!' The words were shouted. The man took a step back, looking anxious, afraid. He looked around at all the faces focused on him.

'Answer the man, then,' Savoy joined in, moving forward, then pushing the man, who staggered back a couple of paces. Savoy's dark eyes gleamed in the semi-darkness, wild with eagerness. 'Let's give him a good kicking, eh. Who's up for it?'

The hapless man stood to his full height, tense: he was now about the same size in this respect as the

McIlroy thug, taller than the one who had pushed him. Those gang members, here in this out-of-the-way spot (no one with any sense came through here at night), who wanted to be involved in this, knew that the man was in real trouble: so did the few hangers-on who really wanted nothing to do with what was about to happen. One or two backed off, wanting to be somewhere else, wanting this not to happen. One of those backing away thought he saw something dark move amongst the gravestones, and then again in another place; the ghosts of the dead? The boy stared hard but decided it was in his imagination, due to his overwrought nervous state.

'I'll give you money' the man pleaded, taking out his wallet, 'Don't hurt me, please.'

'Don't hurt me. Don't hurt me - we'll fuckin' hurt you, all right,' McIlroy said triumphantly, stepping towards the man, who had been slowly backing away. Then he hesitated as the man spoke.

'Then you've had your chance, thug, coward, traitor and enemy of the people and you won't get another one. I'm arresting you, and', pointing to Savoy, 'you. You'll both be charged with conspiracy to maim or commit grievous bodily harm, for gross indecency, and for intimidating a citizen. I am an Officer of the Werod, and I am arresting you.'

Domenic Savoy looked wild, and thought that as the man was on his own, what difference did it make? But as he moved forward, the officer spat in his face. Maddened, he launched himself at the man, whose hand flew like a whiplash to side of Savoy's neck, landing with a sickening thud, like the sound of a cleaver hitting a chopping board. Momentarily, everything went black for Savoy, then he lay gasping and wheezing on the ground, barely able to draw breath. The gang was suddenly aware of black shapes all around them - probably thirty or more armed men: men in black, wearing balaclavas.

McIlroy, Savoy, and four others were separated out from the rest, pinned to the ground, beaten and yelled at. The rest were then allowed to leave, terrible threats ringing in their ears. McIlroy and the other five were dragged off in the opposite direction, the direction from whence the stranger had first come. The captives shouted into the dark night in vain, and struggled, their swearing and anger born of fear. A witness from a nearby house, anxious and disturbed by the loudly shouted dire threats of the officers, and straining to see from their bedroom windows, saw the six being bundled into four vehicles that had drawn up outside the cemetery gates: a confusion of bodies, some scuffling, ending with the slamming of car and van doors. The vehicles, as far as anyone could make out when talking about the event, had been dark, perhaps an aubergine colour, though it had been difficult to tell, since they had been twenty yards from the nearest working street lamp.

Word spread through the community that both McIlroy and Savoy had been charged and would appear in court. The other four in custody were released, looking beaten and afraid, it was said: though in truth, perhaps just afraid. The McIlroy and Savoy families, twenty-three men, women and children in all, had, it was also later said, been moved on. For all intents and purposes, they had disappeared. Nothing more was heard of McIlroy and Savoy. Nothing came to court.

This, it has to be admitted, was a rather minor incident, simply because no one made any real fuss about the fate of these people, at least none that came to the public notice. The phrase on the lips of most people was - good riddance.

The other event took place three months later in the northern reaches of Anytown, on an area of ground that was a sort of no man's land in that it lay between two industrial estates. It was a large area left to nature, a mixture of rough grasses, a few stunted trees and bushes, some fly-tipped items... sometimes an area that someone arranged to have flail-mowed after complaints in the summer about the fire hazard created by dried-out growth. The epicentre of this area was some few hundred yards from the estates that flanked it like two crescent moons: from this epicentre one could, on a clear night, view the security lights of the big rectangular warehouses and the production units, or see out-of-town offices lit up for night cleaning. Large vehicles could be made out, either parked up or in motion, working under powerful floodlights. It was all in the distance: here, it was quite dark on the ground though the sky all around was, as the astronomers would say, polluted.

On this wasteland, this no man's land, bonfires were sometimes lit, and, on occasion, this bonfire was a stolen vehicle being burnt out. The police felt, quite sensibly given their limited resources, that this was not a priority area: residential areas and the neighbouring commercial property itself took precedence. Here, then, drug dealers would sometimes meet, and, unbeknown to the police, come from all over the country to meet. In this instance, this second example of Werod justice, a number of cars were parked in the epicentre of this abandoned field, parked in a circle, their headlights shining inwards, on that dark cold night in early January, just after the festivities, and illuminating in the white-grey clinging mist, scores of figures who were making a film with expensive hand-held cameras.

Most of those present were heavily armed; with hand guns, shotguns, or even machine guns, besides the usual knives. It was indeed a gathering of drug lords from around the country; Anytown being centrally located for the purpose, and close to motorways. This was an unusual gathering however, a sort of temporary alliance or truce between three wholly different ethnic groups, come together for one purpose - to film the executions of seven police informers.

One man, who had had a camera shoved in his face, a close-up of terror as he begged for his life (seen later from recovered footage), lay dead on the ground, his throat cut, the earth staining black. Now, a woman of eastern European origin (again from recovered footage) was about to have her unborn child ripped from her with what looked like some sort of bayonet... Then shooting of another kind started...

The main battle lasted no more than fifteen minutes, though there was some sporadic shooting for another hour as the last of the gangs' members were hunted down one by one across field and hedgerow. The darkness and the heavy clinging mist was no protection against the all-seeing night-vision goggles and the thermal imaging cameras. Those working on the nearby estates heard the gunfire, the explosions, reported it all to the police, but could see nothing, even though they strained their eyes to see. An hour earlier, the Chief Constable had received a communication from none other than the 'Acting' Home Secretary, a member of the Werod Council of twelve, to say that a joint SAS and WSF (Werod Special Forces) operation was happening in the north of the town, and that his armed officers should remain well away until it was over. The Chief Constable was then given the statement that he should read out to the media the next day. His force would be allowed to view the preliminaries to the execution footage - though it was hoped that all the executions could be prevented - but of course none of this was for public consumption.

Seventy-three gang members were killed, along with two informers mistakenly identified or killed in the crossfire. The police kept local people out of the area while unknown agents carried the bodies away.

The official release was that this had been the bloody conclusion of a turf war between rival gangs. It became national news, but news that left a lot of unanswered questions. One question was settled in a lot of minds, however: the widely circulating rumour that a Werod paramilitary force was having direct if clandestine involvement in the elimination of crime surely had some basis in fact. Those involved in organized crime and who had the right contacts were aware that a new and terrible force was at work, that they might find their own bolt holes uncovered, whoever they were, and that it would be the case whether they worked from lock-up garages or penthouse suites.

Alex Quellan, large and smiling from time to time, dressed and looking like an ill-favoured priest, licked his lips with concentration as he pored over a list at his latest temporary headquarters close to Aston University. His high-ranking henchmen sat with bated breath, hanging on his every word.

Leaning back in his chair, he expressed his satisfaction: ‘By and large, a success; so, well done. There is one missing, but we shall soon hunt him down - you will, that is.’ They nodded their appreciation and compliance to a man. ‘Both our agents escaped real injury, I see - good... As for the police informers who died, that is regrettable: I am never happy about the death of an honest and dutiful citizen...’ He paused, and added with purpose, but coldly, without emotion: ‘But those seventy-three, and for the many others like them that we have removed - well, we all know that there never was any reason for their continued existence.’

He smiled inwardly, however, at his last words; he had picked up that expression somewhere along the way: ‘no reason for their continued existence’... Yes, how true, he thought, how true...

As the weeks and months passed into years, there would be no need for all this secrecy to surround the cleansing process. And in any case, even now, there was already a far weightier matter on Quellan’s mind.

15. *Of Government, crime and punishment*

- and a matter truly weighty

It was in all but name a republic, people were beginning to think, this Great Britain. The Royal Family had come to no harm, but constitutional monarchy had not been fully restored as had been promised and there were some restrictions on the calendar of royal engagements. The number of these had been reduced for security reasons.

The parliament buildings were restored, lovingly, to their former glory, with all traces of the 'terrorist atrocity' obliterated save for a memorial plaque to remind the visitor to this place.

The Commons stood empty, except for the droves of tourists, and as for the other place, their lordships had been sent packing not long after the events of June 2030; sent to lead work of national importance, kept away then for their own safety. Those few who complained about the failure of the country to return to the onetime and long-standing status quo, wherein their lordships in the upper chamber had had some say in government, found that there began a whispering campaign implicating them or members of their families in some seedy affair or other, or, more seriously, that they had had after all a hand in the very events that had unseated them.

By 2042, twelve years after the upheaval, their erstwhile lordships, and ladyships, knew, as did everyone else, that they lived in a Werod-dominated state, and under one unquestioned, effectively unchallenged leader, Alex Quellan.

Yet for most, it still seemed like a new freedom. Quellan kept some of the old structure, the county, borough or district, and parish councils. The shift from the familiar to the unfamiliar came in the need for council leaders, chief executives and members of the higher tier councils to report to a nine-member regional Werod panel.

The members of the regional panels held the official and anachronistic-sounding title of Knights of the Werod. These were all highly intelligent people, recruited from the high-calibre graduate pool, and diehard Quellan supporters. The leader thus combined continuity in the business of the everyday, and the functioning of society almost as before, with a flavour of newness, menace and a strange otherworldliness, knowing that in time the people, so long as they could live their lives relatively unhindered, would get used to the way things had developed. Most would embrace the continuing ruthless drive for the establishment of law and order since Quellan's arrival and saw it as a both legacy and a strengthening of Dain Alvis's more extreme policies, that could only benefit the law-abiding citizen.

Quellan had set up twelve regional nine-member panels each reporting to one of his twelve Cabinet or Werod Council (by now the terms were interchangeable) members. The twelve areas for Northern Ireland, Wales, Scotland and England were based on a complex mathematical formula which factored in crude population, demographic profiles, economic prosperity, current and planned infrastructure, crime and health statistics. Quellan had developed a rudimentary form of the model himself, before getting some input from some of the ablest statisticians and mathematical modellers to complete the project. Under the new system a new and geographically large Wessex was recreated, though some suspected that its creation, or re-creation, was in part in honour of Dain Alvis and his obsession with matters Anglo-Saxon.

The decision to have a nine-member panel was based not on a mathematical principle but on Quellan's whim; nine being a significant number in Norse mythology and in other tales of mythical status. Each panel member was too a Knight in the ancient and mythical sense, Arthurian rather than Anglo-Saxon, and in order to become a Knight an esquire had to undergo tasks to prove merit: special forces' training, followed by a series of physical rituals and oath taking, during which process they would swear personal allegiance to the Leader and to the memory and principles of Dain Alvis. The Knights-to-be were as a rule recruited from the intelligentsia, as has been stated, but there were a few exceptions at Quellan's own discretion. The aim of the process was to create a fearless determined elite that would oversee every aspect of government at the local and regional level.

Forty-five chief constables had also to send a copy of their quarterly reports to the Home Secretary to their designated Knights of the Werod panel. In every instance, in every area, Quellan sought to close the information loop; though some might say, tighten the noose.

Education was outside the remit of the panels, being the responsibility of a new government inspectorate, the Office for Standards and Equality in Education and Science (OfSTEES). The regions remained the same, each Regional Inspector a Werod member and academic of note, who would in turn report direct to the Cabinet Secretary within the Central Council of the Werod. A note of interest: the History curriculum in England had always to include a celebration of English history since the time of the Romans, with Anglo-Saxon history prior to the Norman Conquest mandatory. Also core, and unavoidable, was the official version of the events of 2030.

Democracy was celebrated in the classroom, in the media, in the workplace: democracy, its history, its development, its value as a political system. Its practice, however, consisted of a lengthening of the term of government to seven years, and the establishment of ghost parties, properly funded and with a high profile, whose task it was to split the vote of any opposition to the Breakthrough Party: ghost parties being parties set up to fail and blunder and thereby demonstrate the efficacy, worthiness, honesty and absolute necessity of continued Breakthrough Party rule. As there was no Parliament building, or as the old building had been classed as an anachronistic if fascinating and strikingly beautiful relic of the past, in this period of economic prosperity people became convinced that the old parties were equally outdated as were the quaint old ways of parliamentary business. The Houses of Parliament were given over fully as a tourist attraction, as part of the continuing celebration of democracy and national heritage; so, there were subsidized trips for schools, universities, the armed services and any group of people that might be encouraged to apply. But the business of government no longer took place there. Werod secretaries of state and ministers, loosely termed Breakthrough, could be seen occasionally, pacing proprietorially along its echoing corridor flagstones and capacious chambers; but Quellan was rarely to be seen there. The agenda of this most elusive and solitary of tyrants (some would say in private) allowed no time for posturing or gloating: there was still a lot of work to be done.

Civil Service outward compliance and collusion with the new order of things was to all intents and purposes total, though no doubt some individuals and disparate groups thought and hoped that the new apparent status quo would not hold together forever. Nowhere was co-operation more important than that area of the Civil Service which retained its name as the Foreign Office, or the Foreign and Commonwealth Office. Quellan knew with as close as one could get to an absolute certainty, that the greatest threat to his revolution in Britain was from the outside, a foreign power that had the military or economic muscle to discredit and disrupt the rule of the Breakthrough Party; the greatest threat, that is, aside from the assassin's bullet.

The close relationship with the US continued of course, with a veiled promise from Quellan to support US forces active in the Middle East and more recently in South America, support that would mean sending troops - an unpopular move, he knew, if he were forced to make it. He was ably represented on this stage by Sebastian Millar, a great nephew of the newspaper magnate, and a tall, lean energetic man in his late thirties; a Werod Council member, naturally. Millar was tireless in his wooing of the Americans, but equally attentive to the concerns of the Russian Federation, with its dominance of European energy supplies, and to China and India with their vast industrialization and modernization programmes, and their potential, the more so in China's case, for an expansionist foreign policy backed by huge, ultra-modern armed forces. More to the point, for the Russians, there was the ever-present, American-led Western threat. It was a fine line for Millar to tread, under Quellan's guidance; like Blondin over Niagara

Falls someone had said of him. Above all, Britain could no longer afford to indulge in outmoded jingoism and needed more than ever two powerful friends in Germany and France.

Quellan could see these were dangerous times, more dangerous than anyone could guess. He was developing his own agenda, which would be jeopardized by foreign adventures. For this reason, the reason of not wanting to overcomplicate matters now, adherence to religious tolerance was unwavering and must remain so: this message was communicated through and enforced by his legion agents and their associates throughout the land. Let the Catholic Church and the Church of England criticize all they could; let the same be said of the other faiths. In the secular world, in industry and commerce, dissent and criticism of the government were welcomed and encouraged, Quellan said, 'to draw the sting'.

Yet people everywhere knew it was a kind of freedom only: from the richest entrepreneur to the poorest council tenant, from the agnostic city financier who enjoyed his view over the ever-flowing Thames, to the chapel-going sheep farmer in the hills of Snowdonia. Everywhere was the Werod, so to speak, and what the new order achieved in terms of stability, and freedom for and protection of the majority, it achieved equally in its menace to the wrongdoer. And it became clear to the honest and law-abiding citizen, when Quellan's government was in the second of its seven-year terms, just how the evils of society would be dealt with, and just why it was so important to do the right thing - always.

The lists drawn up over the years, and continuing to be drawn up, were ever more important and used to address justice in a much more fundamental, and accurate, way than in the final days of Dain Alvis's government, when Silas Wood had, wrongly it had turned out, been dragged in for questioning.

The nets, intended to capture and eliminate villainy, evil, violence, intimidation, bullying, Quellan said to his closest supporters, to gather up all the filth and vermin who had escaped thus far but who continued to make life unpleasant for the innocent and hard-working who just wanted to live in a polite civilized society, the nets were closing. People, he stated, would be made to behave 'nicely' to one another or face the consequences. Those who did not behave in a respectful way were to be regarded as enemies of the people and therefore enemies of the state. Had Quellan been prone to self-aggrandizing, which he was not, in his casting of the nets he might have seen himself as a kind of St Peter in reverse, hauling in his catch of damned souls.

The lists were long, lists of miscreants and deviants from the age of thirteen upwards, so taking in persistent school bullies, torturers of animals (these people could be of any age, but interestingly had almost always in early adulthood turned their attentions to people, or so the records showed), knife users, particularly those guilty of serious wounding, gang members of all sorts, indiscriminate users of air rifles, drug dealers, motorists who killed, particularly habitual and impatient speeders or drunkards, tail-gaters, dangerous drivers and so on. This would be the second major phase in the freeing of the nation from these worthless people. Further, the lists now included the sellers of air rifles to the under thirties, the sellers of alcohol who had flouted the new licensing and sales laws, and judges and magistrates whom the Werod decided had been unduly lenient in their sentencing.

People would learn the meaning of respect for one another, Quellan would oft repeat, grown larger than life it seemed as he became, for him, impassioned. He truly hated those who got a perverted physical pleasure from making the lives of others a misery, or who were just plain aggressive and selfish in their aggression. Some of these deviants, he often said with contempt, thought self-righteously that they were tough, individualistic, and that their relative might and anonymity made their position secure. He would show them: soon they would be trembling in their bolt holes like the cowards they were - the Werod would wipe them out, wipe them out completely as a destructive and perpetually depressing aspect of society: no longer would these people prove an intractable, perennial problem. Yes, to be disrespectful and aggressive to a fellow-citizen was a crime against the State, a form of treason, an evil that needed to be eradicated. He was committed, he averred, to this course, and he vowed to the Werod Council, to all the Werod members of the Breakthrough Party, and above all to the people that he would eradicate 'this filth from these islands'. Yet even as he spoke to his cadre, and though he meant exactly what he said, he was eager to accelerate his involvement in something else that had to be done, something much more important, something which had occupied his capacious mind for a long, long time. And so, he delegated power on this matter of crime and punishment to two of his deputies, one the bulldog-like Bateman, the other a severe-looking bespectacled man whose loyalty and devotion to Quellan was legend amongst even the Werod elite, and who headed the Werod Internal Affairs Unit, a sort of elevated Secret Police. But, Quellan warned, not a single innocent person must suffer: the Werod knew this and knew the consequences of failing to mark their targets with a one-hundred-per-cent certainty. Mistakes had been made in the past, it was true: to repeat them would be for the Werod to be perceived as no better that the worthless creatures they were educating or eliminating. Punishment should be where there was crime, and there only; and the punishment should fit the crime. This was not some Fascist purge for the purpose of retaining power: this would be a cleansing process unlike anything in the history of mankind. He would review their progress in six months. The urgent business that the Council was aware of, though its detail and true purpose was known to Quellan alone, now demanded all his attention: time was running out.

And so, from page one of the Lists, from page one of every letter that had been discovered, from every e-mail, from every word of every denouncement, from every list of known undesirables, from rumour and from subsequent investigations, the catalogue of perpetrators grew. Many would be crossed off the lists as minor offenders, many would be crossed off for another reason, once and for all - case closed.

Unlike the early days too, when operations against criminal elements had been clandestine, the consequences of failing to respect one's fellow citizen were made plain for all to see. For all to see, because the media were encouraged to broadcast, photograph, report what was happening. The time had come, in the year 2041 (people would henceforth sing a little rhyming ditty about the events) towards the end of a very, very hot August, for the people to be shown that a neighbour, a citizen, by word, gesture or deed, who intimidated another person, would incur the full wrath of the State, of the Werod, of Alex Quellan. This tough action was applied to prisons, where Armed Werod units began carrying out a cleansing process, whereby the worst kind of offenders, those who had operated a rough justice of their own within their walls, were forcibly removed and sent to correction centres at undisclosed locations. Room would be made in this way for minor offenders who could be re-educated in custody without fear of unofficial intimidation. Of course, there remained the Human Rights Act, but whenever this spectre appeared the government denied any involvement in events, said it would launch a full investigation and enquiry and that it would seek out and punish these rogue elements among the Werod, if indeed Werod the perpetrators were. People knew better of course, and no one knew better than the criminals in the firing line.

Into September, still baking hot, with tarmac still apt to melt, and with the fields sun-burnt and the sun blazing, the motorways were targeted: aggressive and reckless motorists were pulled over, dragged from their vehicles and beaten, in full view of passing motorists, and even in front of the TV cameras. There were hundreds of such beatings, and people grew accustomed to this roadside justice - it was like in the days long ago when a pupils were publicly caned for some misdemeanour; though two men had died as a result of their injuries, and one was shot dead for particularly aggressive behaviour and assault, for a crime that was once 'risibly described as road rage', a phrase now banned because it had excused cowardly bullying. Meanwhile, Bateman announced that the sentence for killing a child whilst speeding excessively, the sentence for those with a previous record of speeding or aggressive driving, that is, would be a mandatory forty years in prison and a lifetime driving ban. Such people, the government was keen to point out in a series of public information films, were to be regarded as child murderers, really no different from paedophiles, since they killed children to satisfy their own perverted desires. Whilst being quietly terrified every time they took their vehicles out, many people privately applauded the government's tough stance on this matter: driving, many said, had suddenly become a more civilized experience, less threatening. After all, a car, a van, a lorry, was potentially just as much a lethal weapon as a gun or a bomb and if directed carelessly, or willfully, at the innocent - well, it was an act of terrorism, and the punishment should fit the crime. And was it not true that 1.5 million people across the world were killed each and every year in road accidents, many caused by selfish, evil behaviour?

In this period, this second phase of the New Justice, the Prime Minister, the Leader, made a handful of brief television appearances, though oddly he never really looked the same twice. Perhaps it was the wigs, or the medication for his skin, and he looked older now, or did he actually look younger? He was a chameleon figure and many doubted that they would recognize him in the street if they saw him, except perhaps for his size and evident awkwardness. On television he had a flat humourless delivery that made him unlikeable, even if his policies were welcomed by some, even though the lives of many had become better; an immobile delivery too, except for a rare expansive gesture with his broad heavy white hands that were like great paddles. Occasionally, on these rare television appearances, he would slowly move his head forward hypnotically gazing into the camera and clasping those hands together for effect, hypnotically...

As a final word on crime, before Bateman and his colleague finally took over the management of Phase Two, the Leader announced, in a televised broadcast, that he would 'eliminate knife crime on our streets.'

Anyone found guilty of stabbing someone to death or seriously impairing their ability to lead a full life, would, if it were for their own malicious pleasure, and particularly if they had a record of violence and there were no extenuating circumstance such as the dire need to defend themselves... such people would not be executed: in fact, he smiled at this point, reassuringly, there would be no return of the death sentence as it was previously understood, handed out by outmoded judges placing on their heads a black cap-bewigged. This practice was barbaric, and the method used by a bullying state, and had on occasion been a crime perpetrated on the innocent. This was a benign, benevolent state and in the interests of purity and true justice people should only be killed, where this was necessary, at the moment they were enacting their heinous crimes or celebrating them. The same justice would be applied to any Werod, Army or Police Officer who was discovered enjoying an act of brutality. The State was seeking perfect justice and would remain true to that aim. 'Law, justice and punishment were the burdens and business of the State, to be carried through solemnly and swiftly wherever and whenever the need arises.' And so Quellan went on to lay out his solution to knife crime. No summary execution here, not even a punitive prison sentence. Instead, the perpetrator would be sent to the new, purpose-built clinic in the town of Leamington Spa where Werod surgeons would remove, humanely, under anaesthetic, the perpetrator's offending arm to the elbow, and on his or her forehead would be marked for life the letter 'K'. The perpetrator would then be released, unless still considered a danger and beyond mental rehabilitation, but not allowed any form of prosthetic for a five-year period following the operation, after which period the State would assist and physically rehabilitate the offender. The world would always know of the perpetrator's crime and if the perpetrator were shunned by society then that must be his or her continued punishment. Human Rights activists shrieked their anger and the government let them, encouraged them, and micro managed a media debate, there was even some talk of compensation... but the message had gotten through to most of its target audience. In private, Quellan said: 'This element of justice will be retrospective. People still in prison having committed this crime and, having failed to show the proper level of contrition, will now be punished, unless that is, they have already jumped from their prison roof.'

A few thought that the Leader was not serious in this threat; that is, until a number of young males, missing an arm, with an empty sleeve from the elbow downwards, and a bowed shaven head, showing a livid red 'K' on their foreheads began emerging from the Leamington clinic, looking like victims of war.

Then the Werod government, for it was that in all but name, looked hard at people who stole from the citizen his or her hard-earned money. The crime could be fraud, bogus selling, through internet scams, or on the doorstep... in any way. And judges whose sentences failed to reflect the stress and damage to a perpetrator's victim could find themselves suddenly disbarred...

16. *The people and the Lord Protector*

The following year, in early spring, in which there had been torrential rain following a mild dry winter, three young people stepped out of a small red car in the three-quarters full car park of the supermarket closest to their home. It was a bright day, a relief, a cheering relief from the overcast skies and persistent damp of the last three weeks. Overhead, big white cotton-wool balls of cumulus drifted imperceptibly in the clear blue heaven. The three were Nancy Wood, now seventeen, in jeans and pink tee shirt, with a 'Save the Rainforest' logo, her elder brother Jonas, now twenty-two, dark-haired and brown-eyed, and several inches taller and a little more introspective than his attractive, vivacious and warm-hearted sister, and Jonas's Spanish girlfriend, Carlotta, also dark-haired. Carlotta, her skin a beautiful olive-brown, wore her hair cut short in a boyish style, and had stunningly beautiful dark, deep and black, round eyes.

Jonas and Carlotta were down from Durham University, where Jonas was studying medicine and Carlotta, whom he had met there (while visiting Durham from his Stockton base), was doing a postgraduate course in geophysics. It was Carlotta's first visit to her boyfriend's family: still a big event for the more traditional family, especially meaningful for Carlotta back at home when Jonas had visited for the first time last summer.

They crossed the car park between the rows of cars, noticing a few people moving around with trolleys, going back to their cars or heading for the entrance to begin their shopping: of course, just as you would expect. A handful of people were queueing at the cash machines, cash being back in fashion now after the great card scams of the mid-thirties, now a thing of the past thanks to government action but leaving a legacy of mistrust in the minds of many.

Nancy was joking with Carlotta about her own feeble attempts to resurrect her school Spanish, which she had abandoned in favour of German as her second modern language. Then a thought crossed her mind. 'Joe,' she said, looking up at her older sibling (she often but not always called Jonas by this pet name, especially when she was anxious or worried and needed reassurance), 'Joe, is dad all right? Is he really ill, do you think?' Jonas did in fact know a bit more than she, having talked at length to his father the evening before. 'Yeah, I hope so. You know about his blood tests?' She nodded. 'Well, the fact that they're clear rules out a lot of nasties. I'm pretty certain it's stress-related. Don't worry, the old boy'll be fine.' Nancy was reassured but not wholly so. 'I know,' she said,' we could buy him a bottle of port, and when he gets the all-clear he can indulge, celebrate... Mum'll be pleased if we do...'

They stopped dead, noticing that at the wide entrance half a dozen armed soldiers in camouflage with large berets stood as though on guard, their machine-gun-like weapons resting at waist height, their eyes scanning those coming in and out, and beyond, the vehicles entering and exiting the car park. Close to them were three people, two men and a woman, in black uniforms, one of the men in an officer's uniform. They had all seen pictures of people like these in the media and spotted them at airports, but never seen them in so mundane a place as a supermarket. The soldiers seemed equally out of place here.

Jonas inclined his head and whispered to his girlfriend, 'Soldiers, and... Werod.'

To his and Nancy's horror, as they approached the armed group, Carlotta went up to speak to the Werod officer, a lieutenant, who was at first surprised to be approached thus. Other people, passing in and out of the store, were in the meantime giving the armed men a wide and respectful berth.

Jonas hissed in a loud and ridiculous, and ineffectual strained whisper, 'Carlotta!' so that all the armed men turned to look at him and he could feel himself blushing to the roots of his hair. What could she be doing? She would get them into trouble. Then to his surprise he could see them all laughing, and Carlotta was gabbling away to the officer in Spanish, and he back to her, at much too fast a rate for him to follow.

Carlotta explained that she had recognized the officer; that he had lived in her hometown for a year as an exchange student. He had become friends with her older brother and she was fourteen at the time and had had quite a crush on the intelligent and polite, slightly reserved Englishman Paul. He had just laughed at her, she added, when she had commented that he looked like a neo-Fascist, at which point both Jonas and Nancy were open-mouthed. They told her she must be more careful than that. She in her turn reassured them that her old friend had taken it all in good part, and had been at pains to point out, however, that his people were not Fascists and only criminals had anything to fear from them: they were, he had said, apolitical, and people were free to support whom they pleased just so long as this did not involve intimidation and lack of respect for others. That was their only creed, other than their loyalty to the leader and to the organization. As yet, he had experienced no conflict between these two sides of his office. He was *so serious*, Carlotta laughed, when he had said this, 'so I got him on to talking about my brother'. Unfortunately, this was Paul's last day in the area, or she might have asked Jonas, and Jonas's family, she said, whether he could visit them.

They did their bit of shopping, and Jonas thought long and hard. What after all had this new order done to him? Nothing.... And he looked at the people around him in the busy store... People just got on with things as normal: exchanged pleasantries, studied the prices of things, looked preoccupied (as he was), debated which ice cream or which bottle of wine to buy, mothers complained at their little children, or made a joke with them, old people moved slowly, determinedly, keeping up with the pace of life, the noise of the beeping tills, and so on... It was much as it had always been, and yet... it was calmer, somehow. Was it his imagination or were people more polite and smiling, more relaxed...? He felt positive, and when they left, he went out of his way to introduce himself to the Werod officer and shook his hand. For some reason, however, he decided he would not tell his parents about the unexpected encounter, and for some reason, Nancy, too, thought this for the best.

The elderly couple stood on the motorway bridge, gazing over musingly, intently, at the two orderly, opposing steady streams of traffic below, stretching into the distance, to the next grey-white bridge and beyond: the eight lanes moved as conveyor belts; there was a perceptible slightly faster motion on the outside, but there were no flashing lights, no sudden lane changes and there was no tail-gating, everyone was keeping to the safe distance. The traffic, flowing with a steady hum, punctuated by the increasing rush of sound as the vehicles approached the bridge (the Doppler effect, their grandson had told them once) moved as units of a whole, glinting in the light of the midmorning October sun; a fine, bright and fresh day, where the trees dotting the landscape, in the hedgerows and in near and distant spinneys, were starting to show their varied autumn colours.

The man was in his mid-nineties, his wife ten years younger, though neither looked frail: the old man in particular looked sprightly, the woman younger than her years. They could probably have walked the mile or so from the village centre, to this point, three-quarters of a mile from its northern edge, but their grandson, with whom they were staying, had offered to drop them off there and would be returning to pick them up in an hour.

The old man smiled musingly, then smiled at his wife. 'All that time ago,' he said, 'over eighty years. And now my little grandson, not so little anymore, lives in the same village.' The passing of time, he was thinking, was ineffably sad, and yet for him it had had its many, many compensations, a long life in which he had seen and experienced so much. So, let things move on as they would: he, they, had had a good life.

They stared down at the traffic. 'I remember how we both used to talk about it, mockingly,' he chuckled,' how people used to stop and look at the motorway, just as we are doing now. But over there,' he pointed to the next bridge, people would even bring picnics and set out a picnic table, so they could watch for ages, like people sitting on a beach watching the waves. Do you remember, there would often be a car parked and people just sitting there?'

‘I’m not sure,’ the woman replied. ‘I know your father used to talk about it ... Something some people did in the days when the motorway was relatively new. The first motorway...’

‘Look at it now - endless streams of traffic, even though the new road has opened. ‘

They gazed westward towards the other bridge, three-quarters of a mile distant and could just make out the little roadway that ran down into the field, adjacent to it, where indeed people had used to stop and picnic. Just to the left on the horizon was what in his day the children had called Hob Hill, or Devil’s Hill, though it did not say this on any map. The man pointed due west to this, a low hill, a slight elevation in the landscape, atop of which was a small wood, still there now and turning the red-gold of autumn. ‘We used to think the wood was haunted by the ghosts of murderers... we called the lane nearby, just a farm track really, Cutthroat Lane or Hangman’s Lane... Just boyish imagination really, but it might have been from an old legend or something.’

His wife patted him affectionately on the cheek. ‘Yes, yes, you’ve told me this before,’ she interrupted him,’ every time we’ve passed by on the motorway...’

‘Not every time,’ the old man protested, laughing, knowing he had mentioned the place many times. But he took her gentle chiding in good part, willing back his boyhood days to his mind’s eye.

They looked to their left, toward a nearby spinney, in front of which on a bare patch of ground with a few straggling weeds a black limousine-like vehicle had drawn up. The vehicle looked sinister, with its dark-tinted windows. A heavy-set man was getting out. He was dressed in a long black expensive overcoat and carried a walking-stick. As he came towards them, he seemed to walk easily with his polished mahogany crutch stick (the elderly man's best friend had such a stick), only using it to bear his weight a little from time to time. The man seemed to be approaching them with a purpose, as though keen to engage them in conversation. It was odd: twenty years earlier they would have been afraid of the stranger, on their guard, but somehow, something had changed. It was not that they had become less guarded, less fearful, but that nowadays there seemed less to fear.

The stranger looked vaguely familiar, but then the couple had known hundreds of people in the course of their long lives, and active and interested though they still were in others and in the world around them, memory was perhaps not what it was.

The man, large, and intimidating were it not for the fact that he smiled politely at them and kept a respectful distance, looked a bit odd and both the old man and the old woman separately decided that they did not know him after all. He had a large face, made better by his smile, as could be said of most people, though he did look a bit odd. He had a mop of sandy hair atop his heavy-jowled face, hair which didn't look quite natural - though that was his business - and he wore tinted spectacles that did not allow one, properly, to read his eyes. He was genial enough and obviously keen to idle away a bit of time with the couple, ask them what they were about perhaps or make some enquiries about the area.

'I grew up here. As a boy I used to ride my old bike around a track in that spinney you've parked next to. My friends and I used to spend hours down here, racing around. It's overgrown now.' The old man was responding to the stranger's question.

The stranger smiled, and looked interested, absorbed even. A foot taller, he gazed down with a kindly expression at the speaker.

'In the summer holidays,' the old man continued,' seven or eight weeks of them then, as I remember, we used to go over to Devil's Hill, or Hob Hill - I don't know why we called it that - and down the hill from there to the river beyond. It's close to the source of the Nene, you know, or one of them: like a big stream really - not a raging torrent. I remember, we watched two boys mooring a punt. When they'd gone we stole it and struggled along with it. We couldn't get it far though, because there's an area where we used to camp, with the Cubs, where the river runs over a shingle bed and where you could easily cross...' He shook his head wistfully, remembering. 'It's been a good life.'

'Do you feel safe? Living in this country, I mean. Do you feel safe?' the stranger asked apropos of nothing.

The old man pulled a face but could see the larger-than-life stranger meant no harm. He looked at his wife, who looked back at him. 'Well, yes, as a matter of fact we do. People are kinder, or at least more respectful that they used to be; but,' he thought for a moment,' in a strange way sometimes, as though they're subdued, spiritless. Not always though; often it's a natural kindness coming through. No, I mean,' he was balancing the arguments, 'it's definitely better now because it is safer. Not everywhere of course - it's a violent world and always has been. England's a better place than it was a few years ago; but it always was a better place than most.'

'Well, we've not exactly seen the whole world...' the woman interjected.

'Perhaps your husband is right,' the stranger commented, nodding sagely, a mischievous smile playing about his large face. 'I myself originate from Scotland, sort of...' unassumingly he waved away the apologetic glance directed at him,' No, no, no - no offence. These islands are better: I, too, fully believe that. Look at the traffic,' he pointed to the streams of moving glinting metal below, a permanent soft low roar. 'On average, ten to fifteen per cent slower, so I have read; and no obvious aggression, and fewer fatalities. Oh, I've been reading the newspapers... If you can believe everything you read.' He continued to stare down at the motorway traffic.

'I was about ten years old when they came through here, building this', volunteered the old man. 'I remember my brother I and a couple of friends down here one week-end and messed about on the site... It was raining, and we sat at the bottom of great piles of building sand... We were plastered with sand, with orange faces, and on our way home we had to walk by the headmaster's house. On the Monday he warned the school assembly about the dangers of going onto building sites, saying that he'd seen four boys walking home, and, looking straight at us, saying that he knew where we'd been. He was right of course. My parents really told me off. We never came to the site again though we did walk past and look as the road took shape. I am remembering it as clearly as I see you now... great sweeps and swathes of brown earth...'

'You must be almost a hundred years old, 'the stranger said in kindly admiration. 'Not far off', the old man admitted. In the meantime, the old man was still remembering the sand hills of his boyhood adventure.

The large stranger, too, was suddenly thoughtful, gazing over the bridge at the traffic below, as though trying to understand its kinetic energy, its life force. He sensed a chaotic flow kept under control by self-interest, self-preservation, under the aegis of very real state control - humanity compliant, humanity harnessed.

He turned to the couple. 'How do you feel about the world in general? I'm personally a little disillusioned by all this' - he motioned with a large hand to the flow that ran beneath them, 'by all this modern rat-race.'

'Do you have a family?' the old lady asked.

The stranger pondered. 'Yes, a large family, I suppose you could say.'

'Then you'll know the joys of life, the little things that make life worth living. We have children, grandchildren and two great-grandchildren. It keeps us going; but should our children have come into this world for our pleasure, our need?'

'You're an educated lady, I see,' commented the stranger, as he did so, switching his weight from one foot to the other and leaning a little on his stick. 'Quite what do you mean, though?'

'We've been lucky, I suppose, to get to our age with,' she hesitated, her eyes clouding,' only one or two tragedies along the way in so large a family... Educated, did you say? Yes, I suppose so. A very, very long time ago... But there are such terrible tragedies, things that happen to people; laughing one minute, and then the next... I can't say I understand what it's all for, but we have to just live - once we're here.'

The old man put his arm round his wife's shoulders. A moment, not of complete silence, but just the rushing of the traffic below, a song bird in the nearby hedgerow, and from the spinney, the raucous cries of a gathering of rooks.

The stranger, smiling sympathetically, said at last,' Yes, life can be a hard road, and is for most people in this world at some time or another. The added problem now is that it cannot go on as it is. I can't see it lasting - too many people, too many cars.' He laughed, pointing below.

'And what about global warming,' the old man joined in. 'The ice cap is melting, isn't it; and one day soon the hot summers will kill off the likes of us, unless we get drowned like those poor devils in East Anglia last year...' He gazed across at what he had called Devil's Hill, a dark cluster of trees on the near horizon, as though drifting back to his childhood again. ‘Perhaps,’ he said, almost mockingly,’ it’s all part of God’s plan for us.’ His wife, he was aware, was staring hard at him. ‘I wish I could believe,’ he added, ‘I really do.’

‘Perhaps...perhaps a good thing,’ said the stranger musingly. ‘But let us be positive and look to the future.’ He pointed with a large finger to the wooded horizon. ‘They - the government - are building a new university over there, beyond the hill, at Weedon. It’s going to be called Temple Hill, or something like that, after the Old English meaning of the word Weedon - well, Anglo-Saxon - if there’s a difference... Anyway, by all accounts it will be much more than a university, a sort of future-world. But even as a university, it will be more important than Oxford or Cambridge, they say... though that is difficult to believe, I know.’ He smiled and nodded at them, at the elderly couple, and in a moment, he had turned away and was walking in a shambling heavy fashion back to his car, where, he had told them, others might be impatient for his return.

The old couple watched him go and watched him get into the front passenger seat of the long dark vehicle. ’What a lovely man,’ said the woman. ‘Yes, a nice chap,’ the old man agreed.’ A bit odd, but friendly, and interested in what you’ve got to say. Not sure about all that Oxford business... A bit odd...’

‘Oh, why was he a bit odd? You do find fault. They’re going now. I know, let’s see if we can peek into your old spinney, and have a listen to those noisy rooks.’ She lifted her manicured bony right hand, with its prominent blue veins and turned it over to look at her delicate gold wrist-watch, a cherished eightieth-birthday present from her husband. 'Robert will be here to pick us up in twenty minutes.'

Alex Quellan brooded: his heavy chin resting in his capacious palms, elbows resting on his desk, he gazed across the room with a fixed stare. The main event had yet to unfold, the end game yet to be played. He knew this, and he knew too that as long as there was breath in his body there could be no turning back. Yes, that was the other and far weightier matter. There could be no greater achievement.

For the moment, almost as an *adieu*, he reflected on what had been accomplished by the Werod in its delivery of a series of hammer blows against the criminal elements of Great Britain: ferocious and effective blows dealt out to the barons of organized crime and with equal determination to the little oik, who got pleasure out of seeing the defenceless squirm. Through the executive arm that was the Werod he had taught them all the meaning of fear before they were removed from this life, and in so doing had probably dissuaded many others from following the same path to termination. The work of the Werod, managed by his closest deputies, would continue: you could see the turning of this particular screw even in the faces of the wholly innocent. And this was just: the very thought of wrongdoing, of abusing others, had to be extinguished.

He had enjoyed seeing the guilty squirm and reap what they had sown; but it was not enough, and it had always been for him a sideshow, and not the fulfilment of his *major* ambition, but necessary on moral grounds none the less, and the honouring of his pledge to his former master. And he had been gratified by his personal observations of a range of people across the nation during his recent incognito tour. People felt safer, less threatened by those around them in their everyday lives. Good manners and mutual consideration had returned to the land; that is, if they had ever been there as the guiding principles at any time in history. Nevertheless, even if out of self-interest and a desire for self-preservation, people were 'nicer to one another.' But it was not enough. Quellan had known this from the outset, had thought it when even as a young man so very long ago he had metaphorically sat at the feet of his mentor Dain Alvis. He had had, even then, other, more far-reaching plans.

Lifting a crystal glass up to the window of his room, from where he now stood looking over the Thames, Quellan examined it and its pale, golden-brown liquid contents against the piercing wave/particle beams of morning sunlight. He squinted as if to focus better on the interplay of reflection and refraction as he swirled the liquid round. It was a single malt but more to the point it was his single fiery drink of the day, the continuing ritualistic demonstration of his strength of will, and, it was true, a solitary moment of pleasure suggestive of the experience and joy of life, a bright phial of spiritual light in his darkening world.

He was in this small matter of natural justice happy with what he had achieved. He had paid out many a worthless and vicious sub-human who had thought himself outside the reach of the law; and it was true that it was usually men. His mathematical modelling had shown that there would be a ripple effect from the meting out of justice on the street, and by the very presence, almost omnipresence, of Werod, Armed Werod, and regular Army working alongside Police and Community Special Police, all supported by the intelligence services, including the Werod's own secret police arm. The propensity, the tendency of the UK citizen to deviate from what was acceptable behaviour had been markedly reduced. This had been achieved by ruthless single-mindedness and by ruthlessness when necessary, and again where necessary by the establishment of a climate of fear, no longer fear of the criminal, but of the State. Yet at the same time, whilst it might appear that he had emulated Stalin with his iron grip and a form of the 'Terror', this was not the case: Quellan truly believed that his own form of control was to all intents and purposes apolitical, a genuinely moral crusade, something Werod officers were instructed to impress upon the people of the land: it was all for their own good, not for the good of the government or the Breakthrough Party: it really was well-intentioned. And it was popular, as both Alvis and Quellan had hoped it would be.

Yet for Alvis that had been his major driving force and Quellan, too, had felt this urge to root out the real evils of human aberrant behaviour and its scarring effects upon the innocent, had felt this burning desire to avenge and protect the long-suffering majority. For Quellan, however, the end desired by his mentor could only be achieved by sacrificing some of the innocent, something which in his more reflective moments he acknowledged. This did not really trouble him, for reasons which would become plain for all to see. There was a political element, or for Quellan a far more important reason to hold power in his own hands. He knew too that this experiment in the imposition of a new moral code would not long outlive him. It would fragment: every mathematical model and the lessons of history showed this to be the case; the natural entropy of social systems, the tendency towards disorder. The work put into a system and its output, etcetera, etcetera... In global terms, this social engineering had protected a relative handful of innocent people for a brief span of time.

But time was pressing: it was time to move on. He had said as much, once, though cryptically, to his closest supporters and advisors, knowing that they were buoyant at the power he had vested in them, but not knowing that even they could not be trusted, not yet, if ever, with his most ambitious and far-reaching plans. All he had said was: 'I am developing a novel, and perhaps truly global approach to foreign policy and the problems the world faces,' leaving them for the time being to draw their own conclusions. He wondered at that moment whether, when he was barely dead and gone, they would fight over the scraps of the body politic, just as, minutes after his death, people had stripped the armour and clothing from the body of William the Conqueror. Quellan had no faith in human nature but hoped nevertheless that his Werod, the individuals within it, had developed into something better than the run-of-the-mill example of *Homo sapiens*.

After dictating a couple of letters, one to the armed forces chiefs, the other a congratulatory note to the Regional Hospital Guilds Association, Quellan, alone again, thought long and hard about his global models, pulling encrypted files from his desk drawer. He put on one of his more-played CDs, Rameau: *Castor and Pollux: Choeurs & Danses*, glanced at his most secret of documents; then after twenty minutes put the music off, suddenly finding it irritating, and sat gazing at his plans in deep, pensive mood, a brooding mood that shut out the beauty of the day. Then, after he had finished reading an article from the latest edition of his favourite scientific journal, when another hour had passed, he moved to the window again and gazed out over the embankment from his nondescript anonymous office. The people, distant, seemed to move in an ordered, respectful fashion, as did the vehicles on the road, as did the river traffic that ploughed steadily through the gentle swell, churning briefly the grey-green water. There was, yes, a certain beauty and quiet splendour in all of this. But it could not last: it was on borrowed time. The summertime Arctic ice cap had all but gone and would only be part restored by the next seasonal change in the relative inclination of the planet. Average annual global temperatures had risen by 2.45 degrees Kelvin, since the 1990s. Tipping point would soon be reached, the point of no return. Earth population 8.9 billion... India, China, growing in economic terms too, challenging the envious and ever-watchful, declining United States of America, with its frequent malaria outbreaks, its summer fires and water shortages, its killing ozone pollution, its catastrophic hurricanes, tornados, droughts and floods, and, perversely but inevitably during this global climate warming acceleration, its murderous winters. Britain had consistently achieved, since Dain Alvis's time, its carbon emission targets: the US, realizing the position and feeling its effects, had belatedly begun to make a meaningful reduction, but one made much less meaningful in global terms by the swelling, still-polluting Asian economies and by a resurgent and heedless Russian empire. Billions of words were spent on the problem of climate, but Science and the world would have to find the answers fast and take action.

Quellan knew the truth and it was a terrible truth. He had thus set up scientific working parties of the very best brains in the country, himself included, to address the problem. He was beginning to manage this matter to the virtual exclusion of all other business, trusting his loyal Werod deputies to handle everything else. Of course, the inner circle of science members and regular delegates were diehard Werod, too, but Quellan knew he needed help from a wider group, so these were co-opted through the more obviously official agencies of government.

Everything possible as a solution was being looked at, including the possibility of managing volcanic emissions to cool the planet. At the same time, there was it seemed another problem. Quellan revealed with some trepidation that there were perturbing developments in the United States: influential right-wing politicians and lobbyists there were trying to keep it secret, but he had his sources... They were talking about, urging, pre-emptive action to, on the face of it, reduce the environmental impact of India, China and Russia. What did 'pre-emptive action' portend? A nuclear strike? Quellan voiced what his various senior councils, scientific and military felt, namely that the US feared marginalization and isolation: those vast oceans on two sides that had been a blessing in the twentieth century, that had protected them from the worst of the carnage of two World Wars, enabling them to develop and grow powerful in relative peace, had now become a curse as they began to watch the rest of the world doing business without them. The US was still a massive military power, dangerous and unpredictable in its growing paranoia. Everyone agreed with Quellan that Britain should work closely with the US and support it, if only to determine its intentions. 'We need to be watchful and we need to prepare,' Quellan said.

People long after remembered some of the edicts of the time, such as that from a year earlier:

By Order: 31 January 2041

Whosoever raises his hand against his fellow citizen, commits atrocity against the person through malevolent intent, carelessness, selfishness, or for the indulgence of sadistic, sociopathic or other motivation or other reason that is deemed indefensible, shall be deemed equally to have raised his hand against the State and be punished accordingly.

Alex Quellan, Leader, Prime Minister, Head of the Armed Forces of His Majesty's Government.

The people knew little of the mind of their Leader, however, knew nothing of what now fully occupied his prodigious mental energies. They saw only his evident outward success with Law and Order, knew what he had achieved to date. They sensed his power, and that of the Werod, and they understood the meaning of respect, and in truth most enjoyed a degree of contentment. Many though wondered about the growing problems of the world and were uneasy, wondering how the government could and would respond to the challenges. There was much debate and many views were expressed. There was anger and enthusiasm, sometimes inward looking, at other times directed at other nation states. It was in this year that

Alex Quellan began to keep coded diaries of events and related statistics, linking these data to his hardened scientific view of the most important issue of the time. No one would be allowed access to these observations and scientific analyses; not until the time was right, not until he chose to release this information.

17. *Poor old Briony*

Late morning. Briony Daniels made her way to the ladies' room on the upper floor of the squat but vast rectangular building that nestled in the Hertfordshire countryside, a building surrounded by landscaped gardens, with mature trees, on all four sides, in the middle of a larger open area of scrubland and coarse grass beyond a high inner fence that made surveillance by the company's security people easier. Aside from the generally unimpressive look of the building's main bulk, it did have the redeeming feature of an impressive pentagonal arched entrance of translucent blues and greys which led into the marbled entrance hall wherein spouting dolphin sculptures in the centre of a circular white-marble pool spurted and gurgled water, which pattered and splashed continuously over the rippling glinting surface. To one side, and beneath the spreading enclosing arms of a double staircase there was a big rectangular screen which every seven seconds showed a different picture of snowy scenes from the South of France or the Swiss Alps, until all twenty-seven scenes were revealed to the waiting visitor and he returned to his first view. The scenes were linked, tenuously in one or two instances, to premises owned by the company, Hoffnung-Larousse International.

The building complex was vast with most of it, iceberg-like, below the surface. Its subterranean areas, covering many hectares, housed air-conditioned laboratories and all their support services; and underground too was the maximum-security wing wherein viruses up to and including the latest Level Five entities were researched with the very greatest of care. This part of the subterranean world of Hoffnung-Larousse led via a long antiseptically clean and polished corridor to an above-ground bunker-like building hidden among some dark conifers some three hundred and fifty yards north-east but still within the well-patrolled and electronically monitored triple fencing of the inner perimeter. Nothing and no one could get in or out of the place without setting off the all the alarms, here and in Whitehall and at the army camp four miles to the south where regular army were housed alongside rotating squads of SAS and Armed Werod. Response time for this outside assistance was planned to be three minutes and fifty seconds when a swarm of helicopter-borne special forces would arrive to deal with any terrorist threat. This was in addition to the existing military and 'other' support which was effectively resident at the complex and stood ready at all times for the worst-case scenario. Further, in the event of that worst-case scenario, bomb-proof shelters had been constructed almost a mile underground in the chalk beds where there now existed a facility to destroy the company's entire stock of Level Three, Four and Five viruses, so that there could be no possibility of their survival, theft or escape.

The company, once just Hoffnung Pharmaceuticals in the UK, was now merged with Larousse into Hoffnung-Larousse International, and was, as they say, a major world player, and technically the joint leader in viral research and vaccine and anti-viral drugs development. It was the favoured child of the government: thirty-seven per cent of its sales were linked directly to government contracts as were sixty-seven per cent of its funded research projects; hence the official and massive security presence for what was still nominally a private sector operation.

So Briony Daniels had to please two masters, her company's topmost hierarchy (though she, too, had a seat on the Board of Directors UK) and the government, usually in the shape of officials or representatives of Whitehall and the MOD. It was though a trick or balancing act she had managed many years before over a seven-month period when still married to Daniel Howard, when she was more properly Howard-Hawksmoor, since she had insisted on the retention of her maiden name. It was around then that she had started her second extra-marital affair, this time with Geoff Daniels, tennis and squash player, extreme sports enthusiast, chemist and handsome and charming company climber whom she had finally married rather ostentatiously and gaudily in Antigua at the end of an ill-tempered divorce.

Some days Briony looked her fifty-nine years: others she didn't. Today was a bad day, and if she needed reminding that this was the case, the ladies' room mirror, in the bright lights, the overly bright lights illuminating the normally pleasing pastel shades of the executive washroom provided a cold and clinical lack of reassurance befitting its business-like scientific location in this purpose-built complex. She looked at the once attractive mouth of the woman in front of her: the lips were thinner, much thinner now, and somehow the lipstick she had chosen cheapened their appearance, made her look amateurish in the application of her make-up, like a child experimenting with make-up, as she had done so long ago. Her eyes, still bright and beautiful at times had today lost their sparkle, accentuating the crows' feet at the corners. Her forehead was lined, too - today, it was inescapable, and she could not help noticing. The tension, the inner questioning, the judgement and decisions her position in the company forced her to make were combining with time to weather her face from within. Her hair, neatly done up in a bun, made her look severe, and surely it did need colouring again? She sighed, then nearly jumped out of her skin when a colleague came in, speaking to her in passing, shaking her out of her reverie. The woman in the mirror looked momentarily guilty: Briony herself, turning her back on her reflection, smiled as she answered, thinking that her younger colleague looked at her oddly. But looking again at her own image she felt better, more business-like, ready to face the day, the spell of despondency broken.

There was an important meeting today. Most of them were not: the usual weekly staff briefings and so on, which had become in the main routine information exchanges about such matters as the progress of the post-graduate research students or relatively routine research findings. Of course, given the nature of their work, all the meetings were important - perhaps it was just her state of mind. Today's meeting though was one of especial significance, a red-letter day. It was one of a series of six linked to a top-secret government initiative. And top secret meant top secret: top secret as though your very life depended on letting not a word escape your lips, which was probably how matters stood. This was the second in the series, the first having been held nine months earlier. A senior scientific government representative would be present, and a report would have to go directly to the Prime Minister himself, a report she would have to sign. So, it was important, so important, that the terms of reference of the meeting were right and that at its close clear objectives had been set. Moreover, the purpose of the project, its *raison d'être*, must rest with Briony and Briony alone - top secret. Discussions of political considerations driving this dangerous research were proscribed and must remain locked in Briony's mind and the minds of a half-dozen other people. In her mind's eye, anticipating the event, she could in the bright washroom, the executive washroom, see instead the softly lit, plush, panelled boardroom now.

She allowed herself to think of her friend Caroline Hartson, fifty-eight, calm and stately, and just retired from her practice in Exeter and moved to Lyme Regis. Retirement: perhaps she should have retired. Caroline had been a popular GP. Not a meteoric career, but Caroline had been happy, content, balanced, and had gotten out at the right time. Why had she, Briony, ever this urge to be the high flier, even now against all the competition from her younger colleagues, that endless stream of increasingly younger-looking graduate students, or even established PhDs who looked like they could be her daughters or sons? Thoughts of Caroline, her old school and long-time friend, suddenly reminded her of the set she and first husband Daniel had for a time hung around with. Those dinner parties at the Lacocks.... It was their house that impressed her at the time, but now, she felt, she and her new husband were probably doing even better in a material sense. But at what cost? Simon Lacock - how easy it had all been for him... business and business consultancy and gambling on the stock exchange, compared with the work she had put in ... But would she ever really know how well they had done? Would they renew their friendship? It was unlikely, she was thinking: it was more than seven years since she had bumped into Lizzie in Bristol. Promises of renewing their friendship, of seeing each other again, were made, but as so often happens with such chance encounters, it had come to nothing and the years had passed by.

Her new set, relatively new, included Veronica Newton, widow of the late joint Nobel winner, Patrick. The grim thought occurred to her as she made her way along the carpeted corridors that linked the offices: money, houses, even Nobel prizes - you couldn't take any of it with you. To be remembered - was that all there was?

She shook off the thought, then her mind switched to Geoff, her husband, eight years her junior and still looking good - she could see, and her friends told her, as if to say, watch out Briony or someone's going to grab him. Would he leave her as she had left Daniel? Daniel? A picture of Ambleside and other Lake District images flashed into her mind. Daniel, semi-retired, had gone to live there with his new wife Judith. He had a shop now, selling mint cake, water colours and knick-knacks. Why was she still working? Yes, it was true that she was still gripped after all these years by scientific curiosity, but was it just that or was it the promise she had made to that repulsive man, who seemed to have a hold over her, over everyone?

She had at first been fascinated and flattered in equal measure at the prospect of Alex Quellan's visiting her in her place of work. The mysterious, powerful, enigmatic Prime Minister whose clumsy, odd look belied his much-vaunted intelligence. At least, that was how he had been portrayed, and how others who had actually met him talked of him. She remembered how nervous she had been, standing with her colleagues in reception. She had, she remembered, wanted to look business-like and superior, to meet him as an equal or better; but when he arrived his great bulk surprised her, and his gaze met hers fearlessly and somehow offensively, but in a distant way, as though his eyes were those of a blind man; and when his huge hands had clasped her extended right hand she had felt a wave of revulsion which she felt at once he had actually recognized in her own eyes. She had felt exposed, naked. She had cursed herself at the time for her timidity, a veritable rabbit in the headlights, which was not, she had told herself, the real Briony Daniels. Quellan had apparently not seemed put out of countenance by her instantaneous dislike of him. When they were finally alone, with two strapping men positioned outside the door of her office, he had laughed and joked with her as though to put her at her ease. Though still finding him, in spite of his power, wholly unattractive, she none the less had warmed to him, perhaps out of a sense of guilt that she might have judged him too hastily. She had too, she remembered afterwards, felt grateful that he taken so personal an interest in her work. And he had known so much: he seemed to have a graduate's knowledge of virology, had spoken easily about a number of mathematical concepts and about mathematical modelling, and he had given the impression, without trying to, that he really did know a lot, lot more. It was true then, what they had said about him, she had thought at the time.

That was three years ago. Since then he had been to visit her on three further occasions, each time a long interview, each time more serious, confiding, and deeply scientific than the time before. Most recently, during his last visit four months earlier, on a very hot April day, he had pressed her on the pet project, the government project which, he had said, had absolutely the top priority and in respect of which the utmost secrecy was to be maintained at all times. All her encrypted communications, ostensibly from Thames House and the MOD, confirmed this position. But this was her greatest worry: it was the project of projects and it troubled her the most - how to meet the deadlines that Quellan himself had imposed. The work was urgent, vital in the extreme to national security and for that matter for the security of the world. The Americans were on the verge of creating a truly terrible pandemic virus, with as yet little progress on anti-viral drugs to combat its worst effects. If they completed development of the virus and the drugs to alleviate it, if they got there first... A joint operation, she knew because the Prime Minister himself had told her so, a joint operation by MI6, GCHQ and Werod agents had managed to get sufficient information on the development to enable Hoffnung-Larousse to make a genuine attempt at mimicking the virus, which was remarkably close in certain characteristics to a viral weapon they were themselves already working on. The plan was that Britain got the new virus first, and developed the drugs that would enable people to survive it. It might even be possible to develop a vaccine... Quellan had warned her that the Americans were not to be trusted and that a new right-wing paranoia was sweeping the States, a paranoia arising from a view that the US might soon lose its economic pre-eminence and seek to re-establish it with a military solution. Surely, they wouldn't go that far? she had argued feebly. Yes, Quellan had replied, they would: wars had often been fought for economic reasons - a biological war was no different, and he knew that there were voices pushing for an 'effective solution' to the country's problems. It was at the Leader's insistence therefore that only British scientists, thoroughly vetted, be allowed to work on the project. It was that sensitive, that secret. Only British nationals with an historic sense of the post-Second World War special relationship with the US, and strong views on its imperialist nature and its negative impact on the global environment, could be trusted to work against the old ally, even though this work could and should be seen more as a precautionary measure than a 'working against'. This had given Briony problems: it had meant that she had been unable to use her trio of virologists from Beijing: they were instead transferred to entirely different work in the company's other new facility near Manchester.

Werod security and vigilance around the project was unceasing, separate from and matching in intensity the mixed-force security that the complex as a whole enjoyed, though the Werod agents charged with guarding the project appeared to have only the most rudimentary knowledge of what they were guarding. The agents were in the main unobtrusive in plain clothes, sometimes in lab coats, though there was the weekly visit of a very high-ranking uniformed officer. People had gotten used to this over recent months.

As the project moved to what Briony hoped would be the final stages of the first major phase, it seemed to be ever more secret. A parallel, more mainstream viral agent was required, a smokescreen for the main project. In this way the reports that went to Quellan were encrypted, with coded references for example to the surface proteins of the new virus, a ruse possible because there were naturally areas of common ground between the new super virus and the smokescreen virus. Briony had really begun to worry now, it was true, not about how many people knew about the government project but how few. She was beginning to be uncertain about who the security personnel really were, even though most of her staff seemed unperturbed by their presence. She had initially assumed a combination of Werod, MI5, MI6, Special Police units and so on; but as time wore on she had begun to have her doubts, though she could make no sense of her fears - in any case, she did not have time to consider such matters which were outside her sphere of knowledge and influence. And the personal involvement of Prime Minister Quellan both reassured and unnerved her in equal measure, while behind it all was that terrible sense of driving urgency. She felt isolated at times and at these times she was glad indeed that she still had her old senior team around her: Rupert, Lindy and James were a real source of support and solace, even though they were not allowed access to the whole of the picture, certainly not its political dimension. Nervously, they did as they were asked, knowing only that it was on the highest authority and a matter of national security. The teams supporting her senior group in their turn knew even less: many of the brightest minds, younger ambitious colleagues, had been drafted in from Oxford, Cambridge, Leicester, Durham, Sheffield, Bristol and other UK universities to work on one aspect or another but never in a position to determine with any certainty the possible final product; and there were British colleagues from Switzerland and France. All had been vetted by Werod security, and Briony assumed, British intelligence, with, unusually, Prime Minister Quellan having had access to all of the personal files.

So Briony felt she had the world on her shoulders as she busied herself in her first-floor office, answering a couple of 'urgent' e-mails, getting her meeting notes ready. It was a plush office, with three well-cared-for plants, one sitting on the window sill looking out at the bright world beyond. Her PA looked after the plants, tenderly, efficiently, just as she sought to please and nurture her boss: the job was well paid, and she was indeed indispensable, in Briony's view. A haven of refuge sometimes, this room: today though she was in a hurry. There was a lot of work to do this afternoon, below, in the labs, in the bowels of the earth, as she thought of it, or a cold sterile hell from whence a demon might spring none the less. She looked at her watch and realized she had made a mistake: she had a full twenty minutes to spare - time for a hot strong coffee and a couple of shortbread fingers which her PA duly delivered in no time at all, it seemed.

It was a respite, and the hot milky coffee restored her somewhat. She began thinking of Geoff again, and the eight years difference, though at that moment she was positive enough to dismiss that concern. Geoff had recently made a TV appearance defending the company's huge profits at a time of terrible poverty in the third world, which remained thus in a number of vast geographical areas that teemed with people: some countries, though once considered third world, ought really to consider themselves fourth world, the new economic power houses of the Far East. Geoff had been a hit: as well as actually defending the company well and getting patted on the back, he had been a 'natural' on TV and this had given him the idea of a belated career in broadcasting or writing linked to TV science. He had had already, even before his brief TV stardom, an idea for a book about the management or the processes of the industry. And Briony had been encouraging, seeing the childlike enthusiasm in his eyes, but had wondered at the time whether success or failure in this new venture would draw him closer to her or take him away altogether. Her ace in the pack was that she could lean on a publishing friend to smooth the way for him so that in some way her own involvement would be integral to his progress, just as it had been within the company. But not to worry: she was as positive now as she had been worried an hour before. She had to be careful, however: there was Quellan and the project: it was important that Geoff did not stumble onto something in the dangerous enthusiasm of the amateur. She could manage that, she decided, by setting up a meeting with her friend in publishing for six months' time, and she could point Geoff in a direction other than that she had to traverse.

And there was her only daughter, Christine, now twenty-nine and from her union with Daniel. With an absolute certainty she would marry Charles Vanburgh. It was a good marriage, she often caught herself thinking. Then she would feel odd, like some throwback to the days when such things did matter in New England: 'Have you heard whom Charles Vanburgh of the Boston Vanburghs is going to marry? Yes, the eldest, Charles is the eldest, and stands to inherit...' Yet Briony had often a secret momentary smile of pleasure for that very reason. Of course, Christine was in love with Charles, and she was by anyone's reckoning, not just a mother's bias, a beautiful intelligent girl. Her mother could see her now somewhere in a New England landscape of spaciousness: mature trees, long lawns and great houses that stood proudly under a wide deep sky of new other-worldliness, beautiful autumns with cascades of falling burnished leaves piling deep underfoot... She liked New England, but she hoped Christine would reconsider her apparently final decision to be married over there. How could she, her doting mother, afford the time? Had she really given Christine all the time she could? Could she have given more over the years? Perhaps from thence sprang Christine's determination to be married in the States? The doubts again...

Would Prime Minister Quellan spare her for four, five days with the project at a critical point? She knew the answer would be no, so at that very moment, as she drained the last dregs of her coffee, she hit upon the plan of getting her daughter to visit her in the new year, February perhaps. Hopefully she would bring Charles and there would be an opportunity to work on both of them.

The thought made her feel better than ever about this aspect of her life: yes, it might just work: and, besides, she wanted Christine on this side of the Atlantic for another reason altogether. At the back of all her thinking was Quellan: what he had said, what he might say. At their last meeting, one-to-one, he had hammered home not only the need for secrecy, in respect of this matter of utmost national importance, but also the danger of the developing virus itself, something she did not need to be told.

At that meeting, Quellan had been hard in his questioning. He had been kept up to date by one of his own scientists on the senior team, the thin bespectacled weasel-faced man Babington. She knew that Quellan wanted her view however about the feasibility of the project: Quellan wanted certainty, and he was too knowledgeable to hoodwink even if she had dared attempt such a thing. She had been able to recall Babington's face, with its too-close-together grey eyes, long hollow face and tiny sharp nose, even as she looked at Quellan's large fleshy visage. She had not cared whether Babington's reports had been wholly accurate or that any inconsistency or deviation on her part might get him into hot water: she detested him and his easy supercilious manner with Werod security.

Perhaps even though a scientist of the first rank he was also Werod. He was always so insistent on discussing her every step, her every decision. The clinical, sterile nature of the labs really suited Babington: there was something cold and unfeeling about him. Her own regular team members did not like him, either.

But Quellan was different: Quellan scared her. He always seemed to know too much. It was as though, when he was asking a question, he already knew the answer and was just testing her. One or two of her friends in the past had gone on about the nerve-wracking nature of university *vivas*, but her meetings with this strange all-powerful mountain of a man were something quite different. Every time in her dealings with Quellan she had begun with determined pride in her intellect, achievement and standing in the scientific community, but every time Quellan seemed to get the better of her in one way or another. Next time he needled her, she told herself, she would tell him that he could come in and manage the bloody project himself. Even as she thought this, however, she knew it would not happen.

Development of the virus was nearing completion, at breakneck speed. It was only the second real monster to lurk within the company's Level 5 containment facility, and the closer Briony Daniels came to understanding its potential the more angry she got with her senior colleagues, whose anxious faces annoyed her. They guessed at its possible potential, matching it in their minds with other dangerous pathogens: it could infect cells in much the same way as the influenza virus but the newly created monster was even more unpredictable and more dangerous in the way in which it mutated and in its probable effects on the immune system: it was they predicted more deadly in this respect than the H1N1 subtype which had probably killed 100 million people in 1918, and there was something else... Briony had the whole picture, but even she did not *fully* understand how the virus might operate, and what its mortality rate might be, and no one could determine this without seeing its effect on *Homo sapiens* and how the body would respond; and as her trepidation grew so she projected her anxieties and became intolerant of those around her. What were the Americans thinking of? Like many of the self-proclaimed great and more powerful nations during and after the late twentieth century Cold War, they had worked on biological weapons before, often under the guise of being prepared in the event of terrorist use. Had some of these agents actually been tested on people, say in an out of the way African state or on a Pacific island? It had always been an uncomfortable question scientists working for the military did not want to confront. Briony was aware, however, that what they were working on now was something new, something to be feared. In fact, she was already beginning to apply her mind to an anti-viral agent and sketching out the mechanics and logistics of its distribution. She had not even told Quellan of this, though of course at some point she would have to.

Quellan had made an odd request to her at their last meeting: that he be allowed to name the virus; not the scientific name that it would carry as a result of its structure, its protein coatings and so on, but a nickname, a familiar name, something linked, he said, to the burning fever it would induce, something suitably apocalyptic. It would focus all their minds then on how to defend against it. Such talk had terrified her, but she acquiesced in what she saw as this most unsuitable, unscientific and unconscionable of whims. She had to pinch herself at this point to recollect that Quellan was ultimately after saving innocent lives, something he and his Werod had demonstrated in the application of the new, swift and sometimes final justice.

He had not always talked about the project, even though she had been able to see that that was always the way the conversation was going. His interests in science and mathematics were wide-ranging. She had met no one like him. He name-dropped, constantly; but not as people usually did, wanting reflected glory and status from the link: he appeared really to have met a number of her distinguished colleagues, to know what they were working on. Quellan was all-knowing rather than smug - eerily devoid of any trace of vanity.

A particular interest, he had said, was the Yellowstone caldera, a natural disaster waiting to happen. A full eruption, as had happened around six hundred and forty thousand years ago, would wipe out the US as a major power and affect the rest of the world in terms of climate, creating a ten-year near-dark winter. He knew, he had said, that Briony knew this, but he had gone on to say that his government's scientists had now joined their University of Utah colleagues and those from the US Geological Survey in monitoring the position. He had seemed almost musingly fascinated that, should the catastrophic event occur, ninety per cent of those within a thousand kilometres of Yellowstone Park would die, their lungs clogged with hot ash. Skies over Europe would be red for weeks and the long years of depressing deep winter daylight gloom would begin. In the initial eruptions, Oregon, Idaho, Montana, the Dakotas, Washington State, Utah, Colorado, in the US, Alberta, Saskatchewan, British Columbia, in Canada, all deluged with ash. From Boise to Denver to Calgary, all doomed.

He had watched her face as he had spoken, to see the effect of his words, as in a psychological experiment. 'Our close co-operation with the Americans on these matters,' he had concluded,' has given us the opportunity to get close to them in all research areas, including that related to our friend downstairs.' Briony actually smiled now as she recalled her thought at the time: 'surely that's not what he'll want to call it from now on - "our friend downstairs".'

On the 25th of March 2043 Briony arrived at the complex and looked ill. Her hands were visibly shaking. It was not the sight of four young thugs hanging from the lampposts by the side of the main road that had shaken her (part of the Werod destruction of a local gang), nor the briefly televised events from the Balkans, and in Italy and Spain, where savage fighting over water supplies had broken out, nor the devastating Australian storm surge and torrential downpours which had killed thousands, nor even the direst warnings about the global warming tipping point, though this had been high on her worry list until she heard the news from the US. It was that which had shaken her, perhaps more so, paradoxically, because her daughter, with her husband to be, had only two days before arrived safely in England. A narrow escape, a mother's relief...

The Yellowstone caldera had erupted. Everyone was desperate to know to what extent. Had it been massive, with multiple vents? What was the magnitude? How violent? The British government was busy declaring its unstinting support for the governments and people (US and Canadian) of North America. Briony could not get the memory of Alex Quellan's large fleshy face out of her head as she had heard the first reports, and she had been physically shaken by the image. Was this the beginning of the end of all things, like the detonation of some talismanic weapon of power taking all with it? At least, she found herself thinking when she had begun to calm down, it might be the end of those atrocious unbearable summers, with their heat-induced, strength-sapping inertia, and scuffling sweaty people seeming ready to tip into widespread civil unrest, assuming they had been able to summon up the energy or overcome their very real fear of Alex Quellan's law enforcers. The millions of tons of sulphur would probably cool the planet; but the loss of life, and the unknown global effects, the unpredictability of longer-term climate effects, the global consequences... Perhaps, after all, it was not the apocalypse, long dreaded, but not really expected? She had to know. And she felt she had to know what Alex Quellan, now speech-making in the capital, knew. As she listened for the day's news to unfold, she told herself not to be silly: this was merely an amazing coincidence, and nothing more. She would throw herself into her work. Christine was safe, Christine was safe...

18. *Surt*

It was not the cataclysm many had feared. True, it had left three or four thousand dead and hundreds more were missing; and six million had fled their homes, going in all directions in a radiating pattern away from Yellowstone Park. But it had not been *the* eruption, with multiple vents, a disaster which would have laid waste most of North America. Even so, two huge vents had had opened up, like vast Roman candles, spewing fire, and above which hovered mountainous skies of obscuring, visibly impenetrable, ash. Its power combined with its eventual consequences would make it five times as destructive as the Mount St Helens eruption in the nineteen eighties. But it had not been *the* eruption, Briony repeated to herself - the dreaded super eruption it might have been. None the less, wildlife in the area had been devastated, wiped out; and globally, temperatures would, they said, fall on average by a couple of degrees for two or three years, as sulphur compounds and particulate matter of various sorts circulated in the upper atmosphere, high above the trials and tribulations, the comings and goings of busy humankind. But humankind was about its business again and the global warming trend had received but a temporary check, or such was the wisdom of the world's meteorologists and climate specialists. The detail may have been argued over, but the consensus was that the Yellowstone had given mankind, humankind, a brief respite and an opportunity to address the main threat to life, which was human pollution of the atmosphere.

It was suggested that though there might be another eruption tomorrow, or the next week, this was highly unlikely as, in crude, simplistic terms, the caldera's pressure had been relieved. More likely now was the prospect of the catastrophic eruption postponed to the far distant future, generations ahead. Under ash-laden North American skies such counsel was reassuring.

In sitting with his Parliamentary colleagues, his Werod Council and associate members, Alex Quellan spoke, with stern face and slow deliberate hand gestures, about the precarious state of the world, and with his Privy Council, the leader, the Lord Protector (as some were now calling him), talked of how they should now close with the United States in renewed friendship, to outmanoeuvre the isolationist paranoid elements seeking to control the country's foreign policy. He knew, he said, that the US was looking to see where Britain would position itself in the fast-changing world. His Council agreed and agreed further that the Yellowstone event had provided a natural breathing space, a useful pause for thought for everyone, as much for the British security services and the Russian FSB as for the CIA, as the US looked to reorganize after those few terrifying first days.

As the meeting drew to a close, in camera, where a leaded window looked out at leaden skies, over a sluggish and leaden Thames, Quellan said, enigmatically, 'I think the timing of the Yellowstone caldera's next eruption is unlikely to matter to most people.' When pressed, politely, to explain, he waved a large dismissive hand and added, 'We shall see, of course, and I suppose your god and everyone else's god will see.' This seemed to mean to some that everything was in the lap of the gods. One or two were thinking that their Leader's recent bout of ill health - pleurisy falling hard on the heels of a kidney infection, he had informed them - had temporarily affected if not his reason then certainly his mood. He did not seem quite himself. Quellan, however, did they but know it, smiled inwardly that among those 'one or two', for which read eight or nine, someone might actually be daring to think of the possibility, even in the middle future, of a new leader. There was even a comment or two passed, unchallenging, careful and low-key, barely whispered, and just idly speculative, within the 'Cabinet': 'The Chief's fine - only in his mid-forties.' And the reply: 'Yes, whatever the position, it's not possible really to look beyond the Chief.' And the Chief himself knew this to be the case.

The winter lingered, giving way to a traditional springtime: 'When that Aprille his sweete shours...' And many another poet besides Chaucer had had something to say about life's annual resurgence in the northern hemisphere, a resurgence that in recent decades seemed to have had its normal starting point shifted out of its temporal position by the 'global warm-up', and the absence of regular 'proper winters', the old people complained.

The blossoms, cherry, hawthorn, blackthorn and red-may, loudly proclaimed through scent and sight the full flourishing of spring, a bright and beautiful festooning of white, pink and red seeking to drive away winter's semi-mourning pall of cold grey. Yet there were few really bright days, and the Yellowstone event began worldwide what was an almost perceptible dimming.

Deep within the Hoffnung-Larousse complex a new life was ready, though to be precise not a true life-form, the virus. Quellan had by now 'christened' or named it Surt, a suitably apocalyptic name from Norse mythology. Thought Briony and her immediate team:' Now we *and* the Americans have it'; and frantically they, she and her team, laboured determinedly, painstakingly, unceasingly, and now with official sanction, on the means to combat the virus.

Briony worked now permanently in a state of anxiety, if not terror. The stakes, the responsibility, were too high for any one person to cope with: how much more difficult for a someone, however brilliant, now turned sixty and with her hopelessly small team of close helpers, however supportive. Why was she still doing this? It had been a terrible mistake. She begged Quellan either to let her destroy the virus or else to massively increase the resources, the expertise needed to develop the required anti-viral agents. And Geoff was going to leave her; she could see it in his eyes; she knew it from the increase in the number of presents he was buying her. Overcompensating... Yet even that hardly seemed to matter to her now: it was this potential monster Surt that increasingly preyed upon her mind to the virtual exclusion of all else.

It was the twenty-ninth of June in the year of our Lord twenty-forty-five, and Silas Wood, now fifty-two, stepped out into his south-facing rear garden, and the sun warmed his face as he looked over his day's work. A barbecue next week and the garden was all but ready: just run over the lawn one more time a couple of days before. A period of warm weather forecast, long evenings... it would be a full moon tonight... long evenings, sipping wine and contentedly watching the dying of the light, and the fading of the song birds' calls... contentedly...

There was another reason for his delight in life: his latest blood tests - and he had checked on his health a number of times in recent years - had all come back clear. He had had three, or was it four, bad weeks. He had tried to remember when it had started and had put it down to a night of vigorous sex at the end of which he had been unable to achieve orgasm. Lindy always said that didn't matter; but equally he had never believed her. Silas had at the time put it down to middle age, the various crises of which, he believed, would inevitably include his performance in the bedroom. The event, as on one or two less than satisfactory occasions before, had made him think of ageing and of his mortality. Worse was to follow on this latest occasion: he had had pains, he thought in the region of his kidneys, he was visiting the toilet more, and he had a gripping persistent ache across his pelvis. One of his testicles ached, and though he had previously been diagnosed as having epididymitis, or some such non-life-threatening condition, which periodically caused a lump to flare up in one of his testicles, he thought that this time the lump that had appeared looked larger. He had had a couple of nights too, waking and having to catch his breath, then feeling that something unnatural was coursing through the blood vessels in his chest, arms and legs. How he hated feeling ill, or unwell, in the small hours, when he felt so vulnerable, so weak, so mortal.

Yet all these symptoms had begun to disappear as he started to exercise, a prolonged and vigorous walk each day 'around the block', a rectangle of pleasant summer tree-lined avenues that enable him to start and finish at his house, a circuit of almost three miles. But he had still waited with some trepidation for his blood test results, fearing after all a cancer of the pancreas, of the liver, the kidneys, the testicles or the prostate.

He had been to the doctor's that morning, a pleasant twenty-minute walk during which he had steeled himself for his rectal examination, visualizing himself in the foetal position awaiting the suitably gloved and greased probing digit. He had had such an examination a couple of years earlier, when his benign enlargement of the prostate had been diagnosed.

Lindy had this time been a bit concerned about him, though she usually said that he was 'imagining things' or that he was 'a bit of a hypochondriac'.

In the event, the examination was over very quickly, with the doctor, beforehand, giving him the good news that all his results were normal.

Silas had come back home with a spring in his step, smiling secretly at people out walking, at the bustle around the little shopping precinct, at an elderly couple at the bus stop, and at people out with their dogs on the pleasantly warm summer morning. There were so many delightful people in the world, going quietly about their own business, getting on with life.

He was back home at eleven-twenty and had made himself coffee, and toast topped with a sliced-up large tomato and half a dozen portobello mushrooms cooked in a drizzle of olive oil - a healthy brunch, he thought to himself.

Now, in the garden, soaking up the rays of the sun, squinting gratefully as he lifted his face to the sky, he was looking forward to the long summer vacation, after a busy year at the university. Life seemed good at that moment, a gift to be savoured.

It was around 1pm: Lindy would be home soon. Silas, to celebrate his good news, decided that they would go out to eat that evening. Why not, while it was quiet: the whole family, well, all the children and their partners -though Nancy had just ditched her latest boyfriend - would be filling the house in five days' time. Lindy's parents were not after all coming because Lindy's mother was unwell and might have to undergo an operation. Mortality...ill health... Silas put the thoughts out of his mind as he stood looking up at a gull in aerial battle with a crow.

It was 1.30 pm and Silas had just seen the lunchtime TV news... a new reservoir to be built north of London...perhaps no more riots then... new statues of Dain Alvis to go up in Nottingham and Manchester... the US tornadoes... the Italian flood disaster... Yellowstone aftermath... south of England malaria figures... the cricket... and a trailer for another special on climate change... a new scare story, as if one were needed now... the flood of another kind, refugees from Ukraine... England the best place to live in a world with decreasing levels of violent crime... the official statistics...

Where was Lindy? Silas was impatient to tell her his good news. He wandered out into the garden again, perched himself on a patio chair and watched the birds passing overhead or swooping in and out of the dark branches of his lone conifer... tall, a high-rise dwelling for our avian friends, he would often say.

At 2.30 pm Silas began to worry and could get no response from her mobile. She should have been home at the very latest an hour ago, even allowing for a quick visit to the local shop. But perhaps that was it - shopping: she had said, and he had forgotten. Or perhaps they had kept her working late after all. She was owed half a day too, given all the extra hours she had put in lately. That very morning, she had started work at seven-fifteen.

Silas was relieved therefore, whilst in the process of making himself a cup of tea, to hear the sound of the key in the front door. It was comfortable sound: 'get in and put the kettle on' they often said - like an old couple set in their ways. Silas went to greet his wife with the good news that had kept him in buoyant and then contented mood all morning and into the afternoon.

On seeing her he was horror-struck. The world was out of joint. Lindy stood ashen faced before him, a limp careworn aged doll. This is not my wife, was his first thought; then he rushed forward to embrace her.

Terrible thoughts raced through Silas's mind as he took his wife into the back room, his arm around her all the time, and asking her in a whisper of trepidation what the matter was. He helped her onto the settee which faced the open French doors. The bright day outside, and the warm breeze that moved the curtains ever so slightly, and the noise of the birds, mocked now his erstwhile smug complacent mood: the thought entered unbidden: his earlier joy seemed like a thing he should feel guilty about: he had tempted fate with his self-centred relief. Lindy had begun to shake her head from side to side as she sat on the settee, a forlorn and tormented figure. She could barely catch her breath, alternately crying and gasping for air as she was. A panic attack.

'Lindy! Lindy! For God's sake, what's the matter!' He could feel his courage beginning to fail him: something terrible had happened. One of the children?

He asked the question. She shook her head violently again and again and made as if to speak. Instead she screamed or shouted, at the top of her voice in way which pierced Silas to the core of his being: it was primeval, like the cry a wounded animal. She was like someone demented, not his Lindy. She was so distant from him, locked in with her own wild thoughts. The beauty had gone from her face, which was screwed up in agony: she was like a middle-aged and ugly complete stranger from whom, briefly, he wanted to flee. He watched the curtains stir slightly: something to look at. Then he suddenly had the presence of mind to fetch some brandy that she always kept for cooking and found the half bottle that had been used to feed the Christmas cake. His hands shook and he found himself uttering some prayer-like invocation as he over-filled a silly little shot glass, the brandy spilling over the edge of the glass over the work surface as he turned to hurry back. He almost fell as he re-entered the lounge, and he stared at her rigid limbs and torso and her face, which had now become a mask, set in a fixed stare. Then suddenly, as though trying to ward off what to Silas was an unseen terror, she roared in a deep savage voice: 'Noooo! Noooo !' Two loud and long, deep and angry calls, like a grating sound from the depths of her being...

Silas stared not at his wife but at the face of someone demonically possessed. He did not believe in such things; but he did not know what to think. 'Drink this, drink this,' he urged, holding up the two-thirds full glass in front of her face. In his other hand he held the half-bottle: he guessed there was enough left for seven or eight normal measures.

Her staring eyes were tired and shadowy, her lips thin and pale. She did not or could not look at him. Instead she flung out an arm and dashed the glass from his grasp with such force that it flew across the room.

Silas, at his wits' end, reacted instantaneously and slapped her hard across the face, just like that. He had never raised a hand to her before nor ever before contemplated such a thing.

She looked shocked, and turned to stare wildly at him as though awakening from a dream. She strained to recognize him. Seconds later she felt the hard rim of the bottle being forced between her teeth, and she began choking down the brandy. She could feel it burning her throat, dribbling over her chin as she coughed and spluttered only half protesting. Then she felt him clinging limpet-like to her body, which shook with his sobs.

They sat in silence on the settee for a while feeling the warm breeze of the bright day wafting into the room. He would wait for her to try and speak, and she seemed instinctively to understand this. She tried then to speak, three or four times she tried, but each time tears welled up in her big brown eyes. In the end the words came; haltingly to begin with as she choked still with anger and despair. Now the remaining mouthfuls of brandy were truly a palliative for her mental torment.

'He's going to kill us, Silas,' she said at last. Nearly an hour had passed since she had returned home.

'Who, whaaat...' He whispered in reply, his mind filling with a picture of a knife-wielding maniac about to burst into the room.

'Alex Quellan is going to kill us ...'

'Why us? You must be mistaken. No one in our family has done anything wrong... committed a crime...' He remembered that brief interrogation years earlier and shuddered.' You must be mistaken,' he repeated. 'No.' She persisted, determinedly. It had to be said. 'He's going to kill us all. Not the family... You don't understand.'

Silas struggled to understand; he wanted to understand, and he feared that she would at any moment become frustrated and angry with him for not understanding.

'Silas, Silas, my lovely Silas', she sobbed, controlling herself with evident difficulty. Then she said at last: ‘No, no there is no time: we must warn the children.’

‘It is the family, then?’ he said in wild-eyed alarm, his mind racing ahead to find a course of action that would safeguard them all.

Then she really told him, her eyes fixed in earnest yet pitying look staring into his: ‘He’s going to kill us all -everyone on the planet. No, he has killed us all. He’s released a new... a new virus, the Surt virus...’

Silas looked at her as though she had gone mad, but then shrank back from her as though from some terrifying apparition. Outside, the birdsong sounded as a shrill mocking on the sensitive air and was if from another dimension. The visible spectre of Death seemed about to walk into the room. Silas shivered and went deathly pale. The look on his wife’s face was as the stare of a Gorgon, transfixing, petrifying.

They talked for more than five hours. They found another half bottle of brandy to help them on their way, and in the end, cups of tea: they needed to try and think straight, not have minds fuddled with alcohol. But they could eat nothing.

Lindy spoke, sometimes in fits and starts, sometimes lucidly, calmly and at length, breaking off to answer his questions. He had not even been aware that Alex Quellan had ever visited the Hoffnung complex, had been so interested and involved in its work, much less that his wife's team, or Briony Daniels' team were carrying out such important and dangerous work on his instruction. Lindy had let nothing slip, had dared not let anything slip. If he had known... if only... but what would he have been able to do, a nobody really and powerless... a bio-weapons development... treason if you said a word, he knew that... and of course he was keenly aware, somewhere in the dark and fearful underground of his mind that he had never spoken a word about his own interrogation...if only... the world?...everyone?... it could not be true...God Almighty!

Lindy with a painful effort told all she knew. A dozen people had arrived at ten in the morning, one a woman, but all dressed in the black of the Werod and top ranking, she supposed, Werod thegns, as they were now calling them, with Werod and Breakthrough Party insignia, all the trappings of Dain Alvis's vision of a modern Anglo-Saxon police state, or at least as Quellan had interpreted, created and applied it. Their leader had called the whole of Briony's senior team into the small conference hall underground, wherein there was a large plasma screen and the facility to link directly to the Prime Minister himself; a hot-line in effect with the advantage of two-way visual contact. Its security had regularly been reviewed and thoroughly checked. Briony had had to use it twice, one-to-one communications, updates with and for Quellan alone.

The group of scientists assembled there, twelve in all, were told to expect a communication from the Leader, a communication of the greatest national importance. They would not be allowed to leave the room at all during the transmission: the doors would be locked. They were required to hand over any communication devices... the internal phone would be cut off. It was deadly serious... There was an envelope with a paper in it - for them to read when the telecast was over.

Briony had been absolutely terrified: she was shaking and could barely speak and had not questioned the orders they had been given. She knew that three days earlier 'material' had been taken from the Level Five containment area. She suspected Babington but had been frozen into inaction, checking the containment area time and time and time again until she felt she would go mad. She had told Lindy about it only an hour before the visit of the Werod.

Quellan had appeared on the screen, several tense minutes after the doors had been locked and the room vacated by the dutiful Werod elite. He was in centre screen opposite them in their windowless conference facility, where they had waited silently, the only sound perceptible that of the air conditioning. Nervousness had spread, taking its cue from Briony Daniels. Quellan had been alone, spread in a throne-like seat that looked to be made of granite and carved with something like runic symbols. There had been a collective gasp when he appeared thus; not least because he was dressed in monk-like apparel, with a great dark cowl shading part of his face.

He had thanked the team for their efforts, the whole team, adding that all was now ready. They had looked at one another and at Quellan with stupefied faces: what did he mean, all was now ready? Then Briony, with a shaking voice, her lower lip quivering, had said that development on the anti-virus, new drugs, and a vaccine, was in its infancy. Quellan, sitting like an alien being in his odd perch pulled back his cowl, revealing his great shaven head and just smiled. His facial appearance had sent a chill through them: that fleshy face and shaven head, like a convict or an ascetic monk, a religious zealot... and those impenetrable eyes...

There would, he had said, be no need for such measures. And no, the Americans had nothing, nothing at all: this had been his brainchild and his alone. He understood that Briony had acted in the belief that she was protecting Britain, he said; so, she could not be blamed and he, Alex Quellan, would take full responsibility for all that was going to happen.

The Werod understood only that there was something of world-wide significance about to happen and that they must play their part in a global immunization programme. Lindy broke off at this point while Silas remained a spectator, appalled and silent as the grave. Gathering herself, she resumed. It had been terrible she said: she had been able to smell fear in that room, and a tension building all the time to an unbearable level. Quellan had been icy calm at this point. Two of the team, from an audience of twelve, had already started sobbing. She would never, she said, forget it, the moment when Quellan had uttered those words: 'Surt has been released around the world.' Then

Lindy laughed grimly, bitterly, saying that 'never' was now a relative word.

Mankind, humankind, Quellan had gone on to say, had consistently, over the centuries, proved itself unworthy of continued existence. Had he not striven, he said, to wipe out evil in this country? People were relatively much safer, safer than they were and safer than the actual and potential victims of crime in other countries. Everyone knew this. Then Quellan had briefly become angry; but controlled and lucid none the less. The evil, the viciousness, the cruelty, the sadism of Man had gone on through the ages and had often gone unpunished. Man, in his barbarian state, might have had some excuse but he doubted it: all those cruel, unusual and inventive tortures and methods of execution, from the Vikings, back to the Roman Empire and beyond. Even the half-educated knew of some of the headline monsters thanks to mass communication and the writers of history. But had not his reign demonstrated, highlighted the fact, that there were many evil people in society at any one time? And did not in any case History's mass crimes require mass participation, active participation and a collective blind-eye? Many crimes of war, and peace, crimes of terrible cruelty had gone virtually unrecorded or were conveniently forgotten because they did not suit society's simplistic judgements... society's avoidance of the moral implications of wilful ignorance of evil deeds committed by all nations, evil deeds allowed to go on and not spoken of because this would disturb the feeling of ... 'I can't remember what he was saying here', Lindy groaned, 'I really can't; but it was disturbing: he really made us feel guilty, feel dirty...' There had, he said, been no change: it was still happening around the globe: in Africa, Asia, South America, in Europe, too; often cowardly criminal deviants but sometimes state-supported militias, killing women, children, anything they could get, he said, their dirty mongrel paws on. '" But let us not insult the canine world by calling them dogs..." That's what he said, Silas,' Lindy went on. Selfishness was the watchword of humankind with glimmers of humanity ... but there was no hope under the present circumstances. Keep on breeding and keep on polluting the planet until nothing would be left, until warming accelerated, as it surely would, and everything would be burnt to a cinder. Earth, he said, was on course to become like Venus unless something was done. We could not rely on the greedy self-serving world leaders and their corporate friends because it was too late and he, Alex Quellan would in any case no longer tolerate the hypocrisy of it all. Greed while others starved in their millions: peace and democracy proclaimed by people who were getting money for guns from murderous regimes, by one route or another. There are too many people: there must be the possibility of a new beginning...

'He said that all those wars through the centuries, all that viciousness and vainglory, for ideas, for kings, dictators, emperors, countries, even freedom, were worthless. That was what people wanted to do so let them. And there was what he called the sanctimonious and hypocritical grieving of the state after the event, yet ready to fight again - "Soldiers and civilians killed in their millions for self-serving tyrants or money-grubbing plutocrats" those were his words. He said that an army should have one purpose: to protect its people from the enemy within and never set foot in a foreign land to do it. Could he have lived a thousand years through history, he leaned forward and shouted as if he were on a podium, he could not have satisfied his heart's desire to see all the tormentors, the torturers of history, so often cowards at the core, squirm and die, be wiped out from pole to pole, the world forever cleansed of their degenerate genes. He said those who had escaped justice in the past would now be made to pay through their descendants...

'He grew truly terrifying at this point... Then he had gone on with it, this final lecture for our ears only. And as he had spoken we knew that all the time, because he had told us, and because Briony had told me of the missing cultures... we knew with an absolute certainty, you could see the truth of it in Quellan's face, that Surt was doing its work, replicating itself billions and billions of times in the bodies of its victims and beyond -it's airborne, deadly, it's an unstoppable plague...' She paused, breathless, her heart pounding, seeing still that Silas did not want to understand the words she was uttering. But she went on: it all had to be said. She had probably forgotten something important, she said, because of the shock of it all: you could forget things like that, in shock, as though they had not happened and then recall them years later... 'Years later...'she repeated the words ruefully.

'He had seen, he told us, that there was no way out. Population, industry, pollution, including carbon emissions and methane levels, and global mean temperature - all rising. The millions of words in all the world's journals would have never made a scrap of difference, because it had not up to now. The purpose of life was to increase complexity, to increase the entropy of the universe - I didn't really understand this link -this link - except to think he must have gone mad...' She paused again, repeating the word mad over and over and shaking her head, but the presence of Silas and the fact that he was squeezing her hands helped her to continue. 'This had been the case from the outset, and Man had inevitably through a law of nature and not of his own volition become locked into technological developments which had poisoned the planet and was accelerating its decline. The only chance for Life was in Death, he told us. And Surt, why Surt? Because, he said, it was the ancient Norse fire demon that rose up at the final battle, the Viking Armageddon, whatever - I can't remember the name - and destroys everything, even the gods, so a new start can be made. What new start? What new start?' She was struggling but Silas patiently waited for her to continue. 'He said some would survive, perhaps half of one per cent, though perhaps none. He had left his diaries with a key code, he said, but it would take months to unravel... even for a scientist and mathematician. It was all there; all his thoughts -his vision, he said. They are outside in my car where his bloody Werod people put them... Why me and not Briony? Some would survive: he had made provision for them, for a possible new world. But not for him personally... He would be leaving us, he said, but was as yet undecided on the means.

'He's mad. We did not understand him. There was something else, something odd: it's been blotted out from my mind. I can't remember. It was weird, weird. He, Quellan, looked so weird, so detached from this world reality... as though he didn't belong here at all.' Lindy looked hard at her silent ashen-faced listener and could see tears welling in his eyes. 'He went on to tell us that all matter is sentient to a point and has an inbuilt driving force, and has had from the outset, that hydrogen in its primitive form, not its - never mind. Everything tends to a greater complexity, a higher level of being - inevitability. He seemed quite lost in it all, just as we are all now lost... But that was not it: what else was there? No., it's gone, gone, gone...'

They sat there in silence for several minutes, Silas desperately afraid but still not wanting to believe, still wanting to wake from the nightmare.

The children, the children, the children... they would have to be contacted. Quellan had issued them all, the team, with a supply of poison: a dozen phials each, for them and for their families, delivered by his loyal Werod in a secure box to Briony's office for her to open and distribute. Lindy produced one from her pocket and Silas uttered a cry at this point, turned away and began to sob. But Lindy was determined now on this matter above all others. 'It was an act of kindness, Silas, should the worst happen. Surt is terrible; my God, Surt is terrible. Quellan named it after the fire demon for a second reason... because it burns, it burns with fever and terrible pain. He knew, he bloody well knew all along...'

She had to be strong, exhausted though she was: Silas did not fully understand and would not be able to face the difficult decisions when they came. She had to be cruel. 'It will begin with sneezing like the bubonic plague, and a sore throat. Within hours, a headache like the worst migraine, then shooting pains all over the body. There will be convulsions and vomiting, a burning temperature and pain, external and internal sores, in the nose, the mouth, internally a rapid breakdown of some aspects of the immune system but in some cases an even more rapid overreaction of the system, which we don't understand, there are some completely new proteins, synthesized from replicated genes that... There will be swelling of the joints, haemorrhaging... from the eyes...into the lungs...' She could not go on and began to weep. Silas was glad at the outpouring of her distress, the release from the supreme effort she was having to make... his wife, Lindy.

They must get poison to the children, in case it were needed. Yes, some might, just might have a natural immunity to the virus: a few. But it had been tested: Quellan's Werod scientists had tested it on seven thousand disappeared prisoners imported from Africa, the Middle East and eastern Europe where they had, he had said, been guilty of unspeakable atrocities. Eight different trials hastily arranged had resulted in a greater than ninety-nine per cent mortality rate. Quellan had detailed the progress of the disease, coldly, clinically, his stunned audience of a handful of scientists sitting pale, trembling, mute... unwitting partners in crime. How had it been accomplished? Some material must have been taken earlier, before poor Briony made her discovery...poor Briony... A short incubation period, forty-eight hours or slightly more, then you would take three days to die, less if you were lucky.

Werod agents, some two thousand or more, had been dispatched to all corners of the globe. By the time the World Health Organization and other agencies realized what was going on - a new and terrible virus of unimaginable power on the radar, the doomsday virus, it would be too late. Over ninety-nine per cent of nine billion...eventually... It would take three to twelve months to wipe out *Homo sapiens*. Lindy said *Homo sapiens* and laughed. Then she said: 'No more laughter, no more love, no more science... Science - a filthy word now... No more fucking birthdays or Happy Christmases, no more talk about anything, no more time...'

And Quellan, Lindy told Silas, had just left, telling them that in their own self-interest they should tell no one: it would only create panic that would in turn create more terror. They would only endanger themselves because they would become the victims of retribution-seeking mobs. If his own Werod elite knew the whole truth, he had said, they would tear him to pieces, though he hoped they would be better behaved than that. He did not care for himself, anyway, but he hoped one or two of them might have a natural immunity. It was possible... The lights had then gone out, and when they came back on Quellan had disappeared, as though at the end of some conjuring trick. But there was something else, wiped from her mind as though she had been hypnotized...

They had all stared at Briony for answers, but she could barely speak, waving her hand in front of her face, forcing back the tears, and mumbling,' Do as he says, do as he says...' Then she had sunk into herself, a world of withdrawal, of inner torment. Someone had sworn and shouted at her in their desperation and fear, but she was broken and did not even show a flicker of response. 'Did I shout at her, Silas, did I? I can't remember... '

And Lindy Wood, wife of Silas Wood, was silent, spent. And together they sat for a long time in a soundless deathly communion, before walking hand in hand out through the doors and into the garden, like some parody of the expulsion from paradise.

Silas eventually rang the children and told them that they must come quickly: their mother was dying. He knew it would get them there.

As they waited, Lindy showed Silas a sheaf of papers in a file, the fruits of her own work, carried out with Briony on a possible vaccine. Silas of course understood none of it. But, he supposed, if, or when they were gone someone might find the information useful. How could he, he thought, even consider such matters. Thoughts of survivors brought with them thoughts of those who would not survive...

But Silas began to hope, and not to believe. Perhaps Lindy had temporarily gone insane: that was a better option. More likely, Alex Quellan was mad: what was he? what sort of man or monster? It was just not true: yes, that was a better option. They put the TV and the radio on for news: there was none; at least, not of the sort that they feared. Was it too soon, or was nothing going to happen after all? The news broadcasts linked them to the world, however dire the news... But, as yet, nothing. Perhaps Quellan had been lying, Silas thought. Yes, yes... He had manipulated matters before now: Quellan the Lord Protector, all-powerful Master of the Werod, Quellan the usurper... He would not speak to Lindy about Quellan, he decided... it could not be true... soon the children would arrive and he could tell them instead that their mother had had a breakdown...

It did not turn out that way: at just before ten that evening, as the bats flew like tiny birds in the dying light, and as Silas's grown-up children screamed and ranted and wept, the telephone rang and carried the news that Briony Daniels was no more: she had poisoned herself.

In the days immediately succeeding the traumatic scenes at the house of Silas and Lindy, it seemed as though Silas might be able to breathe more easily. Lindy could not of course go to work: the world was about to end, she had said, and if this were not true then she was anyway in a state of complete mental breakdown and exhaustion. The house was crowded, and none of the family wanted to go anywhere anyway. Lives on hold.... It was a position they dared share with no one else. In any case it would not be believed. Then gradually Lindy remembered with relative clarity the thing she could not bring into her mind when she had first spoken to Silas, and they began to hope.

Lindy remembered now that the lights had gone out at the end, but then they had come back on again, and there was Quellan on that bizarre granite-like throne. His cowl was thrown back still but now he wore a black patch over one eye. He was clutching a glass of brandy or whisky and he lifted it up and proposed a toast to all those who had helped him. If they were good people let them live or die in a manner of their own choosing: if they could bethink themselves of evil deeds they had hidden from the world, then let them suffer at the hands of Surt. He would leave them with the certainty that he and he alone had chosen this path and that his knowledge and wisdom had made his chosen path inevitable, beyond his control, and because of this within his control. It was, he said, the highest wisdom, and he was the High One, or the All-Father. Then he had told them to read what was in their sealed envelopes. Lindy showed the paper to them now. On it was printed the following:

I know that Quellan hung
for all of nine nights
on that wind-blown tree;
he was speared and wounded
and given to Odin,
that is, to myself, to me,
on that tree
who's growth-root
no one knows.

'This is proof positive that Quellan is mad,' Silas proclaimed to his family. His conclusion was also that Lindy and the others had definitely been hypnotized and that it was all a mistake. Briony Daniels, from overwork or whatever, had succumbed to despair, and from what Lindy had told him, had been in need of the supportive family network needed to cope with such bizarre and threatening events. And the diaries, or whatever it was that had been placed in three sealed boxes in the back of his wife's car? Let them stay there until she had recovered from the stress of what had happened, when she was ready to return to work, when Quellan would by then have been discovered to be unbalanced and a new leader appointed. Let no one consider touching those boxes until that day. Silas had come to a decision and in doing so also expressed his relief: that was all there was to say about it.

Jonas ran and ran and ran. His eyes were full of tears and he could barely distinguish anything around him. He knew only that he was in the open - running. He was running madly... He caught his leg on a waste bin and howled with pain. He hoped he had broken it, and that someone would come along and destroy him, extinguish his life. But he could still run, with pain in his leg he could still run, and he would run until his twenty-four-year-old lungs burst...

The Werod had supposedly been a force for good and had done some good.... Now it was all swept away. Had it been just Quellan and a coterie? How could anyone do this? How could his own mother have done this?

It had begun with a report about a new strain of flu, in Singapore, and thus became for a brief time New Singapore Flu or Singapore Flu-45. Then it had appeared in Mexico City. The mortality rate was alarming, but the world had been slow to take action, business intervening to protect its own interests, and questioning WHO dire warnings. Too many times people had cried wolf... This was just as Quellan had predicted. Somehow the name Surt had got out and it stuck: many talked about a US biological weapon, while some blamed the Chinese. No one pointed the finger at the UK and certainly not at a laboratory complex in Hertfordshire.

On that first night, Jonas Wood had demanded, with an incredulous stare and bitter tears, demanded of his mother that she tell him what it was all about, demanded to know how she could have worked on such a project. He had demanded to know, even the very detail of what Briony Daniels had said about the missing material. He had wanted to know everything. Then things had gone quiet and they had waited and watched. There had been those few days of promised reprieve when it had seemed quite plausible that Alex Quellan was simply mad, and that news to this effect would emerge any day now.

Then there were those last days, those last hours, that last night and day at his parents' house, for so long his home. Poor dad, poor Silas, poor mum, poor Lindy... and my God, the handing out of those hateful suicide phials, one of which he now clutched in his left hand as he ran on madly, blindly, blinded by tears, tormented by anger and fear running nowhere in particular, just running, madly...

Silas, his dad, greying, forlorn, ageing before his eyes, helpless, pacing up and down, round-shouldered, despairing... Lindy, his mum, beginning to get sick, really sick...

He had left before the end: he, Leo and Nancy. His father had become resolute at the last and would not be denied. They were not to see their parents' ending, he had proclaimed: they must promise too to use the phials when the virus struck, and its effects became intolerable. And they might just be spared, might have a natural immunity... who knew?

They had gone to his, Jonas's, rented apartment. It had once been an exciting milestone in his life: now it was a meaningless shell; somewhere where they could, the three of them, huddle together and watch the unfolding crisis and just hope... There had been enough food for three weeks at a push, even if it meant at the end baked beans and the last of the frozen loaves. Terrible, gloomy, unrelentingly depressing; a black pall of depression and mourning... And fear, above all fear - waiting for the first symptoms to appear.

Strong-limbed, blond-haired Leo, his carefree self-reliant younger brother, just setting out on his voyage of adulthood was first, the first signs... Then dark-haired Nancy, young, terrified, wide-eyed, not wanting to die; wide-eyed and pleading at the horror of it...

He ran and ran, a searing pain in his leg, his very spirit rent and in tatters, tears obscuring the detail around him under a blinding sun. He was vaguely aware that he was in a park... How many days since Leo and Nancy...? At the back of his mind now, the world's crisis, the pronouncements of governments slow to react, and the desperate advice from the World Health Organization. Hope had been expressed in some quarters: 'no need to panic: by taking the proper, and sensible, precautions...' But, day by day, the picture had become grimmer, the figures geometrically expanding - worldwide. The personal tragedy had wholly taken over, crushing Jonas, crushing every atom of hope within him. He had had to force himself to think what Carlotta's plight might be in Spain: since her second 'very concerned' phone call he had heard nothing. He had tried to remember their moments together, imprisoned as he had been with his siblings, his dearest brother and sister, whom he had discovered at the last he loved more than he had thought possible. But, truth be told, Carlotta was not important to him during those bitter, oppressive, unremitting days. He had been with his siblings, watching the world outside dying and then watching the same beginning to happen to them. Soon the world had no longer mattered: the world, its boundaries consisted of the walls of his claustrophobic apartment with no escape from the horror: it was all his responsibility, how to cope with his brother and sister at the end: no help, no succour, no support... By the time they had become infected the local hospitals had become like war zones, heaving with the dying and the relatives of the dying. He could hope that they might recover, survive the virus, some form of immunity...but it was not to be. Nothing had mattered, nothing but his hateful task that was, that had to be carried out with the utmost love and devotion. When Nancy, burning with fever and screaming with pain had clutched at her phial, the means of escape, the agent of death, he had helped it to her mouth, shared her last gasp, looked on guiltily at her cooling greying face, and wailed in despair.

The despair had not gone away, the tears had not stopped since. He had tried to blot it out, but after trying to eat and drink some hours after her death, he had had to leave them. He could stand it no longer and had run outside, leaving behind the bodies of his sister and brother, and begun to run. He had run and run; for how long he had no notion. It was all a blur: time, grief and the world.

Running still after a fashion, with a shooting pain in his leg, he howled in pain again as the damaged leg struck something else and he plunged headlong onto the baked ground under the midday sun. But his face struck something soft. There was a foetid smell and his senses swooned... He passed out.

The night was long, so long, and seemed cold, fearfully cold to someone in a weakened state and in a state of shock. He awoke from time to time, and moved feebly on the hard ground, a distance he thought until he realized he could still feel that something soft pressing against the top of his head, so that he could not have moved and was only dreaming that he had the strength to do so. Had it been winter this might have been the onset of hypothermia when the sense of danger, the awareness that death might be imminent was ebbing dangerously away into a lulling peace. But it was not that cold; he was cold. Was it the beginning of the virus? Where was the phial? Was he holding it still? What was his head pressing against? He did not have the strength to investigate this ill-positioned pillow that had left his ear pressing on the hard ground, his neck twisted uncomfortably.

His dreams were of a landscape of fog containing some unknown, unnamed terror from which he was fleeing. He was seeking a path that would take him up into the mountains and above and beyond this uncertainty and this awful stench. It was a dark moonless night and he awoke once wondering why the streetlights had failed, or was it the park lights, and there stood a bespectacled council man in a dingy little office telling him that his council tax had doubled and he owed hundreds, if not thousands of pounds, and that was why the lights had gone out, and that was why they could do nothing about the awful stench. The cleaning will be done, the man said, and the man to do it would be Alex Quellan. A huge figure, black, shapeless approached him, and his face became wet as he tried to scream.

He awoke: it was morning. At his start, the black, hungry-looking dog that was licking his face backed off suddenly, nervously, looked uncertain, then ran off. Was it the dog that had been the cause of the foul stench? No, it had gone, and the stench was more powerful than ever. What was that against his head? Painfully, slowly, all his limbs aching and one leg smarting as though from an open wound, he raised himself up and looked behind.

It was a human form, a body that had lain there for perhaps three days. The flesh of the face was yellowing, the lips drawn tightly over the teeth in a deathly grin, and the eyes had become sockets only, two deep-set pools of blackened congealed red. Signs of the virus, signs of the fire demon Surt, but something else had been here. Another body was close by, and beyond a few nervous crows eyed him, hopping and skipping out of his reach. A horrible thought occurred to him and he shuddered with disgust. He tried to stand but was unable to, so he dragged himself along the ground towards the wide green-grey trunk of a great ash tree. He wanted to sit with his back against it. It was huge, incongruous somehow in this park, a lone sentinel, but like a friend, a vague affirmation of life untroubled by the doings of Surt.

He made it to the tree, and though the stench of bodies remained still in his nostrils, the nearest of the decaying corpses lay some twenty yards from him now. Beyond - the hopping, wary crows. He wished he had the strength to throw something at them. Then he thought: why? What had they done? Then it all came back to him and he was in floods of tears, weary tears effortlessly coursing down his cheeks. He could see nothing but a blur, and tasted now the salt tears. He groaned hoarsely and realized then that he had not had a drop to drink for hours. Come for me, you bloody virus, come for me, he was thinking as he slumped against the ribbed trunk of the living tree. He could go on no longer: he was at the end of life's tether, an already dead man in this dead and dying world.

At the sound of a raucous cry from above, he awoke with a start; parched, bereft of energy, his vision blurred. How long had he lain there? It was probably mid-afternoon, perhaps later. The poison phial lay on the ground beside him.

Slowly, with great effort, he looked up toward the blue sky and into the face of an angel. She was dressed in white. Her hair was raven-black, cut to shoulder length and made a frame for her round face. Her eyes were a wonderful unearthly blue, with radiating blue-grey lines, shimmering, like orbs of cold fire. Beneath the mesmeric eyes, lightly freckled cheeks of smooth skin, translucent almost, like the soft skin of a child. He could see now as though by a miracle. It was a beauty that seemed to grip and enrapture his soul. Was he passing at last, floating into a world he had never really believed in? She held out her arms towards him as though to take him up or take up his disembodied spirit.

The little girl in the grubby white dress stared hard at the tall man with the dark hollow tear-stained eyes; the man with the tattered clothes and a bloodstained leg. He was trying to speak to her through his parched cracked lips. She was perhaps six years old and not particularly tall for her age. She had an innocence and a guileless ethereal beauty, however: that was how the hallucinating, prostrate helpless man was seeing her. She held out her bare skinny arms to him again, this time in a jerky, hasty impatient gesture. She needed the dark-haired man to help her: there was no one else.

'Come on! Pull yourself together, man. Get up.' She had heard adults say this. Perhaps it would work. And though the literal sense of 'pull yourself together' puzzled her, she hoped the magic words might do the trick.

Jonas Wood looked bemused, to begin with. Then with a supreme effort he took the girl's proffered hands and lifted himself to his feet. His life was not over.

‘My name is Beatrice,’ said the little girl, ‘what’s yours?’

Above, in the branches of the Ash, a large carrion crow looked down at the scene of feasting, blinking his black insouciant eye - a thing of legend, to be sure.

PART TWO

Beyond Ragnarok

19. *The Argonauts*

Even into the middle of the twenty-first century Lyme Regis still possessed a unique charm, from the pastel-washed terraced cottages of its sea-front promenade to the climbing main street, Broad Street, with its shops, and its historic hotels. The stuff of sometimes quaint and sometimes seductive fiction was Lyme, but also in its last days of the sometimes mundane, sometimes surprising world of modernity, of super-fast communications and a rampant corporate new world incongruously set.

You could, once upon a time, place yourself a quarter way up the rising land upon which the town stood in a terraced manner and gaze down from the 'crazy golf' course to the beach below, to the splendid Cobb, with its sturdy grey outstretched finger curling around the sheltered water and the old stone cottages nestling at the far side of the little harbour: this, to your right hand and out across Lyme Bay. Of course, in this respect you could still recreate the experience of the erstwhile holidaymaker, who would look down with a bird's-eye vantage at the central beach, and to the right, at the strip of sand running alongside the Cobb's broad inner path and see that no one was there on a cold grey morning when the foaming waves drove in noisily and the skies frowned like thunder, and the grey-black body of the sea mirrored its mood. But you could no longer recreate the experience of that same summer holidaymaker who would look out a few days later and see the water blue and the sands and the Cobb swarming colourfully with teeming people, and the Mediterranean blue water with flashes of white from far-out speedboat plumes and colour from the lie-lows and the swimming dots, the ice cream vendor under a striped awning close by at the back edge of the sand, and in front, surrounded by a cluster of young humanity, the Punch and Judy show. The blue sky and the blue waters of the bay and the glistening wet grey crooked stone finger of the Cobb would still be visible, but not so the holiday crowds.

Compared with yesteryear, Lyme was a ghost town. The fire demon Surt had done his work: Lyme had not escaped. He had been here too, in his global rampage, dealing Death to humankind.

Yet there was here still, human life: all had not been erased.

In this place, as elsewhere, the terrible dead, in their houses, their buildings, their sanctuaries, in every conceivable attitude and alignment of limb and torso lay undisturbed still, and therefore, those houses, those buildings, those sanctuaries, remained shut-up, the habitations of ghosts. While the desiccated remains, cobweb and dust-covered, remained within, however, places open to the sky, the streets, alleys and byways of Lyme, had been cleared. A huge burning had taken place three miles to the north-east of the town. That was more than three decades ago, almost four, and had happened two years after the plague. The few who had survived and lived in on the western edge of the town in makeshift shelters could no longer bear the terror or the depressing proximity of those who had fallen victim to Surt. Somehow, with a grim determination akin to that of the mountaineer or the polar explorer, they had laboured at the removal of the dead from the streets, inspired by a new leader, now left and gone to the north of the great island that had been the mainland of Great Britain. Even some of the houses and yards to the west of the town were entered and cleared, for fear of contamination of water supplies. It had been, too, partly a salvage operation, garnering long-life food, materials for building, for survival, until such time as other survivors could be contacted: the desperately determined pioneers of the new world; but oh so few in number, compared with what had been, and so little left of what they had known and become used to. It had been the same everywhere, of course, they had supposed.

Some forty years had passed since the unleashing of Surt. A group of children stood now atop the Cobb staring out across a calm sea, blue-green, lapping transparently over the seaweed-covered boulders that lay in a couple of feet of salt water beneath the steep-sloping outer wall, fifteen feet below. On the same moving body of water, calm now after the terrible storm of two days ago, when eighty-mile-an-hour winds had rushed at the wall, heaving the sea-top spray over the old rampart, they espied a ship slowly approaching. Little more than a dot on the horizon, but for certain a ship...

With whoops of joy the children ran the length of the cambered wall-top and then away left and up the hill to the new dwellings whose broad deep windows gazed out like silver eyes at the expanse of sea. New buildings for the hundred or so inhabitants of Lyme...

The ship anchored to the west, and a half-dozen small boats began ferrying people to the shore, the shore of Mary Anning's dinosaur finds two centuries before, the shore of Monmouth's doomed invasion two centuries before that.

The visitors, some forty in number, were some distance away. They moved closer, most lagging uncertainly perhaps behind a vanguard of a half-dozen who, by accident or design, appeared thus to be the natural leaders. They moved along the strand under the bright morning sun and ahead of a fresh south-westerly breeze. The reception committee, a dozen strong, stood before them, close to the Cobb, as though wanting to draw them away from the terrace of new dwellings up on the hillside along and to their right which the visitors would have to pass by to reach them.

One man was now ahead of the entire group of travellers. A brave man, clearly, as he could not know how he might be received: or perhaps he was a hopeful man: perhaps both. He was lean and a little over middle height but could not be regarded as tall. A rugged, leathery-skinned face with steady grey eyes and ample heavy brows; a hawk-like face, tanned and weather-beaten, a man of the seas perhaps, or of the mountains.

From the small group immediately behind this man a black shape darted and quickly overtook the leader, flying headlong towards the Lyme party. The man bellowed his name, which was difficult to catch on the wind, but the large smooth-coated black hound wheeled about and ran fawningly back to his master, who smiled and patted him - a reassuring sign for those viewing the approaching visitors.

There was a moment of silence when the rugged weather-hardened traveller stood before the tall male spokesperson of the wondering, apprehensive-looking residents.

'My name is Valjean,' said the traveller, extending a gnarled sinewy hand whose grip, as well as its appearance, indicated hard and heavy toil. 'My dog was called Alighieri, but I call him Dante for short. I hope we can be friends. Our party has travelled from Normandy through difficult storms. We bring much with us that might assist you. If we are welcome, I should be glad to tell you our history. We call our ship "The Argo"', he laughed. 'A rather grand idea, but only one of us can claim to be Greek so you need not be afraid of the old adage: beware ...'

'Greeks bearing gifts.' The leader of the Lyme party finished the famous expression, marvelling at the Frenchman or the Swiss with the unusual accent, part-Anglicized and with occasional heavier, more pronounced Germanic consonants. The man was relieved that his much-rehearsed opening remarks appeared to have found favour.

'You are not from Normandy originally. A part of Switzerland?'

The voyager nodded, adding a grain or two of information about his mixed parentage and his unusual upbringing.

'You are most welcome. We made the decision long ago that if the occasion arose, we would honest and open with our visitors. We ask visitors to work for us, and in return we shall be unsparing in our efforts to make you comfortable, and we shall feed you to the very best of our ability.' The would-be host, fair-haired, tall and slim, and with a red-blond fine moustache and chin stubble, spoke now with a quiet confidence born of the new stoicism of the times - at least, in this community - and the apparent lack of threat from the visitors. In any event, if the visitors, travellers, invaders or whatever, were intent upon taking what they wanted by force, they could not realistically be opposed, being too many in number and hardened, evidently, by their recent experiences. What could possibly be done to stop them even if the community had not lived under a vow of non-violence?

The noise of the sea, the soft crashing of the breaking waves close by, filled the brief silences, washing over pebble and sand, an eternal clock marking time and indifferent to the endeavours of humankind.

It turned out that the travellers were themselves well-provisioned and sought only to establish a temporary base on the land, to explore, to meet people who had continued to survive. It was something more than this, to be sure, in the blood and bone of most - a yearning. They were not treasure hunters or pirates; they were not, despite the slightly self-mocking name of their ship seekers after any kind of Golden Fleece. These Argonauts had come not for a single purpose but had travelled as a group for convenience and mutual protection. The travellers were keen to impress upon their hosts that their mission comprised a number of individual odysseys. What held them together as a group was strong, at times fearless leadership and an appreciation of human companionship. This last quality automatically communicated itself to their would-be hosts who, if for their part harboured any suspicions, found those suspicions allayed by the presence on the strand of a group of children from the boats.

The ship had been named The Argo, or renamed, since she was originally the Belle Marie from Brittany and relocated to Normandy. The children had insisted on the new name, taken as they were with the myths of Jason's adventures and favouring those over the adventures of Odysseus, or Ulysses. Confusion had further arisen from their collective failure to find a pun on Jules Valjean's name, a pun that would link him to Odysseus. Theirs was going to be an odyssey they knew, but they wanted to stick to Jason's name for his ship. The adults saw that they often confused or strangely combined different myths but did not want to disappoint them in their determined choice of The Argo. Also, to disappoint the children would, they felt, be tantamount to inviting bad luck, and so it might well have been.

As the groups merged, hesitantly, self-consciously, guardedly, shyly even, as can happen when two groups of strangers meet, Valjean began to observe and remark upon the development that had obviously taken place relatively recently on Lyme's western fringes. He noted the rectangular solar panels on the sloping seaward roofs of the wood-trimmed and brightly painted hillside dwellings; and a larger rectangular building higher up that was the community centre, fortified and strengthened more in case of storms, or anything else that might come along - a place of refuge. Higher up still, a swathe had been cut, continuing down the hill past the centre and towards the dwellings. Atop the heights, the swathe made a gap in the horizon of trees as you looked up north-north-west from the immediate area of the Cobb. It was a sight that held Valjean's gaze for several obvious moments.

'It's a pipeline for water,' the host said, as though in answer to Valjean's questions. 'Some people came fifteen years ago, when I was just turned thirty. We had to move out of their way. Not very pleasant people:

they took over our houses and they must have gotten bored because they just moved off. We feared for our lives and moved inland, to an abandoned village - like most places, abandoned - a village just east of Dorchester. We moved the dead that were there but that was enough for us. When we eventually came back here we were unable to face work like that again. A much greater task too... Oh, and the pipeline,' he added musingly, stroking the soft-red stubble of his chin, 'it works. We try to maintain the pumping station beyond the hill but because of our concerns about the reservoir, which we do not have the manpower or expertise to maintain - the filters and so on - we boil all our drinking water...'

The noisy babble of the mingling groups accompanied by the wash of the tide increased and was now joined by the sound of children from both camps playing together. Valjean, his steady grey eyes sparkling under the cliffs of his brows, clapped a hand like a knot of tree roots on the other man's shoulder and drew him to one side. 'My friend, we shall help you. We have among our number craftsmen, scientists, engineers, plumbers, and just plain toilers who will be only too pleased to help. We should be glad to stay awhile, if you will have us. We outnumber you perhaps: our party is two hundred and forty strong, but the consensus is that our ship will not stand another sea voyage. The days of the Argonauts are over;' he laughed, 'we are here to explore England and beyond. We all have our different reasons for this; but some may wish to stay here as a base from which to explore locally. We shall inconvenience you in no way. We shall, if you will allow us, spend a year cleaning and restoring your town, for our use and for yours...'

The host looked questioningly, envisioning clearly, with a frown passing over his smooth-skinned face, the still, silent horrors that might be uncovered there, in the old town whose houses they had always passed with bowed heads, in reverence and, on occasion, with a hurried step.

Valjean, smiling broadly, showing his crooked teeth and bending down to stroke Dante with his strong gnarled hand, spoke reassuringly: 'Fear not, we have chemical-biological suits. We shall enter the houses of the dead and clear them for the living. If any two-headed monsters block our way, Dante here will scare them off...' The host looked puzzled, but Valjean wanted to move on. 'And your reservoir - is it far? - one or two of our people would be interested. If we can save you from feeling the need to boil your drinking water... Which reminds me; we have some drinks, real drinks, on board, or if you object... I assure you that none of us drinks to excess. Discipline and order has taken us thus far through a number of perils, and we intend none shall deviate from this path... But if you...'

'No, no, we drink alcohol, those over eighteen; that is, most of us. We are careful and watchful. As far as the age restriction is concerned, we have carried through the laws of the old world. It was different, always different in Europe, I know. With the coming of the Werod, everyone saw...the sense...' The host hesitated. A man, strong-limbed and fit-looking, but heavier built and taller than the spokesperson of the travellers, had fixed his stern eyes interestedly on the host. The man it turned out was fifty-nine, but the grey streaks in his dark cropped hair aside, he looked young and robust.

Valjean was aware. He wheeled round. 'Ah, what you have just said will be of great interest to the Captain here.' The 'Captain' smiled, a thin non-committal smile. 'A very serious fellow,' Valjean continued, 'with a quest of his own... We have many tales to tell... and why we call him the Captain...well, that is one of them. It has nothing to do with our ship, or any ship... We shall gladly tell you all about ourselves if you ...'

'We have nothing to gain by withholding our hospitality, which will be freely and gladly given,' interrupted the host. 'There need be and should be no want of trust on either side. New arrivals are not a regular occurrence,' he laughed, 'you are the first large party to arrive by sea in forty years, to my knowledge; and such a large party provides us with endless, or at least very many unforeseen possibilities. If you have provisions to match, to complement ours, we can invite you to a feast to take place tomorrow, once you are rested from your weary travel. We have accommodation for you: it was built in the hope that a day such as this would arise, and in the hope that our community would grow - somehow. But the children are few... that's another story, however. Finally, I will say this: we could of course poison you all and steal all you have: that would buy us a year of extra provisions, and perhaps raise the possibility that some of your friends might come and wipe us out. More importantly, we would lose so much by such an action. We are not a violent community, as I hope you will see. Violence is not the way forward. Of course, we *inherited* a partly cleansed country in that respect...' He stopped, aware of the stern-faced 'Captain's' gaze, aware too of the searching grey eyes of the rugged Valjean. Then he said: 'Quite simply, please join us. You are most welcome.' A few people cheered at this point, and in voices accompanied by the washing of the sounding sea on that bright shore, made known to one another confirmation of their approval.

20. *Number Seven entertains and learns about Valjean and the Captain, and the gypsy Esmerelda; and there is talk of a Messiah.*

The name of the Lyme spokesperson, the first Englander they had encountered, was Jonathan, though he insisted on being called Number Seven, or plain Seven, which was odd, but it was because he was one of twelve people, six men and six women, who comprised a sort of advisory council whose task it was to steer and oversee and guide the activities of the community. Twelve members: it was a throwback to the days of the Werod Councils, themselves based on some historical precedent, though few knew, and fewer cared about such matters, and the council itself was not overly dictatorial or prescriptive in its advice, and many of the positions on the council were temporary, its member 'portfolios' vague. Jonathan, Number Seven, had by pure chance become more of a fixture since everyone seemed to like and trust that he would get things done. It was not known whether the twelve-person 'structure' was repeated across the whole country, though a smaller community near Dorchester, now part of theirs, had also had such a set-up. It mattered little to the Lyme people: it worked, and for them this was the whole country and they feared now to venture beyond a score of miles in any direction.

There was feasting and celebrating on the second evening, a celebration of the arrival of the Argonauts. Many a table was put out and laden with food and drink, and many new bonds of friendship began to form.

The festivities and the story telling took place in the community hall. Valjean and a number of other travellers were interested in its construction and the materials used. Prefabricated, compressed straw blocks and sheets had been used for the inner linings, a supply having been obtained from a warehouse outside Axminster, then painstakingly removed to Lyme. With equal determination, the outer shell had been constructed from local stone, for lasting strength - the bones of the land were not easily broken, someone had said - whilst more modern touches included, as with the houses, the great sloping solar panels of the roof. Energy efficiency, the environment, especially solar power, had been much promoted in the first half of the century, particularly during the days of Dain Alvis, whose statues, spotted and spattered with bird droppings, still stood in a number of local towns, Lyme's own being at the bottom of the high street gazing out heroically to sea. More importantly, there had been a factory producing solar panels at nearby Charmouth.

Number Seven, and several others, listened intently to what had happened over time on the European mainland, and the interest was reciprocated. How had people survived and gotten through the last forty years? How many had perished in the plague, the latter-day Black Death? What did the future hold for the young people - for anyone in fact? These questions came later in the main or were thrown in as rhetorical asides as various tales unfolded.

First, Valjean; Jules Verne Valjean. Born of parents with a sense of humour, his mother was Swiss-Deutsch, his father, French, from Grenoble. They had lived in Lauterbrunnen in the Berner or Bernese Oberland; and Valjean was indeed a mountain man; gnarled and sinewy and tough as tree roots, he clung to the mountain life, and his ambition, before the virus arrived in his land, had been to become a renowned mountain guide; besides this, he liked to paint. His hero was Anderl Heckmair, whose party had been the first successfully to climb the Eiger Nordwand in 1938. Indeed, he had grown to look something like his hero. When the virus came to the valley, he was nineteen, and staying with a friend two thousand feet up the valley wall in Wengen, which for some reason Surt had left alone. Several hundred people had been trapped there, in the famous ski resort, though many had taken trains out to try and get home before the plague really got a grip. When the magnitude of the horror was recognized, however, no one wanted to move out, and suddenly the trains were halted, and signs put up saying that Wengen, to which there were no road links, had become a plague village. It had proved the best way of deterring others from fleeing there. After two or three years people did venture down to the valley and beyond. Like everywhere else there were thousands upon thousands of bodies to dispose of. People realized, as in England, that the cities were best avoided as dwelling places. Many of those who had tried to establish themselves there had succumbed to typhus and cholera...

Valjean was particularly proud of latter-day achievements. They, he and his friends from the mountain village and some intrepid people of the Wengen-born new generation, had managed to re-colonize part of Interlaken, and had even been able to get the old brewery going again, once the water supply had been sorted out and approved for use. This was thanks mainly to a half-dozen people, from an original eight, who had worked at the brewery and were at a conference in Wengen when the world all but fell into the abyss of Hell, as some had described it. The upshot was that he had had for a time a stockpile of his favourite *Rugenbräu* on which to draw, 'properly labelled and everything' he would say, imitating a comment made by a Wengen Englishman.

Valjean, though, was less forthcoming in general about his adventures in traversing the land between

Switzerland and Normandy, a journey of twenty months he and some eighty others had made.

There were English people among the travellers and many of these had come from Switzerland via Normandy and were at the end of a twenty-year odyssey which had seen the birth of children on the way, and also hazard, hardship and death, and the ending of lives. Most of the English had come to see what had become of the old homeland, but within this group, there were intensely personal reasons, a greater intensity than could be generated by idle curiosity. Some hoped their scientific or technical knowledge and abilities could be put to good use here, as had been the case in mainland Europe. It was as Valjean said: there were many experts in their field amongst the Norman visitors. There was even a dentist who, with the help of a team of chemists and access to abandoned pharmaceutical laboratories, had managed to secure for herself a supply of newly synthesized novocaine, a blessed relief for one of the residents of Lyme. Despite the small triumphs, however, none on either side could feel confident about the future: the blow to humanity was recent history and all around them in the present, inescapable.

The music played in the great hall, courtesy of a stock of old CDs, a reliable generator, and three determined and enthusiastic music librarians; and though it was a rather small collection, there was something for everyone. There had been a similar situation in Normandy and in Switzerland, the visitors said. Music was what made many people think, reminisce, be grateful, be sad. It allowed them to think, if only for a short time, that the old world remained and that nothing had really changed. Music thus brought many to tears, always, but paradoxically gave them hope. Music, unlike painting, sculpture and literature, was immediate and alive, and spoke of both limitless possibilities or conjured up old times, for many in its high baroque, classical and romantic forms, or through its great masses or oratorios and motets, for others in twentieth and early twenty-first century popular forms. It did not matter what form it took: whether inspiring soulful contemplation or simple joy, music was music, a friend and solace to all at some time. It was, reassuringly, immortal, or at least an unchanging artefact that could be endlessly resurrected.

Valjean, sipping gratefully from a steaming mug of cocoa as in his younger days on the Alps (gratefully, and remarkably, the cocoa being of a popular very low-fat variety that had been discovered in a cold-store warehouse some years earlier, and which was still drinkable) wondered how Britain had survived the long almost unbroken dark extended winters which had begun two to three years after the plague, and had continued for eight long years. Most had guessed the cause of the darkening to be a catastrophic eruption of a volcano, or a series of volcanic eruptions, or possibly a full eruption of the Yellowstone caldera. Something had caused what had been akin to a mini ice age. It had been bad enough in the south, was the answer, but they doubted anyone could have survived in the north of England, in Scotland, or in the mountains of Wales. On a positive note, someone suggested that perhaps the Arctic ice cap had been restored, and the polar bears were not extinct after all...

One of the strangest things, all agreed, was never to have seen or heard in all the years since the plague, a plane; not a single vapour trail had crossed the blue sky for at least thirty-five years. How many had died, a question often mooted still, whenever and wherever strangers met; a comment to make, a shaking or bowing of heads, even after the passage of years. How many? Not many were left if the rest of the world were like the part of Europe they had traversed. The Earth had had a population of nearly nine billion, and the consensus was that nearly nine billion had died.

Jonathan, or Seven, explained that his group, or the group he had grown up with, had begun with half a dozen people from Lyme and neighbouring Uplyme, and for almost a year, the records showed, that was it; but gradually others had come in from Dorchester and beyond, even a couple with a child all the way from Bristol. He pointed to an animated happy-looking woman in her mid-forties, who was talking to children from the ship.

Although it had become a habit to mention the disaster when meeting, a reminder of hardship shared, equally it was considered morbid and defeatist to dwell upon it after all these years. But as sometimes happened, someone would curse the plague in passing, and curse whichever god had let it happen. It was someone from the guest party this time who made such a comment, at which point a strange thing happened.

One of the Lyme inhabitants, a young man slightly red in the face and tipsy, announced that the Surt virus was nothing to do with any god but a biological weapon released by Alex Quellan. That was what his now deceased father had told him, and the news had come originally from a traveller from London in the early days, a traveller who had said he knew this for certain. He had been, his father had said, quite a young man with something like a religious zeal, a determination to create the world afresh. They all knew this legendary man to be the inspirational person who had given their community the will and purpose to grow. The speaker, in his late teens or early twenties, with an acne-scarred face, intelligent and with an urgent look and blazing eyes that wanted to communicate the wonder of his tale, a tale his father had picked up, he now said, from his meeting with the wandering messiah.

The young man said Quellan had created the virus, and that people had helped him to create it, and that he had even given it its name. Quellan, he added, had seen it as a judgement on mankind. He wanted to kill everyone. Some were embarrassed at this point, but Jonathan Seven and a number of others were frowning, hoping the young man would be quiet. The boy did stop, aware that he was spoiling the atmosphere of the evening, aware that really, he was mouthing someone else's words. He did not know for sure, he mumbled at the end. The Captain, the heavy-set, square-shouldered man, stared with mute barely contained incredulity, then annoyance, at the boy. To become truly angry at a mere annoyance, to be angered by impetuous youth would be to make him break a vow which all the voyagers had made to one another. He quietly left the circle therefore. Valjean watched his strong square retreating figure and fixed on the cropped black hair which showed some grey-white flecks of age. Still a powerful man, however: a man to be reckoned with. Valjean knew why he had left. When the boy had finished and was sitting in a far corner with his immediate family members, out of earshot, the Swiss quietly explained the Captain's reaction to Jonathan and three others who happened to have 'council' or 'elder' status. They spoke quietly, half listening to a man nearby who was singing a tuneless song about Rome's Piazza del Popolo and then talking about a Pope of the 11th Century who had had a walnut tree cut down because it was a source of evil. It was an interesting tale but a distracting one.

Valjean explained that the Captain, just before the time of the apocalypse, had been sent as an emissary, and as an outstanding Werod officer cadet and potential future thegn, to Switzerland as part of a European recruitment drive for the planned expansion of the law and order initiative. He had taken a solemn oath to defend the Law, to obey unto death Alex Quellan, the Leader, adhere to the Code of the Werod, and defend every innocent citizen. It was something his uncle, who had brought him up after the murder of his parents, had done: his uncle had sworn his oath to the Werod and the Breakthrough Party, headed then by Dain Alvis, and had had to take another oath when Quellan had taken over, the second time an oath of personal loyalty to the Leader. His uncle, totally loyal and unquestioning, had not even considered the possibility of Quellan's involvement in Alvis's removal, conditioned as he was to focus his entire being on the destruction of criminal degenerates. Thus, he had become in the end a high-ranking officer close to the Werod Council. It was all gone of course, but his uncle, after having contracted the virus and being close to death, had given him cause to hope: in his last telephoned message he had said that ten thousand Werod elite soldiers and their young families had been sent by Alex Quellan to a place of safety, to a vast underground shelter, with provisions for years. At some point they would re-emerge into the light and re-establish order in the land, if anyone were left behind and in need of help. He, the man they all now called the Captain because of his paramilitary background and because he was a determined fighter and a natural leader whom their fifty or so 'security' volunteers were glad to follow, had come to England at last to search for the fabled next generation of Werod elite. It was clear, however, that the strange story about Quellan had shaken him, even though he probably thought it fantastic.

Valjean, aware of the doubts passing through his English friend's mind, eventually crept away to join him.

The Captain stood close by, his wife in all but name, Esmerelda, hanging on his arm. She had, like Valjean, seen him leave the hall, and, saying a brief goodbye for now to the Lyme children, who had really taken to her and with whom she had quickly established trust and rapport, a friendship, she had quickly followed her husband outside and followed him down to the beach. Esmerelda was still a beautiful woman, with large, brown, 'Spanish' eyes her husband said, and long naturally curling black hair that tumbled over her shoulders and down her back. She was now in her mid-thirties, having been rescued by the Captain some eighteen years earlier near Grenoble when she was sixteen or seventeen. She was being abused then by a group of bandits or brigands notorious in the region for some years, but alas for them no match for the Werod Captain (as he had now become) and the dozen hard men he had trained and who travelled still with the group, apart from one who had been killed in the brief battle and another who had since died suddenly from natural causes. Esmerelda was a Romany gypsy, a fact which sometimes caused incredulity, especially when linked to talk of her escape from bandits and brigands: thus, she might seem to some not real at all but more like a character from a nineteenth-century romance. But Esmerelda she was, and the mutual love between her and the Captain was a bond that could be broken on one side only by death; on the other not at all: the survivor would cling onto that love until his or her dying breath.

They stood at a point on the beach where the tide was close in, and they stood and looked up at the stars in a silent communion, while about them the sea washed in hushed tones. A score of yards distant, and beyond, along the beach to their right, the locals had lit three bonfires. The light from the closest of these showed off the fulsome figure and olive skin of the gypsy woman whose face shone in reds and golds beneath her tumbling mane of raven hair which lay over her shoulders. She wore a plain white silken blouse and long red skirt and had wrapped around her a colourful shawl. The Captain looked into her face and smiled. Valjean approached and so the three of them stood and looked out to sea. The Swiss felt that he would wait for his friend to speak first about the Quellan tale, which had clearly rattled him.

They were joined at length by Jonathan Seven who kept for a time the same respectful silence. Eventually, however, the subject was broached. The Lyme man was keen only to keep everyone happy, as indeed they all should be, given this opportunity for new friendships. The Captain in the end relented and became less brooding, Jonathan reassuring him and the others, saying that any story coming out of the traumatic end to the old civilization might have an element of truth in it, but that that element had possibly been distorted by time and in the repeated telling of the tale. Was it not too, he said, at that time a world in which there had been no one who was concerned to document anything for posterity. And even this was not true, he added, since the young man they had spoken of had gone north to find the mysterious sanctuary the Captain had been told about by his uncle (Valjean looked a little embarrassed at this point and could not meet his friend's enquiring gaze) and had said he wanted to bring learning and hope back to the world, and so on.

'I cannot properly remember him,' Jonathan said, 'but by all accounts, he was a visionary, or even a saint, if you hold such beliefs; and he was completely unafraid of what was in front of him. When he left, with three of our people, he had spoken in riddles, saying like any agnostic I suppose that though he did not believe in any one god in particular, he believed in a god of some sort, or at least a destiny... He said he had with him a spirit guide who protected him and whom he would also protect. I don't have to remember this: we have it written down. He was not alone... but you will see. Read for yourselves and draw your own conclusions. It is not much of a record, but it is something.'

The others looked at Seven in quiet amazement, soothed by his words, and beginning to think that this brought another dimension to their quest: a search for this godless messiah, who, it was true to say was probably dead anyway, but equally true to say that this did not really matter - it was a mystery to be solved.

The wonder and joy of the evening was what was important, and all felt it: new life in the community and a safe and prosperous haven for the travellers. As the day closed the music sounded mutedly from the heights above, to those standing on the beach. A slight chill had closed in and a calm sea showed a silver path to a full large moon, and thousands of stars shone in an unpolluted clear black sky, as the nearby fire warmed the watchers. Close by, the dinosaurs lay in their eternal resting places.

21. *Goodbye, Lyme - for now*

The face looked out of the mirror, the face of the Captain. The eyes were green-hazel, with a deep hue about them, almost beautiful, like those of a woman, some said, but on first waking, as now, betraying some signs of middle age, something accentuated by the lines around, and to the sides, and by the light furrowing of the of the forehead over the dark brows. The black hair of the head, cut short, close-cropped, with flecks of grey... The ears stood out slightly, with the tiniest, barely perceptible flat mole on the lobe of the left one. The face was square, a little fleshier now, but with a firm square jaw. A long, ragged scar ran pink, red and grey beneath a day's growth of greying whiskers, ran diagonally from the left cheekbone, reaching almost to the corner of his thin-lipped mouth. The nose was symmetrical though slightly broadened at the bridge, the result of years of sparring in his twenties and thirties in the makeshift mountain training camp.

Despite this, the Captain did not look anything like his fifty-nine years, something peculiar to some but not all of those who had come into contact with the virus though not obviously contracted it, in its full, virulent, deadly form; though perhaps in his case he was just destined to remain young-looking into his late fifties. As usual, a wash and shave in this clean tidy little bathroom would restore the youthful glow to his strong dependable and, some would say, stern countenance.

The Captain stretched his head upwards and massaged his neck, then moved his head from side to side, a habit picked up years before, and part of his pre-fight warm up. The upper torso still looked strong and toned under the square head, wide neck and broad shoulders.

The Captain, elected to the rank rather than commissioned, but elected because of his fighting prowess, his grasp of tactics, strategy and logistics, his practical knowledge of the motives of men, and above all for his dedication, effective dedication, to the organization of the whole group, which had begun as a smaller entity back in Switzerland. Since his mid-twenties he had served and protected and led many of these people, in Switzerland and in excursions beyond its borders, then later through the saga of their many adventures in the crossing of Europe, their incorporation into the Normandy community, and now, to this English venture. He was Valjean's closest friend and most tenaciously loyal supporter, though no one would have thought it sensible to challenge theirs, his and Valjean's effective joint leadership, as it had served everyone so well through almost three decades. There was a Norman element to the leadership, but this third number of the would-be triumvirate was happy to let the two close friends steer their best course. They were proven survivors, having come through some lean and dangerous times.

Now a hardened veteran of travel, fighting, and sleeping under the stars when necessary, the Captain was no stranger to or churlish eschewer of the creature comforts when they came his way. He was a friend to soap, a good hot shower or a soaking bath. He was particular to a fault in his toilet, as though he might with soap and water wash away forever from his mind and soul the horrors he had witnessed in his life.

He remembered the world as it was, full of human life: the comradeship (he still had Valjean and one or two others, thankfully), the challenges, the laughter, and the tears, the bustle, the packed and noisy cities, the constant passing of cars, the airports and their duty-free shops and wide concourses with all manner of people clutching cases or huge holdalls, piles of luggage, the schools, the crowded busy hospitals, the quiet side wards, the sports events, the crowds of thousands, the televised events, the traffic jams, the bright weddings where people grinned self-consciously or laughed with abandon, the solemn funerals, and the duties... of having to deal with the few bad people, at times, too, the gratitude and the smiles of the good... Such a busy world, always in a hurry, but not always... the quiet moments of contemplation, gazing out of a window, or looking out at the tide and far out to the boundless sea, or gazing at a lake or down into a mountain pass, or simply up at the floating clouds or a passing bird or the vapour trails of planes. It had gone, all gone; at least, as he, as all those of his age, had once known it. The young ones knew no better, which was just as well.

'Coffee, *mon Capitaine*?' suggested a tall, thin, sandy-haired Englishman whom the man addressed and now standing in the spacious dining area knew well, the biologist and virologist Peter Jones. Jones, who was his own age but older looking, freckled, with a high forehead and sandy thinning hair with a receding hairline. He smiled a yellow-toothed smile. The Captain had never really understood why the good-natured Peter often dropped into French, and not very good French, when he spoke to him, since both of them were English. He put it down to the cosmopolitan influence of the old Wengen community, which at the time of Surt's dominance had comprised a multitude of multifarious visitors as well as those who provided the hotel services and those who provided services for them, such as plumbers and electricians and the railway staff, utilities engineers and so on... and a couple of priests, one of whom travelled with them still, a decrepit old Swiss-Deutsch who, despite his arthritis managed not only to put on a brave face but to bring cheer to others. But Wengen was long ago now: even Normandy was beginning to fade after their eventful and tortuous sea journey over the grey mountains of waves. Just to say, Peter Jones had been trapped with a whole host of scientists in Wengen, the group having travelled up from their convention base in Interlaken: 'Such are the vagaries of fate', Peter Jones had said many a time.

It was a fine morning. Out on the boards of the veranda was an uninterrupted view of the broad sea, with the grey wall of the Cobb stretching away to the left and providing a point of reference. Gulls wheeled and cried overhead. Off to the right, the Argo, so named, swayed in the bosom of a quiet swell: soon she would sink, but along the shoreline at some point they would find another ship when they needed it. Off to the left, somewhere in the town, a muted car horn sounded several times, bringing a smile of surprise to the faces of the half-dozen travellers standing outside now with the Captain, taking in the morning air. They all sat down at a couple of wooden tables, and coffee, toast, marmalade and eggs were brought, and a big jug of cold milk.

'I'll tell you all about it, my friend,' Valjean said, his gnarled kindly face breaking into a smile. 'Jonathan and I have had a long talk. They have worked miracles in this settlement over the years.'

'It's just a mixture of what we inherited - what was provided for us - the practical knowledge we acquired, some tender care for the livestock, some knowledge, er...'

'In other words,' Valjean interrupted,' you really have done a lot. We should visit your farm, your water pumping plant -which we have promised to get working again, your vehicle maintenance station...and so on and so on.' He laughed without constraint or hidden intent, laying a hand of friendship on Jonathan Number Seven's sloping shoulder. 'But we can still help. We made you a promise to open up the old town and enter the Houses of the Dead, and so we will.'

'Much was left from the old world,' Jonathan mused, 'much we could use. One day there were more than sixty million, the next only a few hundred or a few thousand were left, or so we think. We have never desired to explore the interior, or perhaps have been afraid to; but the when the young visitor came all those years ago, to truly inspire the community, to give us hope, he did take three of our young people with him, as I think we told you. I suppose one could indeed call them disciples. Perhaps they are long dead,' he added, staring thoughtfully out to the watery line of the horizon, the terminal straight line of grey under the blue canvas of a clear sky. 'Including our three young people there were nine of them. He had brought five with him, gathered up along the way, he said, waifs and strays, I suppose. But he had hope, they say, and not fear. An inspiration... is he dead, I wonder...'

'Do you see many ships pass?' asked the Captain, interrupting the quiet musings of the elder.

'In all these years, I think we have seen five ships,' six, another corrected him, 'Yes, perhaps it was six, but yours is the first, apart from one lost soul, to land here. You can see the reason for our celebrations. The violent strangers who came, came from further along the coast, we think... They did some damage, stole some things, that was all; the women and children, the young and old, and some of the men, escaped inland and then we sent for them when it was all over. I truly mean this: I never held out much hope for the intruders; they were, we felt, certain to destroy themselves in the end. But we don't dwell on such matters. We focused on what we could achieve and were fortunate in that we inherited much that could be used...'

The wide empty sea, with its plumes of white horses bright in the morning sun, testified to the end of the regular passage of man over its surface.

'The world looks sometimes as it always was,' Jonathan continued, sipping from a mug of coffee, coffee from the old days, preserved, vacuum-packed, drinkable still. 'The sea has always been the sea... so calm today. I notice your ship is beginning to list, 'he commented, lifting his left arm and half-heartedly pointing in south-westerly direction.

'We have someone here who will interest you, Captain, 'he suddenly recollected. 'Roland here, whom we also call Number Six, left the village community some six years ago and travelled briefly into the interior; as far north as Oxford. He had perhaps - only perhaps - better news of your old order. There was, he will tell you better, some rumour, among the handful of survivors on the outskirts of Oxford, some rumour of roaming bands of what were called the Weird Huns ... Let him explain...'

A small bespectacled figure, whose dark-rimmed glasses had been 'discovered' ten years earlier in a search through a Dorchester optician's, edged forward on the bench seat, closer to the broad-shouldered man in the fur-trimmed leather coat, the Captain. The rather yellow-skinned emaciated man - he must have been seventy or so - smiled and squinted as he spoke. The glasses helped but were evidently not of sufficient strength. Speaking slowly, deliberately, he related the detail, or some of it, of his relatively brief sojourn those half-dozen years earlier, when he had travelled beyond the spires whose dreaminess, as elsewhere, oversaw the macabre nightmare of a corpse-ridden cityscape. Perhaps it was different now, but he could not see how this was possible.

The Weird Huns of recent 'folklore', might well have been a contraction of the Werod Hundreds, a small army supposed to have been a last reserve in the event of a breakdown of society, incredibly well-equipped in a subterranean fortress somewhere underground in the Midlands, where they had room for their families, if such people had families, and where it was rumoured they would be able to continue on for three or four generations.

The Captain listened with interest, and without interruption, his head cocked to one side. He would rather listen to this than what he had heard about Alex Quellan.

'Perhaps this is nothing: perhaps something,' he considered afterwards, pushing his booted foot between the angle of the boarded veranda floor and the weathered upright of the table leg. But this land still offered the hope of something: his instinct told him this.

What was clear was that, in the midst of its second generation, the Lyme group had become established and had prospered in its small way. But was there a need to do more? For the travellers, or for many of them, it was not enough: they had come to Britain for a purpose, even though the purpose was as yet lacking form. The history of the land immediately prior to the visitation of Surt did promise that those left alive might on the whole be less prone to the sort of lawlessness which had accompanied mainland Europe's dissolution, and in some places, descent into barbarism. Wengen and its immediate environs had by chance remained civilized, but the group had had at times to fight its way to Normandy with some losses that still grieved them sorely; that is, when any want of activity gave them the time to think about it.

The Werod Hundreds and the talk of an inspirational leader who had once upon a time gone north to find something, was enough to encourage the Captain. More than that: the mention of this Master or Messiah was a tale that grew in the telling. People had come forward with either their own recollections, if they were old enough to have been there, or those of a parent. He had come among them, this Messiah, among the despairing remnant of this coastal town. People now began to say about this moment in history that it had especial significance; that not long after this man had been accorded mythic status. It was said, they now fondly remembered, that with a touch of his hand or even a look he had been able to heal the sick. When he had arrived with his few followers, including children, he had radiated calm and inspired them from the outset. They had listened to the story of how he had survived the virus, and how his followers had likewise contracted it and survived, fleeing in the end from some makeshift hospital, on the edge of London, where thousands had lain dead. Thus, the story had grown, or perhaps fondly grew now in the retelling, that the Messiah had not only survived the virus but had cured the others, the most worthy and the innocent, and thereafter had begun to travel England doing good works. This was utter nonsense, Richard Jenkins, ruddy-faced Argonaut with a shock of silver-white hair and a robust frame, had grumbled to the Captain, who had with a wave of his hand and a frown subdued the vociferousness of his criticism. But, paradoxically, Jenkins was in a sense himself inspired, because the consensus now among the scientific group, of which he was a key member, was that this so-called Messiah had probably been heading for the provisional destination they had set for themselves, and the most likely place for success in finding a society which had done more than just survive the plague. That destination, which they had all agreed to make the objective of any expedition inland was the university-cum-township that had been the dream of Prime Minister Dain Alvis, who had laid its foundation stone in 2015. The place was one time called the University of Mercia and West Anglia, and though he had never been there, the Captain for one knew of its history, its planned purpose, and its location: it was he remembered at Weedon Bec in Northamptonshire, otherwise called by

Alvis's successor (because of its Celtic and later Saxon history and the probable original meaning of its name), Temple Hill, or Hill Temple. Temple Hill had a particular ring to it: they all liked the idea, perhaps because it would give to their quest a quasi-religious dimension.

People had other agendas, desires: to see what had become of Oxford, to perhaps see Stonehenge, to see the White Horse...but it was useful to determine a provisional end point.

A peel of church bells came from the old town, repeating tunefully over and over again, a fond reminiscence of childhood for those English among the travellers old enough, taking them back almost bodily to their days of growing up. Many smiled but were sad as they lifted their heads to catch the sound on the cooling sea breeze, drifting over the town, a siren sound.

'Every Thursday, morning and evening, and the same on Sundays,' explained Jonathan proudly. 'We inherited a bell-ringer who taught others, and we also have a band of sorts. Every twenty-fifth of March and every twenty-ninth of June we play the Dead March from Saul, among other things... in remembrance, you know, of all who passed away. The twenty-ninth was a date handed down, though we don't know its origin.'

The death throes of many rising unbidden to his mind, Valjean re-registered 'passed away', a euphemism he had not heard in a long time. Then he urged the assembled group of some thirty voyagers and their dozen or so hosts present to think hard on the planning of their activities, including the planning related to their expedition into the interior.

And so, after days during which men and women in white suits, looking every bit like astronauts, began the removal of the desiccated and dusty dead from the old town, preparations began for the journey inland.

It was decided that there would be one group only; a large group, men and women, fifty-six strong, comprising assorted scientists, craftsmen, medics and immediate family members in certain cases, though only five children were allowed, these between the ages of eleven and fifteen, three girls and two boys. Most had a skill or specialism to such a degree that the host community began to be accustomed to the travellers' gifts, achievements and abilities and were no longer surprised that someone or other of their number could turn his or her hand to just about anything.

The expedition would be led jointly by Valjean and the Captain, not really any sort of concession by the Lyme people since it was self-evident that these men would have the ability and decisiveness to make the best choices in time of peril. Valjean and his stern friend would be supported, in terms of the security of the enterprise, by six of the Captain's men and one woman, who was as tough as any of them, with a sinewy grip of steel developed through years of solo climbing in the Alps. A well-armed (much to the council members' consternation) contingent of twenty-five fighters would remain in Lyme as protectors of the original inhabitants of this community and of the greater part of the voyagers from Normandy, who had chosen and been chosen to remain there to build and renew, to fulfil the promises made to their hosts.

A planned date was set for the expedition's return; seven months hence, with the instruction that no one was to follow. This was understood by the Argonauts, based on precedent and thus the instruction was redundant, a mere formality. It was really for the benefit of the inhabitants of Lyme, some of whom had already found friends among those preparing to travel inland.

And so final plans were drawn up and provision made. A half-dozen milch cows were to be taken, though it was uncertain whether a life on the road would suit them, and a number of chickens in a large coop. The wayfarers on their leaders' advice took only a couple of horse-drawn carts and some newly constructed hand carts; the former taken long ago from a farm museum, the latter built by friends of Valjean. Petrol and diesel vehicles were still available but the Swiss and his fellow-leader advised against reliance on these, given the probability of overgrown or impassable roads, the uncertainty of fuel supplies and the importance of stealth, the importance of not being noticed by a possible enemy. In any case there were not enough serviceable motorized vehicles for all.

There was a great feasting day before the departure, with bonfires, outdoor games including wrestling, tug-o-war, and racing, and in the bay close to the shore competitive swimming. The festivities went on until just after midnight, with the plan being to set off at noon the next day. Then the party spilled out onto the soft sands under the Cobb wall, or along the beach, and people sat around the harbour wall with drinks clutched near the burning torch lights under a star-filled sky. Lights reflected and winked below in the slopping and slapping water that caressed the old stone as it had done for countless years of the comings and goings of people. The next day, however, brought torrential rain that thundered and lashed a boiling grey-black sea that crashed foaming white into the Cobb fortress. Yet the storm passed in a day and delayed them only for a day: they left with many a sad farewell as a nearby clock struck two o'clock on a fine afternoon: the hopeful but wary motley of humans and their animals moved out and up the hill, and then moved steadily through the abandoned village of Uplyme, which the sign showed was in the next county: from Dorset they had entered Devon.

Valjean, his hand loosely holding the reins of the lead horse, was thinking again of the strange sight Jonathan Number Seven had shown him three days earlier. The Captain, too, had been there with them, as had Esmerelda. They had, the four of them, been driven to Dorchester in an old Ford, and Jonathan had suggested that they get out and take a closer look at something just visible from the old main road, a road the community had worked hard to maintain over the years.

They had been able to make out the doughnut-shaped arrangement of lush green ancient earthworks which Jonathan told them, and the Captain knew to be Maiden Castle, fold upon fold, of man-made encircling ramparts and ditches, like piled-up inland waves of a verdant sea. On closer inspection, after a brisk walk, and the climb of the ramparts, they were at last able to make out, at its interior, the nature of the incongruous grey object they had discerned vaguely from the road. It was a cone-shaped body consisting of hundreds or thousands of discarded computers and their peripherals; monitors, some with smashed screens, keyboards, printers, and so on. Maiden Castle was not known to be an especially holy place, more a place of central defence for the Iron Age community that lived here - though close by there were the remains, stones growing out of the ground, of a Romano-Celtic temple; but this seemed none the less an act of sacrilege, an eyesore some sixty feet high. Was it a comment on the failure of the technological age, or simply an act of vandalism? Who had done this? It was a mystery. Valjean for one thought it odd that their quest should begin thus, with a riddle occupying his mind. The sun had come out as they had stood there looking at the grey-black jumble of weathered and dirty plastic and wires, and it cast its warming golden light upon them as they had stood in the shelter of a great rampart.

'What does it mean, old horse?' he said aloud now in English, laughing and affectionately rubbing the animal's nose. One of the Lyme people smiled at him just at that moment. A good sign, thought Valjean.

22. *A man in love*

He had gone into the wilderness and had been tempted by the Devil. Or had he been tempted by the Devil before he had gone into the wilderness? Or was this all a form of self-aggrandizing deceit; the setting up of some externalized tempter to put some space between himself and his decision, if indeed he were able to make such a decision?

It was a hot summer's afternoon, and not even a wilderness in the strictest sense of the word. But it was outside, some way outside, the outer-ring perimeter, which itself now lay out of sight beyond the dark hill-top wood that he had passed on his way down to this place.

He lay on the spare grass, and on the dry dusty ground close to the continuous babbling of shallow water over sparkling pebbles...water from the source, or one source of the River Nene. It was shallow here, but deeper over yonder, a few yards upstream, with reeds and bulrushes clustered below steep banks either side, silently mirroring the sky with its high cotton wool floating clouds. Away from the deep pool the river divided as it passed either side of a tiny raised patch of ground, a pebble-strewn ironstone sandy island upon which thistles and a few rough grasses clung to life. The water gurgled and bubbled in a continuous indecipherable pattern, yet a melodious accompaniment to the outward sounds of birds and buzzing insects and the inner sounds of busy thought.

The ground was bone dry and uncomfortable at the end of a long day of summer sun and a week without rain. He shaded his eyes then sat up. One most certainly could not think matters through in a prone position. He idly pushed at a large stone close to the edge of the grass, such as it was, moving it a few inches over the sandy soil towards the plashing, tinkling water. It, the water, was fulfilling its destiny, making its way downstream.

He had once read a whole book about water. The way the stream sparkled and danced in the light, in the foreground; beyond, the green fields and the old hedges unkempt, full of life. Water was a wonder... complex: the quintessence of life and the life process. He had read and studied so much over the last eight years of long winters which had merged into spring and begun again in late August, trapping them all for months at a time. He could not apply science or philosophy to his current problem, however; nor even logic, though he knew he would go over today, time and again, the arguments for and against, and the possible consequences of action or inaction.

The more he thought about it the more difficult it became, the more remote and nebulous the answers he was seeking.

He actually shook his fists in front of him, in a sort of hand-wringing gesture, as he stood up then paced along the river bank, as if to say, 'Come on, think!' But thinking, he knew, was his downfall. He needed instead to access some kind of emotional intelligence, which all his recent duties in and for the community, all his voracious acquiring of knowledge, seemed to have driven from his being.

He ducked to one side and swung a hand clumsily, comically, at an insect that buzzed in his ear, or close to it; and he had to do so three times before it would leave him alone. 'Of course, I'm close to the river,' he thought, 'always insects.' It had been a reflex, his initial attempt at swatting the insect, for in truth he would not hurt anything living if he could help it. He had seen enough of death in all its guises, and for this reason he had chosen to eat neither meat nor fish. At the same time, he knew that the plenitude of other foodstuffs he had access to had made this decision an easier one to make, unlike the one he had now to work towards.

The sun was so bright that the light reflecting from the water hurt his eyes almost, but it was a comfortable sort of discomfort. He walked now in the opposite direction, going upstream the few yards that would enable him to look into the deep pool of still water, or seeming still water. This was a holding place only: in its depths a current stirred as the water moved towards shallow fork around the little island before its journey downstream.

The water was still and deep, sky-reflecting, but giving no answers, as a magical mirror might. He hardly processed this thought consciously, but moved from the lush grass here, back to the sparse growth beside the fast-flowing shallows.

This place, this whole area, had been covered in snow, four and five feet deep, with thirty-foot drifts, snow that hung around for months: he could probably still find some dirty clump of snow-ice if he searched in the shade of hedgerow. He couldn't remember whether scouting reports had stated that the river had entirely frozen over this year: he thought not, which probably meant the winters were getting less harsh. What had caused them? The consensus in the community was that it had all been caused by a huge volcanic eruption. Some said that it had been Yellowstone. He remembered the diaries which he and a few others had had access to. My God, *that* philosophy of life, *that* world view was difficult to grasp. An understatement... Quellan... He shuddered. It was a study in itself, and it would be a long, long trial of mental strength. But that was not what he was here for.

He watched some birds moving overhead, and behind and around him, low, quite close to him at times, moving quickly. They were swallows; yes, without doubt, they were swallows. How had such life survived these winters? He knew little about bird migrations; perhaps that was it. He and his original companions would most certainly not have survived had they been out in the open, in the almost empty countryside, in the dead and abandoned villages, littered with vehicles standing still and gathering dust and bird droppings, mocking the very technological progress and prosperity they had once been emblematic of.

Did he love her? Did he love her with a passion that both could adjust to? He had been shocked by his sudden feeling of desire and lust. The whole business had made him feel dirty, degenerate, and older, much older than his thirty-four years. At the same time, he loved her.

Her deep blue eyes were radiant, stunning: they always had been. At the outset their gaze had pierced his soul, as though she were an angel looking at him: but he had never before, until now, thought of her in *that* way. Since then they had been through so much together. She was, as they used to say, pure as the driven snow. At eighteen, almost nineteen, she was quite tall now, almost as tall as him. She had straight, black, shoulder-length hair, if one were prosaic about it. Her face was too strong and broad for some to call her beautiful, perhaps her forehead too high but he loved the porcelain clarity of the smooth skin of her forehead, the shape of her mouth, the slightly snub but symmetrical nose, and the faint but noticeable freckling of the skin of the cheekbones. She had for so long been his great friend and they had laughed together and understood one another, together against the perils of the world. To other males, boys, and men younger than he was, she seemed distant, reserved, aloof and unfriendly even.

He had seen them look at her as she passed, as though they were in awe of her, not daring to approach her, then turning away, losing interest as though she were cold and alien, some sort of ice maiden. In some ways she was ordinary, if he was honest about it: her speech was ordinary, with a trace of a regional accent, but he could not be objective about it: her voice haunted him now. And when she looked at him now, he wondered whether she could see it in his eyes - the change.

This had been going on for six months now, ever since she had returned from a short expedition. He had been so relieved to see her, and she him, that they had embraced. But he had without thinking embraced her as a lover would, and he had kissed her soft hair which was cold and damp from the night air. He had felt at once a change between them, immediate on his side as he considered his feelings; and on hers too: she had seemed to know, but then, had he been imagining this? For his part, from the moment of that embrace he knew he loved her and must never let her go, his companion, his guide, his deliverer.

So how could he declare his love now? Could he do so without betraying his lust?... because it was a physical love and not some high-minded spiritual fancy... Would he be risking losing her companionship for evermore? On the other hand, could he bear to stand by and watch a boy, or a young man of her own age go through the process of winning her, taking away all hope that she could ever be his? Crisis point: yes, it was the crisis point, now, by that river.

Idly, abstractedly, he picked up a smooth pebble which he launched at the deep pool. A good shot, it landed dead centre. He watched from his slight distance and thought he could make out the spreading and increasing concentric circles of the shock wave. He remembered his school days when water ripples were used to demonstrate the actions or the properties of sound waves. Learning was getting in the way of his emotional decision making. Were intellect and emotion contradictory? Could they exist simultaneously?

He could reason this out. He would give himself up to reason, and to work. The celibate: yes, at least for the time being. But why? He had read a passage somewhere from a foreign novel, with a translation to hand, when he was struggling to learn German - yes, it had been a German novel - in which a psychoanalyst had suggested to an audience of sick people that suppression or denial of the sexual urges led to actual physical illness. The character's name: was it Korohov, or was it Karensky? What did it matter? And was that the author's view? What did that matter either? It would be like a sentence of living-death to deny his love, to deny that it really existed. It was probable that it had been there for some months, a latency, waiting for his mind to come to the conscious realization.

He stared across to his left, looking downstream as he moved to the water's edge, his faded dark canvas shoes, with their white trim, almost touching the rippling surface, watching the play of the light, hearing the rattling of stones, trying to understand the chaos of the tiny currents, searching for minnows in the quieter shallows, if any had survived. He turned from this and looked downstream to a darker place, shaded by trees close to the bank, a place where another dark pool had formed. Light and dark: a moment of frozen time.

He was suddenly aware of something, and he looked up into the blue vault with straining eyes shielded by his long-fingered hand. A bird, majestic and high, very high, heading parallel to the stream, south-eastward: a huge bird, a sea eagle he thought.

Birds held a special significance for him. A sea eagle, a messenger of Neptune... He smiled, then actually laughed exaggeratedly, out loud, at his fanciful notion.

He looked around. Still alone, on this bright afternoon... down by the river. A fanciful notion, but probably a sea eagle, none the less.

Who was that character? A German novel... Then he remembered something else he had read in translation, in one of those useful dual language books that had once been popular, a short story about an attorney, a story by Goethe. The attorney had lost his daughter or son: the child had died, and he was inconsolable in his grief, and nothing, not world travel, nor any experience, could wipe it from his mind. Nothing could: nothing would. A sob came unbidden, catching him unawares, as sometimes happened, even after ten years; a picture in his mind of the people he had lost. Was he feeling sorry for himself? Did he wish to die? Was he being tempted? The proximity, the interaction, or the conflict between Eros and Thanatos, Freud's Love and Death drives, linked to war, to the death wish...

'Freud!' he said, throwing another stone off to the right, hearing it land with a 'ploop'. 'Not convinced by what you said. Go and sink to the bottom of the class.' This gesture made him laugh, so he picked up three more stones, intending likewise to dispose of Kant's Categories, Hegel's synthesizing hypotheses, and Schopenhauer's idea of art as a form of intuiting the unknowable and the role of the universal will. But he dropped the stones to the ground, tired of his irreverent gestures, slightly angry that he was pleased with himself for remembering things that were of no use to him at that moment, and, in any case, concepts which he had never really engaged with, and so never really understood. The decision he had to make was as far away as ever.

A breeze got up and he suddenly felt cold. The thin cotton shirt he had felt quite warm enough was no longer adequate to the task. He pulled out an old grey sweater from the rucksack he had abandoned nearby and took from it a drink of fruit-flavoured water which immediately refreshed him.

But it was getting late. He would be expected back. They would be worrying about him and soon sending out search parties. He was important to them, he knew, and that made him feel better. Should this, too, form part of the basis for his decision?

Was that it? Thinking of others would help him to choose, the act of thinking of others, that is. It had been his maxim in life, ever since he had contracted the virus and survived, just as she had done? Surely this had been a sign? He was strong and youthful and forward-looking, despite his experiences, his personal losses; and who had not had to endure such things? She too was strong and healthy: they, both of them, might look forward to many years of life - together? She was beautiful in his eyes. She was still eighteen; and though he was almost halfway through his thirties, they had so much in common... Fate had after all thrown them together ...

He must not allow it to get too late, both in the hour and in his life - a metaphor for life, his life, a prompter of his decision? The hour was late, and he might leave this matter until it was too late. The hour: it might inconvenience those who would worry and who would decide to come looking for him. Being out here had spelled danger in the recent past. Only two years earlier he and a group of others had saved her and her companions from a pack of wild and ravenous dogs: two summers ago, when it had seemed still like the midwinter... His life: too late if he lost her through vacillation and indecision.

They were coming down the hill, tiny dots emerging from the spinney to begin with, crossing a field, then appearing on his side of the hedge, following the hedge-line in the field he was in, and moving down toward the place by the river where he stood, approaching him from the oddly named Hob Hill.

There were perhaps a dozen of them, his people. The very idea of *his people* made him smile.

He had been packing up his meagre belongings anyway, almost without realizing it. He had made his decision. He turned and left the friendly river, with its pebbly little island, behind him. The hour was quite late, but the sun was still up, beginning now noticeably to cast longer shadows; but the birds were still singing, and he saw in their songs the joy of life. That was his mood at that moment, so was it not the right decision?

And what of her? Living close to him as she had grown up, she had seen him with two different women over the years; a long relationship in one case that had come to a mutually agreed amicable end. Yet her devotion to him had seemed not to waver, and it had become more powerful as she approached womanhood. He would no longer torture his mind, he had decided, because of the nature of that devotion. He would tell her of his love, and he would tell her too that he would wait three years for her, to see whether she felt the same way. She was and would be, he thought, sensible enough to see that this period of waiting was important. She was a serious girl and had grown even more thoughtful of late; something perhaps of his doing. She probably sensed this time approaching. Whether she wanted or dreaded it, he had to follow his decided course of action.

She was not among the search party and he was glad of that; but he intended to speak to her this very evening. It was difficult to look beyond this and at the very thought of it his stomach churned; but tomorrow, with his reading partner, a former avionics engineer, he would sit down and read through some pages of those chilling notes, diaries, musings and statements of intent of Alex Quellan: an early exploration of these writings was planned, no more than that: it was estimated that close knowledge and understanding might take years. As a key member of the community he had agreed the rule, a rule for the time being, that no person should alone have access to these writings, nor any group that might form a clique; such was judged to be their terrible and corrupting influence; and yet these writings were also judged to be a window of wisdom on the follies of mankind. This last view was something he would struggle to come to terms with, though the consensus was that this thorny path to a possible universal truth was one they should all follow. But first, there was the matter close to his heart.

So, the man, lean and long, and looking more at ease than when he had arrived at the riverbank, was mentally preparing for the difficult and serious task ahead of him, even as with good humour and back slapping he greeted his companions.

23. *What they had seen and done*

Old England and older still... They had arrived at a place called Longcot on a wet September's day. Through the morning drizzle, which had followed thunderous downpours that seemed to have drenched them and all they had in despite of the protective awnings they had erected, they thought they could discern some of the chalk markings on the hill southward whereon they knew they must find the ancient White Horse.

The drizzle was a drenching curtain, a mist before their eyes as they looked across the grey-green vale towards what should be Dragon Hill and White Horse Hill. Mere undulations these hills, it had to be said, to the men and women who had spent so many years in the Oberland, but still something of interest here in this foreign empty land.

Of immediate concern was the condition of a young man originally from Dorchester, who had come along as one of the Lyme contingent. The friendly, gangling youth, whom Valjean had likened, without originality, the English wryly noted, to an eager young puppy, had been feverish for some days and had had a faint rash of indeterminate nature. The medics were four in number; though, aside from the eldest, they had, of necessity and because the times were such, been trained in a makeshift sort of way. They were in agreement on one point: it was not pneumonia.

Adam was feeling better, however. He was awake and chatting and smiling, and sipping, if weakly, at the meat and barley broth that had just been prepared for him. By his side, still looking concerned, was a pretty and petite French girl with dark saucer eyes and a Cupid's bow mouth. She was herself by turns animated and exhausted, relieved but worn out by her night's vigil. In spite of their contingent of medical experts, both travelling with them and at their new base on the English coast, and the fact that they were well provided with medicines, the travellers from the Argo always feared illness, that or disability that might arise as a result of accident. Beyond their small communities, as far as they knew, there was no help that they could call upon. For that reason, any expert in this field who could be gathered up or gleaned from the scattered remnant of blasted humanity was usually a welcome addition to any group.

The fact that the boy Adam seemed on the road to recovery - his rash of tiny pink-red spots had begun to fade, his temperature almost back to normal - lightened the mood of the travellers, a mood which had been dampened by the whole business of his illness and by the incessant rain, which had also now begun to abate.

As the morning progressed the grey curtain lifted, and they could see the lines, or some of the lines, of the Horse. It was true, the elderly female doctor said, that you could not really see the whole of the chalk figure from the plain but needed an elevated position.

'If you want to see it properly, at its best, we have to become airborne again,' she said earnestly, addressing the Captain, who stood tall and dark above her under the porch-flap of the south-facing tented enclosure that was serving as a makeshift hospital.

The Captain stared down into the slightly wizened bespectacled, heavily freckled face. There was something in this ageing academic's enthusiasm for the little, arcane details of such matters, something that amused him. He had known her for years and in truth was very fond of her.

'We can get a good view from that hill on the left - perhaps, 'he said.

She thought for a moment. 'Yes, Dragon Hill... A hobby of mine, as you know - early English history.' She looked a little self-conscious, as she often did when enthusing about her hobbies and interests, but as usual her enthusiasm got the better of her. 'It's the White Horse of Uffington. It's a genuinely old chalk figure, unlike many in the country... probably three thousand years old, from the Bronze Age. Some people claim it's not a horse, but in the eleventh century an Abingdon cartulary, which was written on vellum by monks of the order...' She stopped, noticing that the Captain's normally stern gaze had changed to one of polite concealed amusement; but she felt compelled to continue... 'However, the monks referred to it as *mons albi equi*, meaning White Horse Hill. What is exciting is that now the mist is clearing we can begin to see that it has been regularly scoured...'

'Scoured?' A number of others turned their heads, including the nearby Valjean.

'Yes,' said the doctor excitedly,' it was always done every seven years to keep the lines clear; and even from here they look clearer, cleaner and sharper to me than forty years of neglect would have made them, do you see?'

Yes, they did see. If it were really true, then another community of people was active in this area and had the time to expend energy on such matters.

Closer inspection later that morning showed that the monument had indeed been scoured, the wide chalk lines of its three hundred and seventy feet long figure had been was cleared of grass overgrowth and the lines topped up with pounded limestone chips. The work had been carried out in recently, probably in the last two years. This was encouraging, something to offset the strangely disturbing and pointless discovery at Maiden Castle.

They needed some new hope on this expedition. Winchester, Andover, Newbury, had had a depressing similarity about them, even though it had all been as they expected: buildings, empty of life, eyeing them as they passed by; shops with broken windows, traces of the final desperate scenes of looting perhaps; cars and other vehicles, abandoned and at odd angles, littering the streets. In Newbury, near the racecourse, there had been a coach full of dead people, people long dead of course; desiccated corpses, lots of dusty bottles aboard, a mystery.

Everywhere had been so quiet, so empty, and yet they had picked up three new people on the way, people who had been eking out an existence in the dead towns and villages. Two were in their forties. It was usually the case: children at the time of the plague, who had grown old watching their parents or other relatives grow older and give up the ghost, falling victim to malnutrition, bad water, or the visitation of disease, or a sudden acute problem such as appendicitis. The voyagers, and the people of Lyme, had had on occasion to carry out appendectomies; but for isolated people there was no hope - a horrible painful death.

Whenever they were in the towns, outlying estates with functional but soulless mini shopping areas, or Victorian terraces cluttered with cars, and in one case, black wheelie bins ready for a collection that never came, it had been the silence which oppressed them. In the countryside, too, abandoned farms, the skeletons of dead animals... There were other animals too; feral dogs, and wolves which the shrunken, ragged old man they had chanced upon, their third survivor, in his sixties now, had told them about, repeating wildly that he had seen them with his own eyes. The man talked to himself a lot: isolation, decades of isolation and solitude, had driven him close to madness. But he may well have been right about the wolves: possibly their antecedents had escaped or been released from Whipsnade Zoo in the Chilterns, a place with a chalk figure of its own, a lion on the hillside created in the twentieth century - people had been able to see it from the train as they travelled south on the Rugby-Northampton to London Euston line. The man added to the wolf stories with tales of lions and polar bears, which he said had come down from the far north in the long winters of a score and more years ago. Most doubted that there was any truth in this however.

In the countryside too, ancient defunct monuments to the last gasp of the drive for green energy, like grim grey-white sentinels, clusters of wind turbines standing idle, their blades twisted or smashed by a succession of destructive winters, ice-damaged with no one to come and repair them.

That evening, they came to the market square at Wantage, and a score of yards in front of an estate agent's smashed windows, crumbling brickwork and now pointless weather-stained displays, there stood proudly with scroll in one hand and long sword in the other, on its base, the marble statue of the only English king labelled Great, Alfred of Wessex. They marvelled at this because everywhere else, in many other towns, including Lyme, they had seen only statues of Dain Alvis, erected in most cases on the instruction, directly or indirectly, of Alex Quellan.

The old king, warrior and law-giver seemed a comfort to them somehow. Golden rays of the westering sun cut obliquely across the white-grey weathered face, almost lending animation to its frozen stare.

The statue had been there not much more than two hundred years, the doctor-historian eagerly told them: it had been moved from St James's Palace, its original site. The sculptor had been a nephew of Queen Victoria. That was, she said, all she really knew about it.

Did it really matter? Valjean was thinking as he poured out water for Dante into a metal bowl. The sturdy black dog determinedly lapped at it, his pink tongue working furiously, his deep brown eyes looking wild, excited, the whites showing. Valjean pondered: a moment's reflection. The statue, the silently gazing buildings about them, they were all from the dead past. The chronology, the passage of humankind seemed lumped together into two elements: the whole of history, the past, and the struggle for continued survival, the present. No continuity: it had been thus ever since the plague; the daily, weekly tactics of survival, and the strategy, the strategic planning of sorts for the longer-term survival. Then he realized that this had always been the case; that which is now and that which can never be recovered, gone forever. The old king, the great king of the ninth century, was no comfort to Valjean, but did appear to mean more to the English contingent, brought up in this century on the radical history championed by Alvis, and by his successor, the enigmatic Quellan. He reminded himself that he must speak to his friend, the Captain, to make sure he was not brooding about that particular matter.

'The crowds lined the streets here in 1877 and the Prince of Wales attended... he unveiled the statue, 'someone ventured, emboldened and encouraged by the doctor-historian's snippet of information. She went on to say that when she was a child her parents, who had had relatives here, had often spoken about visiting Wantage, and had told her about the statue.

On a more practical note, and as the sun started to sink in a red-gold glow, the Captain, seconded by Valjean, instructed that their camp be spread out at the edges of the square, close to the buildings on either side. They would all be too exposed to view if they crowded together for the night close by the statue. It was important, given that *someone* had been around to renovate the White Horse. Better to assume foe rather than friend and so avoid unnecessary risk.

At bottom was the suspicion on the part of the Captain, Valjean and one or two others that they were indeed being watched. It was a sixth sense that had rarely let them down in the past and had prevented catastrophe on more than one occasion in their crossing of the European mainland.

The leaders quietly discussed the matter, so as not to alarm the whole group, and agreed upon the doubling up of the night watch, and the sending out of a two pairs of reconnaissance scouts, one pair on each of their flanks as they advanced, further forward from the main column than was usually the case, this arrangement to begin the very next day.

Thus, they journeyed on to Oxford, drawn by the spires, the ancient butter-coloured stone buildings and the prospect of some form of welcome. The ancient seat of learning offered the possibility that someone over the passage of four decades might have been around to resurrect a community of some description.

But it was not to be: they were disappointed. In many of the streets they had to pick their way between dusty windblown piles of rags which may or may not have contained skeletal remains. Crows and a few pigeons watched their passing from the high rooftops. No one really wanted to enter the buildings, and those who tentatively suggested this were discouraged, whether the suggestion related to the Bodleian Library or two of the more famous old pubs, The Eagle and Child and The Lamb and Flag, gazing at one another over a wet and desolate St Giles, whose tarmac surface, as elsewhere, was scarred and pitted here and there with potholes sometimes six or more inches deep - unrepaired damage caused by a decade of long hard winters and four decades in all of total neglect. The winters had done a lot of the damage in the years following the dreadful passing of Surt, and now life, the undeniable sunlight-seeking life of plants, had found its way to the surface and was beginning to erase the efforts of humankind.

Though some were certain they were being watched, they saw no other signs of life, aside from the birds, and a lone feral cat which nervously ducked into the shadows to avoid them. A city of ghosts.

They turned north-eastward, then followed the desolate, deserted M40, with its abandoned vehicles and pitted surface. Vegetation on many stretches was already pushing through the outer edges of the tarmac, and in places self-seeded sycamores and other young trees had begun clustering at the once-called hard shoulders. It was becoming a grim and nerve-straining odyssey, and the leaders noticed that people were beginning to look tired and dispirited; though no one as yet had suggested turning back. There was still the prize, or the grail, of the rumoured new settlement in the heart of Northamptonshire, which the most recent English history they had, that which they had picked up at Lyme, suggested to them that this place they sought had been the destination of the young spiritual leader who had once visited and inspired the survivors of the southern coastal town. But that tale was set almost forty years ago. Perhaps the story, if not apocryphal, was overblown. Even if it were true, the man might have died en route, or found nothing when he arrived, or could not find the place he was searching for... And now he would have 'sixty or more winters on his head' as the Irish poet would have it: the more they thought about prospects for success, whatever that might be, the more doubtful they became that the journey would have a good outcome. Still, as they had done in the past, they would persevere: there was nothing else to do, no other acceptable course of action.

It was decided that they would make a short detour to Brill, around whose old windmill they could camp and whose elevated position might reveal signs of human life in the distance. But it turned out there was nothing: no one moving across the plain below, not a puff of smoke, nor any sign of human life, just the wheeling birds, and a single eerie animal shriek they could not identify.

They moved on, using the M40 again: slow determined progress, until they arrived at the old, silent and still junction eleven near Banbury. From here they headed north-north-east along a decaying, empty A-road, overhung with handsome old trees.

They had re-provisioned at a satellite estate north of Oxford but would need a source of fresh water in the coming days.

They were discussing the water situation and the longer-term food provisions, the Captain, the rugged Valjean and two of the Lyme contingent, as they turned a corner on an elevated stretch of road when suddenly they stopped dead and just gazed, speechless with wonder.

They could, all of them, smell it now and wondered that they had not noticed it before. There was the scent, the rich earthy odour of the wheat harvest in the air, filling the air; and around and in front of them as far as the eye could see, field upon field of stubble dotted with neat bales of straw. A palpable wave of excitement, amazement and unbounded joy swept over the travellers, who all rushed forward to see the fields of gold all about them. The sun was shining as though to light them on their way. It was the promise of a new Eden.

24. *Seat of Learning*

Just as a medieval community lay clustered by a parish church or huddled up against the wall of a Norman castle, so this community radiated outwards and downwards from its central building complex on the hill.

At the epicentre of the set of buildings, which spread out over the surface of the hill in an imperfect circle, was an ornamented castellated octagonal red-brick tower three hundred and fifty-seven feet high. As it was built on the topmost level of the high ground upon which the township stood, the tower's rooftop observation area seemed a giddy height, a height from which could be surveyed wide tracts of countryside. Nine miles or so to the east and visible on clear days was the crumbling lift-testing tower on the edge of the town of Northampton, a straight and broken finger of grey pointing up to a sky that looked over the gloomy prospect of a still abandoned town that could have been any town in the land, any town except this place, the inhabitants supposed. Close by the grey tower on the eastward skyline, and more elevated because of its position on a high ground was a campanile-style clock tower, the centrepiece of a housing estate, but once upon a time the centrepiece of a massive red-brick complex of buildings that people had called a lunatic asylum when it was built in the late nineteenth century: close to this tower was a large vivid white building, once a residence for nursing staff, it was said, subsequently converted to luxury flats when the hospital was demolished. These were the landmarks of the eastern skyline. All around, there were rises and depressions in the land, large arable fields, a meandering river, dark spinneys and nestling parish churches in long abandoned but no longer entirely dead villages, a picturesque panorama.

In the near distance beyond the old canal which ran close to the eastern perimeter wall, and beyond the sparkling ribbon of the river in the valley, eastward and north-eastward, lay the village of Flore, partly obscured by another wooded hill. It was said that Charles 1 had paused here for a time, coming down the hill to Weedon Bec, to view the terrain before moving on westward to the town of Daventry, once called Danetre and once part of the Danelaw lands, where the King would spend the night before the fateful and decisive encounter at Naseby. A hill at Danetre, Borough Hill, was where Charles's army made its last camp and was higher than the hill that overlooked Weedon Bec, the hill upon which the tower stood; and from Borough

Hill it was said, in a line due eastwards you could find no higher point until your impossibly scanning eye, like that of some supernatural being, lighted upon the Urals of Russia; unless you were to count in this reckoning the roof of Temple Hill's tower. Temple Hill, University and Township, on hilltop flourishing, where, it was said, goodness reigned.

From the tower in one direction you could look to the township's eastern gate and thence down the hill beyond the ribbon of canal and the parallel line of the inevitably disused railway to what had once been a High Street with thriving shops and heavy traffic passing through, down to the crossroads and to the meandering river, narrow at that point, only a few miles from its source - the Nene. If you looked immediately below from the tower you could see the new 'town' and its plan for the surface dwellings: seven concentric circles, each with a protecting wall, and between the rings of walls pleasant places to live with ornamental well-tended gardens, places of rest and contemplation, and of work. Much of what was here though was below ground.

The central positioning of the tower was no accident. Aside from architectural considerations, the vision was thus: the university was the town and the town the university, so that the tower served as a symbol of unity expressive of the whole philosophy of the community. The complex had been built as a place for learning and a place in which to survive and live, built for a future which had elsewhere, as far as they knew, all but disappeared. This was not exactly the case: some finer understanding of the purpose of this town in miniature, more substantial, more active below ground than above, was held by those who exercised what can only be described as a benign control over all matters here, academic, spiritual, pastoral and corporeal. Control was the wrong word, the leaders would say: it was case of steering the ship, to avoid the type disastrous collisions which had befallen humanity on countless occasions. A few, including the beloved Leader, Master, Guide, as he was variously called, knew most of the real story of the twenty-first century's plague, a story and a truth accessible only to those inhabitants who had passed through a long and painstakingly designed course of study that would minimize the possibility of their being corrupted or disturbed by what was contained within the library. People, it was agreed, had to be spiritually as well as academically prepared for what was truly shocking...

Many of the inhabitants liked to refer to this place, this hilltop community, as a township, though some called it simply a university, others a seat of learning, others their living space. It was also called the Centre... It had once been called the University of Mercia and West Anglia. This had been proposed during the early phases of its building under Prime Minister Alvis, and though the foundation stone near the south gate commemorated this, the title had been dropped by most of those who lived there...

In short, what was important was that it existed, and continued to exist. In its way it thrived and was home to some three thousand people, many of whom explored no further than a dozen miles from its prominent tower and were content to be thus contained, perhaps waiting for a time when the world would recover, perhaps fearing the world. For many of the young, they knew that the memories of their living parents harboured visions, recollections of the apocalyptic plague, and of the eight years of terrible winters when even this place was hard put to it to survive. The parents, some of them, were survivors of both ordeals: it was difficult to believe that there was much left of humanity beyond the sanctuary of a place such as this. Perhaps too this place had been uniquely created, the last refuge... humanity's last hope...

The Department of Alternative Histories, in the School of History, Subterranean Level 1, with natural light reflected in, down through wide tubes, from above...

Seven teenage students, four of them girls, and one of whom was stealing furtive, sly, half-glances at one of the boys, who with equal shyness returned them from time to time, as the mentor, a woman in her forties, but looking no more than twenty-five, spoke again, this time selecting dark-haired and serious Lucas.

'Lucas, if you apply the methodology we've discussed to the Battle of Hastings, what happened?'

Lucas, a bright boy, though everyone here was considered bright or having the potential to be so... Lucas, a bright boy, then, considered for a moment, wanting to speak well but mindful of his tutor's guidance.

'The Battle of Hastings,' he began slowly, looking upwards to the light, that was the diffusing end of the tube that brought natural light from the surface, 'the Battle of Hastings might have taken place either much earlier in 1066, much earlier than October, or some days earlier than the event that unfolded... I shall assume the latter... that William, Duke of Normandy, landed in mid-September, before King Harold could have had news of the Norwegian King's invasion in the north. The tides were favourable to the Norman invasion which went ahead before it's fated date, with the same level of men and materials...'

He hesitated but was given confidence to continue by the tutor's smile and nod of encouragement.

'King Harold had not even stood his army down for the winter and had been expecting William's invasion attempt. His army, in a state of readiness and strong, did not have to make a forced march towards York to defeat Harald Hardrada, or march all the way back down south, all in the space of three of four weeks. Harold defeated William's army: the Duke of Normandy was killed. There was no invasion, the battle did not even take place at Hastings, but at Pevensey. There was no Norman Conquest, as I said, no Norman castles were built, and Saxon rule continued. England's remained a northern culture with closer links to Scandinavia than southern or mainland Europe, even though there had been and remained Saxon links to the Roman church.' Lucas halted, wanting to say more about what did not become of England. 'With the possibility,' he continued with the tutor nodding encouragement,' or the probability that England played no major part in European intrigues, wars, and benefited not at all from the inspiration of the Renaissance, neither in Science nor the Arts, because there was no great Elizabethan age, no Shakespeare, no scientific revolution, no colonization of North America...

'No American War of Independence, and so on,' his tutor suggested. Her smooth-skinned grey-eyed face melted into a kindly smile, so that Lucas thought she looked both sympathetic and wise at the same time. 'I want to see you all to write down your thoughts on this subject and see where your flights of fancy take you. But remember: they are not necessarily flights of fancy in one respect: History is full of turning points: kings, queens, parliaments, dictators and democracies alike have made choices whose consequences they could but vaguely have predicted. So that's your out-of-class work... though do remember the other side of the coin, as we have said: the past is the past, she added in a businesslike manner, out of habit, though herself lost in thought. She was thinking all History, always and everywhere, hung on single moments.

'To end today's session, and since you've all looked at this a little already, Katherine' - the girl who had been looking at the boy quickly focused her attention on the woman standing in front of her, 'take us through the invasion of the Soviet Union... in a few sentences.'

'Well,' Katherine began, confidently, 'events showed that the Soviet Union did much of the fighting on the ground against Nazi Germany, though it needed supplies from its allies and a second front to achieve victory: it was a combined effort... a world effort... I have considered the possibility that Japan, as Germany's ally, attacked the Soviet port of Vladivostok, instead of Pearl Harbour. This meant Stalin's Siberian divisions which came to the aid of Moscow were instead pinned down in the east. America, the United States, did not declare war and Stalin's decision to stay in Moscow led to his death when the city eventually fell. The subsequent swift collapse in the medium term of Soviet resistance left the Germans in a position to again attack Britain and successfully invade. The US was subsequently annihilated by a nuclear attack, delivered by submarine or more likely by some form of V weapon from the Caribbean., without war having been declared. The US itself had never worked with the British and Jewish refugee scientists on a nuclear weapon themselves... The Nazis got there first.'

The tutor was encouraged by these speculative attempts, and concluded: 'As a final thought, you might consider the choices open to us now, as individuals and as a community. As well as alternative histories, we can dream of alternative futures: rather more difficult without the benefit of hindsight...'

And so, to Science, a floor lower and close to an acre of laboratories that served not only the university but the community in all its manifestations and in all it needed. Some of its labs were out of bounds to students. There was piped-in natural light here too, supplemented by electric lighting for prep rooms and three photographic dark rooms.

'This is what you have to consider,' the Professor, an honorary and affectionate title for this animated round-shouldered little man whose wild mop of iron-grey hair resembled that of his hero Albert Einstein, shook his hands in front of his face, clenching his fists as he hammered home his point, showing that it was really important to him that his score of students grasp the truth, in this, the introductory first session of the year. 'You have to consider that the labelling of science into neat divisions of Chemistry, Physics, Biology, for example, is to an extent arbitrary, a mistake possibly, a mistake of history. Of course, our tendency to classify or rank things in order, is natural to us and helped us to develop as a species, so the word mistake is a being a little unkind to us all' - a ripple of laughter - 'but do consider that all chemical reaction is dependent on electrical and physical energy in some form: electrical energy, and the strong and weak nuclear forces, electromagnetic interactions, all of which combine to govern the lives of sub-atomic particles. Of course,' he said after a moment and a drink of water, 'we have to have some form of terminology to work with. As Kant suggested, though I won't dwell on Philosophy,' - he took more than a passing interest in this, however, as he well knew - 'and the term he used, as it has been translated, is actually Categories, and it is a way, according to Kant, of giving form and structure to our perceptions of the world, linking the inner being to the outer universe. A philosopher might put it better and keep you all here for three days and nights...' Again, a ripple of laughter around the class...

At the very time the Professor, so-called, in his enthusiasm, was temporarily losing the thread of his opening lecture in his Introduction to New Science, the Captain and Jules Valjean stood with three companions just in front of the porch of All Saints Church in the village of Flore, and barely more than a crow's mile from where he was speaking.

The travellers' main encampment was on the recreation ground or playing field of the historic old village, out of sight of the church and beyond the grounds of a large, Georgian-style house built of Northamptonshire stone.

The expedition leaders were, however, focused with a keen intensity only on present-time matters, except that is for a surprising revelation on the Captain's part.

As they stared out over the overgrown churchyard, with its leaning stones commemorating the dead, stones now deep in coarse grasses, over the stubble field beyond the iron railings, and southwards to the line of hedge that marked the course of the river, the Captain, in a sheepish manner for him, and with an awkward smile that wrinkled the scar down his cheek, said suddenly to Valjean: 'I was a boy here. I know this place well.'

'*Mon Dieu*! Are you serious? How is it that you said nothing before, except to say that you were familiar with the land? I had no idea...' Valjean smiled his crooked-teethed smile, patting Dante who was standing on his back legs, his front paws on his master's chest, gazing upwards, expectantly.

The Captain explained that he had lived here for two years and had attended the primary school, which stood at ninety degrees to the Georgian house at the end of a wide road, which itself ran for eighty metres or so from the school to a patch of waste ground close by the churchyard gates, a secluded spot where hearses would park when such times arose, or where parents would park their cars when picking up their children from choir practice, the Church in general having gone through something of a revival in the twenty-thirties. If you stood at this point you could look back towards the mellow, sandy-ochre stone of the older part of the Victorian-period school, with the large house on your right hand and a high ivy-covered wall to your left. Immediately to your right, too, a winding little road ran down for a quarter of a mile to the picturesque old mill and mill race. The Captain, Valjean learned, had been at the school from the age of nine to eleven; then the family had moved closer to London. As they gazed southward, viewing in the autumn sunshine the thread of a worn dusty path that ran from the iron kissing gate on that side of the churchyard, through the stubble field and down to a footbridge known to the Captain in the old days, but out of sight from where they stood, Valjean learned to his amusement that the Captain as a little boy from a church-going family had often sat with his school-friends on one or other of the two tomb chests that stood close to the church entrance. There he had sat, swinging his legs, and trying to scare his friend by saying that through the narrow dark cracks between the stone joints he could see a dead body. The Captain was secretly pleased that his mountaineering friend, so far away and unknown to him in his childhood, should now be standing here smiling and chuckling about his past.

'This is continuity, my friend,' Valjean said in his heavy mix of accents. 'This is a good sign. I have not felt so,' -he searched for the expression - 'light of heart since we left Lyme Regis.'

There was another reason for hope. A messenger had visited them at their encampment an hour or so before sunset on the previous day. He had been the head or spokesperson of a party of six men, rustic in their dress someone said, and with a monk-like respectfulness and modesty in their demeanour. It had been agreed that they, a representative group of the travellers' leaders, were to be escorted from here to what they called the Centre, or if they preferred to call it so, the university township of Temple Hill. An approach would be made from the river and up to the church, so that the newcomers could see from afar that their guides offered no threat. This had seemed at first to Valjean's group overly submissive and perhaps not to be trusted; but this opportunity was after all the very reason they had come here, so fears of this kind were all but dismissed. Just in case, they had left behind the main contingent of their toughest heavily armed fighters. But in truth they did not sense a real threat; and they were usually right about such matters.

The party approached at last, a small stirring at first against the hedge line in the valley, some five hundred metres away from their vantage point. It became apparent as they watched their steady approach, up and along the dusty worn path that traversed the field, that their welcoming committee from Temple Hill comprised eight people, three women brightly dressed, with one other, like the four tall men, in a mottled green that looked like combat fatigue, though they also wore bright green beret-like caps. The military-style dress made the men waiting in the churchyard edgy, however, until they realised that, like them, none was armed. This much was clear by the time they reached the kissing gate. As they approached, the Captain, Valjean and the others moved towards them along the church path.

A woman from the group spoke first, moving forward in a stately fashion in her blue garb, which was long and had a ceremonial look about it.

'Welcome, strangers. Welcome to the Centre, and, we like to think, the future of humankind in these islands.' Then she laughed out loud, but not in a mocking way, either to allay their concern or at the openness or strange formality of her own speech. She then introduced herself as Eleanor, and then introduced her companions. The men, all tall and strong and taciturn, taciturn except for the smiling ebony -faced man who had taken to calling himself Tashtego, and who echoed Eleanor's welcome. He was, he said, like the other men who had come to meet them, a ranger, adding that they should not see their paramilitary dress as a threat, because it was not intended as such.

When Valjean, in mixed, heavy-accented tones, and with his crooked-toothed smile, introduced the Captain, first by his name, and then by his usually used title of Captain, Tashtego, obviously the senior man if there were one, said: 'A Captain, sir, a Captain indeed - of the Werod, unless I am much mistaken.'

25. *The First Conversation with the Master*

The travellers put their trust in their hosts. This was after all, they agreed, the place they had come to find. It was probably the presence of a half-dozen or so children running around and playing happily in the second zone, or second ring of what they were already calling the city that reassured them, just as the residents of Lyme had been when the Argonauts had come ashore there. They were themselves in the spacious outer zone and could look at the children, and they them, through a screen in the wall. Possible infection could not be allowed to pass from them to the inhabitants of this place; so, like those who had volunteered to greet them, and all who spent time with strangers in this circle, they were in quarantine.

A bright sun beat down from a blue sky in which a few white clouds floated as they, Valjean and the

Captain, gazed across the countryside with its dark trees and hedges and yellow-brown fields of stubble that appeared with crystal clarity in a quality of light that was typical of September on a clear day, when everything is lent a sharper focus than in the hazy, steamy days of midsummer.

'This is not really a fortress, 'began one of their hosts, a fresh-faced young man of about twenty, who had joined them on the outermost walkway atop the castellated perimeter wall. 'It never needed to be. A defence force a thousand strong was housed here, sealed in, protected from the virus. The complex was provisioned with weapons which would never really be needed. Power was supplied by the wind farm to the west and by our own generators here. The town, the university, call it what you will, was begun in the days of Prime Minister Alvis but it was really fully developed by Lord Protector Quellan; no expense spared, as they used to say. I was born here of course and have grown used to it; but I'm sure you will be impressed. We are lucky: I can't imagine how anyone outside survived the winters of twenty... thirty years ago... even we found it difficult, so we are told by our parents and teachers... and certainly limiting, having to rely on our stockpile of foodstuffs; though, of course, we also had fresh produce from our underground orchards and gardens, in the terradome, as we jokingly call it...' The young man laughed with evident pride, seeing the effect he had had on the strangers. 'You will see all in three weeks, should your people confirm your decision to stay... But I marvel at how you have survived... We are so pleased...'

Valjean's craggy weather-beaten face broke into a smile. Visualizing the white mountains and the green valleys of the Berner Oberland summers as he spoke, he said: 'Most of us were in Switzerland or Normandy during the worst of the northern winters. In Switzerland we lived in a place that was bypassed by the plague. But some of those among us now, it is true, come from your south coast. It seems there was a narrow strip of land, perhaps thirty miles deep, that escaped the worst of the long winters.'

'I can see you have plenty to tell us,' the young man respectfully interjected. He was impressed by these people: they had had obviously led a life of adventure far removed from his own experience. He was not envious: he had been taught the danger posed by Envy, that it was a threat to the welfare and stability of the community; but he was interested.

'I am amazed, so amazed by all this,' Valjean said, throwing out his arms in an expansive gesture expressive of that amazement, and smiling a crooked-toothed grin, this tough man of the mountains.

'And of course,' added the young man as he took his leave of them,' in three weeks, after your quarantine, you will be invited to meet our beloved Master.'

Quarantine, in the form of solitary confinement, with visits six times a day from masked and gowned volunteer nurses, was the lot of young Adam, whose recent brief and sudden illness had passed but had given cause for concern, and, moreover, the nature of which was unknown. This young Adam was separated temporarily from his newly discovered Eve. For the other travellers, without exception, there were blood tests and brief questionnaires to be completed related to recent fevers and rashes.

It was of some wonder to the visitors that anyone from this place would volunteer to live with and assist them at this stage: after all, if they were infected these people would share in their fate. Their hosts seemed to take such considerations in their stride. Adam's case in the meantime was viewed with the utmost seriousness; what they called a 'disease event.'

The three long weeks of quarantine passed very comfortably; the travellers were unanimous in this view. The quarters in the upper ground ring of the complex were well-appointed, and the fact that the outer perimeter wall enclosed a circle of almost a mile in diameter meant that a circular walk of some three miles was possible, with, every so often, steps up to the wall-walk or rampart, which ran the whole length of the wall. From here were wide panoramas of managed farmlands, or, turning back, the inner concentric rings of walls and buildings they would soon have access to, and the great central campanile-like tower.

The walking during this period was not always pleasant. A change in the weather, some heavy autumnal downpours over a three-day period with water constantly dripping off the eaves, followed by days of heavy, chilling, blanketing fogs that refused to lift until well after noon, kept most people inside. But this was more an opportunity than a problem. In the wayside places, on the circular walk, there were covered shrines, well-heated and serving all manner of foods; in fact, the smell of cooking food, of hot meals being prepared would drift daily over the complex indicating that this place was one of plenty. A mile or so from their cluster of lodging houses, by the circular path, there was something else: a small concert hall adjacent to a fifty-seat cinema. Almost all the quarantined visitors found themselves in one or other of these buildings at least once during the period. Some visited many times, and never stopped pinching themselves that they were listening to and watching a live performance or a recording of a Mozart quartet, piped in from the Third Circle (theirs was the First Circle), or seeing and hearing historic footage of Iron Maiden tours or of the twenties band, Achilles Four, and perhaps pinched themselves even more that they could sit in comfort and watch, for example, *Citizen Kane, Double Indemnity* and *Ivan the Terrible*, or films in French and German, and films by the Italian masters of the mid-twentieth century (all showing in Classics Week), or alternatively, in the following week, action and adventure films from the late twentieth, early twenty-first century, or the mishaps of Laurel and Hardy. Whatever they saw, they would often emerge from their cinema experience, into the light of the afternoon, blinking in disbelief. Old newsreel footage was not available, since it was a rule there that everyone was briefed and assessed before being exposed to the events of the past. Even the visitors' access to some of the films available had been discussed beforehand, and some films were considered to present a danger and not shown. Mostly, the audience response, the response of those fifty and over, was that it had been an experience so unexpected, so redolent of the days before the end of things that they could barely take it in. In truth, it rather upset them, and in a way the younger members of the group were unable to comprehend.

The three weeks of waiting were eventually over, and they were welcomed into and shown around what to them had all the feel of a city in miniature. The above-ground areas were impressive, but below ground was a complex vast and deep, seventy per cent, in terms of floor area of the whole. This place had been built for a community of intelligent, knowledgeable, skilled and resourceful survivors; a place more than sufficient for their every need with plenty of room for them to expand when their numbers increased. As the eager little figure of the bespectacled historian-doctor reminded them, the word university had its origins in the Latin *universitas*, and *universitas*, well.... a community of scholars... and so on...

The people sent here, many being leaders in their field, some great minds, were intended as progenitors of a superior and pure people; and as their defenders, the defenders of the future nation, the nine hundred or so fighters who had been given the title of The Werod Hundreds. In the succeeding years they and their children had helped maintain and develop the life support systems of this community: from the wheat fields, some as far away as twenty miles, to the hydroponically grown crops of the biodome, or terradome, from the wind farms to the in-house generators, from the old petrol and diesel vehicles to the new hydrogen cars, from the safety of the complex to the security of the potentially wild frontier, their contribution had been immense and unceasing. The Werod themselves, or the sons and daughters of the Werod, had become in their own right, as far as the circumstances allowed, engineers, doctors, mechanics and farmers, and a few had also become rangers. Membership of the Order of the Rangers was popular, and though the oath sworn at the passing out parade bore some resemblance to that once upon a time taken by the Werod, its focus was on protection of the community only and spoke of no obedience to a leader. The rangers were expert trackers and foragers, survivors, and trained but in most cases unproven fighters. Most of the rangers were too equally at home in the laboratory, at the library and archives, on the farm, or fending for themselves in the wild. It had been four of their number who had tracked the caravan of strangers from the White Horse to their arrival at the neighbouring, long-ago mostly abandoned village of Flore. When they had met their quarry one of their number had instantly recognized the Dagaz tattoo on the Captain's neck, the same as that carried by both her father and her mother, and had communicated this to her companion Tashtego.

And so many things were explained, but some things, they were told, were best left to the Master, who would talk to them soon, very soon; their leaders or their chosen representatives first, and then any individual who had anything pressing to ask.

In the meantime, the visitors marvelled at achievements as disparate as the successful keeping of bees and the production of honey, or the production of hydrogen for fuel; or the continuance of academic life from kindergarten teaching to studentships in advanced mathematics. They marvelled too at both the openness of this society and its freedom from any real constraints, its unwavering discipline and its commitment to progress.

One day, Valjean saw an old man, shuffling along with a stooping posture, slowly cleaning off tables in one of the many refectories, so called. The man rather solemn-faced, tired looking, and at first sight broken in spirit, had only one arm, his left. He had placed a wicker carrier on one of the chairs, and slowly took from it a spray bottle with whose contents he wet the table's surface. He returned the spray bottle to the wicker carrier, then lifted out a blue cloth with which he began slowly to wipe over the table. It appeared to Valjean that he moved from table to table, laboriously, gracelessly, notwithstanding his age and his having only one arm: it seemed to Valjean as though he would take forever to clean the twenty or so tables. He approached the man and spoke to him. The man was old: he gave a tired smile and replied courteously, but without enthusiasm, which was unusual in this place. Valjean noticed a still clearly visible old scar on his wrinkled forehead, a letter 'K'. It turned out that the man had been rescued from the wild thirty years earlier, close to death's door, having travelled days through the snow looking for help but with no hope of finding any. He had made no real friends here, but people were kind to him, and physically he led a comfortable life. Valjean learned from the Captain that the man had been punished for stabbing someone; hence the scar and the missing arm. Valjean was shocked, and though he had heard of such things happening in England he had not wanted to believe them. He pondered far into the night and through the next day on the nature of that society and that justice. The Captain, for his part, was without sympathy and saw that the man's punishment had been inevitable and just: moreover, he resolved not to discuss the matter with Valjean. He certainly did not intend to fall out with his friend over such a thing.

The time had come: the Master would see them on the morrow. That night Valjean slept like a log in the comfortable little room whose walls were made from compressed fireproofed straw. The incongruous sound of a guitar being played in the distance, playing some wistful Spanish air, did not disturb him but rather lulled him into a pleasant deep slumber. Valjean could sleep anywhere: on more than one occasion in his youth he had bivouacked in an upright position on a freezing vertical face with nothing but a tent-sheet covering him; once, most memorably, he had slept thus during his failed attempt at the Eiger *Nordwand*: even there, like his fellow climbers, in a poor way and in real danger from a sudden storm, he had managed to doze off.

The Captain, in an adjacent room, was just as different this night: he tossed and turned. Usually a good sleeper, he lay awake listening to the same guitar music that went on for a couple of hours, probably. It was a well-played guitar certainly. Then he realized that its perfection with no stops and so on, probably meant it was a recording. As he lay there he thought that was a pity: he would have preferred a live if flawed performance. It had been some weeks since he had picked up a guitar himself, and though he knew he was not that good, it was something of his own, a way in which he could lose himself and at the same time connect with others, and without the need for the spoken word. A song, and his voice was not that bad, did not belong to the realm of the spoken word, but rather to the realm of music, or something like that, he was thinking.

He was missing Esmerelda, who had stayed in Lyme having befriended the locals, especially two young children and their family. He thought of her now and wanted her. His mind was troubled, and had she been there she would have turned her head on the pillow and gazed at him for a while before asking him what was wrong. He was staring corpse-like at the ceiling, white-panelled and still retaining a deep grey shade from the reflected street light. So the Weird Hun were indeed the Werod Hundreds - or had been once, long ago. Perhaps there were more; another settlement somewhere? One place such as this was enough, enough to generate a host of questions. He was not that certain he wanted to know the answers. That tale he heard at Lyme Regis bothered him still. Why would the man he had worshipped as the bringer of law and order and justice have unleashed a virus that spared neither the innocent nor the guilty, as though they were indistinguishable? When he had left England at the age of nineteen, with the fire of justice and truth in his veins, Alex Quellan had already become for him, and for the other officer cadets, the stuff of legend. Quellan had been in total control of affairs at home: what had he to gain by such a mad action? It made no sense, and the Captain as he lay there, knew that his thinking about it, keeping himself awake, would not help it to make sense. It simply was not true: so what was he worried about? He lay there, staring at the ceiling until it became a lighter grey at the dawn of a cold autumnal morning whose mists clung to the hilltop township.

They were led through the complex, down from the surface to begin with, from their new quarters in the third circle. They passed laboratories, seminar rooms, a medical centre with two operating theatres, a maternity unit where one baby lay in an incubator and was attended by three nursing staff, a subterranean herb garden, lit from above with natural light, and Mediterranean in ambient temperature, and then up and into the open air again, until they were standing at the centre of the complex and at the base of the red-brick tower, its plain wooden entrance door facing them. They were: the Captain, showing no ill effects from his sleepless night; a smiling and expectant Valjean, and three women; a nervously excited and awed chemistry major (if such terms could be applied) , Christina Papas, who had a shock of dark wavy hair and whose spectacles moved upward when she spoke earnestly and caused her to wrinkle her nose, Christina who was slim and tall and of Greek and Tunisian parentage; Monique Dubois, petite, black hair in a neat coiffure, dark-rimmed glasses and a business-like manner, Monique, linguist and biologist, not looking her forty-eight years, and Barbara Eagleton, the chief medic and amateur historian, lifting her spectacles with one hand as she gazed up at the tower... These were the five whose names were either put forward or who had volunteered: Christina alone had had to draw lots with some of the other younger travellers for the honour, if honour it was to be. It was in a way fitting that she had been successful because she had made a point of chronicling their journey from Lyme up till now, not missing a day.

The sun broke through, briefly, a few warming rays... Their guide, a man in his fifties, and below average height, stooping somewhat but energetic, seemed to be either running in front of them or stopping to point something out. Now his job was all but done as he ushered them through the entrance at the base of the tower and into the lower vestibule.

'There are over seven hundred steps to the top - a stone spiral staircase. We don't use the lift unless absolutely necessary'. He smiled, as though privy to something he had not yet told the visitors. 'Both the Master and the Mistress are in residence and are eager to see you. Please - be yourselves and don't feel you need to stand on ceremony'. His words had the opposite effect: all felt that they were going to be pitched clumsily into some regal presence whereby they could say and do nothing but make the most embarrassing *faux pas*. The Captain found himself polishing his right shoe on the back of his trouser, something he had not done since his schooldays. Valjean looked at him, frowning.

The lower vestibule was bare except for tables with flowers, a large bookcase and a couple of wall-hung tapestries, each depicting a medieval scene. It was somewhat baronial, but, all in all, quaint and anachronistic. They began the ascent of a wide staircase to their left and within a few steps were on a second level, a sort of mezzanine hall, with the spiral staircase beginning in front of them. A rope was attached in loops to the left-hand side to aid the ascent.

'There are seven landings,' their guide informed them as they began the climb between chilly brick walls, a stair whose turning spiral obscured the way ahead, ‘seven, including the topmost one, the roof. At each level before that there is a viewing window, should you need to stop and rest... and a shrine...’

And so it may have been, but they stopped after a few steps and were shown through an arched door on their left, and into a cosy antechamber. ‘My little joke, I’m afraid; just to put you at your ease. The Master and Mistress have their quarters on the second level - quite a spacious apartment. They don’t like so many stairs - any more than you or I.’

The man bowed and smiled, then knocked firmly three times at an inner door and cocked his ear to listen. The visitors engaged in a bout of surreptitious quiet frowning, smiling and eyebrow raising, wondering now if the Master and Mistress might prove decrepit; another 'joke', that is.

And so they were shown into a spacious, carpeted, lightly furnished room with one large double-seat sofa; facing this, a half-dozen upright chairs with red suedette upholstery, and in between a low table. The room, one of its walls partly forming the arc of a circle, had a window facing the east and another facing north. A tallish man was getting up from the sofa to greet them: he had a flowing mane of dark hair, streaked with silver-grey, and was dressed in white, probably ceremonial robes. Likewise, moving forward to greet them, a woman who had the most beautiful of blue eyes and whose hair was raven black. She was almost as tall as the man, and dressed in a long silken blue dress which shimmered in the light of the room. But it was her eyes, the irises radiating blue-grey that had a penetrating gaze that captured the attention of Valjean in particular.

The Master, the skin of whose rather dark-complexioned smooth face contrasted that of the Mistress, whose skin was alabaster pale, but glowed with the same healthful lustre, ethereal almost... The man, the Master, greeted them all by name then motioned them to be seated.

The woman, the great lady of this most hospitable of places, spoke then, enquiring after their health and comfort, and asking them to speak briefly about their history, hearing again what she already knew; that all but Christina, the young chemist, had lived long in Wengen, in Switzerland, in the years after Surt.

Then the Master spoke in calm, steady, unhurried tones that were expressive of thoughtfulness and even wisdom, or so it seemed to those listening, who found themselves, mentally, trying to guess the ages of their host and hostess.

'I have been here almost thirty-nine years,' he said, as though reading their thoughts, smiling under his dark brows, his warm face framed by that mane of hair. 'I passed through Lyme Regis in the early days.' He noticed the dark, strong, Captain's concentrated focus on him as he spoke. 'I still marvel that I am here now, after all these years. You should know, by the way, that although people call me master, or guide, they do so out of kindness or perhaps because they see in me the proof of possibility of life beyond this sanctuary. But their faith in me was always misplaced:

I owe everything to my wife.' He turned to the woman at his side, smiling. 'Yes, we did have a formal civil ceremony: we insisted on this for ourselves; though people here are free to choose the way they run their lives, as long as they make a contribution to the life and workings of the community, and respect others.

'But you must have many questions,' he said, 'Some, I can answer, but for most of the very technical, practical matters there are people at the university or the centre who can serve you better. I was trained in medicine once upon a time and I suppose too I am a mathematician and physicist of sorts, but not really a practical man. I also, for my sins, make it my task - with two others now, on a regular basis - to pore over the many texts and manuscripts we have that can shed light on the catastrophe that befell the human race...'

The Captain looked troubled and was forced to speak: 'The role of Leader... of Alex Quellan, Master?' he began awkwardly.

A shadow, barely perceptible, seemed to the Captain to pass over the incongruously smooth and youthful face of the softly smiling host. There was a noticeably long silence before he answered.

'Forgive my hesitating, Captain. You are necessarily interested in Alex Quellan. I will speak with you presently, and just you, if that is your wish, about Alex Quellan.' He turned to the others. 'You will all be interested, and it may or may not change your view of life... At this point, all I will say is that we owe our survival here to the foresight of Alex Quellan, who developed this university complex far beyond that envisioned by his predecessor... It also fits in...' he added mysteriously in an undertone, as though speaking to himself.

Again, he stopped, looking thoughtful for a moment, before turning to smile at his wife.

'But in my case, it is not wholly true to thank Alex Quellan alone.' His wife took his hand and squeezed it. 'I owe my life, my very sanity, to this lady, who saved me from absolute despair, who lifted me up body and soul from the pit of Hell. Those of you old enough will remember, like me, on your own account that time, the time of terror: it claimed my parents, siblings, all my family and friends.' He spoke calmly, as though he were reading some historical account by someone else: he could see also the distress it caused, momentarily, in at least three of his listeners.

He invited the others, if they so wished, to be open as he had been about their remembrances. Time had been for him a healer of sorts: likewise, those who had similar memories and who had suffered thus, they, too, had probably been able to distance themselves in some degree from the events of the past.

Refreshments were brought: wine, fruit juice, dainty sandwiches, and some little cakes. Valjean commented that they were all much obliged to them both, and to the people there, for the kindness and open-handed hospitality they had received. He added that he was amazed still at all that had been achieved here, that they were so well provisioned, that this very meeting could be taking place forty years after the world as they had known it had ended.

'Well, it wasn't quite the world's end,' the Master said. 'We still remain, older, and hopefully a little wiser. I myself am content. That is all any of us can hope for. We must all work to try and make it a permanent state of being for all. Of course, we know this is not possible: we must, however, persevere...'

Christina the chemist, now that she had grown in confidence in this relaxed congenial atmosphere, asked smilingly how old the Master was and whether they might know his name, since no one had told them.

The Master laughed; his wife smiled broadly, and the young chemist blushed - noticeably so, despite her Mediterranean complexion.

'Well, we have no real secrets. The people here like to call me Master, and my wife, Mistress, so as to feel they have leaders of some description, non-threatening leaders perhaps; but leaders are a legacy of the old world and maybe a human need, a subject that some of us have had long discussions about as we look back over history. I am sixty-three years of age...' he added suddenly, as though just at that point recollecting the question.

'And I forty-seven, volunteered his partner, without the same hesitation, and smiling reassuringly at Christina, winning her affection instantly. 'We do not trouble about age here.'

'Is that because you look *so* young?' the Captain suggested gallantly, perhaps wanting to make up for his forthright question about Alex Quellan. 'Both of you, that is. Not a day over forty-five, Master; and your wife, I would have said she was barely more than thirty. Of course, in your case, Master, a little grey in your hair, a problem I have...'

The host laughed and almost knocked over his drink, as with an expansive gesture he said: 'A rather back-handed compliment in my case then, Captain.' They all smiled, and then the Master added: 'I said no secrets and I meant no secrets; though I might if I may defer some revelations in your case, Captain, as I have already indicated. But there is no mystery to our appearance; or rather there is a mystery. To explain: we attribute our youthful appearance and exceptional good health, our good fortune in this respect, to our close contact with the Surt virus. We both fell victim to it, but in both our cases the virus took an unaccountably mild form. We don't yet know why and perhaps we never shall. Our scientists here, in which number I rather fancifully include myself - that is, I try to keep up with things -, still work for an answer. My hair? There is some grey resulting I think from a long, a protracted period of stress, I suppose, but now thankfully in the past. This lady beside me has rescued me in more ways than one...'. A light shone in his brown eyes, the recollection that she had literally saved first his life and then his sanity.

'She was a child when she rescued me, barely seven years old. I was literally at death's door and literally lay among the dead. She held out her little hand and commanded me to rise, and, like Lazarus, I did. We became companions on the perilous road in a terrible landscape of death and despair, but I never despaired when she was with me...'

'That was because you were protecting me: you had no time to worry about yourself.' The lady turned her radiant gaze on her guests, and without a trace of self-consciousness or sentimentality said as a matter of truth: 'He protected me, and I looked up to and respected him; and, eventually, I fell in love with him.'

'And I with her. Ten years later I discovered this and truly agonized over how I should tell her so, after our long years of companionship, and the difference in our ages. It seemed wrong somehow, and yet when I spoke she thought it perfectly normal, and we agreed to wait three years. We held a ceremony of sorts... I cannot imagine a world without Beatrice...'

Beatrice smiled, the Captain noticing her high forehead and the strong line of her jaw. He thought her quite a beauty in her cold northern way and was comparing her in his mind's eye with his dark Esmerelda. Beatrice was still speaking, directing her gaze at him now, as though reading his thoughts. He lowered his gaze, this fearless Captain. 'They often call me the Lady Beatrice, or Mistress, but it is, as Jonas says, that they choose us as leaders, feeling the need to defer to someone in the community, giving life more of a structure, as in the old days. Yes, I'm sorry,' she suddenly added, recollecting herself, 'my husband is called Jonas.'

'Feel at your ease to address me as Jonas,' the Master urged.

'I think we should feel more comfortable with Master, at least for the moment,' Valjean offered. 'Your people will otherwise think us disrespectful. No,

I should feel more comfortable with your title: that is how we have come to know you. Perhaps,' he smiled his crooked-toothed craggy smile,' we, too, need to think of you as our leader or our guide.'

'We are honoured; but should you change your mind, should any of you... We try to avoid all conflicts here,' the Master continued,' especially conflicts stemming from damaged egos. We are all equal here. What you feel comfortable with in this respect is for the best. Naming and status, the legacies of the old world do still have a place, but such things are taken much less seriously, unless of course it should become a matter of disrespect. The community will not tolerate this; but given the low level of dissent and dissatisfaction here, such issues do not really arise. We are ever watchful, not wanting to return to the old ways. In any case, everyone knows that his or her fate depends on the success and continuance of this little world of ours. Naming and labelling is still important in science - and we continue on here with research and learning as best we can - but as far as titles are concerned the world has seen many a perilous precedent set.' Here, he looked at Valjean's friend. 'But, unless you wish otherwise, we shall not change from calling you Captain. I'm afraid you are something of a curiosity to our rangers, our children of the Werod...'

A brief silence, after which Valjean asked: 'Are there other places - like this one?'

'We don't think so,' the Master replied. 'We have an extensive, a truly extensive library and records office. Many records were brought here and secured in the basement areas even before completion of the buildings, which everyone thought odd at the time.... No matter... I myself have searched and searched: some hints, some references perhaps, but no real evidence, I'm sorry to say.'

The Master appeared circumspect, hesitant, all of a sudden, it seemed: Beatrice looked at him. Then it was explained. 'But here I shall stray into areas in which the Captain has a particular interest. Another meeting, Captain, just you and I, if Monsieur Valjean, Doctor Eagleton and the other ladies have no objection... What the Captain learns he can pass on, though I fear what I have to say might trouble him, unless...' There was a scuffling noise in the adjacent room. 'Well, you may all learn more than I planned to say at this stage...'

No one had any objection to the proposed one-to-one meeting; though they were puzzled by their host's last remark. Jonas, the Master, continued. 'We do have plans to expand our operations, explore and if you like re-colonize the wild; but it is a question of numbers. Here, we are secure and strong and can produce all we need: we feel we are making progress. It is a gradual process and the young in particular can become bored. We hold a number of celebrations and festivities throughout the year, but we are the same three thousand people this week as last, and this week as next, and in the weeks following. We are aware of how many, or how few, children come along... the gene pool, you understand. Some couples seem able to have only one child, others are childless. At times we have thought gloomily that we have here the whole of western civilization - all that is left; which is why we overjoyed rather than merely pleased to see you all. Our rangers have, over the years, managed on their travels to pick up a few people, but all too few, and of those many have been ill or depressed. Lyme Regis is excellent news. I am glad they survived and that they have flourished. We worried for them, those living beyond the protection of our walls, when the desperate winters came. I think,' he added enthusiastically, 'the winters did spell the end of malaria on these islands, though we have no means of knowing for certain...'

'The people at Lyme had had no new cases in their area since that time...' the Doctor interjected. 'But we can't be so sure about the levelling out of the climate; we don't know with any certainty that warming, man-made warming, has ended; but the drastic reduction in... together with the winters...'

Another silence whilst they digested the implications of what was being said. The elderly doctor, meanwhile felt obliged to remove her glasses and clean them, a habit she had developed in social situations when there were gaps in the conversation.

They talked on for another hour.

Jonas and Beatrice began to speak about their three children: Silas, named after Jonas's father; Briony, so named to honour his mother's dying wishes, and Hope, the younger daughter, still only eleven, named after Jonas's beloved doting aunt. Jonas spoke almost reverentially about his father, a stoic at the end of things, he said.

Whilst they were in their turn listening to some of the trials and adventures of their visitors' long trek across Europe from Switzerland to Normandy, the visitors themselves stopped and listened. They could no longer ignore the sounds emanating from the adjacent tower room; they were the sounds of some strange animal.

'Ah!' said Jonas Wood. 'I can see he will not leave us in peace. You must all come and meet our resident raven. I brought him back from Anglesey nine years ago. I call him Balder, back from the dead, like the favourite son of Odin and Frigg; not that we really believe in the old Norse gods, you understand.'

26. *The Ravens of Anglesey and the Master's Terror*

As Jonas Wood briefly related the story of the rescued bird, his mind flashed back to the time he and Beatrice, with their escort of some forty rangers, made the longest journey the couple, or indeed anyone had ever made from the purpose-built centre or university since the onset of the plague.

Nine years ago, they had left their sanctuary, their island, their paradise, for a purpose. It had been a mission to restore Jonas's mental health, a mission carried out at the insistence of Beatrice. For almost a year after he had been rescued by her, he had been tormented by dreams about black birds feeding on the carcases of the dead, the human dead, the charnel house that was the city of London, its parks, its buildings, its famous landmarks... It was not surprising that he had been tormented thus, as, in a half-dream state, desperate, dehydrated and wholly exhausted he had lain slumped against the ash tree and had looked out on this very scene. And so afterwards it had haunted him. The dreams had eventually gone away, his mind and life occupied in the Temple Hill sanctuary with the physical difficulties of his and the settlement's survival during those eight long years of winter. Then came his tortuous decision eventually arrived at to declare his love for Beatrice; but this was followed by years of happiness and optimism, and three children. In his early fifties, however, he had decided after years of study that he would try and really grapple with the writings and last testament of Alex Quellan; Alex Quellan, who had murdered his family and who had all but wiped out human life. As he began this endeavour, after his years of study during which he had prepared himself for the task he had set, Jonas knew that it would be a difficult journey, emotionally and intellectually. As he began this task in earnest the dreams began to return.

He could perhaps have coped with the dreams alone, but he worked so hard at his task, in the deep vaults at the lowest level of the complex, that he was becoming physically and emotionally drained. At first, he did not work alone, and found in any case that he needed the help of real scientists to try and grasp what was being said, to try and understand what Quellan was trying to prove, what supposed truth he was working his way towards. The scientists, a dozen or so, half of these in their declining years and much respected members, fêted members even, of academia in the old world, were themselves hard put to it. Quellan seemed to have made quantum leaps of understanding backed up by the most abstruse and arcane mathematical proofs; but interspersed with this were philosophical and moral lengthy discourses, that, or simple asides that deviated from the main theme, or diatribes about the baseness of humanity, rants that grew ever more strident. The scientific complexity was one thing, the chilling haunting comments about the nature of mankind another; but Quellan had linked them in his mind and turned his writings into the darkest of visions. In short, Jonas Wood became obsessed with the task and ignoring much of what he should have been doing in the community and with his family, he withdrew from life and entered this dark world; alone in the end, stealing away to the vaults to carry out his own programme of reading, to wrestle alone as best his could with the mind of Alex Quellan then returning exhausted to his suite of rooms, unable to sleep properly and gazing from the tower soon after dawn, still wrestling in his mind with the spectre of Quellan, as though Quellan were a haunting physical presence.

In addition to the diaries and the writings of Quellan were the files and the endless lists of the enemies of the people and their case histories. The lists had been collated and, in a few instances, drawn up by senior members of the Werod organization, the organization that had infiltrated every important part of the country's mechanism of power and control and made that mechanism its own.

Among the papers, after months of searching through the rank upon rank of archive files (a distraction he could have done without as began to look through the diaries - except that the diaries had made reference to the security files), he had found his father's file, stamped in blue: 'No Threat'. Therein, he read the transcript of a single interview at a police station, the one not far from the family home, so long ago. It had sickened him to his stomach, every word of it, and yet though he hated the name Werod at that point, the notes showed that his father's interrogator had himself been reprimanded and demoted for intimidating an innocent. This was under the governance of Dain Alvis: later, under Quellan, it might have cost the man his freedom or even his life. This matter, too, gnawed at him: they had made a mistake with his innocent father, but they had dealt with their mistake. He had gone on to read how harshly the Werod, under Alex Quellan, treated their own people if they showed sadistic pleasure in the dispensing of justice. To Alvis, and to a greater degree under Quellan, these Werod deviants were regarded as the lowest of the low: the damned. Few in number because of rigorous recruitment methods and thorough indoctrination, those who failed to live up to their oath to protect the innocent and to carry out their war against crime in a just manner, ran the risk, under Quellan, of summary execution.

Jonas could see a consistency of justice in all of this, and in his youth he had never understood those people who hated the very presence, or the omnipresence, of the Werod. For him, they were there to protect people from themselves. But for him too this matter was a distraction, a diversion: Quellan himself remained the person responsible for the death of his mother and father, his brother and sister, the death of Carlotta and no doubt her family... billions of souls... This burned in his mind as he returned to those red leather-bound volumes, written in the man's own hand.

He had found the diaries and other volumes of writing including the volume with the key to encrypted passages, all bound in that same manner, in the back of this mother's car, as she had said he would: that was three weeks after her terrible days of torment and her eventual suicide. Early on, on that first night, the day she had come home from work, his mother had told him of their existence, those books, and that they might explain something... but too late for a cure. Jonas had promised to keep them if all she had said turned out really to be the case; and of course, if he were to survive. In the end, close to death, she had forgiven Briony and had realised how she had been manipulated by Quellan. Before her death, and feeling guilty at Briony's suicide, she had made him promise that if he did survive and lived to have children, he should call one of them Briony. Reluctantly he had agreed, but he had not shown his reluctance.

And so, after returning home with Beatrice, the two of them had travelled west in his mother's car, the Quellan volumes in three boxes in the boot. They, he and Beatrice and some other waifs and strays, had come, eventually, to Lyme Regis, from whence, in one of two fresh vehicles, they had travelled north to find the University which his mother had told him might offer some hope, some sanctuary. Briony Daniels had spoken often of its development...

So the books had remained, after early uncertain attempts to grapple with them, shut up, locked away, for many years, cloaked in the darkness of the vaults, but somehow ever present to the mind of Jonas Wood. A score of times in the early years he had toyed with the idea of opening and studying those books, bringing them to the light of day, but a score of times his nerve had failed him. And at his request, others, too, had shunned them. Then, finally, he had given in to curiosity and a feeling that this was unfinished business. At the outset he had not worked alone, and there was a long gap of years when they remained shut up in the dark; but more and more he became obsessed with the task and thought it was his mission to come to terms with all that had been set down in writing by Quellan.

And so, the dreams, the night visions of the black birds tearing and poking at the flesh of the dead returned, at the very time his mind was vainly struggling to cope with what he was studying. He even began to take the soft red volumes to the tower, to his study. The combination of these two things, the nightmares and his obsession with the Quellan writings, was making him ill and irascible. He was too beginning to lose faith in and make cynical comments about the work of the community. It was as though he were being taken over by Alex Quellan. Beatrice could see this, but he could not; and so she acted. With help and encouragement from their closest friends, she commanded Jonas to cease his work on the manuscripts, have a period in which he could recover, and above all place some mental and physical distance between himself and that awful testament. They had found a way to do this, and at the same time to drive the black birds from his mind. He had always believed in her, and in her wisdom and good sense: she was still a figure of shining white light illumining the darkest recesses of his mind, a force opposing the dark prophetic dreadful shadow of Quellan who seemed, through the written word, to paralyse his will.

And so it was that they left their home, and their children, and travelled into the west under the protection of the rangers.

The annual gathering of ravens on the island of Anglesey had long been known. Every year, the great black birds, usually to be seen as individuals or in pairs, would head along the western shores of England, or even cross the Irish Sea, to visit a communal roosting ground on the island. The gathering took place in late autumn, when the community of ravens in Newborough Wood and its environs would number anything up to a thousand. Why they came had never been clearly understood. The scientific community adduced one theory among others that it was all about widening the gene pool, whilst some among the less scientifically minded perhaps, and certainly of a superstitious nature, assigned mythological status and meaning to the event. It was without doubt a spectacle when the day began to fade and they returned to the roost. What was important to Beatrice, however, and to those whom she counselled to this effect, was that it was a possibility that prolonged exposure to such large numbers of these essentially harmless and impressive creatures might drive away Jonas's unreasoning horror of black birds. At the same time, the journey would keep him away from his obsession with Quellan.

For the double purpose, then, they travelled.

They had journeyed slowly westward, in that cold clear November of early frosts, from their ordered little community and its ring of satellite farms, and into what they regarded as the 'Wild', from whence little or no news came. It was a silent and empty land; that is, devoid of the noise and bustle of humanity. The evidence of that humanity's passing was there, to be sure: weather-worn roads littered with vehicles; cars with dulled paintwork upon which a layer of dust had settled and would never be removed; dead-eyed town houses looking out vacantly on their passing; looted garages with weed-strewn forecourts; gaunt and ugly abandoned industrial estates with lorries that had been parked up long ago; broken windows; tipped-over bins long ago raided by marauding rats; scattered rusting tins and other debris in supermarket car parks, rubbish that had been picked over by gulls, pigeons, magpies and jackdaws; crumbling roofs; tarmac split apart by growing vegetation; abandoned farm buildings; but above all, a deafening eerie silence, the absence of human activity, of speech, of the sound of machines, a silence punctuated only by the sounds of birds or a distant bark or howl of a feral dog, or something they could not identify. Whether there were people and they just fled at their passing they would never know; but as far as they could see, and hear, the trail to Anglesey was through a world of the dead, a world which neither recked nor reckoned the passing of the sun, or moon, or seasons of the years. For all intents and purposes, Jonas and Beatrice, elected figureheads though they were, were king and queen of a near empty, desolate land. The silence, the stillness, oppressed them ever more as they passed on into the west.

They came at last to Anglesey, over one of the two great bridges from the mainland, a bridge for many years now with its own quota of abandoned vehicles, a bridge surveyed by group of noisy gulls spiralling and wheeling on the air, their harsh cries rising to a cacophony.

They had found near Newborough Wood a large abandoned stone house: no desiccated bodies; just abandoned, a base of operations for Jonas's foray into the unconscious and into the dark wood, where he must face his fears.

The first cold day, he had ever after fondly remembered, had been in part devoted to a walk along the strand, south of the woods; on a brisk and breezy day which helped churn the choppy waves as they rushed and hissed to shore. And it had not been long before Beatrice had pointed out a pair of ravens heading inland, with powerful if laborious direct and purposeful flight, seemingly indifferent to the humans moving over the sandy strip.

On the second night, Jonas had sat in a fold-up chair, which he had dubbed the director's chair even though he was not of course directing matters, a chair placed on the springy grass close by the edge of the woods, close to Beatrice, who stood behind him, with both of them under the protection of a half-dozen rangers camped in tents some fifty yards distant adjacent to a vigorous but slowly diminishing camp fire. Jonas, for his part, had stared at the dying light of the sky above the treetops, a sky growing orange, red and indigo by turns. This was to be the first of his cold nightly vigils, of communion with what his subconscious had told him were the messengers of the underworld.

The livid skies, spectacularly hued, until it grew perfectly dark and the stars would become visible in a sable mantle, were busy with the comings and goings of the birds beginning to fly in to settle for the night. Every night a cacophony of cries, deep hollow 'cronking' sounds, repeating discordant choruses with intermittent, sporadic stops and 'pruk-pruk' obbligatos, and clicking and rattling sounds; until it grew quite dark, when thereafter the occasional clacking croaking 'pruk-pruk', a ruffle of feathers as though the whole roost might suddenly erupt on this island that legend had it was the last stronghold of the Druids and a land where human sacrifice had been practised.

For Jonas, that first night (the second of his stay on the island) had been the ordeal he had, if he were honest, truly been dreading. He could not have endured the close proximity of those dark creatures had not Beatrice been by his side. They were not the crows of his experience long, long ago, the crows which had haunted his dreams: they were not crows at all. They were of the same family of carrion birds, the *Corvidae*, but larger, with distinctively heavier curved beaks than the carrion crows, and bearded. And to Jonas they were the feasting terrors of his imagination grown larger and more threatening. They were impressive and terrifying, and he could not have faced being there, on that first vigil, in the gathering darkness, completely alone. He had felt that at any moment there would be a deafening demented uproar, followed by the thunder of two thousand wings beating the air.

But, he persevered, as Beatrice had hoped he would, and a change had gradually come over him. By the sixth night of watching he had come to relish the prospect of his task, his watching, gazing at the changing hues of what had fortuitously been kind skies free of rain clouds and clinging sea mists, as though this stage had been prepared just for him... the timeless skies of changing mood, the patterns traced by the ebb and flow, the dark flights of the birds...

At the end his vigil had been trance-like and he had begun to see and feel in these creatures a link with a primeval era before the coming of Man; and yet here they were still, when Man, or Humankind, had all but gone. He watched the birds by day too, sometimes on the sandy shoreline, through the flurries of snow, as they foraged for scraps of stranded sea-life jetsam, where they hopped and jumped in ungainly fashion in running scuffles with competing gulls or with their own cousins, the crows, the jackdaws and the magpies. The ravens, big, black, bearded creatures with heavy black shiny beaks and powerful claws... he could see clearly, as he watched this primeval squabbling for food scraps, that like all birds they were descended from the long-vanished dinosaur, and so were in fact the still-existing dinosaur, a continuity across millennia. So, at the end too, he realized he had undergone a metamorphosis of sorts, a change of mind and outlook: unaccountably, he felt strong and whole, a survivor like them, simply a survivor: his fear of the birds had gone, and he felt only respect for them, for their determination to survive. Like them, for this time here, he knew he could be free of imagined horror, and simply live. He would, and did, disturb this transient feeling by what he *planned* to do: *Homo sapiens*, he knew, could never be free of mischievous thought for long; but he felt renewed and would be ready, on his return, to meet the mental challenge of the writings in the red books. But those writings did not matter, did not disturb any more. He had achieved much more than the banishment of nightmares: he had achieved a kind of wisdom and acceptance he could never have anticipated. He had had Beatrice to thank, and the person who had advised her of this course of action that she in turn she had urged upon him and supported him in: and the noisy ravens, of course, at their annual gathering here, had played their rôle: a gentle reproach, he had said to Beatrice, would be his response to anyone who spoke of 'an unkindness of ravens'... They might have fed on the dead and near dead of history's ancient battlefields, but that was what they were supposed to do.

On the last day, bright but chill, after the last night of watching, they had been walking in the woods and had emerged onto a sandy heath close to the strand and the noise of the sea, where they found an injured or sick raven. It looked a pitiful thing: it had not tried to get away but had just stared dejectedly. It was quite large, but looked bedraggled and did not have the purplish, green-blue sheen to its plumage that a healthy bird would have had, and that they had seen in other ravens when close to them. It was not, one of the rangers said, a juvenile; the blue-grey eyes of the early stage had changed already to the deep brown of the adult.

They had picked it up, riskily in truth, not knowing the cause of its inertia, but sensing that it could not survive other than by their nurturing of it. It was surprisingly heavy for a creature whose like they had seen gliding on the wind, albeit without the natural grace of a raptor but nevertheless with an amazing range of aerial acrobatics. This poorly specimen could do little, however, and had made a slightly muted and feeble 'pruk-pruk' sound as they lifted it, and the nearby gulls had cried noisily at their interference, sensing a lost meal.

One of the rangers had known how to nurse the invalid and had understood its need for scraps of raw meat, snails, and when it was recovering, some handfuls of grain. And so Jonas had brought home at last a living souvenir of his spiritual regeneration. Balder was now a fine specimen, his shiny jet feathers iridescent with those hues of purple, green and blue. The community's leading scientist would refer to him as, 'the living, thriving dinosaur dwelling among a bunch of near extinct hominids.' Jonas, when he first heard this said, had raised an eyebrow in disapproval, but this was soon followed by a benign smile of self-deprecating, self-mocking humour at the dignity of Man.

27. *A Second Conversation with the Master*

The snow had lain for some weeks, blanketing fields and buildings alike. The latest heavy fall had again dragged down, with pendulous soft white clumps, the hedges and the trees which stood out as lightly sketched black features in a winter landscape. But a thaw was beginning: the snow was melting and thinning, imperceptibly for a time, until in the fields the furrows began to show through. On buildings, each of the great cornices of once frost-encrusted snow began to fall to the ground with a pattering thud. The walkways in the hilltop university township had long since been cleared of their thick loading of snow and had been flanked with mounds of dirty ice-snow which had, until now, become repeatedly re-frozen. But a thaw had definitely begun and the old diehard shards and slabs of ice atop these mounds, once glistening with frost and hard as broken bottles, were now softening and relenting under the winter sun.

The two men stood at the summit of the tower, gazing out over the whitened land. The fields glistened in the morning sunshine and on the east-facing walls and fences of the town the evaporating snow sent up a steady smoke-like steam.

'Yes, reluctantly, Master. We promised, Valjean and I, that we should be back by the twenty-fifth of March.' The Captain still used the title and for some reason could not move to calling him by his name. Valjean, he had noticed, no longer had this problem, in private at least: when others were present, he would still address him as Master.

Jonas pondered for a moment. 'Beatrice has a mind to travel with you, Captain, and so have I; if you would welcome our company and that of our rangers...?'

The Captain smiled: he had a look of boyish delight almost to the point that those who knew might have been able to picture him fifty years earlier, sitting on that tomb only a mile from where he now stood, see him then, swinging his legs and teasing his schoolmates. 'I'd expect your rangers to pitch me from these battlements if I said anything other than a resounding yes... Everyone will be delighted... And you, both of you, will be able to meet Esmerelda.'

'And at the same time fulfil at last my promise to the people of Lyme. They will think me an old man now, and from what you've all been saying, something of a disappointment: if there are such things as miracles, they are beyond my capabilities.'

The Captain said that the university town and the work it had done there and was continuing to do was a miracle and the Master must know he did not look his age.

Jonas accepted the compliments gracefully, then walked to the parapet and pointed eastwards to the ribbon of road that ran away in that direction.

'You probably know already, if our people haven't said anything. Barbara - Dr Eagleton - will have, I am sure. That is the Watling Street, the old Roman road, a major artery. Along there somewhere, beyond the town of Towcester, Boudicca's army was destroyed and it was said that she took poison. Well, in truth, it's just one possible site. The place here, this university, this town stands, unremarkable really except that it was the home of the cavalry until the beginning of the twentieth century, before it became an ordnance depot in the Second World War - you can still find some of the ruins close to the perimeter - this place was once selected as the bolt hole for George the Third and his royal entourage in the event that Napoleon should invade Britain. Close by, too, on the old High Street, a shrine to the goddess Eostre was supposed to have existed. Bede, in his *De temporum ratione*, said that the celebrations of the spring equinox were linked to the goddess Eostre, hence the pagan origins of Easter, as celebrated by our distant ancestors. The point of all this, Captain? I'm not sure, except that we can sense a long, long history, of people's lives, thoughts and fears, their living and their dying. And all that conflict, all those wars, fighting and killing for what was right, in somebody's view. Our little world is submerged in a void, an infinite ocean of darkness inimical to life; yet here we sat and squabbled for millennia, in our haven, in our protected bubble, despoilers of our own good fortune. I read something along those lines: it's almost a quote and might be from Quellan for all I know, or something he quoted. The past is gone and we can only really know what we experience now: our learning is our experience and no one else's, even though someone else, someone from the past, has written it down for us. I sometimes think that what we do here is so small, so insignificant when seen in the light of all that history; but then I think that this would be the case whatever we were achieving here. On the other hand, we are so few, one tiny remnant of a global civilization crushed down to a point of singularity, as the physicists might say.'

Jonas became thoughtful, eyeing the Captain. 'Ah, yes, I mentioned a shrine, and I know I have not told you this: we have a shrine here, too, of sorts...' he pointed to what was a brick-built outdoor oven opposite them, on the roof garden-cum-observation area, there at the top of the tower. It was type of oven popular in Britain in the early part of the century as the climate began to produce long, hot summers. It was fixed against the western wall and almost six feet tall: a place below for fuel, coals or wood, and above an arched opening and a surface on which to place the food. A small vase containing crocuses had been placed in front of it, on the ground; within, just discernible in the shadows, was a jumble of artefacts.

Jonas explained. 'We encourage people to come up here if they wish, and place within the shrine, the oven, any little trinket they have found that has any meaning for them. They can say a little prayer for the future or in remembrance of the dead or of the lost world. We leave the items in there for the six months of autumn and winter, then on the twenty-fifth of March, weather permitting, we, the inhabitants of the tower, with a few helpers use the oven for its intended purpose and bake bread and make pizzas and so on as part of our Festival of Life, which goes on for a week. The items we removed are placed in our little history museum. It does no harm, the placing of these offerings. People can quietly pray for fine weather, a good crop, or a successful fishing trip.' The Captain laughed at this, thinking of trawlers and the like: they could hardly be further from the sea. 'Well, you know what I mean,' Jonas added with a smile. Their at times light-hearted and easy conversation was a far cry from the second conversation they had had, five months earlier, a few days after the Captain's first visit to the tower...

The Second Conversation: Jonas Wood's version and understanding of the Writings and Last

Testament of Alex Quellan, Genius or Madman, as discussed with the Captain.

'Sit down, Captain.' As he spoke, he sat down himself, on a low wooden bench, and with a motion of the hand inviting the newcomer to sit beside him.

'Some things you already know,' he began. His dark soulful eyes, the Captain thought, looked earnest and concerned. 'I shall begin with what I am sure you know: the Werod grew out of the Breakthrough Party and was always intended as a force for the good. Dain Alvis created it and it began to grow. He had the odd idea of some Anglo-Germanic resurgence based loosely on his view of pre-Norman Conquest history - I am sorry if you think I am a little suspicious of this. I am not mocking the concept: it is as valid as many a belief expressed through the ages. People were burned to death disagreeing with the interpretation of a word or two in the Christian Bible or whether they thought it should be read in Latin or in English -diabolical...' The Captain shrugged his shoulders at the mention of the Werod as originally conceived by Dain Alvis, indicating he, too, was a little sceptical about Alvis's ideas of history or qualities judged purely on nationalistic or racial grounds; but this worldview, as embraced by Alvis, had, he truly believed, been used effectively as a springboard to a potentially better and more just society...

'Its focus,' Jonas Wood continued, 'was the establishment of law and order at a time when lawlessness was perceived as a major problem and was a major problem that governments before that of Alvis had shied away from. In effect, governments, even though they constantly interfered with their ever-changing performance targets and charters and so on, had ceased really to govern in a way that took account of the problems that ordinary people were encountering on a daily basis. This was true of law and order, and equally true of health and education. It was abdication of responsibility - many people, as I recall, felt this way: it wasn't something Alvis made up; it was something he tuned in to and addressed. At the same time corporate entities became like robber barons sucking the life and the wealth of the nation while governments effectively turned a blind eye or made bland comments such as the "trickle down effects of wealth". This was Dain Alvis's political platform, and as I said, the people saw more than a little truth in his message...

'Alex Quellan was a shadowy figure, almost it was said a wholly self-effacing disciple of Alvis. Interestingly, you will find no statue of him in this land, nor any portrait in any gallery. He was a chameleon figure and a solitary one. He was, however, no *eminence gris*, seeking to rule behind the throne, and he had no real authority or influence, officially, until he seized power; though he was of course a key person in the Werod elite, who subsequently became the power in the land. Quellan did not care about himself or what people thought of him: in that sense he had no ego to bruise. That is a truth his writings bear out. Had he been a little more human in this respect...' He paused, considering himself such a possibility and how things might have been different; but of course, they were not. 'He was wholly focused on what he had to achieve, and not at all how this might benefit him personally. For him, Alvis had not gone far enough; and the first evidence of the new leader's thinking came in the ruthless pursuit of a pure form of law and order, a vision of a world in which intimidation, in any form, and selfish behaviour adversely affecting the lives of others, such as, he states, using a vehicle as a weapon, would not be tolerated....'

The Captain did not look surprised or perturbed by this: it had been part of his conditioning and his belief system. There was nothing to disapprove of thus far. He let Jonas Wood continue.

'We who lived through the last years, as you yourself did, agreed with an approach that had made it safer to walk the streets, or safe to walk the streets, even though some people may have been squeamish about the methods employed...' He noticed that his listener frowned. 'Please, I intended no criticism. It would have been easy to criticize. The Werod, your people, made us safer. Over the years I have tried to examine my conscience on our benefiting from the work you did; but it is easy to forget what an increasingly vicious and selfish world we were living in before Dain Alvis appeared. All this you know. But did you know Alex Quellan, and the Werod, took power by force, that he was in the end a betrayer of Alvis and his murderer? He came to power by means of a coup...'

The Captain smiled ruefully. He looked up at a grey squirrel scampering in the branches of a nearby tree, and up at the tower from the pleasant cloister in which they were sitting, in the seventh circle. 'We all guessed as much, though I was a child when it happened and learned about it later and believed it to have been for the greater good,' he said at last. 'And we had sworn an oath: the oath meant everything to us -loyally to serve Alex Quellan and at all times to protect the innocent. There is, there was, an inconsistency in this, in the way power was achieved. However, our work was important…' He would add no more and leaned forward, his forearms resting on his knees, looking up, ready to hear what else the Master had to say.

'It is clear from Alex Quellan's diaries and his other writings, that he was a solitary man who, as he dreamed of a better world and as he meted out punishment to bring that world into being, held a poor opinion of his own species, often referring to humankind as degenerate apes. He would speak thus, to himself, as though he were an observer entirely cut off: not human at all - something else entirely. You raise your eyebrows: I am not really suggesting anything supernatural, but we shall come to that, in a manner of speaking. Quellan was odd, and as we now know, terrifyingly dangerous: he killed Dain Alvis and removed and replaced society's ruling elite, *not* out of envy, hatred or personal ambition, but simply because he had to fulfil or bring to fruition a plan that was in his head, gnawing at him all the time. He actually respected and admired Prime Minister Alvis, and years later, he says as much in his writing. In the end, however, the man he admired was having to proceed too slowly for his liking and he knew with an absolute certainty that the revolution would be over as soon as Alvis lost power by the usual means. So, he coldly reasoned that both Alvis and the system that would replace him with a lesser light would have to go - lock, stock and barrel, just like that. He planned to sweep it all away and did so: it was for him a necessary act of evil for the greater good. He felt guilty about Alvis, there is no doubt about that, as far as his form of humanity would allow; and *that* is why you will find in this land so many statues of his mentor.

'Quellan was obsessive in his attention to detail in regard to how the laws should be imposed and enforced. Execute people on the spot, yes; but torture was out of the question: "a form of bullying and therefore the way of the coward", he wrote.' The Captain nodded approvingly but solemnly. 'Towards the end, before he became engrossed in the project that would consume all his thought, demand all his focus, he was considering the development of a brain implant to be trialled by Werod volunteers after it had been thoroughly tested on criminals. It was to be called a Purity of Law Implant, a device that could be triggered remotely and destroy the brain. It would have ensured that no one deviated from the path of justice, especially those charged with administering it.' The Captain pulled a face that showed he was beginning to feel less comfortable. 'Quellan was just as hard on himself. No one really knows what happened to him. He wrote that one day he might have to knock a nail in the wall and hang himself from it...

'He was odd, Captain, but his intellect was vast. We here have had to wrestle not just with the morality and the implications of his view of humanity, but also with his brilliant and innovative scientific work. Oh, not me, on that score: I have to be guided through the mathematical maze by others here; but everyone has struggled, our best minds. His scientific arguments seem at times quite fantastic, but there is a chilling logic about all his work, and though no one can prove or validate his theses, or hypotheses, or conjectures, none is able to disprove them either. That such a mind could have focused on something which has brought the world, or at least humanity, I should say, to the brink of the abyss, to the brink of extinction, is almost beyond comprehension in itself.'

The Captain watched his host stand up and pace around a little before being able to resume his seat in the sheltered cloister beneath the tower. He had not looked upset but rather was preparing himself.

'Quellan believed,' Jonas Wood began again, 'Quellan believed and sought to prove many things, drawing on a plethora of scientific thought from a number of disciplines. Some of what he looked at was useful to him, some irrelevant in the end. He had a few of what we should call perhaps overarching ideas. One obsession was entropy: entropy and its application to astrophysics, for example. You might be familiar with it as explained in thermodynamic modelling, not that

that model is of particular importance, but it is a universal law... You must forgive my imprecise wanderings, Captain. Quellan linked entropy to what he called " the drive to complexity", something he posited as inherent in the diversity of life forms and the state of human society.'

'Evolution? Darwin?' the Captain suggested. 'I studied the sciences at a basic level as part of my cadetship...However...'

'Evolution, yes, Captain, but only in a manner of speaking: with absolute conviction he went much further than Darwin. Quellan had a novel idea, taking life itself as one step in a different kind of evolutionary process, which he described in various terms but eventually settled on as "the drive to complexity". This drive he said was a property of inanimate matter, or what we have always called inanimate matter. What he claims is that inanimate matter itself seeks to become more complex, is driven to become more complex, and this seeking is predetermined by the structures at the subatomic level. The subatomic particles have in them and in the arrangement of their forces, Quellan said, a drive to complexity that stems from an original imbalance, and this imbalance, down the line, is reflected in the first element, hydrogen. Hydrogen without a neutron in the beginnings of matter as we usually encounter it, at a level we can work with, was he says the obvious driving force that gives rise to a search for complexity, and also that it is the missing hydrogen neutron that also gives rise, ultimately - though with links to an opposite form of matter-less energy or negative state matter, to the supposed dark energy and dark matter of the universe. When Quellan begins in his writings to formulate this hypothesis he loses us with his mathematical leaps which seem sometimes intuitive at best. But what we do see written down, makes sense, so our best mathematicians tell us; though we are too few here... There are too great gaps in his workings as though he is trying to keep something from posterity. It's all either brilliantly innovative, a quantum leap in our science and our understanding; that, or complete madness.'

'I don't really understand,' the Captain said with complete honesty. It seemed that the Master was straying far from the point he himself wanted to arrive at. But he would be patient. 'But please continue.'

'Quellan's intelligence, his cold objectivity, was matched at times, increasingly often in fact, by his impatience and his anger. I say this because it is true and perhaps because I don't want to appear to be praising him in any way: he murdered my family, destroyed so many -but I digress. Even in the pages of his most intricate and abstruse mathematics are marginal notes expressing this anger, this impatience; and, too, his hatred of the worst kinds of human behaviour. This is a recurring theme: the speeding motorist who kills a child is a paedophile; the drug baron who murders and maims to retain control of a mini empire, who poisons the young, is just the same as the politician or bureaucrat who blocks spending on life-saving medicine, or his like who fails to condemn a murderous foreign regime to secure political or economic advantage... Those who created, tolerated or permitted the suffering of the innocent were enemies of the state, and, more importantly, corrupt - the damned. It is all couched in terms of protecting the people. You will agree with a lot of this. But it is not always so clear cut... Sometimes his anger betrays a propensity to strike at humanity as a whole for its failings. This same man, who can on the one hand become interested and empathetic with the poor person suffering abuse in some God-forsaken outpost, so to speak, of this or any land, is capable at the same time, in his frustration and anger, of saying that he will if necessary carry out a series of nuclear strikes on the Afghan poppy fields, or a city in Columbia, to crush the opium trade. At a stroke he can promise to protect and threaten to destroy. Such anger at, such impatience with, the failings of humanity...

'His was a dark world: a world of growing but unchallenged scientific certainties, but a world inhabited by evil that needed to be destroyed. But we come to the point at last: Quellan ultimately wanted to save the world; not for humanity but from humanity. It was probably always there, that dislike, hatred even, of the human condition. But I run ahead... Quellan could always improvise within his grand plan. For example, he wooed the US as a necessary part of his plan to retain power here and did not forget its capacity to undermine his revolution: he was aware that he was perceived by the US as a volatile, potentially dangerous element in its own plans for a world that was beginning to move away from its economic control. He knew at the same time that though he might himself influence the world beyond these borders, the Werod's work could not really be exported, not in his lifetime, not in a dozen lifetimes. Asia, Africa, the Americas, would ever remain outside the scope of his revolution: the protection of the people, the innocent, 'from pole to pole', as he desired it, could never happen. He is clear that he was beginning in his isolation and impatience to confuse sub-humanity, the criminal deviants, with the common run of humanity, the innocents; or what most would call innocents. At the same time, he suspected, he had intelligence reports, that the CIA was beginning to question whether his presence was a good thing after all. Quellan then talks about , in his words, "killing two birds with one stone - a metaphor I detest, expressing as it does humanity's arrogant overweening sense of its own superiority, its assumed right to dominate other life forms" - this, I remember it well, Captain, is written as a marginal note as he discusses and calculates the effect of climate change, of global warming. I remember it because it was beginning to signal the end of things for the greater part of humanity... In short, Quellan, coldly, objectively, and driven by a new scientific certainty, was beginning to turn on every one of us. First, he had to check the US: he did this, under the cloak of the joint scientific survey programme by getting his people to trigger the Yellowstone volcano...'

The Captain was stunned by this announcement. 'But that just happened - it was a natural occurrence! Are you sure?'

‘It is true. Quellan’s leading scientists had planted at Yellowstone devices that were sheathed in layers of heat-resistant materials and planted close to the magma chamber: ostensibly measuring probes they were timed to detonate and create multiple pressure waves. It may have been a coincidence, and in any case did not result in a full eruption. There has been a possible later eruption, we now think, which has countered the warming of the planet - of course, this was in combination with the sudden elimination of polluting humanity as cause of the accelerated warming... We cannot be certain that the second and bigger eruption was Yellowstone... It could have been another caldera, or something else happened... we don’t know...

‘Yellowstone was the key. Quellan saw an eruption as serving two purposes: the lesser one, to prevent the US from undermining his revolution by making it focus on something much more important, or perhaps wiping it out as a major military and economic power; and secondly, and more importantly, to counter global warming temporarily by creating vast clouds of sulfur compounds and so on: a chemistry experiment carried out on the planet’s climate... His eye had wandered from justice, crime and the deviant elements of humanity, as we commonly understand those things, to something else - the way in which the whole species was careering headlong into a catastrophe for all life on Earth, turning it into, as he puts it, a waste world... complete devastation, planet wide, an extinction-level process for all life forms...

‘The writings tell it all. Examining the efforts of the world to tackle climate change, he pours contempt on the word “sustainability”, so often used by corporations in the early years of the century to brag of what they called then their ‘green credentials’... It was another way of making money, and if money could not be made that way then it need not be spent in dealing with man-made climate change, the sceptics said, because climate change was not really happening. There was an attempt early in the century to devalue the science of climate change, as we know, but by the time there was almost global acceptance, still no government would lead the way, make significant changes. In one place Quellan writes “sustainability” then crosses it through with such force that he almost tears through the paper. Then he scrawls beside it: “LIES! LIES! LIES!”. Then his calculations begin again. Throughout all the talk global carbon emissions were rising, methane emissions from the thawing Siberian permafrost were increasing, the summer Arctic ice cap was all but gone... great shelves had broken off from the South Pole, you remember... Temperatures, global mean temperatures, despite local weather-related dips, were beginning a steady but slowly accelerating climb overall... Quellan writes with scientific certainty that the end was near while world leaders focused on the problems created by heat waves, by water shortages. They put their faith in scientific innovation, or so they said... Quellan saw something else, and probably others did, too: the real danger that no one could or would contemplate. Quellan of course had developed a chillingly objective theory about life and came up with an equally chilling two-part equation. The first part was based on the drive to complexity. There was the drive to complexity of the mental process itself, resulting in the needs of the individual human organism. This in turn, leads to its attempted integration into ever more complex society, a socially interactive world, marked, since the Renaissance, by accelerating scientific and technological progress, ever driving forward. Early in the century lip service was being paid to the fears about carbon emissions and warming and so on: and Quellan and a few others - one of the few instances where he praises himself - were brave enough to state as much. He knew, he said, that nothing would change: he argued that the world leaders were acting as the proverbial ostriches, and their condition of life, as he called it, their drive to complexity, in its manifestations such as world economic development, completely blinded them to the danger that was facing the very Earth itself. There was, Quellan stated, no open-ended agreement with the planet's atmosphere, so that temperatures could rise steadily with a bit more inconvenience, making things a bit more uncomfortable for some in terms of rises in sea levels, and so on, or an increased incidence of malaria and other diseases, which was unfortunate for some but could be avoided by others, with mainly the world's economically disadvantaged the victims... No, Captain, Quellan saw in his isolation, from his self-imposed scientific distance, something he could not ignore... His labyrinthine but to him crystal-clear calculations on climate convinced him that the world was almost at the "tipping point", a point from which there could be no return. At the tipping point, the planet's atmosphere would become locked into a cycle of positive feedback. The heating-up would accelerate, be out of control. There would have been no way out, he knew this with an absolute certainty, a terrifying certainty. Within two or three centuries, or perhaps even within a decade - because massive climate shift could be as abrupt and sudden as this - he clearly states, Earth would become rapidly begin the transformation towards a planet like Venus, a poisonous hot house of a world, inimical to life, all life, even the ants and cockroaches.

'And so Quellan turned to his only solution: the extermination of a species, a humanity which he viewed as a self-deluding biological complexity, driven by demands set long, long ago at a molecular level, demands that could be traced back to a pre-animate state. There was no free will at all in this world, simply the illusion of it: humankind was driven like the spawning salmon, by its nature, and to its doom. So Quellan turned his intellect to virology, even though he retained his interest in geophysics and kept one eye on the events at Yellowstone and the impact of his attempts to interfere with its life cycle. Had he succeeded in destroying the power of the US and at the same time checked global warming he might, he states, have relented, and allowed humanity more time. But, by the standard of what he wanted to achieve, Yellowstone was a failure. Population would continue to rise and with it accelerating pollution leading to inevitable and imminent catastrophe: *Homo sapiens* had failed to address its real problem, that of its numbers.'

Then Jonas talked with great dignity and forbearance of Surt and the final events at Hoffnung Pharmaceuticals; of his mother's involvement in the development of the virus and of the last days of the Wood family, the recriminations, the horror, the grief and the sadness. It was the story, too, of the demise of the old world.

The Captain was shaken by the revelations, even though he had anticipated and feared this truth. Surt, so named by Quellan in honour of his murdered predecessor who had had a love of all things Saxon and Norse.... Surt, the fire demon of the ancient world, destroyer of mankind and the gods in the Norse Armageddon - *Ragnarok*... Alex Quellan, well, Alex Quellan...

'So, it is true', the Captain said at last, his dark face looking drawn and pale; but he was not selfish in his brooding thoughts. 'You were so close to those final events,' he added sympathetically.

'Not final, Captain: we are still here.'

'Nine billion people across the world - wiped out. As your mother knew Alex Quellan, you must have been all the more tormented by what you read about his reasons for all this...'

'Not least by the fact he might have been correct in his analysis. But we shall now never know the truth of that unless we recreate the old world, with all its complex problems, which might take a million years... My mother did not know him, probably no one did, but she saw him twice close up and then a third time on screen when he announced his intention to destroy humanity and that his plan had already been put into operation. It was Briony Daniels, for whom my mother worked, who carried the terrible burden and who was crushed by the turn of events, inconsolable, a 'wretch in a living hell', my mother said. That was why she made me promise to name a child after Briony. She felt guilty for screaming at her at the end, for blaming her: but no one, no one in the world, was a match for Quellan: Briony Daniels was as much a victim as anyone else. But there is that strangeness at the end. Alex Quellan, as I have said, dressed himself as the Norse god Odin to make his final dramatic appearance. He left everyone in the room part of a poem from the *Hávamál*, or *The Sayings of the High One*, lines he had changed, distorted, identifying himself with Odin. In one of the last entries in his diary he said that he would "show a degree of madness in this respect so that Briony will not blame herself". Do you see? He felt sorry for her: he was being kind. And in the same way, he felt he had to provide some scrap of hope for the future - this place, Captain.'

The Captain had hoped until this meeting time that it was a fiction, that Quellan had not released the virus, that somehow there must be another explanation. Jonas Wood left him time to reflect: they would meet again many times. For now, he watched the Captain pacing up and down, gazing up at the tower, vainly struggling with what had been said; especially those words, 'he was being kind'.

So, he, the Captain, and those of the newcomers whom he chose to tell, knew what the inhabitants of Temple Hill had always known, or had known since the arrival almost forty years earlier of Jonas and Beatrice and their rag-tag band.

Jonas and the Captain became great friends, swapping stories of their past. The Captain on one occasion revealed to Jonas and a group of rangers that he had in his time killed twenty-seven people; one in Switzerland, the remainder in their eventful and dangerous journey through France. France was a place with no history of the cleansing Werod, no eight years of prolonged and destructive winters, a lawless place compared to England, but still with few inhabitants. His listeners were shocked at first by this revelation of determined if probably necessary ruthlessness and found themselves momentarily alienated from the tough dark-featured man with the great scar running down his cheek. Mostly second generation, the rangers had practised the art of self-defence but had never had to deal with what the Captain, in the language of the old world, still referred to as 'cowardly, murdering scum.' As he uttered them, the words sounded crude and awkward to his own ears, not belonging to this place and this time, a blasphemy almost. It was one thing to know from the records, as many of them did, that the Werod, in its time had over the years had summarily dealt with, that is, executed, over thirty-seven thousand criminals, and sent scores of problem families to an island off the coast of Scotland that had once been used to test anthrax as a potential biological weapon: it was quite another to meet a hardened, resourceful and phlegmatic killer face to face. And the population? Judging by what they knew of France and Switzerland, and now England, the population of the world was probably between one and two million. There were probably just enough people left in the whole of Western Europe to fill a large football stadium.

Jonas was at pains to point out, in case there should be any doubt remaining, that he was not a Messiah. Death still visited from time to time: but life persevered. His greatest fear, he confessed to the Captain and Valjean one day, was that life had in one sense become stale. They lived happy, ordered lives there, in Temple Hill, but like other communities, he supposed, they feared to venture forth from their miniature earthly paradise. It was for this reason they had avoided contact with the wider world. They had not sought to develop communications, means by which they could advertise their presence. The Captain said this was probably wise and Valjean nodded his agreement, knowing what they did about the lawless lands. On the other hand, they had some good defenders and a useful arsenal, should this be needed. They added that the situation had been the same in

Normandy, until a large group of them had decided to make the crossing to England. Jonas said he would give some thought as to how they might create a corridor of civilization from Temple Hill, to Lyme and on to Normandy, perhaps even to Switzerland.

People made the best of things, had their entertainments and above all, their imaginations. The little river at the bottom of the hill, only a few miles from the probable source of the Nene, could have been, and was for some, the River Styx. People had, as Jonas Wood had pointed out, died at Temple Hill. Some had been cremated, others buried in a little cemetery just outside the perimeter on the south-facing lower slope of the hill. It was a well-tended place, reminding Valjean of graves in his home village of Lauterbrunnen and typical of the Oberland in the old times, where flowers sat against almost every stone and memorial, pretty and colourful so that the tourists could often be seen taking photographs there.

But Death was singled out for special treatment at Temple Hill. Every twenty-fifth of March, at the beginning of the Festival of Life, and every twenty-ninth of June to commemorate the beginning of the plague and to remember its victims, a small well-practised band would play the Dead March from *Saul*. It was moving and sad, always; but not for long. That evening, the evening of the March ceremonies, effigies of Death, as a skeletal robed and hooded figure, usually wooden, with skull and ribs painted on, clothed and carrying a wooden scythe, would first be mocked by the inhabitants, by then merry and perhaps slightly tipsy, who would throw all manner of things, rotten vegetables and so on, and even sealed wooden boxes containing animal faeces at the evil one before setting him alight. It was all about putting Death in his or her place, depending on one's belief system. No one celebrated Guy Fawkes' night any more: there was nothing to celebrate in the supposed narrow escape of some Stuart king, when so many more worthy people had perished in this world's recent history.

Valjean's dog Dante disgraced himself by repeatedly setting the free-range hens and by chasing a flock of sheep. One of the Normandy visitors said that someone should sit down and write a poem in *terza rima* about these canine exploits.

Valjean himself found a new friend in the tall and strong black man Tashtego, one of the ranger leaders, who told him in French that he spoke six languages fluently, had lived in seven countries, including in deepest Africa and Amazonia, and had sailed the seven seas, fighting pirates and hunting whales on the way. Then he told Valjean that not much, in fact virtually nothing of this was true: his name was really Dwain, 'plain Dwain from Brum,' he joked, though he meant that his parents had come from there: he himself was born at Temple Hill. He confessed that, and he had never set foot outside England, and would never wish any whale anything but a long life. Still, he liked to be called Tashtego, he could speak fluent French - his mother was French - and he was good at carving things, including toys, which meant he was in great demand at Christmas, which was celebrated with enthusiasm, and with its Christian religious message, even though it had originally been a pagan celebration, and even though there seemed to be, in this small community, people of every denomination. The point was to celebrate: as such, it was another festival of life.

The scientific community meanwhile debated the theories of Alex Quellan, some wholly opposed to such nonsense, some beginning to see that they made sense: but in one thing they were beginning to agree upon: there was a big question mark now over the validity of the Big Bang theory of the universe's origins, because as Quellan had said, it all depended on what one really meant by the universe. 'As though it really matters,' Valjean said to the Captain.

A surprise was planned for the visitors. It was decided that the long overdue completion of the renovation of the public house-cum-inn, at the crossroads at the bottom of the hill, would be carried out in time for Christmas. Thus, a week before the big day, the Captain was astonished to hear the Master, the sought-after and newly discovered Messiah, say to him, 'Fancy a pint, Captain? We're off to the pub.' He could not believe his ears at this anachronistic outburst and his first instinct was to ask Jonas Wood to repeat what he had said. But that was what he had heard, and he could see this from an incongruous mischievous look in Jonas's eye. Then he could not stop laughing, and it was from that moment that he and Jonas became firm friends. And so, the old pub with the flagstone floor had been decorated for Christmas and was full of people: the beer was good, and it was a time of wonder; but it took some getting used to - a surreal experience.

So, they stood atop the tower, in the last days before the people from the south would have to return. In a few paces Jonas crossed the roof area to the brick-built oven-cum-shrine. He pulled out a few items into the bright light to show the other man.

'As I said, people like to place things here; a sort of offering to the Earth goddess perhaps: a primitive superstition, a memorial to the past, a hope for the future - who knows?'

Jonas had retrieved four items from the dark recess. One was a pocket French/English dictionary, its cover decorated with the colours of the French *Tricoleur*, its pages yellowing, curled and stained, at one corner with mud, and throughout with black spots of mould. Jonas stared at it with the Captain looking on: there was no inscription inside: it was just part of a school child's daily baggage, but he handled it reverentially. The second item was a pair of blue plastic compasses with short metal points, a design introduced in the latter part of the twentieth century; attractive, safe, 'mathematics is fun' design. The third was a plain golden ring of eighteen carats, someone's wedding ring perhaps... Like the child's book, the child's compasses, its adult owner, or possessor of the ring was long gone. 'Valuable, yes, Captain; but in truth all of equal value, the plastic, the printed word and the gold. We value things that link us with the past, treasures that belonged to the now dead that we, the living, can hold in our hands. Generally, we are not overly sentimental over such matters, but it makes one think...'

The fourth item Jonas lingered on, turning it over in the pale palm of his hand. It was an old credit card, the signature on the reverse side smudged and all but obliterated by time. Where it had lain for so long and who found it he knew not.

It was yellow on its face, approximating to gold and with the word VISA and another word and some sort of blue device in one corner. Jonas ran his forefinger over the sixteen-digit embossed number broken in four groups of four. Below, it said, 'VALID FROM' and the embossed numbers 02/11 and 'EXPIRES END' 05/14.

'From the early part of the century,' the Captain said, handling it respectfully. 'I remember, I remember.' A vision of the old days, long ago, of queuing in banks, of credit card statements, of purchases and pin numbers, of information and advertising of interest rates, of savings accounts, and transfers, of information, so much information, so much data, all around the movement of money and the focus on wealth and poverty. He shuddered: it was all gone. He knew that bustling and hustling, complex, information-laden world never return. The silence around him, the slow and sure movement of the skies and the permanence of the land beneath, cloaked in white, told him it would not.

With reverence almost, the Captain read aloud the name on the card, the last piece of embossed information, the letters standing proud still but with a grubby dark substance filling the ‘O’ and extending to the ‘E’. He took a deep breath, drawing into his lungs the fresh snow-melt air. ‘This was a person once who perhaps worried about his bills, his income tax, his pension, how much a litre of petrol was, who got annoyed by what he saw happening in the world; a young man, an old man - we shall never know. Perhaps a woman -did they have titles on credit cards? Here is the name of a person, almost certainly long gone: “H. LATTIMORE”’. For a moment they both stood, there at the top of the high tower, trying to imagine the busy old world and what this person’s experience of it was. ‘Lattimore,’ the Captain added, his hand to his face drawing his index finger over his old battle scar as he was wont to do when struggling to remember something. ‘Lattimore was the name of a verse translator of Homer’s *Iliad*: Richard, I think. No, it was Richmond, definitely Richmond... I owned a copy when I was eighteen but never got around to finishing it. It was one of the texts we officer cadets had to learn something about, and then give a critique. Events overtook us,’ he said musingly... ‘The world of ancient heroes...’

Jonas saw an opportunity, a chance to mention something he had not before told the Captain, something that gave him both pain and pleasure to recount.

‘That reminds me, Captain, there is something I have to tell you about my father Silas. Silas Wood was a hero, too: my mother said that he once saved a little boy from drowning.’

28. *Valedictory*

Jonas Wood was as good as his word, and he and Beatrice journeyed to the south coast with the visitors who had been with them for almost six months. Their children, Briony, Silas and Hope, went along, too, excited by the prospect of walking by the sea, and the prospect of adventure.

They were all warmly welcomed by the people of Lyme who were equally relieved and pleased to see the safe return of their own people and the people from Normandy. The Captain and Esmerelda embraced whilst Jonas and Beatrice were for a time regarded with reverential awe.

They had returned in time for the twenty-fifth of March and the beginning of the week-long Festival of Life, the annual celebration Jonas had suggested forty years earlier as he had passed through the town, subsequently taking the same idea with him to Temple Hill. So, along the sea front a procession followed the brass band to the sound of the 'Dead March' from *Saul*. It was a time of remembrance and solemnity, and people still shed tears as the music played, and the first day of the festival was given over to rites and rituals that seemed to wallow in the losses of the world. The mood quickly changed on the second day and endured for the remainder of the week. It was all about the triumph of life and determination in the face of adversity, and joy. Handel would make another contribution: there being no choir of sufficient numbers and quality, people would listen to a CD of the final chorus from *Saul*; its libretto was martial certainly, with talk girding on swords, but the music was celebratory and inspiring. Valjean wanted to hear it three times over: it got the Dead March out of his system, no doubt as Handel had intended.

The travellers stayed into that year's long and balmy summer and brought away good memories of new or renewed friendships, of feasting under the stars, of the rhythmic crashing of the sea on the strand, of music and laughter, of the celebration of the birth of a child and the cry of a new voice in the world; and the people from Temple Hill would come away with the knowledge that their little township to the north was not the last hope of humanity.

In June, on the sixteenth of June the records showed, Valjean said goodbye to the Captain and Esmerelda. They had decided to remain in Britain, the Captain's homeland. Valjean, for his part, said that though he had agonized over his decision, he would be putting even more distance between himself and his friends, as he was intending, he said, to return to Switzerland where quite possibly he would end his days. The Captain at first blamed himself for this with his own talk about England being the land of his birth, his homeland. Valjean, however, would have none of this and said it was an idea that he had had rattling around in his mind for some time. The Captain relented and agreed that he must follow where his instincts chose to lead him, but he added that he would give a written order that twenty-five Normandy fighters must travel with him -it was a dangerous journey across France. Valjean thanked him, adding that the ranger Tashtego, too, intended to travel with him, to see the lands he had only learned about, until now, from books.

And so, in a new ship, most of the Normandy party set sail, so to speak, from the southern shore of England; and Valjean was with them. Some had remained in Lyme, and a few of the Lyme people, it was said, later travelled with Jonas and Beatrice back to Temple Hill.

Valjean, as his own diary later recorded, shed a tear as he watched across the grey expanse of sea, a sea that slapped against the ship's side as he watched the receding shore, and his friends, at first diminishing, then merging into the waving crowd, then almost indistinguishable from the features of the land. He clung to his loyal dog Dante who also strained up to look out, his black paws hanging just over the gunwale. The ship rocked and tossed on the choppy sea but held its steady course. For Valjean it was the ship of life, his life, leaving his friends behind, ever diminishing in his sight, consigning them to his past.

So Valjean, man of the mountains, had one more adventure at least to look forward to: the crossing of Europe and the return to the Berner Oberland. There he would seek out his remaining friends and distant family members; there he would stand in the summer, in the lush meadow grass of the long flat valley, and gaze up at the white peaks, the Jungfrau and the Silberhorn, at the lofty snows of the high Alps, icily caressing with still cold purity the immensity of sky.

Yes, there would be friends there still, and a few relatives - he hoped. By now, after the passage of years, even the trains might be running. He had, strangely for someone who had in his earlier days sought out the solitude of the mountains, no longer a desire to avoid all but a few people. He did not want to be alone in this near-empty world. He remembered fondly, if he were honest, adoringly, as a worshipping pilgrim, the radiating beauty of the blue eyes of Beatrice. Like circles of cold fire, they had seemed to pierce his very soul. He would remember her kindness too, and her wisdom and intelligence. He felt that she, not Jonas, was the guiding spirit of Temple Hill; something Jonas himself had been quick to admit.

He hoped that one day the Captain would make the long journey to see him one last time. Then his next thought would be that it did not really matter: they would remain friends to the death whether or not they ever saw one another again. And Esmerelda would look after him...

A tough, fearless man, that Werod Captain, that Englishman, Valjean would often think. Such a man could have stood loyally, unselfishly, in the shield wall at Hastings, defending his King with his life, defying any odds and contending with the very Shadow of Death until the last gasp of his being.

Was that the Captain? Valjean would often then ask himself. Or was that the story the Captain used to tell? Not all can so well contend with that Shadow when they meet it. There could be no ultimate victory in this life, but what did that matter? As the Captain said: 'Hold hard! Let not the shield wall break!' And in so saying he had often laughed as though to say in self-mockery: 'What pictures we conjure of ourselves!'.

Printed in Great Britain
by Amazon

23521752R00270